Ambition

Millennial Mind Publishing
An imprint of American Book Publishing
American Book Publishing
P.O. Box 65624
Salt Lake City, UT 84165
www.american-book.com
Printed in the United States of America on acid-free paper.

Ambition

Publisher's Note: *This is a work of fiction. Names, characters, places, and incidents either are the product of the author's imagination or, are used fictitiously, and any resemblance to actual persons, living or dead, events, or locales is entirely coincidental.*

Library of Congress Cataloging-in-Publication Data is available upon request.

ISBN 1-58982-024-X

Ambition

This book may be purchased directly from the American Book Publishing on-line Bookshop at www.pdbookstore.com For more information e-mail: orders@american-book.com, 801-486-8639.

Ambition

Peter Verinder

Dedication

This novel is dedicated to the memory of my beautiful sister Maggie, who provided the inspiration for *Maddie*, and my great friend, Edna (Terri) Sullivan, who was always my *Billy*.

Chapter One

It was a wet evening at the end of an equally wet Sydney autumn day. The rain had finally stopped, and the reflections from the streetlights were beginning to give the pavement a silvery-black hue. It was time for Marc Braddon to leave the safety of his car and confront the men who now held a vice-like grip on his life.

Marc crossed the street and pushed open the door to Alan Wilkin's real estate office. Everyone else had gone for the day. The lone light from Alan's rear office cast a ghostly glow over the orderly collection of desks that filled the main office. As Marc followed the light, he observed that Alan was already in deep conversation with Vic Hastings, who was sitting in one of the two chairs facing Alan's desk. The two self-made businessmen appeared to be hatching another grand plan.

Marc took a deep breath, checked his stride, and straightened his shoulders. As he entered the room, both men halted their conversation in midsentence and cast patronizing glances his way. Marc sensed a wall of negative energy forming all around him.

"Good evening," he said, projecting a rehearsed confidence.

"Hello, Marc," they replied in eerie unison.

After an awkward moment's pause, Alan appeared to remember his role as host. "Take a seat," he told Marc, motioning him to the chair next to Vic's.

The three men sat eyeing each other, waiting for someone to speak first. Finally, Vic's pasted-on smile twitched into life.

"OK, this is your show, Mr. Braddon," he said. "Please tell me why you've dragged us all out on such a miserable night."

The moment Marc had been anticipating so keenly had finally arrived. He fixed Vic with a serious look and waited until the older man's grin began to fade.

"To express my disgust for the way you've treated me," Marc delivered quietly.

"What?" Vic snapped. His thin, pale face flushing as he leaned menacingly toward Marc.

Marc's body position remained defiantly upright in his chair. He tilted his head and focused a depreciative gaze at Vic. "I'm talking about cutting me out of ownership of a company I helped to form," Marc replied, delivering the words slowly and carefully. He knew he must control himself if he hoped to make a proper stand.

"Oh, not that again!" Vic said, rolling his eyes before sitting back in his seat. "I thought we'd sorted that out ages ago."

"Only to your satisfaction," Marc retorted cynically, the unfamiliar smell of battle now stinging his nostrils. "You're just happy to keep your little con game going for as long as you can, aren't you?"

There was a small noise. Out of the corner of his eye, Marc could see Alan, shuffling in his seat and suddenly looking vulnerable.

"I don't know what you mean," Vic replied dismissively.

"Oh yes, you do!" Marc shot back with a vengeful glare. "Pointer Homes Pty. Ltd. operates under my builder's license and uses my copyrights to sell its products. I intend to withdraw both immediately. There's no way I'm going to let this company operate for another minute; not unless this whole matter is resolved tonight!"

By now, Vic was visibly shaken. He evidently hadn't expected this sort of attack from a novice, and Marc had been counting on it. As for Alan, a typical real estate salesman with an impressive repertoire of catch phrases and sales pitches, he was unusually quiet. His large frame, condescending manner, and superior dress were often all he needed to control his suburban real estate situations; now, he seemed to be completely out of his depth.

Sensing that he was already gaining the upper hand, Marc pressed on. "You should also know," he continued, "that I haven't yet certified several of the houses under construction. The houses' foundations can't be inspected by anyone else, because you've built well beyond that point. Without my engineering certificates," he added quietly, "you won't be able to collect the progress payments from your clients' banks, which will soon starve you of cash and eventually bankrupt you."

Alan and Vic now seemed lost in their own worlds, and their silence was deafening. Marc knew that he already had them on the ropes, but suddenly wanted more. He instinctively followed an idea that had just popped into his head.

"I've also instructed my solicitors to begin legal action in the District Court tomorrow morning to recover my share of the value of this operation," he informed the two men with steely resolve, studying their faces as he delivered his last volley—"the part the two of you tried to cheat me out of!"

While it may have been a spur of the moment attack, Marc was betting that the prospect of a protracted and expensive legal battle would scare the living daylights out of Vic and Alan, if they weren't fretting enough already.

It was worth a try, Marc thought as he got to his feet, preparing for a dramatic exit.

But the battle wasn't over yet. As Marc started for the door, he could hear Vic's chair swivel in his direction.

"Well, Marc," Vic said in a voice filled with quiet menace, "I suppose you think you hold all the aces."

Here it comes. Marc stopped in his tracks and turned to face Vic. He moved back toward Alan's desk and leaned his thigh against it to brace himself for the expected counterattack.

Suddenly, Vic paused. As he took off his wire-rimmed glasses and rubbed his eyes, he looked more tired than angry. "Look—maybe there's room for compromise in here somewhere," he said in a placating tone that barely masked his resentment. "I'm sure we can reach an agreement, provided that you haven't already done something foolish that'll sink us all."

Marc felt a sudden rush of accomplishment, but quickly suppressed it—he knew that Vic wasn't that easily beaten. He also knew that Vic saw him as an ungrateful upstart who had been allowed into their inner circle and who now sought to dictate terms. Looking at their pained expressions, it was clear to Marc that both men had wrongly assessed his willingness to be manipulated.

Vic turned to his ally for support. "You've been very quiet, Alan. What do you think?"

As Marc glanced over at Alan's passive expression, he knew he had done the right thing to get Alan secretly aligned with him before he went into battle. When he had informed Alan earlier of his plan to confront Vic, Alan responded by doing just what Marc had hoped— indicating a desire to break free of Vic's tight grip if he could become part of Marc's future plans. This allowed Marc to sideline him in this fight and treat him as a kind of milquetoast personality.

"I don't see that we've got much of a choice," Alan said with resignation as he stared at the wall.

Vic shot Alan a slightly puzzled look. In the same instant, he seemed to accept that he would have to do all the talking.

"Come on, Marc; sit down and let's try to work this thing out, shall we?" he suggested soothingly, his grin looking more and more like bared teeth.

Marc remained on his feet, his jaw thrust out resolutely.

Vic sighed as he resorted to the nice-guy approach. "Look, we obviously don't want you to stop any of the ongoing work, but our business affairs are far too complicated to allow ownership to a third person," Vic explained as Marc's expression hardened. "But there has to be some other way we can achieve what you want."

"If we are to agree on anything tonight, it must be put in writing, preferably by my lawyer, so that there can be no further argument," Marc demanded.

Vic and Alan exchanged an uneasy nod and motioned him to sit back down. Marc decided to stand for a little longer.

"Well, what are you guys offering?" he asked.

Alan's role was now put into motion. He spoke hesitantly at first, as if the idea had only just occurred to him.

"What if, in exchange for you licensing the company and allowing us to use your copyright on the house designs at a set price per job, we fund you into a parallel branch of the company?" he suggested. "This would be in an agreed territory, under your management, and with my sales team to make all the sales."

Vic fell back into his chair, aghast at how quickly his partner had fashioned such generous terms. A cloud of suspicion crossed his face before he finally resigned himself to the inevitable.

"I think I can live with that," Vic said with a heavy sigh.

"I'm sorry, gentlemen, but it won't do," Marc responded. "There will always be trouble between us if we're both selling the same product in parallel regions. There's bound to be cross-border disputes, and we'd just end up crossing swords again."

He paused. "What I really want is for you two to fund me into a completely separate building company, giving me half of the current Pointer Homes sales just to kick things off."

"But this would give us no share of the operation, and would instead create a competitor!" Vic exclaimed, his jaw dropping.

"Yeah, that's right," Marc agreed. "But you'll still have a business—one that you created on my back, based on deception and false promises!"

Alan looked over at him quizzically. "Aren't you being a bit hard, Marc?" he asked.

"No, I don't think so," Marc answered with a dangerous glint in his eyes. "If you guys had just honored the original partnership agreement, it would have cost you a whole lot less. This way, I'm taking back what you owe me, as well as what's really mine anyway!"

Now that he had indisputably taken control of the proceedings, Marc sat back down. He felt he had earned the right to relax and watch his foes squirm as they reluctantly started negotiating a settlement.

* * *

As Vic and Alan began the unsavory process of splitting up the company, Marc's thoughts raced back to a series of meetings he had had with them a year earlier, when they were clients of the engineering practice he managed. He realized now just how green he must have appeared to these guys.

"You know, Marc, I reckon that you'd be ideal for a new building company we have in mind," Alan had told him at the conclusion of one of their many meetings.

"You seem to handle this place easily enough," Vic observed with a grin. "Maybe it's time you thought about starting out on your own!'" He suggested that Marc could design the homes, do the engineering on the building sites, and use your his degree to provide the corporate building license the company had to have before it could sign up building contracts.

Marc was flattered that two of his firm's most valued clients were taking such an interest in him. Although only twenty-four at the time, he had felt for some time that he was ready to take his next step into the commercial world, and the idea of a partnership with two experienced businessmen sounded ideal. He was intoxicated by the idea of entering a brand new area of business, one in which his own creations would be tested in the marketplace. He soon started dreaming about all of the trappings that would come with fabulous wealth. After thinking about it for two days, he accepted their offer.

Vic immediately offered him a directorship of the new building company. The company would be called "Pointer Homes," because the others felt that this new venture would point the way forward. Marc knew that the directorship didn't grant him equity in the operation, as it would if he were a shareholder. But he liked the prospect of becoming a one-third owner of the new business, so he accepted the offer anyway, retaining his other job to play it safe.

Marc began focusing on providing technical support for the new company, with the expectation that his ownership would be formalized later. At Vic's suggestion, he agreed to use his name and qualifications to secure a corporate building license for Pointer Homes.

Designing project, or "model" homes—which were standard house designs built many times over on different owners' land—wasn't a skill Marc then possessed, so he spent most of his free time researching the state-of-the-art through home design magazines and visiting other builders' display homes. Marc spent most evenings and weekends at his drawing board, experimenting with home layouts and façade designs. Finally, after months of hard, grinding work, tinged with a few flashes of inspiration, Marc had a new range of designs ready to market.

Remarkably, the sales and building sides of the operation took off: In no time at all, the fledgling company racked up its first fifty sales, with homes popping up all over suburban Sydney. Marc's designs seemed to strike a chord with the home-buying public, and everything pointed to a successful partnership, with enough money for everybody. Buoyed by the success of the new venture, Marc eventually quit his job as manager of the structural engineering design firm so he could devote his full attention to Pointer Homes.

The months passed, and Marc remained somewhat awed by his new partners. Vic, the senior partner, was an urbane, semi-retired businessman who impressed Marc with his apparent command of the business world. Marc saw him as dynamic, bold, and highly effective, and he was sure that Vic had only his best interests at heart.

The other partner, Alan Wilkins, was "thirtysomething" and always seemed to be juggling the demands of his long-suffering wife and young children with those of his clients and the endless stream of sales leads they represented. Alan's thickset frame made him look older than his years, and his thinning hairline bore testimony to the long days he had put into making his suburban business work. After only a short time, Marc concluded that Alan was tired of working and looking for a way to coast.

When Marc began pressing his partners to formalize his ownership, Vic always kept putting the discussion off until another day. To make matters worse, Marc was only getting a trickle of money—less than half of his previous wages—from overseeing the company's house plans and engineering inspections, and he was starting to feel the pinch.

Whenever Marc tried to address the money issue, Vic would say that this was part of the short-term sacrifice they all had to make in order to succeed. This only added to Marc's suspicions, which turned into deep concern when Vic finally refused to discuss ownership or money altogether.

"I really need to know when you two guys are going formalize our arrangement. I can't go on living on a promise; I want my one-third ownership put down in writing," Marc told his partners when he finally cornered them.

Alan looked away while Vic prepared to deliver the blow. "This company belongs to Alan and me," he explained coldly. "You only draw the plans and provide the builders license; we could have paid anyone to do that for us."

With that, Marc's world started to crumble all around him. "You...you're joking, aren't you?" he stammered in disbelief.

Vic shrugged. "Frankly, I don't understand your surprise. I thought we were giving you the chance to work for yourself. Surely you didn't expect to get an equal share of Pointer Homes for just drawing up the plans and providing the license," he uttered scornfully. "Whatever made you think we'd agree to that?"

You rotten scumbags! Marc stood there in shock as the words sank in, confirming his worst fears. As the days passed and the new reality sank in, it became abundantly clear that these men had always meant to trap him, exploit him, and then steal the fruits of his labor.

Marc wasn't about to allow himself to be duped so easily, and decided to hatch a plan to turn the tables on these rogues. He knew he would have to execute it with stealth and purpose if he hoped to win. He also knew that he had to find a way to extricate himself from his partners' control without destroying himself in the process. He knew that he could never work with these men again, but the prospect of being cut adrift from the only secure arrangement he had didn't appeal, since he had no other immediate employment options.

He swore that if he ever became part of any other business deal, he would do so only after signing an agreement. He now realized the value of the old saying, "Verbal contracts aren't worth the paper they're written on!" Unfortunately, he had realized the truth of this wisdom a little too late.

*   *   *

Maddie Braddon sat in her cozy Surry Hills apartment, toying with her simple meal and trying not to look at the clock on her kitchen wall. She was still dressed in the navy blue business suit that she had worn to work that day, too nervous and distracted to change into something more comfortable, as she usually did.

It was now just after seven-thirty, and she visualized her brother fighting against the odds to get his life back from those two shysters. Her concern could not have been any stronger had her own existence been hanging in the balance.

She shared her trepidation with a big black tomcat that had found her two years earlier, and now answered to the name of Yindy. He, too, seemed to be watching the clock from his comfortable place on Maddie's lap.

Her apartment was filled with photographs of her family. She had borrowed heavily from the family album, and had blown up and framed several photos of her and Marc at various ages. All of her visitors remarked about the striking resemblance between the siblings. Maddie's huge brown eyes and determined chin were just as apparent in those early photographs.

Her favorite picture was the one in which she and Marc were each holding up a bunch of Muscat grapes that had just been cut from the laden vines that filled their elevated courtyard when they lived in Algiers. Although they both held their bunches at shoulder height, the grapes still trailed on the ground. She was only four when the picture was taken, but Maddie's admiration of her older brother already shone through. It was clear that she worshiped Marc, and would gladly follow him into any adventure.

They had both grown up together in Algiers, England, and now Australia. Although she was three years his junior, Marc had always treated her as his equal—she would never have tolerated anything less, especially now at age twenty-two—and they were now closer than ever. She found it easy to be available for him, whether on the phone or for a quick cup of coffee. She was always there for him. That was just the way it was.

Marc and Maddie had spent most of their spare time planning every aspect of this denouement. Her support helped him to focus during the days leading up to the meeting. She was his sounding board as he played all of the major roles, countering his enemy's imagined threats and responses before delivering a well-rehearsed tirade that would whip his opponents into submission.

Intelligent and resourceful, Maddie was the mastermind behind several of Marc's strategies. "Why don't you meet with Alan first and suggest some sort of ongoing involvement?" she had suggested during a recent conversation. "You don't know how he really feels about Vic—maybe he's looking for a way out, too."

Marc smiled at his sister's intuition. "Yeah, that might work."

"It might be a way of dividing and conquering," Maddie remarked with a disarming smile.

The image of Marc leaving the scene of a great battle with the vanquished in his wake comforted Maddie now as she pushed her food around the plate and tried not to look up at the clock again. As the minute hand dragged reluctantly forward, she smiled nervously at her cat, praying that her brother would emerge victorious.

*　*　*

After an hour and a half of grueling negotiations, the three men had finally settled on the details. Vic and Alan looked drained, while Marc remained as collected as when he'd first arrived. Alan's desk was strewn with paper, as a result of the men working through every suggested scenario.

"OK, so we write Marc a check for $50,000, which will provide the working capital for his new company," Vic said, wearily rubbing his eyes. "We will also give him twenty-five of our most recent sales. He will operate separately, but can use some of our tradespeople and accounts during his start-up period if he chooses. In exchange, he agrees to license us for six months before taking away his builder's license.

"Marc also agrees to let us use his designs for a fee of $2,000 per house for six months while we get our own designs done. Oh, and Marc will now issue those outstanding engineer's certificates."

Finished, Vic drew a breath. "I hope that this makes you happy, Mr. Braddon," he added sarcastically.

"Yes, it does," Marc replied with a smile. "Thank you very much, gentlemen."

As he got up to leave, he delivered his last joust. "Just one more thing," he remarked casually. "I took the liberty of making an appointment with my lawyers to firm up whatever we agreed on tonight. Can I rely on you both being there tomorrow morning at eleven?"

Vic's face darkened into a scowl. "I thought they were ready to go to court against us in the morning," he noted.

"Only if we couldn't reach a satisfactory arrangement tonight," Marc replied firmly. "So, can I rely on you both being there in the morning?"

"It doesn't appear that we have much choice, do we, Marc?" Vic answered bitterly.

"So I take it that you'll *both* be there?" Marc pressed.

"Yes," Alan said, shooting Marc a furtive glance.

"Here's his address," Marc said as he offered each man his lawyer's business card. "I'll see you both in the morning."

With that, he rose and shook hands with both men, leaving them to quarrel amongst themselves about what had gone wrong. In the space of ninety minutes, Marc had made the transition from Vic's patsy to his master.

* * *

As Marc made his way back out into the street, he looked around the dreary little outer suburb of Cravenwood, a cluster of about a dozen shops on each side of a wide main street. A railway station and a level crossing, whose boom gates regularly blocked one end of the spartan main road in response to the comings and goings of the suburban trains, completed the bleak landscape of this commercial backwater.

Once back in his car, Marc slumped over the wheel and finally exhaled the stale air trapped deep in his lungs. An overwhelming sense of relief washed over him and somehow he felt as if he'd been remade, like part of him had been changed forever.

He now felt equipped to take on the whole world.

Chapter Two

Marc was thankful that most of his twenty-five mile journey home was on the freeway because he couldn't wait to tell Maddie what had happened. He could think of nothing else as he wound his way through the darkening suburban streets that led to the freeway.

He knew Maddie would be pacing the floor of her apartment, worrying about him, and he wished he were already there, recounting every glorious moment. She would want to hear every single detail, and he was so imbued with victory that he could feel his blood tingle.

Marc turned up his car radio when he recognized *I Come From A Land Down Under,* the inspirational song by Men at Work that was all the rage during Australia's unprecedented win of the America's Cup. As he started to sing along at the top of his lungs, he decided right then and there that 1983 was also going to be his year.

He looked in the rear-view mirror and saw the tired, but handsome, face of a young man, framed by dark brown wavy hair and punctuated by the same determined chin as his sister's. His blue green eyes, now bloodshot, and thick eyebrows were inherited from his father. His tanned skin was still smooth and tight, darkened only by his after-five shadow.

Marc peered through the fading twilight at the houses dotting the hillside on each side of the freeway. Their lights were beginning to dominate the landscape as the black of night came creeping in with finality.

Without warning, a car careened across Marc's path. Shaken out of his inner thoughts, he broke hard and swerved to avoid a collision. As his car skidded and just missed the guardrail that protected the shoulder of the road, Marc suddenly found himself fighting for his life.

With another swerve, he was back in the middle lane again, his heart pounding heavily against his rib cage. *What sort of lunatic would drive like that?* Marc tried to get a look at the driver of the other car, but the darkly tinted windows made it impossible. His mouth went dry as he realized the car looked a lot like Vic's.

Just as suddenly, the car lurched out of his lane and into the vacant lane next to his. Marc slowed to allow the other car to get ahead of him.

No, it couldn't be Vic. Vic was smarter than that, and besides, he wouldn't have had time to catch up with him after sorting things out with Alan. *I'm just getting paranoid,* Marc told himself, trying to steady his nerves as the car sped ahead, swerving between lanes yet again.

He spotted a freeway off-ramp, and decided to take it. Sighing with relief, he was soon feeding coins into a gas station's pay phone. Maddie answered on the first ring.

"Hi there!" he said cheerfully, putting his brush on the freeway out of his mind for the moment.

"Well, come on, tell me what happened," she pleaded.

"We won, Maddie, we won!"

"That's brilliant!" she screamed. "I hope you're coming over."

"I'm only about half an hour away. I just had to pull off the freeway to get to a phone and tell you as soon as I could."

"That's wonderful news. I'm so glad you called. I've been sitting here going out of my mind."

"Oh ye of little faith!" Marc said mockingly. Then, his face grew serious. "It was tight, Maddie, but we got there. I don't want to think about where I'd be if it had all gone pear-shaped on me."

*   *   *

As Marc filled up his car at the self-serve pump, he felt a cool gust of wind wash over him. *It's an ill wind that blows no one no good!* he thought as Billy Kennedy's face flashed into his mind. Marc saw the value in his old friend's favorite saying, especially after all that had happened tonight. He knew Billy would have pointed out that if he hadn't met these nasty types and fought with them, he might never have gone into business for himself.

Marc smiled at the prospect of telling Billy all about it. Then he sighed, realizing that he would be able to talk to Billy only by phone, and then only if he could get the time zones right.

When the two men first met, Marc was a shop boy, a junior unskilled laborer who ran errands for any of the tradesmen in the foundry where Billy worked. It had been Marc's first job after leaving home at fifteen, and Billy had been the first kind person he had met after he began living on his own. He had quickly become the father figure Marc lacked, and they struck up an instant friendship.

Billy had then been in his late fifties, with a craggy, well-worn face that was nonetheless friendly. His shock of snow white, tightly curled hair always made it easy for Marc to spot him in the crowded lunchroom, and make his way to the seat Billy always reserved for him at the long luncheon table.

Billy loved going to the football every Saturday. His beloved rugby league team, Balmain, was one of the oldest teams in the Sydney competition, and Billy always knew somebody who had a spare ticket. Almost every winter's Saturday, Marc would be Billy's guest at the football. Under Billy's tutelage, Marc became quite expert in the subtleties of the code. This gave the two men one more thing in common.

Marc always remembered one particular talk, when he was helping Billy to clear his workspace of a number of disused timber pattern boxes. During a break, after they had loaded ten of the heavy boxes on to a trolley, Billy leaned against his workbench and rolled a cigarette. Marc moved closer, hoping that Billy was going to tell him another story.

Billy's face broke into a kind smile as his exhaled his first drag. "If I had an apple tree laden with ripe, juicy apples, and I told you to take any apple you wanted, I bet that you'd pick one from the very top of the tree rather than off the ground."

As he paused and took another long drag, a knowing look crossed his face. "Well, it's the same in life, m'boy. You should reach up as high as you can and do the very best with what you've got. Sometimes it means you'll have to stretch a little farther to reach the best apple, but when you do finally reach it, it'll taste all the sweeter!"

Billy's smile became more benevolent. "You shouldn't stay here as a shop boy, young Marcy. You should go and get yourself an apprenticeship in something worthwhile. It might be hard to start with, living on apprentice's pay, but if you stick it out, you'll have a trade for the rest of your life." Billy's voice suddenly became a bit gruff with emotion. "Anyway, you're way too good to be sweeping floors, m'boy."

Billy's opinion meant a lot to Marc, who had longed to be as close to his own father for as long as he could remember. Unfortunately, his father's indifference had seemed only to widen the unspoken gulf between them. Meanwhile, Billy was missing his only son, who had gone to work in the States several years earlier as an insurance executive after Billy's wife had died. Marc always figured that he had somehow been sent to fill that void in Billy's life, and was glad for the opportunity.

Marc took Billy's advice, and was soon apprenticed in a workshop that fabricated structural steel for multi-story buildings. Although he had fulfilled Billy's wishes, he dreaded having to tell his mentor goodbye. As it happened, Billy didn't like the idea of being separated from his surrogate son either, and asked Marc to come and live with him.

Surprised by Billy's generosity, Marc insisted on paying rent. Billy had reluctantly accepted, taking only half of what Marc had been paying in the cold, impersonal boarding houses he'd been forced to call home.

Billy was not much of a cook, and had only three dishes in his repertoire; baked beans on toast, grilled steak with salad or baked beans, or bacon and eggs with baked beans. "I only cook food that'll stick to your ribs," Billy used to say, and it didn't take long for his cooking to have that effect.

After Billy retired from the foundry, he seemed to make it his business to steer Marc along life's road. Billy knew all about the impetuosity of youth, and was one of the rare few that had learned not only from his own mistakes, but also from the mistakes of others. The two of them would debate for hours about anything and everything, from football to the meaning of life. Billy subtly polished most of Marc's rough edges during those long conversations, and got the young man to see some of the other points of view that exist in complex issues.

Billy's inner calmness and evenhandedness were just the right foil for Marc's aggressive and impulsive nature. From then on, Marc blossomed. He studied part time until he finally earned his engineering degree. Then, he immediately got a job as a design engineer in the Sydney Central Business District, or CBD, as multi-story commercial precincts are called in Australia. His new job gave him his first exhilarating taste of commerce.

* * *

Back in his car, Marc peered into the dark night for any sign of the car that had nearly knocked him off the freeway. He felt a hint of trepidation and tried to quell it with reason. *It was just a coincidence; nobody's out to get me,* he told himself as he prepared to reenter the freeway traffic.

As Marc got back onto the road, his thoughts returned to his good friend.

Six months earlier, out of the blue, Billy's son asked him to come and live with him and his young family in America. Billy was apprehensive about telling Marc of the offer. But when he finally did, Marc was happy for him and encouraged him to go.

When Marc saw Billy off at the airport, he realized that they had not really discussed how they were going to get on without each other. The bustle of the crowds, the noise and excitement of all those about to depart on their different journeys, seemed oddly out of context with the way Marc was feeling. Billy looked at Marc's face and sensed his turmoil. "You've been like a son to me, Marcy. I've seen you grow up from a scrawny kid into a fine young man. I mightn't be your dad, but I'm still very proud of you." He smiled warmly. "It's high time this old man got out of your life—at least for a while, anyway—so that you can get on with it!"

Marc felt a smile spread across his face. This man was more of a father than his real father had ever been. Marc knew he owed Billy a debt he could never repay.

"Billy, I'm sure I wouldn't have made it without your help. I've learned so much about life from you that I could write a book. If I did, I'd call it something like "*Standing on the Shoulders of a Giant*," because that's what it's been like for me." As Marc continued, his voice began to quiver. "It was as if you hoisted me up on your shoulders every time you wanted me to see something that I couldn't see for myself."

Billy tried to swallow, but couldn't. "We need to make a pact, Marcy. We must always keep in touch and call each other at least once a fortnight. I've given you my son's New York number, haven't I?"

"Yes, it's right here," Marc said, tapping his chest pocket.

"OK, wish me luck," Billy said stoically as they reached the immigration gate.

"You know I wish you that and a whole lot more, Billy," Marc said, feeling the words choke in his throat.

"I know, I know."

The two men embraced for a full minute, patting each other on the back. Billy then pulled back and looked Marc in the eye. In that moment, Marc saw Billy's depth of feeling for him. Billy then turned abruptly on his heels and disappeared through the gate with only a half-glance backward.

* * *

Madeleine Braddon—Maddie, as Marc always called her—was a lady of natural beauty and grace. There was a genuineness about her that people immediately accepted as real. Everything seemed to come easily to her, and her life followed a direct and sensible path—a complete contrast to her brother's.

She was by far the youngest and probably brightest person in her class, and had finished at the top of her high school before going on to graduate university at age nineteen and a half with a bachelor's degree in business, majoring in marketing and management.

She had a considerable talent for selling and organizing, and immediately secured a position with one of the biggest real estate firms in the city as a sales and marketing executive. She had worked there for the past three years, and was steadily working her way up their corporate ladder.

However, all of Maddie's personal ambitions seemed far away as she stood in her apartment doorway, peering over the edge of the carpeted landing for the first glimpse of her brother, whom she had just let into the building through the security intercom.

"Come on up, my little gladiator!" she cheered as she saw the back of Marc's head come into view on the stairs.

"This heavy armor is slowing me down, m'lady!" Marc joked, turning to face his sister before negotiating the final flight of stairs that led directly to her front door.

"You look beat!" Maddie said as she scanned his battle-weary face. "Never mind; I have something that'll put some life back into you. How does a hot meal sound, with a chilled bottle of Bollinger that I've been keeping for a special occasion? I think this is about as special as it gets!"

A few minutes later, Marc had his feet up and was finally taking stock of his victory. "I still can't believe I did it, Maddie. I got everything I wanted! Here's to us," he said as he took a sip of celebratory champagne.

"All I can say is that it's *brilliant*, Marc," she said, hugging him around the shoulders after putting his meal down in front of him.

"Right now, the whole thing feels so surreal. It'll take me time to accept that I'm finally free of those parasites, and I have you to thank for great part of it, Sis. I can't tell you how important you are to me— you made me believe I could pull it off."

"I was only a small part of it. You had to have the guts to face those guys on your own," Maddie replied modestly, rounding the dining table and sitting in a chair opposite. "Now that you're free to decide your own destiny, what are you going to do next?"

"The first thing I want, Maddie, is for you to join me in my new company. That way, we can work together. I can't think of anything I want more."

Maddie rocked back in her chair and threw her brother a look of disbelief, which soon softened into a thoughtful smile.

"The prospect of running our own company is almost too good to be true," Maddie mused dreamily. "But...you're not ready to hire anybody yet," she cautioned. "You've got to put a whole lot of other things in place beforehand. What about stationery, sales brochures, advertising, not to mention subcontractors to build your houses..."

"Come on, Maddie, you and I could handle all that standing on our heads."

"But I have my job..."

"This will be better than any old job," he coaxed. "We can conquer the world, you and I. Come on, Maddie; just say yes."

Maddie looked hard at her brother for a couple of minutes while she considered all her options. Before long, her face broke into a wide grin. "OK, Marc—count me in!"

"Fantastic! That makes you my first official employee, Maddie," Marc announced with a laugh. "God, if only everything that I have to decide is this easy."

They refilled their glasses and drank another toast: this time, to their new building company.

As Marc shared another broad smile with his sister, he felt sure that she would add some much-needed glamour to his fledgling company's sales office. She was nearly five-foot-nine, with a perfect figure and a lovely face highlighted by huge brown eyes. Her honey-brown hair was always beautifully styled, and she dressed stylishly in a way that emphasized her inner beauty and elegance.

Marc had watched silently from the sidelines over the last few years as Maddie transformed from his kid sister into a confident, worldly woman. To him, she had become the personification of class. He knew he could also depend on her business sense and a brain that worked with Swiss-watch precision.

Marc felt sure that Maddie would take to selling houses like a duck to water, because she could so readily empathize with people. Her quick wit would allow her to rapidly assess a client's needs and tailor a specific house design to meet or exceed those needs. Somehow, the uncharted waters of the building business held less trepidation now that Maddie was going to be by his side.

Her cat, Yindy, moved off Marc's lap and climbed his chest, putting a paw on each shoulder before nestling his face in the small of Marc's neck. He and Maddie smiled at each other as the cat began to purr loudly.

*   *   *

Marc had decided to spend the night at Maddie's place, having drunk a little too much to drive home safely. She put him on the sofa, but he didn't care—he didn't sleep well most nights.

His sleep was often interrupted by a recurrent dream he had had for nearly ten years. In the dream, he was a young boy again, wandering through a magnificent forest. So vivid was the dream that he could actually smell the wet eucalyptus leaves as he trod the rain-soaked forest floor.

The sky would always be clear and blue. He'd then look up through the thick canopy to see the sky begin to cloud over. With the clouds came the wind, gaining strength within seconds to become a forceful gale that bent the trees in all directions.

Frightened, Marc would start to flee, but instead found himself going deeper and deeper into the forest. Trees began to fall all around him as he dodged and weaved his way through the rain of timber. No matter which way he turned, a tall tree would snap in half and fall to the ground right in front of him, blocking his path. Every time he changed direction, another tree would fall within inches of him.

Finally, Marc would trip over one of the fallen logs to end up, face down and exhausted, on the ground. As he rolled over and realized that a massive tree was about to fall on him, he awoke with a start, drenched in sweat, just before he would have been crushed to death.

Whenever Marc had this dream, he cried out in his sleep. As soon as he awoke, he wanted to tell someone about the dream and how it made him feel, but with the morning's first light came a feeling that it didn't really matter anymore. Daylight seemed to relegate those lingering concerns to the depths of his subconscious mind. Tonight, Maddie was at his side within seconds, holding his hand and calming him down. "Shh, Marc, shh."

"What...what...where am I?"

"You're here with me; you're safe. You were having a bad dream, that's all."

Now that he had an opportunity to talk about his nightmares, Marc found himself stalling. "Oh...was I?"

"Yes." Her big, brown eyes filled with concern. "Do you want to tell me about it?"

"No. No, it's all right," he told his concerned sister, not wanting to involve her in this painful part of his life.

"Was it about Vic and Alan?"

"No."

"Does it have anything to do with...the accident?"

"No. Yes. Probably. But I don't want to worry you, Maddie, it's just something I have to sort out for myself," he said, wanting only to put the lingering strands of the bad dream behind him. "Maybe we could have a cup of coffee, now that I've awakened the whole house," he suggested ruefully.

Maddie knew not to push him for an explanation. He would tell her in his own time, although she silently wished that this were the right time. She turned on the kitchen light and started to brew up a pot of coffee.

Chapter Three

Marc couldn't help feeling that he had wasted the past six months working with Vic and Alan, but consoled himself with the thought that at least he had been able to use the experience as a springboard to start working for himself.

A month after confronting his former associates, he was becoming accustomed to living without the security of a steady income—that in itself was an achievement. The certainty of his victory was finally sinking in and Marc was beginning to accept his new circumstances as another piece of his own particular reality.

Their new company had to have a name and Maddie and Marc considered dozens of names and their derivatives before finally agreeing on "Highmark Homes." The siblings felt the name offered a number of benefits while minimizing opportunities for negative marketing by their competitors. "Highmark Homes: the high point of your new life." *Not bad for a first attempt,* Marc thought.

Marc couldn't afford to hire many employees right away, so Highmark's staff was comprised solely of him and Maddie at first. For a while, they shared every high-sounding title in the company. "Big things sometimes spring from small beginnings," they kept telling each other during those early days.

Maddie worked part time initially, helping Marc to set up every aspect of the business from scratch. Many things had to be organized before the business could ever hope to operate properly. Sales brochures and stationery had to be designed and printed, ads placed, and houses sold.

Marc decided that Highmark Homes' first home would be a speculative, or *spec* home, because he needed something to build while dealing with all the red tape associated with the houses he had inherited from the settlement with Pointer Homes. Highmark could build a spec house quickly, because it didn't have to meet a specific client's needs or wait for lending approvals. Marc only had to obtain building approval through the local council, meaning that he could be building within a few weeks of drawing up the plans.

Eventually, Marc and Maddie planned to sell the spec home as a completed package. While the property awaited sale, it would be used as a model, or display, home from which to sell similar building contracts.

Now, it was time for Marc to face another challenge: He had never built a house before. In his previous arrangement with Vic and Alan, they had had a carpenter who acted as the building supervisor. With Highmark Homes, Marc was on his own.

As an engineer, he knew a lot about foundations and structural strength, so this was as a good a place as any to begin. His structural engineering degree had allowed him to automatically obtain a builder's license, and now his assumed building knowledge was about to be put to the test.

He cautioned himself to start with what he knew. *Let's see. First we need a site preparation; then a concrete slab, followed by the timber frame, windows, brickwork, roof tiles, and then the finishing touches.* Just as in Tennyson's "Charge of the Light Brigade," he rushed bravely into the "valley of death" otherwise known as the cottage building industry.

As fortune would have it, Marc knew a group of excellent Italian concreters with whom he had worked on one of his engineering projects. He spent a lot of time talking them into coming to work for him. Milo, Claudio, and Umberto had a high work ethic and could solve any problem related to concrete.

Milo was the leader, a balding man of medium build with a ready smile and a good, practical brain. He was still fit enough to play soccer at forty-two, but admitted to a few aches and pains the following day.

He looked like a thinner version of one of the Mario Brothers, complete with handlebar moustache.

Claudio and Umberto were good workers who relied on Milo to do the "undesirable" work, like setting out the foundations, preparing the invoices, and collecting their money from slow-paying builders. They were happy working through their existing subcontract arrangements, and naturally suspicious of the financial strength of Highmark Homes and its ability to provide them with secure, long-term work.

Milo jumped at the chance to work for Marc, but first had to convince the others of the advantages of getting in on the ground floor of the new company.

"I'm telling you that this man knows where he's going," Milo told his team. "You know I'm never wrong about people; we should grab this opportunity with both hands."

Milo always made good sense to Claudio and Umberto, so the trio soon finally agreed to become Mark's concreters.

Highmark Homes' first house was to be built on a fairly level site, meaning that it would suit a concrete slab foundation. Thankfully for Marc, concrete slabs were right up Milo's alley. *That'll get us off to a flying start,* Marc thought as he breathed more easily.

After that, Marc decided to cross each bridge as he came to it. He spent every day on site with the concrete crew, checking ground levels, helping to set out the formwork for the slab, and watching the placement of the steel reinforcement.

After two days of preparation, the slab was ready to be poured, and all four of men cracked a couple of bottles of Lambrusco as the last section of concrete was finally smoothed off.

Maddie arrived at the last minute, dressed to the nines and wearing a pair of impractical patent-leather high heels. She tiptoed across the soft, muddy site, just in time to propose the toast: "To the first of many Highmark Home slabs and to the team who'll be behind them all!" She beamed.

*   *   *

"I know we're working like dogs, but I love it, don't you?" Maddie asked her brother on one of their late-night sessions after they had been in business for three months.

"Yeah," Marc replied with a tired grin. "Everything I did today was a first."

"It's a wonderful feeling, isn't it, being able to conquer new horizons every day? I never thought it would be this much *fun*."

"Fun?" Marc repeated with a look of disbelief. He had been secretly hoping for the day when things would become a bit more predictable.

"Once we set everything in place, it'll run itself," Maddie said with a determined look and a right-hand air jab. She smiled as she acknowledged the look on her brother's face. "I know it's harder for you, because you have to be on hand to control the guys on site—but it'll get easier, you'll see."

As time marched on, Marc developed some innovative approaches that allowed Highmark to build its houses in twelve weeks, rather than the eighteen to twenty-six weeks it took most other builders. Marc's coordination of the subcontractors was superb; no sooner would one trade finish its task than the next one was on the job. This eliminated nearly all of the time traditionally wasted on home building sites, and the whole industry sat up and took notice.

Maddie happily exploited this advantage to her clients, and was soon selling contracts at the rate of one a week. After numerous conversations, she and Marc agreed that Highmark Homes should have at least two permanent model homes with which to drive more sales, and Marc set about making it happen.

At the end of its first six months, the new company was completing its twentieth home. The majority of Highmark Homes were being built in a new housing estate in Edensor Park, a suburb in the southwest of Sydney that was the keystone to an even larger group of brand new suburbs. This central location was fertile ground, presenting plenty of opportunities to procure ongoing work. This was where Highmark Homes wanted to locate its display homes, so with this in mind, Marc scouted every new land subdivision for a possible model home site.

As he warmed to this task, Marc decided to build a display village of five model homes. He and Maddie figured that the larger group of homes would better feature Highmark Homes's range of designs. They also recognized that a larger exhibition village would create a real presence, which in turn would attract more people and make a statement about the financial strength and solidity of the company.

"Right then, we'll 'ave one of those!" Marc and Maddie joked in mock Liverpudlian accents as they compiled their wish list. Marc wasn't joking, though, as he set out to find such a site.

He looked for weeks, and just as he was beginning to lose hope, he noticed a new subdivision starting up on a patch of vacant land. It had substantial street frontage to a main arterial road, and seemed ideal for his purpose. Marc quickly tracked down the developer and arranged to meet him in his office.

* * *

Patrick Morrissey was an old hand at land development, and it showed. Tall and thin with a weather-worn face, he looked as though he had been in many a battle. When Marc arrived to propose buying a five-block parcel of land within Patrick's latest subdivision, the first thing he noticed was Patrick's slight limp and the way he seemed to lose his balance on occasions, as if he was not yet used to his disability.

"I can see a mutual advantage in you selling me these five blocks in one line," Marc noted persuasively. "Each of them would be difficult to sell to the general public because of their main-road frontage, while their location is actually attractive to me."

Patrick rubbed the point of his chin with his thumb and forefinger for a few moments. "It makes sense, Marc," he finally replied.

As Patrick continued gazing at the young man sitting in front of him, his face grew pensive. "You know, not that long ago, I was probably the biggest land developer in this city," he said, peering over the top of his bifocals to gauge Marc's reaction.

Marc kept listening, sensing that Patrick wanted to let him know that he was not dealing with just any land developer, but someone of real pedigree and experience. *I don't want to upset this guy; I'll just go along with him,* Marc thought.

"Yes, things were different then," Patrick mused, swiveling his chair to look out the window. "I had a tiger by the tail, and couldn't let go of it. I must've worked a hundred hours a week and had almost no other life. And what for?"

Don't look at me, Marc thought, hoping that Patrick had just posed a rhetorical question. After all, that was exactly how he operated. *Doesn't everybody who's in business for themselves?* he thought, a puzzled look stealing across his face.

As Marc snapped back into the present, he saw Patrick smiling at him before resuming his monologue.

"Yes, I had everything going for me," Patrick murmured thoughtfully. Then, his expression grew bitter. "But in the end, the bank got most of the benefit of my hard work." Patrick's voice changed tone; he took his glasses off and waved them in front of his face. "They forced me to sell most of my assets for a fraction of their real worth, just because they got nervous during the downturn of '78. It took me years to recover. I only do small subdivisions now, using only my own money."

Patrick paused, looking Marc squarely in the eye. "You're about to grab on to the tail of that same tiger," he warned, "and I want you to think about where it can lead. Ambition's not always a good thing!"

Marc felt a wave of panic break over him as Patrick swiveled back toward the window. *Great. Now he's going to back out of the deal,* he thought.

Just as suddenly, Patrick swiveled back so that he was facing Marc again. "I'm inclined to do this deal on the land with you, Marc," he said with an easy grin. "I'll tell you what: I'll hold the property while you take a couple of days to think about whether you really want the sort of life I had. If you still want to buy my land, then I'll sell it to you and won't sell it to anyone else in the meantime. You have my word on that!"

This was all too strange for Marc. He had come here only to buy this fellow's land, and now found himself being asked to consider the meaning of life. Well, at least Patrick had in effect said yes, and that had been Marc's main objective.

As Marc rose to shake Patrick's hand, the seasoned developer said with disarming honesty, "You know, I liked you the minute you walked into my office. You remind me so much of myself twenty years ago— so full of ambition, ready to take on the world and everybody in it. Just mind how you go, young man, because you might end up with everything you want and a whole lot more."

With an uneasy smile, Marc left Patrick's office with a little more than he had bargained for.

* * *

"Maybe Patrick's got a point, but I think that between us, we can make sure you don't fall into the abyss," Maddie told her brother with a broad smile after he finishing telling her about his meeting.

"Well at least he said he'd sell us the land, and that can't be half bad."

"It's going to be brilliant," she gushed. "It's more than we dared dream about."

Maddie's face lit up with enthusiasm as she imagined herself leading a powerful sales and marketing team. "I can see the whole thing now: A brand new display village with hundreds of customers lined up around the block!"

They stayed back in the office until late into the night, talking about what it was going to be like to have a five-home display village. Maddie eventually tired and finally went home, leaving Marc, who was still high on adrenalin, alone.

He looked at the clock and realized that he could now talk to Billy Kennedy, who would be just getting up for the day on the other side of the world. In recent times, as business began picking up, Marc had gotten lax in phoning his friend. Here was an opportunity to make it up to him.

"Are you sure that's what you want?" Billy asked Marc from his son's home in upstate New York, after Marc had described his meeting with Patrick.

"Why not?"

"It's like that man said Marcy, ambition *isn't* always a good thing. It can steal your life out from under you when you're not looking."

"I'll be careful," Marc replied, slightly miffed by his old friend's concern.

"It's not always in your hands, Marcy."

"Come on, Billy, it's me you're talking to. You know I can handle anything."

There was silence on the line for a moment as both sides prepared for another round.

"Look, Marcy," Billy began, "have you ever asked yourself what you really want out of life? An expensive car? A big house? Plenty of money?..."

"I want to be successful. I want everybody to be able to say that I made it with my own two hands and the brain that God gave me. I want the respect that comes with being a self-made success."

His answer revealed only part of the truth. As he talked, Marc's head filled with images of a white mansion like the one where he and Maddie had grown up in Algiers. Deep down, he longed to return to that huge house, and the carefree days he remembered as a child. He now had Maddie with him again, and that felt like the first crucial step toward getting there.

"I think this Patrick fellow might have summed you up," Billy chuckled. "You're in real danger of trading your life for an impossible quest."

"I thought you were on my side!" Marc said indignantly.

"Of course I'm on your side, Marcy, but that doesn't mean I want to go over Niagara Falls in a barrel with you."

"What?"

"Come on, son, wake up. There's more to life than just chasing money and a notion of success. What about your friends and family?"

"I don't have time for friends right now. They will come later, when I succeed. Maddie's my only real family, and she's right here beside me."

Marc's comment about Maddie being his real family stung Billy. After a short silence, Billy spoke again, his tone sounding slightly wounded. "If you ask me, you're taking on a huge risk with your life, Marcus. I've seen it so many times with other people during my working life. Even my own son seems to be falling victim to the never-ending search for more."

"But he's not *me*, Billy."

"Sure, but if you buy this land and build all those display homes, the whole thing will start to run your life. Once you learn to run fast enough to survive, you'll find something else and you'll end up running even faster to catch up with it."

"I come to you for support, and this is all you can say!" Marc growled into the phone. "I'm going to hang up now, before I say something we'll both regret."

"OK, Marcy. I'm just worried that you won't recognize what this obsession is doing to you until you're too far gone."

"Don't worry, Billy, I'm a big boy now. I'll ring you later," Marc said, slamming the phone down as if it had suddenly become too hot to handle.

*   *   *

The next morning Marc decided to do a little background check on this Morrissey fellow. He called his friend, Jim Daniels, who was a building products rep and seemed to know everybody in the industry. He and Marc had become instant friends on the first Highmark home.

"Yes, that's the fellow. About fifty, medium height with sandy gray hair, walks with a bit of a limp," Jim confirmed. "He's been in the business for ages, and has got a pretty good name in the industry."

"That's good, because I'm relying on his word," Marc replied wanly.

"Oh, if Patrick's given you his word, then you'll be fine. He used to do a terrific amount of land developing, but now he only does small stuff."

"What happened to him?"

"I don't really know, but I think he got burned in the credit squeeze of the late seventies. He got through it all right, but after that he seemed to scale down all of his operations."

"Well, if you vouch for him, then that's good enough for me, Jimmy," Marc told his friend. "I owe you lunch next time we get a chance."

"I hope you don't mind if I keep bringing a cut lunch," he replied with a chuckle. "Getting you away from that company of yours is like...well, trying to get shit off a blanket."

Jim Daniels was a rough diamond, and nothing he said could ever be taken as an offense. He just called a spade a spade, and that was what Marc liked so much about him.

"OK, you old rouge, what about next Thursday at noon then?"

The chuckle grew into a hearty laugh. "Suits me. I knew if I stirred you up enough, you'd spring for lunch!"

"That's what I like about you, Jim, you're a *thorough* rouge!" Marc said, his face splitting into a grin.

* * *

Marc called Patrick Morrissey exactly forty-eight hours after their meeting. "I really want to buy the land, Patrick. It's very important to me."

"Why am I not surprised? As long as you know what you're doing, Marc, but I can't help thinking that you're blinded by it all."

"Look, Patrick, I'm a young guy keen to climb the ladder, and that's all I can think about at the moment. I'd be lying if I told you anything else. Tell me honestly: Could anyone have told *you* anything when you were on your way up?"

"No, I suppose not," Morrissey said reluctantly. "Look, I'll accept your offer and agree to delay settlement for ninety days. I'll have my solicitor supply yours with the contracts today. Good luck! I know that treadmill you're about to get on, and I know you're going to need it!"

"Thanks, Patrick. You've been terrific. I really appreciate your help," Marc said, unable to conceal his delight now that the deal was done.

The small deposit was all the spare money that Highmark Homes Pty. Ltd. had in its bank account. Taking on such a large undertaking with such limited resources was either very brave or very foolish or both, but Marc felt that he must take the risk if he was going to get anywhere.

Marc called Billy later that evening, and quickly apologized for losing his cool.

"If I don't understand you, Marcy, no one does," Billy said with his familiar, disarming laugh.

"I need your blessing, Billy. Wish me luck."

"I do wish you the best of luck, Marcy," Billy replied sincerely. "If anybody can make it work, you will. Just try to remember what I told you, even if you don't agree with it right now. Time is a great teacher."

*   *   *

The next few months were a whirlwind of activity as the five-home display village was financed, built, landscaped, and furnished. At the same time all this work was being done, the company's main building program had to be kept on track in order to maintain the cashflow that was its lifeblood.

Maddie predicted a major jump in sales once the homes were complete, and if the interest signaled by the passing traffic during construction was any indication, she was going to be right. A little more than a year after starting the business, the siblings had the display village they had dared only to dream about.

Suddenly, in June 1984, the village was ready to open, and everyone's hard work finally paid off as the company's sales skyrocketed. Within a year of opening the display village, Highmark Homes was ranked as one of the top twenty homebuilders in the state.

Marc was now twenty-seven. Two years after leaving full-time employment, he was well on his way to becoming a millionaire. Although it didn't matter to him, since everything he made went right back into the business.

Almost daily, the new company was gaining a stronger reputation for delivering a high-quality product at a very competitive price, well ahead of any other builder's time lines. The company had dozens of satisfied customers, all of whom gave glowing testimonials about Highmark Homes's quality, reliability, service, and integrity.

The volume of work the display village generated was nicely matched by the company's ability to build the number of houses it sold. And Highmark Homes was also able to employ just the right number of subcontractors to keep its production levels in balance, moving them smoothly from job to job. Marc also recognized there was an incentive for subcontractors to work for just him, as it allowed them access to a constant stream of well organized work, without having to worry about where their next job was coming from.

With the balance of sales and construction in such good order, Highmark Homes was enjoying a golden period in its young existence. Maddie and Marc were an incredible team, and now they had something tangible to show for their teamwork.

In short, life was finally becoming sweet.

Chapter Four

When Maddie returned to the office after attending a sales and marketing seminar at the Regent Hotel in town, her eyes were brighter than usual.

"He is about your height and build, really good looking, and he's intelligent and a real gentleman," Maddie gushed.

"Did you get anything *else* out of the seminar?" Marc asked her, somewhat miffed.

"Of course I did, silly. But we just *clicked*. We have so many things in common."

Marc's eyebrows started knitting. "Where is this guy's business located?"

"Well, his name is Robert LaPont, and he has a business north of Sydney on the central coast. He works in the development field, subdividing land and building retirement villages." Maddie's smile slowly faded. "Aren't you happy that I met someone nice?"

"Yes, of course I am, Maddie," Marc answered, somewhat unconvincingly.

"Well, then…give me a hug, big brother," Maddie said, preferring to ignore her brother's less-than-enthusiastic response.

Who is this guy to just elbow his way into our lives and unsettle the natural order of things? Marc thought as he held Maddie close. *I'm not sure I like him, and I haven't even met him yet.*

"Look, I'd love to stay longer, but I've to go out," Maddie said with some urgency. "I just called in to pick up some quotes and see if you wanted to have dinner with me and Elisa Zubreroff. You know, the archaeologist friend of mine who just came back from Egypt? I've told her all about you, and she said that she'd love to meet you."

"Not tonight, Maddie. I'm not in the mood," Marc said, slowly filling with resentment at his sister's sudden emphasis on her social life. "Besides, I've got too much work to do," he said, strongly hinting that she should follow his lead and make work her priority instead.

Maddie eyed him critically. "You're such a stuffed shirt sometimes, Marc. You should really get out and meet some new people. You can't spend your whole life working. It's just not good for the soul!"

"Tell Elisa I'd like to meet her too, but some other time, OK? Right now, I've got a few things on my mind, and I don't feel much like rushing out to dinner."

"But she'll only be in Sydney for a couple of weeks before she heads off to Crete on another dig..." As Maddie took in her brother's pout, her face grew resolute. "Oh, well, it's your loss. Must fly. See you in the morning," she said, planting a kiss on his cheek before heading for the door.

Marc's world had taken a knock. It wasn't just that Marc thought no man was good enough for his sister; it was that he had dreaded the day when someone else's shadow would come between he and Maddie, taking away the opportunity for them to be together every day. He knew that his fantasy of he and Maddie living happily ever after in that huge white mansion would have to hit the wall of reality one day, but he had grown accustomed to using it as a point of refuge when things got tough, and he wasn't quite ready to give it up yet.

As Marc considered the unpalatable prospect of replacing a key salesperson and a trusted confidante, he shuddered. *Life without Maddie!* He tried to convince himself that it would probably never happen before settling down into more paperwork.

*   *   *

Elisa was already waiting for Maddie at a smart York Street café in the center of the city. She had selected a table on the sidewalk and positioned herself so that she could spot Maddie as she approached. It was a warm night at the end of a very hot day, and Elisa was thankful for the breeze that flushed the city streets of the day's stifling heat.

Turning in her seat, Elisa caught a glimpse of herself in the side window of a car parked next to the curb. The reflection revealed a classically beautiful lady with finely chiselled European features, long, dark tresses and shining, crystal blue eyes. In short, she appeared to be the same confident, happy young woman whom Maddie had known from her university days.

Elisa had been a positive force in Maddie's life for a long time, and vice versa. They had helped each other through some long nights when things were not going well at university or in their personal lives. In the years since, they maintained a strong friendship, and often sought each other's opinion on important matters.

Turning her gaze back to the street, Elisa could see Maddie approaching. Her friend's gait was slower than usual, and her face looked a little haggard, as if she was trying to work something out in her mind. Elisa knew not to ask if anything was wrong; if Maddie wanted help, she would ask for it.

"Sorry; I'm always late, aren't I?" Maddie remarked apologetically as she hugged Elisa.

"You're only a few minutes late. Anyway, I've been enjoying the breeze. I hope you don't mind if we dine *al fresco* tonight; it's too nice to be indoors."

"No, this is lovely," Maddie said, putting her bag down on an empty chair before ordering a glass of Perrier from the hovering waiter. "Now, tell me all about your dig. Did you have a good time in Egypt?"

"It was hot and dry; murder on my skin, my fingernails and my love life!" Elisa joked. "But seriously, it was darn hard work. Going overseas for one or two years at a time plays havoc with every aspect of your life; it takes me six months to get things back to normal when I return. This time, I've only got a couple of weeks before I'm off again to set up our new dig in Crete."

"Sounds like you're getting tired of it all, Elisa."

"No, not really; you just caught me at the end of a bad week. All I've been doing this week is unpacking, cataloguing, and attending debriefing meetings. I dread that part of coming home, but once I'm all unpacked, I soon get itchy feet again." Elisa sensed her friend's misplaced concern, and her face lit up with a smile. "Don't worry about me, Maddie. I love archaeology. It's what I do!"

"I believe you, but thousands wouldn't!" Maddie replied, smiling back. "How are things at the university? Are you getting any closer to that elusive professorship of yours?"

"You mean the Holy Grail, don't you?" Elisa said with a smirk and a roll of the eyes. "Oh, I don't know; I must be getting closer, I suppose, because I'm forever writing papers on my findings and heading off to present them at an international conference somewhere. Maybe I need to unearth the Dead Sea Scrolls again, or something equally earth-shattering."

"It must be hard for you in such a male-dominated bastion like the university," Maddie said. "Remember how we used to lament the lack of women in our faculties?"

"Yeah, but if you're good enough, you eventually make it."

"That's the spirit, m'girl; just keep on chipping away," Maddie said, lifting her glass of mineral water and clinking it against Elisa's.

"Anyway, how's that brother of yours? I hope he's not working you too hard?"

"No, he's OK," Maddie replied, her face darkening. "I think I may have upset him tonight when I told him about this fabulous guy I just met. I think it sort of knocked him off balance."

"Fabulous new guy! I need to hear all about him. Tell me everything, Maddie, and don't leave out a single detail," Elisa said, her interest piqued.

After Maddie had finished telling her friend about Robert LaPont, her eyes clouded over. *Here it comes,* Elisa thought, leaning forward to listen.

"I'm worried about Marc," Maddie confided. "He doesn't seem too keen about Robert. Marc and I have always been close—always there for each other through all the hard times. Even though I have no idea what will happen yet with Robert, I suddenly feel torn between being there for Marc and creating a life for myself."

Elisa's face glowed with compassion. "Maddie, if your brother is anything like you, he will only care about your happiness," she said firmly. "You should talk it through with him. I'm sure that he would only want what's best for you. He'd be crazy not to."

"Yeah, you're probably right, Elisa," Maddie told her friend, although her brow furrowed.

"Come on Maddie, it's not going to be that tough," Elisa said with a warm grin. "Time will sort everything out; you'll see. If it's meant to happen, it will."

Maddie pulled out a tissue from her handbag to dry the tears that had suddenly welled in her eyes. Elisa leaned across and took her friend's free hand.

"Now you know I'll always be there for you, Maddie, any time you need someone to talk to. Even when I'm in Crete, I'm still only a phone call away. Remember that."

"Thanks, sweetie," Maddie said with a brave smile. "Why am I getting so upset? It's not as if I'm contemplating eloping with the man—I've only just met him."

"I know how strongly you identify with your brother. But you owe it to yourself to make the right decisions for *you*. If you're not there for yourself, how can you be there for Marc?"

"That's true," Maddie replied, her face brightening.

"Now come on, we're out here to have good time. What do you want to order for dinner?"

*   *   *

Alone at his desk, Marc couldn't shake the uncomfortable feelings that Maddie's news had given him. Every time his mind wandered away from his work, he found himself wondering what he would do if his sister married and moved away. He finally decided to call Billy.

"How are you?" Marc asked when Billy answered the phone.

"Great, Marcy. I'm just getting the grandkids ready to go to the zoo. And after that, I suppose I'll have to sit through another McDonalds meal. Thank God, they have free coffee for senior citizens. I don't think I can face another cheeseburger."

"At least I didn't drag you off to McDonalds when you were babysitting me," Marc smirked.

"Yeah, but you were still a handful," his old friend and mentor returned with a laugh.

Billy was philosophical when Marc told him about Maddie's news and his fears about the future.

"Look, it might never happen, Marcy."

"Yeah, but it might." Marc's fingers drummed on the desk.

"You're going to have cross that bridge when you get to it—no sense in worrying yourself to death about it now. Just get on with your life and let time take care of everything else."

"It's easy for you, Billy; you're on the other side of the world. Here, where I am, it feels like someone's undermined a part of my foundation."

"Life has a way of quickly getting things back into perspective, Marcy—just allow things to take their course. I know how important your sister is to you, and you should consider her feelings in all of this as well."

"Yeah, I guess you're right. I'm thinking only of myself, but it's hard to let go. It was hard enough when *you* moved away."

"Ah-ha, so you *do* consider me part of your family," Billy crowed.

"Of course I do. Why did you say that?"

"Oh, nothing," Billy chortled. "Well, don't let a misunderstanding grow between you and your sister—tell her how you really feel. Don't let a festering silence create a divide between you two."

"I hear you, Billy. But it's hard not to be selfish and want to keep her all to myself. Oh, it's all too hard, Billy, and it's getting late. Maybe I'll feel better in the morning."

"Sure you will, and remember, I'm always here if you need a sympathetic ear."

"Thanks 'dad,' I'll talk to you soon," Marc laughed.

* * *

That night, his dream about the falling trees returned with startling intensity—so much so that he woke up feeling disoriented.

At work the next morning, Marc called Maddie into his office before she even had a chance to put her bag down. This was the first time he had ever contemplated telling anyone else about the extent of his torment, and it was the only thing Maddie didn't know about him.

Maddie listened intently as he finally unburdened himself about the nightmares, and reached for his hand. "Marc," she replied huskily, "I don't know how you're going to do it, but you have to get over this thing somehow. We all know it wasn't your fault. You've got to stop punishing yourself like this."

"Maddie, I've tried," he said, dropping his face into his hands. "But how do you get over the fact that you killed your own father?"

Maddie broke into tears, her pretty face contorting with anguish. "Everyone knows that it was a tragic accident. It's bad enough we both lost our father that day, but if I end up losing you too, then it would be an even bigger tragedy. You have to be able to beat this thing, Marc. You just have to!"

Marc shook his head resignedly. "I seem to have lived my whole life denying it ever happened. I've been so single-minded in everything I've done since that day that I thought I'd shut the whole thing out forever. I guess it didn't work."

"I know you're strong enough to beat this thing, Marc," Maddie replied tenderly. "You just have to have the same belief in yourself that I have."

"What you think is very important to me, Maddie. I know that our mother blamed me up until she died, but you really believe that I couldn't have done anything more to save Dad, don't you?"

"Everybody knows that, Marc! Mum didn't blame you, really. She simply could never come to grips with what happened. It was as if the light of her life went out, and neither you or I could have done anything about it."

"I could've at least stayed and helped, instead of leaving you alone with her while I ran away to the city!" Marc yelled, as he pounded his desk in frustration.

Maddie quickly moved around his desk and took his wrists, encouraging him to stand up. She then cradled him in a warm embrace.

"You have to stop beating yourself up, Marc!" she whispered into his ear, tears rolling down her cheeks. "None of it was your fault—you were just landed with an impossible situation. You dealt with it the best way you could."

"I just wish it were different, Maddie," he sobbed into her shoulder. "I wanted it to be so different for you and me."

Maddie stepped back and looked into her brother's eyes. "I'm very concerned for you," she murmured, "and, quite honestly, I've always been concerned for you. Why didn't you tell me about your terrible nightmares before? We've always been able to tell each other everything."

"I don't know," Marc replied sheepishly after wiping his eyes on his shirtsleeve. "I guess I figured it was something I felt I had to handle myself. Consciously, I know that I'm not to blame, but somehow my subconscious keeps taking me back to that horrible day, again and again."

"You know," Maddie began cautiously, "maybe you should see a psychiatrist, or someone else who can help rid you of your guilt. You should've seen someone right after it happened. Maybe I can help you find someone if you like."

As he considered her offer, Marc's expression grew stoic. "No, I'm OK now, Maddie. I've come this far without a shrink."

*   *   *

Over the next few weeks, Maddie and Marc talked about everything: his fears for her, her concerns for him, and the future of the precious bond between them.

But Marc was still refusing to seek professional help, which was a source of frustration to Maddie. She and Marc had their first argument in ages when she accused him of not wanting to see a doctor as a way of prolonging his suffering, and that he was using his suffering as means of stopping her from moving on with her life.

"You can't be serious!" Marc told his sister.

"How else can you explain it You know you need help, but you won't look for someone to help you—in my book, that smacks of self-pity."

"No, Maddie, it's not like that at all!"

"Well then, show me."

In spite of his initial protests, Marc soon started seeing Dr. Paul Williamson, a reputed specialist in deep regression therapy, about his nightmares. On his second visit, the doctor told Marc he wanted to try hypnotherapy and hoped that it might be a way to effect a long-term cure. But first, he wanted Marc to describe in detail what he remembered about the accident.

This was a dark place that Marc had fastidiously avoided visiting over the past years, and he found himself reluctant to relive that day again, even for his doctor.

"I can't help you unless you allow me in," Dr. Williamson told him firmly.

"It's not that I don't want your help, doctor; it's just that I'm balking at the thought of having to recount that terrible day," Marc said nervously.

"Maybe we can try a state of semi-hypnosis. That will put you at ease and allow you to be a little more detached as you describe what is happening to you."

"Sure, if you think it will help."

The doctor told Marc to focus his attention on the image of a spiral mounted on the wall and not to let his focus wander, not even for second. He told Marc that in a short time, he would feel his eyelids getting as heavy as lead; so heavy they would want to close.

At first Marc was slow to go under, but finally succumbed as Dr. Williamson's melodic voice guided him into a light hypnotic sleep.

"I want you go back into your childhood, to a time when you were a young boy," the doctor said as he started the process of regressing Marc to that fateful day in the bush.

After the doctor had brought Marc to a time just before his fifteenth birthday, he asked his patient to describe the scene.

Marc told the doctor that he had gone into the bush—a wooded area on their property in the southern highlands—with his father to fell some trees for firewood. They always used a chainsaw for this work, and Marc had used it to drop many a tree, becoming quite an expert with the dangerous tool.

Marc had relinquished control of the day's decisions to his father, Richard, who had spent a lifetime in the Army. Richard was still an active colonel at the time, and had had his British Army commission transferred to the Australian Army.

As Marc breathed deeper, more sights and sounds from the past began to fill his head. His body jerked slightly, and his expression made it look as though he was straining to hear something. "What's that noise?" he mumbled.

"Only you can hear it, Marc, so you will have to tell me what you hear," Dr. Williamson said. "Take your time."

A minute later, Marc's face relaxed. "It's just the wind, that's all. It's windy, but I can only really notice the wind when it catches the treetops and sends a whooshing noise down to the forest floor. Dad wants to fall a large, girthed tree that is standing in a small clearing. He reckons that the tree is big enough to provide firewood for the next month, and that this will make the whole exercise worthwhile."

A few more seconds went by. "What's happening now?" Dr. Williamson asked gently.

"I tell my dad that I don't like the way the tree is leaning," Marc answered, beginning to squirm. "I feel it will be difficult to make the tree fall into an area where we can get to the trunk. The tree has a twist halfway up its trunk, and I figure that it will be difficult to make the tree fall the way we want."

"It's all right, Marc," Dr. Williamson murmured soothingly. "Just keep talking. What happens next?"

"My father ignores my advice, which is nothing unusual," Marc replied bitterly. "He's starting his cut at the base of the big old tree. I'm just standing there and watching him cut a 'V' into the base of the tree on the side that he wants to hit the ground. He's going to make a horizontal cut on the other side of the tree, just above the "V," which will sever the tree and allow the 'V' to trigger and control the fall."

Marc paused, and his face became ashen.

"Go on," Dr. Williamson urged. "You're safe here, Marc. Keep talking. What is going on now?"

"Dad has cut the 'V,' and he's turning the chainsaw to the far side of the trunk and beginning to chew into it. As the chainsaw eats into the trunk, a sudden wind change is causing the tree to rock back, gripping the saw's blade and locking the cutting chain." Marc, breathing hard, paused again for a moment.

"Dad leaves the chainsaw idling in its jammed position while he steps back to ponder another plan. He doesn't want to lose his chainsaw, and he still hasn't given up on getting the tree down. Dad's telling me to man the saw and give it full throttle while he stands over me and pushes the tree forward."

Marc's hands began to shake. He was only dimly aware that he was beginning to talk faster and faster.

"I do as I am told while my father imparts a series of pushes that frees the chain long enough for it to cut a bit more with each push..."

Suddenly, a look of terror crossed his face, and he began to tremble violently.

"What is it, Marc?" Dr. Williamson pressed. "Tell me!"

"A huge gust of wind just caught the top of the tree," Marc choked out in a voice that seemed more like a teen-ager's. "The tree is pivoting at the cutting point, and kicking back as it splinters up its shaft. The tree is pummeling my chest, throwing me and the chainsaw about twenty feet."

Marc's voice then broke. "The tree is spinning...now, it's splitting and collapsing to the ground, catching my father and throwing him into its path," he managed between ragged sobs. "I see my father's body, trapped below the fallen timber. He isn't moving. I'm trying desperately to lift the tree, but can't budge it. I'm just not strong enough," he whimpered. "The forest is spinning around me faster and faster...now everything's gone black."

"This wasn't your fault, Marc," Dr. Williamson said quietly to his patient. "You did everything you could. You were a loving son who tried his best to keep his father from making a mistake."

"I couldn't stop him!" Marc howled into his fists, his emotional scars now fully exposed.

"No, you couldn't," the doctor replied. "A fourteen-year-old boy is no match for a giant tree, or a chainsaw, either. I think you were incredibly brave to risk your life in order to save his."

"B...brave?" Marc stammered through his tears.

"Yes, brave, Marc," Dr. Williamson replied firmly. "And wherever they are, I bet your mum and dad think so, too."

As Marc's face smoothed into a peaceful expression, the doctor smiled. "You are now safe and sound," he told his patient forcefully. "You're back in the present, and you're in control. You will begin to feel better now that you have finally got this off your chest. Now we can begin the healing process."

Chapter Five

Based largely on what Maddie told him, Marc supposed that Robert LaPont could be considered "old money," if such a thing existed in Australia. The LaPonts had held massive landholdings for several generations, and been one of the leading families on the central coast of New South Wales for all of that time. Maddie telling Marc that Robert had had a fairly privileged upbringing and had attended the best private schools in Sydney only cemented Marc's preconception of Robert as a stuck-up, private school type who was not able to get past his eternal loyalty to the old school tie and the fellows who attended the third grade with him.

All this made Marc very suspicious of Robert. He couldn't understand why someone from a wealthy family would get serious with someone who didn't have the same financial standing or social pedigree. He only hoped that Robert wasn't a cad who was about to shatter his sister's heart.

The next week, when Robert dropped in to see Maddie at the office on the spur of the moment, Maddie couldn't resist the urge to show him off.

"Marc, this is Robert," Maddie said proudly.

Although Marc was taken aback at this unexpected visit, he couldn't help being impressed by Robert's presence. He was about six feet tall, with a strong athletic build. He had a crop of black wavy hair, a tanned and unlined face, and his voice had a low, soothing quality.

"Pleased to meet you, Marc," Robert said as he offered a firm handshake and a friendly smile. "I feel I know you already, from all that Maddie has told me."

"Likewise, Robert," Marc said, still recovering from the shock.

"Maddie tells me that you're very busy down here."

"Yeah, we are," Marc replied as he got his bearings. "So, how is *your* business going? You're up on the central coast, aren't you?"

"I'm pretty busy, too. I spend most of my time doing land subdivision and dealing with bankers. It has its moments, but it's nothing like the hurly-burly of running a building company. Sometimes I envy you that, but only sometimes," Robert finished with a laugh.

"Can I make you two a cup of coffee?" Maddie asked, her brown eyes darting eagerly from one face to the other.

"Yeah, why not?" Marc said as he motioned Robert to sit down on the lounge in the corner of his office.

Marc found himself easily engaged by Robert's conversation and his laid-back approach. They quickly found that they shared common interests in sports as well as business. Robert was a big fan of cricket, and he and Marc began sizing up the relative merits of the upcoming Test series between Australia and England.

"You know, we've been playing five-game test series against the 'Poms' for over a hundred years, and even if we beat them, it still feels like we're in the middle of a never-ending battle. They just keep coming back again! You'd think it would get boring, but I'm just gripped by the contest—I find it hard to concentrate on work for those few weeks every couple of years," Robert confessed.

"I like the cricket, too," Marc said. "I'm always willing Australia on to win, even though my heritage is English, but I'm an armchair fan—I watch the highlights package on TV at night rather than go out to the ground."

Robert shot him a look of surprise. "You don't know what you're missing, Marc. The atmosphere at the ground, when two teams are playing any sport at the highest level, is unbelievable."

"Well, maybe one day I'll get out to a game."

"Maybe we can go out together. I've carried on my father's membership of the Sydney Cricket Ground Trust, and watching cricket from the member's pavilion is enjoyment in its purest form."

"You guys aren't talking sport, are you?" asked Maddie, returning with their coffee. "It's like the great Aussie barbeque, with the men in one corner talking sport, and the women in the other talking about their kids." She giggled.

"You didn't tell me you had any kids, Maddie," Robert joked.

"Only Marc," Maddie joked back.

"What can I say?" Marc said, offering his open palms up to the heavens as they all shared a chuckle.

*   *   *

A few weeks later, Marc received an invitation from Robert to attend the opening day of the Sydney cricket test as his guest. Robert had obviously gone to a lot of trouble to get another seat in the member's pavilion for one of the city's most eagerly awaited sporting events, so Marc couldn't resist taking him up on it.

They sat next to each other from the opening over at 11 A.M. until the last ball was bowled at six. During that span of time, they talked about many things.

"I went to boarding school, and we played a lot of cricket to kill the time," Robert explained to Marc during the course of the afternoon. "I suppose that's how I became hooked on the game."

"Which schools did you go to? Marc asked, turning to look into Robert's face.

"I went to the Lords School and Knights College," Robert replied without a hint of a brag. "I was school captain of both and captain of the cricket team." He shook his head and smiled. "Thank God for this glorious game—it's the only thing that kept me sane. Boarding schools can be terrible places for young boys." His smile disappeared, and he shifted uncomfortably.

So he's human, after all, Marc thought smugly. "Really?" he offered, affecting concern. "We public school boys always heard that the private schools were crawling with bullies. Was that true?"

"Yeah," Robert remarked with a laugh. "I suppose bullying was the worst aspect of my time at those schools, if you discount chronic loneliness. Most people left me alone, but some of my friends took a terrible shellacking. I used to have to step in and try to protect them with negotiation, fists, or anything else available to me."

"Is that why they made you school captain—because you fought for the underdog?" Marc asked, warming to the idea of Robert's selfless exploits.

After a moment of thought, Robert shook his head. "I don't know, Marc. I've never thought too much about it. I think I was too busy trying to make sure we all got through the day. Don't believe what they say about soft, private school types—some of them are absolute horrors!"

"Yeah, the future captains of industry," Marc smirked.

Another disarming grin spread across Robert's face, but his eyes were earnest. "Seriously, I think that's why I hold Maddie in such high regard. She has such unaffected beauty, elegance and charm, but I can picture her going in to bat for her friends in a heartbeat."

"She did it for her brother often enough," Marc remarked quietly.

By the end of the day, Marc decided that Robert certainly had the style and class that came with good breeding, but none of the off-putting pomposity that so often accompanied wealth. In fact, Robert consistently came across as one of the most down to earth people Marc had ever met. Marc found Robert to be a man easily judged on his own merits rather than on his inheritance, and was soon convinced of the genuineness of Robert's feelings for his sister.

After the day's play, Maddie had arranged to have them both over for dinner. She had worked feverishly to prepare a baked lamb dinner for the two hungry men.

"You really are a great cook," Robert told her reverently.

"Yeah, she's a special lady, this sister of mine," Marc said with a big smile, but nevertheless sending Robert an important message.

"My mother always said that a way to man's heart is through his stomach—cook you a baked dinner, and you'll follow me anywhere," Maddie said with a teasing smirk.

"I think I'd follow you anywhere on a empty stomach!" Robert replied spontaneously, causing Maddie to blush.

In spite of how well things were going, Maddie still seemed to be seeking a nod of approval from her big brother. Marc gave her a hand to clear the table before she served dessert in order to get a few minutes alone with her in the kitchen.

"Look, I really do like him, and if he makes you happy, then I like him all the more," Marc reassured her. "Anyway, you don't need my approval, Maddie!"

But they both knew she did.

Maddie and Robert soon became inseparable, and even Marc had to conclude they were made for each other. After his sister had given him so much of herself over the years, he couldn't allow her now to sacrifice her chance at happiness because of his selfishness. Marc knew that if Maddie married Robert, she would move up to the central coast and help her husband with his business, leaving him and Highmark Homes behind.

In the months that followed, Marc tried to convince Maddie that her work with him was coming to a close. He was slowly being cured of his nightmares, and she had played an integral part in helping him straighten out that aspect of his life. He knew that whether his sister left or not, he would never be able to repay her for the huge part she'd played in helping him establish his own business.

"I'll be fine," he told his sister every time she raised the subject. "I have to stand on my own two feet sooner or later. Anyway, there'll always be so much of you here that the place will run as if you were still around."

He didn't believe a word of it, but he had to say it.

* * *

Even before the prospect of losing Maddie, Marc had a sense of impending doom. Everything had been going exceptionally well till now, but experience had taught him that just when he started patting himself on the back, fate had a way of suddenly turning around and biting where it hurt.

His problem was that he had chosen the building industry, which was very cyclical. With every new upturn in the economy came a virtual armada of new building companies. Ninety percent of them would be wiped out by the time the next recession came around because of poor management, undercapitalization, or both. A builder could almost set his watch by these recession waves, which occurred every three to five years, and knew he had to make enough money in the good years to cover himself during the bad ones.

Marc became aware of a slight downward trend in the economy as he watched the business reports every day on the morning news. After operating for almost three years, Highmark Homes was only now really establishing itself and could do without the spectre of a recession.

He realized that first-time homebuyers would soon be under pressure, with unemployment figures on the rise. This meant he would have to focus his company's sales on second- and third-time homebuyers by redesigning many of the homes and adding more options and features.

He increased his advertising budget in an effort to reach a wider audience and slashed overheads and unnecessary costs, wringing out every last drop of efficiency from the building process in a determined effort to weather the economic storm that loomed on the horizon.

There was now a noticeable drop in the number of people visiting his display village, which was a more immediate concern. Marc knew the shelf life of these centers was only a couple of years before the model homes became stale with homebuyers. His village was now in its third year of operation, and if he were going to stay in the project home market, he would have to build a new center.

Now, more than ever, the survival of his operation depended upon it achieving mainstream general public exposure. Marc recognized this would happen only if he could get into something like a larger, better-publicized display village containing a group of similar builders. That in itself would be difficult because he also faced the added challenge of a dwindling real estate market, making it extremely hard to sell any of the five homes in his own village and severely restricting access to his own capital.

Marc felt his luck was changing when he heard about a huge display village that was planned for an adjacent suburb. The organizers were looking for new participants to fill out the village, which would feature as many builders as possible in a showcase environment. *Sounds promising,* Marc thought.

*　　*　　*

A public ballot for positions in this new village was to be held, and Marc had contacted the organizers to gain accreditation to attend. The organizer had assured him there would be plenty of land to go around, and he was also told that everything was in place to allow him to bid for several sites.

On the appointed date, Marc found himself sitting at the back of the ballot room, mouth open in disbelief. All the other builders who had had a presence in the previous display center had been given first option, and had tripled or quadrupled their previous holdings to shut out any new participants.

When he finally recovered, he started to walk out of the room and was approached by another builder who had also come to bid. He introduced himself as Bill Williams of Chantelle Constructions. "So, you missed out too?" he inquired.

"I'm afraid so."

"I heard that a lot of these builders had gotten together to keep you out."

"What...why would they do that?" Marc asked incredulously.

"They were genuinely scared of the competition you would have created."

"That's crazy. I thought this was supposed to be a civilized cooperative."

"This isn't Mother Russia, you know! I guess you can't blame them. They were just trying to protect their livelihoods," Bill said.

"What about you, Bill? Don't tell me that they wanted to lock you out too."

"I'm only a small builder. I really just came to have a look and maybe pick up some crumbs. But the others seemed so worried about you and Highmark Homes that they made sure that there was nothing left for anybody else."

"Funny, I don't see myself as a threat."

"The building industry is a lot more parochial than people think," Bill said as they both walked through the door. They shook hands and headed off on their separate paths.

*　　*　　*

Marc immediately found himself between a rock and a hard place. The deeper he ventured into business, the more difficult his decisions became. There was no respite, and he had to deal with the fact that sales of his project homes were diminishing to the point where it was getting hard to make the weekly payroll.

He knew he had to make some tough decisions—downsize the Highmark Homes operation to a trickle and operate it himself, or try a bolder new approach.

This issue occupied his mind for weeks. Finally, one Monday morning, Marc walked into his office and announced that he was going to shut down the display village and sell it off. He would take Highmark Homes into the prestige end of the contract-building market, which was still relatively strong.

Marc decided to employ an estimator to price the specialized work he planned to take on, and soon found a fellow who could start immediately, speeding up the whole process and forcing him to release his sales team sooner than expected. Luckily, he was able to place them all in good jobs with several of his real estate friends, and gave them all generous severance pay.

He then prepared a smart marketing package highlighting his company's achievements and background, and sent it, along with a letter of introduction, to every architect in town. He hoped that this approach would allow him to pierce the so-called "yuppie" market that, according to financial commentators, was the only group expected to have any real disposable income in the coming downturn.

During that period, many architects took up Marc's offer to price their clients' building work, and soon Highmark Homes had a full order book again, but this time it comprised one-of-a-kind architect-designed, homes or tricky renovations. With every confidence, Marc prepared himself for this new endeavor.

*   *   *

Maybe it was coincidental, but Marc's recent bout of decisiveness paralleled a breakthrough with his psychiatrist, Dr Williamson.

On many occasions over the past twelve months, the psychiatrist had taken Marc back to that fateful day in the bush. Each time, he had helped Marc recreate a little more of what had happened.

As a result, Marc was finally able to consciously remember how, after he had been hit by the tree, he had concentrated only on fending off the flying chainsaw with its free-spinning cutting chain as he flew through the air.

The doctor said this was the real source of Marc's guilt—he blamed himself for not saving his father because he had been too busy saving himself.

"It's going to take a little while, Marc, but I'm sure that you will eventually be able to see that there was nothing you could do," the doctor said at the end of their latest session.

"I think I can see that now, at least in the conscious world..."

"Yes, and in time you'll come to believe it in your subconscious mind. But you shouldn't expect to overcome the trauma of such an event without going through the proper healing process."

"Yeah, I guess so. At least I am sleeping a little better these days, Doc."

"That's a good sign, Marc, so let's keep going. Same time next week?"

"I'll be here. I think my car can just about find its own way here."

"That's not a bad thing," the doctor laughed, as he saw Marc to the door.

*   *   *

The work Highmark Homes now quoted and won was far more complicated than the basic stuff the company had been dealing with before. Thankfully, the initial surge of cash coming from deposits on these new contracts relieved the company's financial pressures. Marc was now well and truly in a new market, and there was no turning back.

With this batch of new work came the need to adopt a different building philosophy. Unfortunately for Marc, many of his project-home subcontractors were not up to the challenge of building esoteric projects—deserting him just as he was coming to the end of that project-building phase, and before he could start the new specialized homes.

Being deserted by people he had worked with for years gave him a sinking feeling, particularly when he realized that all his subcontractors had been spoon-fed ongoing work and had made good money as a result of his industry and risk-taking. Slightly miffed, Marc decided to supervise the construction of the new, more complicated homes himself, developing whatever new skills he needed along the way.

He wasn't looking forward to putting himself in the front line with clients and tradespeople, but what else could he do? He understood this was the price he had to pay to save his company, and just hoped he'd be able to tread his way through the minefield of uncertainties before him.

That thought was filling his mind the day his trusted friend, Jim Daniels, came to visit his office. Jim had since been promoted by his company to the position of business development manager, a role Marc felt Jim had earned because of his helpful and positive attitude.

Jim was a genuine sort of a guy who would do anything for anyone. He went out of his way to help Marc on many occasions, and Marc had returned the favor whenever he could. Theirs was one of those genuine friendships that spring up quickly against the strangest backgrounds. From that first day on a building site, they had felt an immediate rapport.

Jim had arrived at the Highmark offices to discuss his company's prices for the upscale products Marc was required to provide under his new contracts.

"It's good to see you, old mate," Marc said as he warmly shook Jim's hand.

"Yeah, it's good to see you too, Marc."

After spending half an hour going through the new price list over their second cup of coffee, Jim asked Marc about his foray into a new part of the building industry.

"Just watch out, Marc. Some of these upmarket clients can cause you more trouble than you ever imagined. They'll make you wish you weren't born if they get on top of you."

Marc's face grew somber with apprehension. "I'll see that I watch out, Jimmy."

Chapter Six

Maddie and Robert decided to get married in the following November, and what Marc had expected to be a low point turned happily into a high. Soon after agreeing to give Maddie away, Marc found himself caught up in most of his sister's wedding plans.

Maddie made Marc an integral part of the preparations and included him in as many of the lead-up arrangements as he would go along with. Knowing his sister, Marc suspected that she was doing this in the hopes of easing the pain of their eventual separation.

"You know, I sort envy you, Sis—getting married to someone you really love, who will look after you forever," Marc told Maddie one afternoon in a coffee shop, as they took a break after visiting the caterers.

"There's someone out there for you, Marc," Maddie declared resolutely as she poured cream into her cup. "She's probably right under your nose."

"Oh, I don't know; I never seem to attract anyone interesting."

"It's because you put out the wrong vibes. You're always so preoccupied with work that you create this sort of impenetrable barrier that's hard to get past."

"Hmm, maybe," Marc mumbled.

"It's only a mindset, Marc. Once you open up to the possibilities of the universe, your whole life will change…just like mine did."

Marc couldn't help but burst out laughing. "What's this 'possibilities of the universe' stuff?" He managed in between gasps. "You sound more like a tarot-card reader than my sensible kid sister."

"Laugh if you must, but I know I'm right," Maddie nodded knowingly.

"Maybe; we'll see," Marc said, without conviction.

"Same old Marc," Maddie sniggered.

* * *

The wedding day soon rolled around. It was a beautiful sunny spring day, with not a cloud in the sky, and Marc felt the optimism of the season as he arrived at Maddie's apartment.

He checked his attire in Maddie's living-room mirror while his sister prepared herself in her bedroom with the assistance of her three bridesmaids. He straightened his tie and tugged at the sleeves of his hired morning jacket. Although he looked the part of the dutiful elder brother about to give his sister away, he still felt a little ill at ease in an apartment overrun with primping women.

When Maddie finally emerged from her bedroom, she took her brother's breath away. She looked radiant in her pure white wedding gown and veil, holding her wedding bouquet in front of her in a full-dress rehearsal of the coming ceremony.

"Maddie, you look unbelievably beautiful," Marc said as he smiled at her in wonderment.

"You look pretty terrific yourself, sweetie," Maddie told her brother as she eyed his morning suit.

"Yeah, but you look *angelic*, Maddie," Marc whispered, the reality that his little sister was about to be married hitting home in earnest.

"I might look glamorous, but under all this makeup, I'm as nervous as a cat," Maddie joked nervously.

Sensing that his sister needed some reassurance, Marc gently guided Maddie out to her balcony for a few private moments.

"You've planned everything down to the smallest detail— everything will go off like clockwork, don't worry," Marc told her soothingly.

"I'm so disappointed that Elisa can't make it today. I really wanted her to be my maid of honor," Maddie fretted. "It's such a shame that her dig is so remote. I'm sure she would have come if she could have afforded the time, and it if wasn't going to take her three days to travel each way." Maddie started biting her lower lip, but once she tasted the lipstick, she winced and stopped.

"I'm sure she feels terrible about it, too," Marc murmured as he took her hands and squeezed them. "You two go back a long way—she'll make it up to you, I'm sure."

"I wish Mum and Dad could have been here," Maddie said as her eyes slowly filled up with emotion.

"I know," Marc said softly as their eyes locked. "That's what I was thinking, too. They'd both be so proud of you."

At that moment, Marc suddenly realized that even though Maddie was dedicating her life to someone else, he would never really lose her. No matter where life took him and Maddie from this day onward, there would always be a part of each other that knew what the other one was thinking. The link between them had survived many changes up to this point, and it was going to survive this one, too.

Marc's eyes shone with joy as he squeezed his sister's hands again. "Now come on, don't let any dark clouds get near your happy day—it's all sunshine and smiles today."

"Are you going to be all right?" she whispered in his ear.

"Yeah, I'm made of steel. Everything bounces off me," he sniggered.

As Maddie drew her head back to look into his face, her expression was somber. "Seriously, Marc, I need to know that you'll be OK."

"Maddie, my sweet sister, I'm fine with everything," Marc insisted. "I'm excited about you getting married, and having fulfillment in that part of your life. I just want this to be the happiest day of your life, so please don't worry about me...I'm with you all the way."

As the two siblings hugged again, Marc looked at his watch and realized that the bridal party was already a few minutes behind schedule.

"Come on ladies, our chariots await us," Marc announced, motioning the bridal party toward the three-car convoy of white Rolls Royces waiting in the street below.

Twenty minutes later, the church doors opened, the organ burst into the bridal march, and the congregation stood and turned to see Maddie, resplendent in her wedding gown and long veil, being escorted down the aisle by her brother. Her three bridesmaids marched in single file behind Maddie's trailing veil.

As they approached the altar, Marc saw the loving look on Robert's face. In that second, Marc shared a part of their feelings, and was finally reassured that this was right for Maddie.

As Marc passed his sister's hand to Robert's, he whispered, "Take care of her; she's a precious flower."

"I will," Robert said with conviction.

At the reception, Marc sat at the bridal table and was separated from the bride and groom by Robert's best man and his two groomsmen. Maddie's bridesmaids filled the other end of the table. All three bridesmaids were old school chums and formed part of Maddie's tight circle of friends.

Marc had met them all many times before when they were still college students. None of these ladies had ever interested Marc who, from the little he knew about them, believed that they were not his type. Now, on the happiest day of Maddie's life, he found himself looking out into the sea of guests and wondering if there really was someone out there for him.

* * *

After Maddie and Robert returned from their honeymoon in Europe, they decided to set up house at Whitefeather Cove—an estate that Robert had inherited from his parents, who had passed away several years earlier.

The beautiful old home, perched high atop an emerald green escarpment, stood on five hundred and fifty acres of prime land that ran up to the cliff's edge and had unobstructed views of the coastline and the Pacific Ocean. It also overlooked a beautiful private white sandy beach, which was really a crescent-shaped cove totally inaccessible by land to anyone other than the owners. Looking down on the beach from the house seemed to make the scatter of well-weathered rocks appear as if they were cemented into the fine white sand. This collection of blunt, protruding rocks provided refuge for the seagulls and other bird life that frequented the foreshore—hence the property's name, "Whitefeather Cove."

The place had been in the LaPont family for five generations, since Robert's great-great grandfather, Francois, had emigrated from France in 1822. The house had a lovely, homey feel about it, due to the generations of LaPont women who had left their indelible mark on the place.

Robert's great-great grandfather must have been a very astute man indeed. He had the foresight to identify and claim this special parcel of land, even though it was then a long way from civilization and the young settlement of Sydney Town. He was clearly a man driven by his own vision, one who was prepared to think outside the accepted norms of his day.

In those early days after Australia's settlement, he not only saw the potential of this wonderful location, but also bought large tracts of land in the surrounding area for a song. He built the small mansion with the balance of the money he brought with him from France, and eked out a living as a farmer after wresting his farmland from the tough virgin bush.

In recent years, Robert's father and later, Robert himself, had developed large parcels of their inherited land into rural and residential subdivisions. Robert had taken the family development business to another level and had been actively purchasing other land in the area to fuel his larger ambitions.

Maddie was a perfect wife, and the new couple seemed deliriously happy. She was also able to help Robert with his business because, although he had great wealth, it was all tied up in land. When Maddie examined her husband's books, she was shocked to find that he had to quickly sell off most of the two hundred blocks of land in his latest subdivision in order to appease his pressing bankers.

Robert's real problem was that none of the local real estate agents he had hired over the previous eighteen months had been able to sell more than ten blocks of land in this particular subdivision. This had caused the bank to doubt Robert, a situation that grew worse with each passing month.

Maddie decided to take control of the marketing herself. After firing all the local agents, she set up a new marketing campaign that targeted city investors. She then linked a number of local contract builders with a group of well-heeled business people looking for investment properties.

Through these means, she managed to sell all the property herself within six months. Not only did she get Robert's business back on its feet, but she also saved him almost half a million dollars in real estate commission in the process.

Robert soon realized why Marc had been so reluctant to lose Maddie's business skills, and considered himself a very lucky man. Not only had he found the love of his life, but also one of the best businesswomen he had ever met. Like all great relationships, theirs existed on several different planes.

* * *

With Maddie married and now living on the central coast, Marc was now running Highmark Homes on his own, more or less. Maddie rang him nearly every day to chat and offer whatever advice the situation warranted, but Marc found himself standing more and more on his own two feet.

This was a time in his life when Marc began to feel like he could control his own destiny. His sessions with his psychiatrist, Dr. Williamson, were now at an end and he had finally come to accept that he was not to blame for his father's death. His nights were more peaceful than they had ever been, and he felt better about himself than he had for a long time.

Armed with his new self-belief, Marc single-handedly met a whole range of building and people problems, but noticed that the harder he worked to solve each one, the harder things became. He also saw his cash flow drop behind his actual costs. Most of his well-heeled clients were slow payers, and this was stretching his working capital.

He went on undaunted to his next job and the challenges that it posed. The Grimm brothers' job was one of those ongoing sagas that had started when he had first entered his new specialized building phase and, in one way or another, ended up occupying the next eighteen months of his life.

Grimm was their real name. Better yet, they were identical twins. Michael Grimm was an architect, while his brother Colin was a lawyer. They were short men, with smarmy smiles constantly painted on their chubby faces. They wore cardigans, and seemed addicted to brown corduroy trousers.

Michael had designed Colin a dream home that Colin was happy with until the brothers sat down one day and decided to redesign it. They then scrapped the whole thing and designed it all over again before redesigning it a fourth time. *Two of the world's worst ditherers*, Marc thought when they first met. As the brothers explained their building needs, they took turns finishing each other's sentences.

"We're very happy with the price you've quoted to build the house," Colin told him.

"You do understand that my price is based on the specifications that Michael has provided?" he asked them.

"Oh yes," they confirmed.

"We can sign up today if you want," Colin added, "as long as you're prepared to sign a building contract that stipulates that an architect—Michael in this case—be appointed to supervise the works."

"Sure; I don't have a problem with that," Marc said.

When the work started, Michael insisted on visiting the site at the end of each day. He was very diligent, arranging weekly construction meetings with Marc. However, it wasn't long before he started changing things almost as quickly as Marc could build them.

"Don't worry about it. Anything I change from the original drawings will be a variation to the contract. Colin will happily pay you for these changes," Michael said, his hand firmly placed on his heart.

This house was unique, to say the least. In fact, Marc often described it to his friends as the sort of house that only a mother could love.

It turned out that Michael had no real idea of how to build many of the features that he had incorporated into the design. Marc was amazed to find that all of these details were left to him and his tradesmen to work out. Nothing on this particular job was straightforward. There were curved walls everywhere, extending upward to meet an elaborate system of exposed cathedral ceilings. Further on in the house, the walls and ceiling changed shape yet again. As it turned out, the owner and his architect wanted everything in this house to be of a higher quality than that allowed in the quote, and the cost of construction escalated dramatically.

Michael stopped coming to site meetings but kept up the communications by phone, still reining in the changes and upgrading the finishes. It got to the point where Marc would arrive on the job in the morning to find Michael's fresh messages scribbled on the wall, such as, "remove this section of plaster" or "move this door opening," but still no sign of Michael or Colin themselves. This went on for months, right up until the job reached its final stages.

Then all of a sudden, Colin Grimm started showing up and began making even more changes, freely ordering bigger and better ones. He had an annoying habit of getting to the site just as Marc's workmen were about to install an item ordered months earlier. Colin would then tell the subcontractors not to use that particular item, because he now didn't like its color or design. He then expected the men to drop everything so that they could rush off to the nearest hardware store and change the item. The upheaval that this caused was almost too difficult to quantify, because everything was hectic enough in the final stages of a job, as people ran in all directions trying to finish off all the bits and pieces.

Marc was beginning to smell a rat with the two-man, tag-team antics—nothing he could readily put his finger on, but experience had taught him that money was usually part of an owner's motivation when acting this way. He decided to call his friend, Jim Daniels, to see if had heard anything about the brothers.

"Sorry, I can't help you, Marc," Jim told him after a moment's silence at the other end of the phone. "But then again, I wouldn't expect to have heard of these people unless they were serial rip-off merchants. My intelligence network relates mostly to people who work within the industry."

"Thanks anyway, Jim," Marc said resignedly.

"You'd best err on the side of caution and make sure that you don't let them get behind in their progress payments. By the sound of them, you don't want people like that owing you money."

Marc took his friend's advice and decided to prepare his final account for this job before it was due. When he summarized all the extra costs, he was amazed to see that Colin's spending spree had increased the costs by more than fifty percent of the original contract price. Colin Grimm now owed him a quarter of a million dollars after including their variations and the amount outstanding against the contract.

Their changes had significantly extended the construction time, which meant that Marc had to pay extra for overhead and supervision. It also meant that he couldn't get off this job and move on to a more profitable enterprise. He knew that builders were entitled to claim reimbursement for such costs under the "prolongation" provisions of the contract. But when he calculated this figure, he was horrified to see that it had increased his costs by an additional $100,000.

When he presented his bill to the brothers at the nearly finished house, they went ballistic.

"You never told us anything about these extra costs. Where do you think I'm going to get this sort of money from?" Colin shouted at Marc.

"What did you think—that all the variations you ordered would be done free of charge because you're nice people?" Marc thundered back.

"There's no need to let this get personal," Michael whined in an effort to mediate.

Marc swung around to confront the other twin. "You're right, Michael. There's nothing personal about letting you two put your hands in my pocket, is there?" he replied, his anger rising.

"I don't think there's any point in talking about this while you're in this mood," Colin said dismissively.

"How very nice of you, Colin," Marc spat sarcastically. "If I had $350,000 of your money, I'll bet you wouldn't be as relaxed as you appear to be with my money!"

As the twins' phony veneer crumbled, their pasted-on grins were replaced by conniving, contemptuous sneers. "It seems to me that you have a bigger problem than we have," Colin told Marc as he and his brother stood up to leave. *"You've* got to get the money from *us."*

It was clear from their response that the Grimms weren't about to pay up. Gone was the go-ahead-we'll-be-happy-to-pay attitude.

Oh no, not a building contract dispute, Marc thought. He had been lucky so far, and had always been able to avoid these sorts of disputes like the plague. But if the twins didn't pay, then he'd have to fight fire with fire and keep them out of their new house.

Marc knew that there wasn't much more a builder could really do because, in the final analysis, the finished house stood on the owner's land. If they broke into the house and took possession, there would be no alternative but to take them to court and battle for his rights in an expensive judicial system heavily slanted toward the consumer.

It soon became apparent that the Grimms were past masters at ripping people off, and had used the legal system to their advantage many times before. Sure enough, they broke into the completed house and took possession. The Grimms now had the house, and Marc was about $350,000 out of pocket.

So much for the big end of town, Marc thought. He'd never had bad debts with any of the so-called "blue-collar" workers for whom he had built basic project homes. They were hard-working, honest people who always honored their commitments. There were always those who couldn't pay part of their final bill, but he had always been able to reach an agreement with them and sometimes even forgave part or all of the debt, depending on their circumstances.

These so-called "professionals" were a different breed and seemed prepared to use every trick in the book to get what they wanted without meeting their contractual obligations, clearly choosing to abuse the legal system rather than pay up.

With no other option available, Marc went to see a solicitor recommended by the President of the National Builders' Association.

"I believe you have an open and shut case," William Munro told him.

William was a man in his forties who looked eager for battle. His was a tall, thin man whose wrinkled forehead and prematurely gray head of sandy hair bore testimony to many similar legal fights.

"How long will it take to get these dirtbags into court?" Marc asked.

"Probably two to three years," William said with a shrug.

"What!" Marc recoiled.

"Yes, Marc, the courts are full to overflowing with these sorts of cases. Judges hate building disputes because they're so complicated."

"There's got to be a better way, William," Marc said as he rubbed the back of his neck in frustration.

"There's always arbitration, or conciliation," William suggested. "After all, you're a member of the National Builders' Association, and an arbitration could probably be heard within twelve months. It often produces the same outcome as the court system."

"Twelve months is no good to me," Marc spat. "I'll be broke by then!"

"Well, under the building contract, we can force them to conciliation almost immediately. It's not as regulated as arbitration, but the outcome is binding on both parties, and with the other side's agreement, lawyers can be used to put the respective cases. It'll be a lot cheaper than arbitration, too."

"If it's that quick, let's do it," Marc said eagerly, his face lighting up.

*   *   *

Armed with boxes of files, he and his solicitor found the room designated for the conciliation. The National Builders' Association, the NBA, often used this room for their regular meetings. Marc recognized it by the ornately framed portraits of past presidents, dating back to 1895, which filled its dark, timber-paneled walls. Its rectangular shape made the collection of portraits appear as if they were hanging in the back room of an art gallery.

The room's modern, concealed lighting contradicted to its period decor, and was so dim that it was difficult to make out the facial features of the person sitting opposite, let alone read the papers that were spread out on the table. Thankfully, after a while, everybody's eyes got used to the lighting.

Across the arbitration table sat the Grimms and their legal people. Jonathon Hastings, a senior partner in the firm of Hutchings and Wilmont, and an attractive junior associate represented the Grimms.

Marc's $350,000 claim against the brothers consisted of about fifty points of claim, and included a claim for an extension of time to the contract completion date and its associated prolongation costs. It was critical for Marc to win this part of the claim—not only because it represented $100,000, but also because the brothers had lodged a cross-claim for the same amount as their damages for the job not being finished within the original contract completion time.

The Grimms had also come up with a lot of spurious demands to offset Marc's claims against them, but were obviously pinning most of their hopes on their $100,000 damages claim for late completion to offset the prolongation claim against them.

Once the conciliation got under way, everybody settled down and was very cordial to one another. Every now and then, things would erupt, and the conciliator would referee the fight by scampering around the table to calm the warring parties.

The battle raged for about two weeks, and Marc progressively won most of his fifty points of claim, netting him just under $250,000.

The next real test had to do with the extension of time, which both sides knew would determine the final value of the case, depending on which way the conciliator ruled.

The conciliation proceedings were a lot less formal than a court proceeding, and evidence was taken in an almost conversational format. Both parties' lawyers made arguments as to why their client should prevail.

After listening to legal argument for three hours, the conciliator rose and advised that he would hand down his determination after the luncheon adjournment.

*　　*　　*

Marc stayed on to pack away some of the papers he had brought to support his position. This left him sitting opposite Jonathon Hastings's associate, Loren Wilmont—who, he had been told, was also the daughter of one of her firm's principals. Loren was a tall, slender woman of about twenty-five. She had fiery red hair, which was neatly tied at the back, and emerald green eyes that stood out against her pale, powdered skin.

Throughout the proceedings, he had noticed her sneaking glances at him. On a couple of occasions, Loren had permitted a half-smile to flash across her face whenever she caught Marc gazing at her across the heavy oak table that separated the warring parties. There was something about her face, Marc thought. It was as if she was hiding a secret that she was dying to share with him.

She's the enemy, he kept reminding himself while concentrating on the battle at hand. As the hearing progressed, he started to dismiss her little looks, preferring to think she was just bored with the endless details brought out by the parties.

"Tough going, isn't it?" she said, rocking back in her chair to expose the soft flesh of her inner thigh while flashing him a suggestive smile. When she had spoken during the proceedings, she sounded educated and confident. Now, her voice was low and sultry.

"It sure is," Marc replied, motioning to his solicitor that he'd shortly join him outside the room.

"Look, the rules don't allow me to say too much, but it would be nice if we could have coffee together after this is over. Purely personal, you understand," she said with an impish smile that revealed fetching dimples.

Marc was surprised by her fast approach. "I'd like that, Loren," he delivered instinctively into her hypnotic gaze. "It'll give me a good reason to get this trouble behind me, won't it?"

"Well, I hope so, Marc. Look, if it gets too hectic when the conciliator returns and if we end up missing each other, will you call me at the office?" She handed him her business card.

"Yes, of course I will." Marc felt his knees turn to jelly.

As their hands touched, he could feel the sexual energy ignite between them. Marc was both amazed and intrigued that within a few seconds and with only a few words, this woman had sent him into a spin. He could hardly believe this was the same woman who had sat opposite him every day for the past two weeks. *Where was I?* Marc wondered.

"It will be great to finish this bloody battle and get on with the rest of our lives, won't it?" she said in a way that made Marc wish he had her in bed.

He had to change the subject quickly, as he felt his heart pumping blood to parts of his body that had no place in this forum. "You know, Ms. Wilmont, I can't say that I'm impressed by your choice of clients."

"Come on, Mr. Braddon," Loren replied with a smirk. "You know that lawyers have to take all comers. We're duty-bound to do our best for our clients. I assure you it's nothing personal."

"Of course, I know that. I just thought that I'd get a rise out of you while we were still on opposite sides of the table," he said in a failed attempt at humor.

"There'll be plenty of time for that later," she said, as her eyes lingered on his zipper.

They both let out nervous laughs as they walked out of the room together. No doubt about it: They had made a connection in those few minutes that sent a wake-up call to Marc's senses. He felt as if he had been cattle-prodded rather than awakened! *Just as well all this is going to be over soon,* he thought. He wasn't sure he'd be able to concentrate for much longer with an overtly sexy Loren sitting opposite.

He escorted her to the door, pressing his hand gently against the small of her back as all sorts of sexual fantasies danced across his mind.

She half-turned and smiled back at him as they parted, and he moved off to join his solicitor, who had been waiting for him in the hallway.

William Munro smiled knowingly. "You look a little flushed, old boy."

"It has nothing to do with the case, but I think I just got picked up!"

"Well, half your luck, Marc. That Loren is a real looker, but she makes it a rule not to date lawyers, so yours truly didn't stand a chance!"

"I'm not surprised. The way you lawyers talk about each other, the poor girl would be pilloried in an instant! Your lot has no appreciation for a woman's charm," Marc remarked with a laugh.

Although he'd had many sexual encounters with women over the years, Marc had never gotten seriously involved with any of them. *Who needs it?* he used to think. He always ended up satisfying himself with the thought that his work prevented him from becoming involved with anyone, but in truth, he had never found anyone who understood him and his lifestyle.

Loren seemed different. There was something very attractive about her that was hard to define, a sort of impishness. From the little he'd seen of her in the arbitration room, he'd formed the impression that she was quite intelligent. *Why not? Maybe it's time I took a chance on someone*, Marc thought as he and his solicitor walked down the street to their now-regular lunch spot to buy a sandwich.

*   *   *

After everyone returned and the room came to order, the conciliator announced he had found in favor of the owner on the issue of prolongation. He said he believed that as the builder, Marc should have known to file his extension of time claim within a reasonable time of the delays becoming apparent, regardless of the architect's actions. He also stated that a "reasonable time" under the contract was no more than fourteen days.

This had the effect of crediting the owners $200,000 against his claim, and effectively meant that the Grimms had managed to turn a claim of $350,000 against them into one of about $150,000. Not only had they managed to avoid over $100,000 worth of prolongation charges by forcing him go to conciliation, but they had also used this point against him to reduce what he'd already won by an additional $100,000.

The Grimms had somehow managed to win by losing. No wonder they liked going to court so much!

"Some advertisement for justice!" Marc said in disgust. His solicitor agreed.

"We can appeal, Marc. I really don't know how this guy found for the Grimms on the extension of time," William said. "You were clearly set up by these scoundrels. It sticks out like a sore thumb."

"What would be our chances on appeal?" Marc asked.

"Difficult to say. The Supreme Court wouldn't overturn something that had been decided on fact, but they would certainly look at denial of natural justice as a proper basis for appeal. We must have come close to that today!"

"We'll talk about it later, William. I'm not really thinking too clearly at the moment," Marc said, as he gathered up his files. He thought he'd prepared himself for the effect of such a loss. He thought he'd be all right if everything went against him, but he wasn't, and it was like dropping into an emotional freefall.

It started with a sick feeling in the pit of his stomach that spread through the rest of his body, affecting all his thoughts. He just wanted to get out of that room and leave behind what he perceived as a failed attempt to get justice from an unjust legal system.

He'd had enough of tilting at windmills for one day. It was now time to retreat under the cover of night.

*   *   *

Marc's lived in the inner city suburb of Glebe, in an old three-story walkup that had heavy cedar doors, high ceilings, and oversized rooms. The building had recently been renovated and was painted a stark white throughout.

Marc's freshly painted second-floor apartment overlooked a narrow, tree-lined street—a view Marc often found himself gazing at late at night as he turned over the day's events in his mind.

Tonight, Marc was sitting in his living room, licking his wounds. He found himself staring at the blank wall as he sipped at his third neat scotch of the evening, still trying to come to grips with the events of the day.

It still irked him that the brothers had managed to rip him off, but he was slowly getting over it. He kept conjuring up images of them and their legal team at a drunken victory celebration somewhere in the city while he moped around at home.

He wanted to get that image out of his head, and the scotch was slowly beginning to help. After all, he had to accept that such an outcome was possible. His solicitor had told him as much on several occasions, so why was he surprised? That rhetorical question put an end to another round of mental recriminations, but within another five minutes, Marc found himself starting the whole process again.

This is a good time to take stock of my life, he thought as he completed another continuous loop of unproductive thought. He had been in business for just under five years, and was now nearly thirty years old.

During that time, he had established a building company, been forced to change direction by a recession, redeveloped the business, and now had just about come to the end of that two-year cycle with the completion of the last couple of jobs.

Marc realized that he still had the wherewithal to stay in business because, in spite of the losses he had suffered on his latest venture, he still had several valuable assets and some cash reserves left. He was also on good terms with many of his suppliers, and they were still prepared to provide credit and support him if he chose to continue in the building business.

His recent experiences had given him a healthy mistrust of well-heeled professional clients, and he resolved to never again build for such people. *Maybe I should build larger houses, but on a speculative basis,* Marc thought, as the third scotch started to kick in. After all, he now had all the building expertise that he needed.

It would probably take a lot more capital than he presently had, but it would give him the independence he sought from bad clients and unfair building contracts. Anyone who purchased one of his houses would have to pay full price for the completed house and land package.

He was still sober enough to realize that he would have to deal with these clients only through his lawyers. Although he liked that idea, he still wondered where he was going to get the needed funds.

It's too hard to think about today, he concluded. He could feel his brain shutting down as his double-malted scotch took hold. *I'll think it through tomorrow, when I'm in a better frame of mind,* he thought as he tottered off unsteadily to bed.

Chapter Seven

Loren sat in her office, wondering why Marc hadn't called her in the five days since they had met. *He seemed so keen at the time. Well, if he doesn't want to call me, then why should I care*, she thought.

She let that train of thought dissipate as she opened another of her client's files and started to make some notes on the yellow legal pad she had strategically placed on her desk.

I don't know why I have this fatal-attraction thing going, she thought as she scribbled. *Maybe it goes back to my childhood—maybe it's got something to do with the way my mother is.*

Loren put the end of biro she was holding to her lips, immediately visualizing herself as a high school senior sitting at her desk in her small bedroom, studying dutifully for her final exams—although they were then still six months away. Loren was doing what her mother, Margaret, demanded—study, study, and more study. Loren going to a university was a given in the Wilmont household, even though Margaret received little help from Loren's father to pay for their daughter's upbringing.

She could still hear her mother's favorite catchcry: "If you get high enough marks, you'll be able to choose whatever university you want. I haven't worked my fingers to the bone to support you for all these years just to see you fritter away your God-given talents!"

Loren could also hear her anguished response. "It's not as easy as you think, Mum. Why don't *you* try doing some of my calculus problems?"

"Don't be so disrespectful, young lady."

"You're always hounding me. It's not as if you're *so* perfect!"

"And what's that supposed to mean?"

"I've heard you telling your boyfriends how you walked out on my father with his best friend, just because he shouted at you for flirting. How *could* you! Thanks to you, I've had to grow up without him to look after me."

"I look after you, don't I?"

"Yes, Mum, you do. But how do you think it makes me feel? My father has been a virtual stranger since I was five."

"I didn't stop him from seeing you. He's got another life, and another daughter, and I suppose he's just forgotten about you."

"Maybe," Loren replied. She had gotten used to her mother's brand of tough love, and had learned to turn off and not to allow her ego to be crushed by Margaret's caustic thrusts.

I don't care what you think, you old cow. If you could keep your hot pants on he'd still be here, Loren thought, picturing the dozens of men who had traipsed through her mother's life and how they had tried to rule her and her mother in one way or another. She turned up her nose in disgust.

The tug-o-war of emotions left her in a constant quandary and gave rise to a rebellious streak, which she found harder to suppress as she approached womanhood. On her more introspective days, she wondered if she was rebelling more against a dysfunctional mother than a father who had forsaken her.

I'm going to be eighteen soon, and then I'll be out of her control, she thought as her imagination ran wild with images of everything she'd heard about sex, drugs, and rock and roll. Although she had never had sex, she knew she had the body for it and liked the power it seemed to give her over men.

*　　*　　*

As Loren relived her last days at high school, she remembered how she would modify her pleated school uniform each morning as soon as she was out of sight of her mother, tightening her belt and transforming it instantly into a much more provocative garment by lifting the hemline and folding the excess material over the waist-splitting belt. She would then unbutton her blouse to exposure a hint of soft white cleavage and lace before teasing her hair up into a more daring style. Her naïveté and inquisitiveness was a potent brew that had already drawn her irresistibly toward the faster side of life.

Looking out her office window, Loren's mind flashed up the image of the day she had arranged to sneak out in the dead of night with her best friend, Cathy Kendall.

"Come on, Cathy; it'll be fun!" Loren remembered saying.

"What if we get caught? We'll be grounded forever!"

"Don't be such a chicken. I'll be there, too. We'll have a fantastic time!"

"OK, OK. I'll meet you at eleven at the bottom of your street."

"Are you sure? I don't want to get there and find myself alone."

"I'll be there, don't worry."

Tonight's the night, Loren remembered thinking as she worked studiously at her desk to hide her plans from her ever-vigilant mother who might burst through her bedroom door without warning. Tonight, she had decided, would be the start of the next stage in her quest to sample what the world had to offer an attractive young girl—one filled with a sense of wonder and just starting to come into her own as a woman.

Loren planned her escape through her ground-floor bedroom window. Until then, she had to force herself to study until about ten o'clock, when her mother would stop by to say good night before going to bed. She would then allow another half-hour or so for Margaret to doze off before starting to dress for her big night out. She decided not to put her make-up on at home, reasoning that if her mother came in unexpectedly, she could explain away trying on a dress, but make up would leave her mother with little doubt of her intentions. If everything was still quiet when she finished dressing, she would slide open her window and make a silent getaway to a world beyond her mother's suffocating grasp.

After meeting up, she and Cathy planned to make their way across the park to a local service station, borrow the key to the restroom, and put on their makeup before heading off to sample some of the local nightspots. Loren didn't know what the night had in store for her, but she was determined to meet it head on.

* * *

Loren remembered silently sliding her bedroom window up, taking care not to ladder her nylon stockings as she straddled the window. She lowered herself until she hung from the sill. Holding that position for a moment, and with her head still inside her room, she listened for any sound from her mother's room before dropping the last few feet to the ground.

Her stocking feet landed softly on the lush lawn and, after brushing herself off, she checked for any sign of nosy neighbors before scampering across the lawn, high-heel shoes in hand, toward the end of her street.

It was 10:50 P.M., and she hoped that Cathy would already be there as she hurried to their meeting point. She kept looking for her in the shadows where the dark edges of the park met the half-lit street, but there was no sign of her. After waiting impatiently for another twenty minutes, Loren realized she was on her own.

Well, OK, she told herself as she started across the dark park. *I'll do this myself. This way, there'll be no one to tell me that I've gone too far. Yeah, it's probably better this way!*

She strode purposefully into the service station on Barrenjoey Road and easily got the key to the restroom. She was young and beautiful, and the attendant knew that the flush of freshness in her cheeks was not that of a hardened streetwalker or drug addict. He readily gave her the key, figuring she probably just needed a pee.

Loren spent the next thirty-five minutes locked away in the tiny restroom, putting on her make-up until she was eventually shooed along by the attendant, who, fearing for her welfare, rattled the door until she yelled that she was all right.

She was soon on her way again, walking along the ash-white concrete footpath that ran next to the main road, all the while drawn to the bright lights and bustle she imagined was just over the next rise. A number of drivers rode their horns as her shapely and unexpected form came up in their headlights, the monotone of the blasts stretching off into the night to be absorbed by its blackness.

Loren ignored the coarse comments yelled from the vehicles because she was in another place in her mind. It didn't dawn on her that she was putting herself in any danger. She was going to test herself tonight, determined to see if she really could control her destiny out in the real world.

She soon got her wish when she caught the attention of the leader of a gang traveling in the opposite direction. Although cars and engines were the gang's main passion, they still found plenty of time to cruise the streets looking for "fresh meat," as Jimmy Ring liked to call all young women. As soon as he spotted Loren in his headlights, Jimmy told his boys to make a U-turn. She was the best thing he'd seen all night, and certainly worth a closer look.

The red, over-customized 1964 Chevy pulled over to the curb. All four men were in their early twenties and worked in blue-collar jobs in the motor industry, but as tough and single-minded as these boys were, they all valued their freedom and were not about to give it up for the sake of a "quickie" with some girl who would cry rape the next day. One look at Loren, and the three other boys saw trouble.

Unfortunately for them, their leader had a bad case of night blindness. Jimmy was a good-looking guy with a small frame, tight jeans, and slicked-back hair. He saw himself as God's gift to women, and didn't care who knew it.

"Hey there, beautiful. Where're you going?" he asked her from the passenger side window as the Chevy tracked the curb.

She didn't reply and just kept walking, eyes fixed straight ahead.

"Surely you've got enough time for a little conversation with the Ringer and the boys? Come on, baby, we're not going to bite you."

"But I might bite you!" Loren spat.

Jimmy jumped out of the car, took Loren by the hands and spun her toward him. He then held her before him as he propped himself up against the front guard.

"If it's fun you're looking for, me and the boys can oblige!" he said.

"Oh, yeah? What sort of fun did you and 'the boys' have in mind?"

"We like all sorts of fun," Jimmy replied suggestively.

"What makes you think I'm that kind of girl?"

"Well, maybe it's the way you walk, the way you talk. And that body, oh yeah!"

"Really?"

Taken aback, Jimmy suddenly toned down his approach. At least Loren hadn't smacked his face and run off, so he decided to try talking to her so they could get to know each other better.

"What's your name?"

"Cathy. Cathy Campbell."

"Where do you live? I haven't seen you around before."

"I'm new to the area. Just moved in a few weeks ago," she lied.

"My name's Jimmy, and that's Spanner, Becky, and Skades," he said gesturing toward his entourage, still seated.

Loren eyed him up and down and decided he was someone she could have sex with. She always liked to categorize men into two groups: those she could readily do and those she couldn't.

Jimmy was a fast worker. He already had "Cathy" in his grip and started kissing her. She kissed him back, allowing her tongue to dart invitingly in and out of his mouth. He then spun her around so that she was now propped against the car, and pushed his body into her groin as his passion began to rise. She took this as her cue to exercise control over the situation.

"Want to go for a ride?" Jimmy asked her urgently.

"No."

He reeled back in amazement. "What do you mean, no?"

"I mean, *no*."

"That's not what your body's telling me!" Jimmy said incredulously.

"I'm not getting into a car with four strange men. If you want me, then you find a way to get rid of your boys."

"What do you mean? We go everywhere together."

"You make up your mind. Either you deal with it, or I'm out of here."

"OK, OK."

Jimmy went over to the car to talk to his gang members. They all piled out of the car and started walking back to the service station from which Loren had just come. "I'll come back for you," Jimmy shouted.

"I'm impressed," she said, smiling as she realized how easily she had made Jimmy bend his rules for her.

"Yeah, great. Jump in, then. Let's go down to the lake," he said, opening the passenger side door for her. Once they were both inside the car, he handed her a small bottle of bourbon in a paper bag. "Here, take a swig; it'll get you in the mood."

Jimmy pulled up on the edge of the Narrabeen Lakes in a secluded spot he seemed to know well, rolling up all the windows so that their hot breath would steam them up and give the couple additional privacy. He then asked her to join him in the back seat. She obliged, and they immediately took up where they had left off before he'd dumped the gang.

Loren had no intention of telling Jimmy she was a virgin. Tonight, she was out to change the status quo, and she didn't want to be treated with kid gloves. She wanted to taste all the power of wanton sex for herself. She wanted to know if it was all she'd read about. Jimmy was relatively expert in the art of seduction, and Loren found herself surprised and delighted as he ran her through his repertoire.

The grown-up Loren winced as she remembered the pivotal moment: How she had braced herself as Jimmy entered her, absorbing the pain with only a widening of her eyes as she looked into the black space over his shoulder. She remembered not knowing whether to laugh or cry as she tried to isolate the feeling, so she just made little pleasure noises for his sake while filing the sensation away.

Suddenly, Jimmy reeled back in horror. "You're bleeding," he said, pointing to the small pool of blood gathering between her legs and staining the white vinyl seat.

"Oh. I must have got my period."

"Well, you'd better get dressed. I'll take you straight home."

"Yeah, that would be good. I live on Rednal Street."

"Wanna see me again?" Jimmy asked smugly when he stopped outside her door.

"Maybe," she answered coyly.

He noted her address, but unfortunately for him, he had dropped her five streets away from where she actually lived. She smiled as she got out of his car, realizing he wouldn't recognize her once she was back in her school uniform. He'd served his purpose, and she had no further use for him.

Turning back to her office desk, Loren smiled as he remembered how easily she had manipulated Jimmy, and nearly every other man she had bedded since. Her brow furrowed when she thought about Marc's apparent reticence to call her, and decided to ring him herself if he didn't call her by the end of the week.

*   *   *

It took a few days for Marc's thoughts to return to Loren and the powerful feelings she had stirred up, but it was still too soon for him not to associate her with his loss. When he thought about those events, he rationalized that she wasn't really part of it, but no sooner had he convinced himself of it than he would lapse back to his former position. He wasn't inclined to phone her while in that frame of mind, resolving each time to let it go for a few more days.

About ten days after their last meeting, Loren called his office. "I thought that you'd forgotten all about me, you nasty man!" she said playfully when he answered.

"Oh, hi, Loren. I was going to call you." It sounded hollow, even to him.

"That's OK, I understand. Look, I don't want to let what happened at the conciliation come between us. I promise never to mention it unless you bring it up first. But frankly, I'd be happy never discussing it again."

"OK, you've got a deal," Marc said happily.

"Now, how about that cappuccino?"

"When are you available?"

"I thought I'd made it clear the other day that I'm available anytime for you!" Loren whispered sultrily.

The ball was now in Marc's court, and this time, he couldn't fail to get her drift.

*   *   *

The coffee shop was a cozy little place, situated right on top of Circular Quay. Marc and Loren sat at a table in front of a huge, plate-glass window and watched the world go by.

"So your father owns the firm you work for?"

"Don't say it like that, Marc. You make it sound as though he's doing me a favor by employing me," she giggled.

"I didn't mean it that way, Loren. I'm sure you're very good at what you do."

"I'm good, but I bet I could learn a lot from you," Loren replied suggestively.

Marc flashed back a worldly grin and asked, "How did you get into law?"

"My mother's a bitch and she drove me away my father after they divorced. He was lawyer, so I guess that's why I decided to become one, too."

"To get close to him?"

"Yeah, probably," she mused as she pushed her empty cup in idle circles. "He remarried, and I have a half sister who has no interest in the law, preferring instead to spend daddy's money on the social scene." Her upper lip curled in disgust. "After my dad and I reconciled, it turned out that I was closer to his expectation of an ideal daughter than my half sister, so here I am. What about you? What made you want to be builder?"

Marc blinked. It was the first time anyone had asked him that question. "God knows," he answered reflexively. "I just seemed to fall into it. I looked around one day and I was a builder. I am an engineer by profession, but building is my business, and one day I'll be the biggest builder in the state."

"A lofty ambition," she nodded approvingly. "I suppose your work keeps you single, too?"

"Yeah. Does that matter?" Marc asked with smile as he leaned toward Loren.

"Not to me," she whispered as she took his hand and looked into his eyes. "So, Mr. Braddon, master builder, do you have time for a bad girl in your life?"

"There's no such thing as a bad girl."

Loren's eyes flashed with excitement. "Wanna bet?" she shot back with a seductive pout.

They became so wrapped up in each other's company that they didn't notice the afternoon slowly fading into evening. After their third coffee, they decided to walk along the Quay, and found themselves on the concourse leading up to the Opera House. They reached the base of that wonder of the modern world, and drank in the magnificent view of the bridge, the harbor, and the city that lined the shores.

"It's magnificent, isn't it?" Marc said.

"I love it. I think Sydney's the most beautiful city in the world. Where else can you leave your office and walk down to such a magical place?"

They didn't speak much for a while, but just stood there, watching whatever activity caught their attention. For Marc, it was the ferries that were coming and going from the Quay. He watched their progress as they made their way across the harbour. Loren seemed mesmerized by the flotilla of small craft out on the water and the clusters of tourists milling on the grassy banks of the harbor bridge.

"Well, I suppose we'd better go, although I have really enjoyed this time with you," Loren said with marked reluctance.

Marc, too, had enjoyed her company, and wasn't keen to let her go. He found himself saying, "How about we have dinner together? I know it's a bit early, but we can go somewhere for a quiet drink first."

"I'd love to!"

They strolled back down the concourse, arm in arm, glad to have found a way to stay together—anything to keep the magic going was foremost in their minds.

They stumbled upon a little French restaurant tucked away in one of the back streets. Its decor featured brick floors and huge exposed beams, and red tablecloths that set off the black tables and bare wooden chairs to perfection. Open metal candleholders, with four black prongs shaped to form a rose, housed short, thick, red candles at every table. The flickering candlelight danced provocatively on their faces, reflecting in their eyes as if to mirror the smoldering fire building within them.

Loren took off a shoe and started to rub Marc's calf with her stocking-clad foot. They looked deeply into each other's eyes as they sipped their full-bodied red wine.

Their meals were consumed in a similar way, with their eyes fixed on each other rather than on the fare. They picked at the Chateaubriand for two and fed each other selected morsels. The act of passing their fork into their partner's mouth only added to the seductive atmosphere, dragging each of them in a little deeper with every bite. Even though he was part of it and hopelessly engulfed by it all, Marc could sense the eyes of others upon him as he and Loren went though their overt mating ritual.

Raw lust overtook him, and Loren did nothing to cool those fires. If anything, she fanned the flames with the unmistakable message that she was ready and willing to handle anything that might happen between them.

Her breathlessness suggested anything but caution, and they found it impossible to remain long enough to order coffee or dessert.

The cab driver took them directly to Marc's place, and had trouble keeping his eyes on the road due to the open display of wanton lust going on in the back. The sexual tension between them made the air feel heavy and damp. They climbed out of the cab, Marc fumbling through his pockets while Loren kept kissing his face; then, she dragged him away from the curb and toward the apartment's entrance.

The wine, the food, and Loren's lips created a mix that lifted Marc up to another plane. He kept asking himself if this was real or imagined, but his mind and emotions were so out of control that he couldn't even hazard a guess.

* * *

Marc spun the key in the lock and pushed the front door open, carrying a clinging Loren across the threshold. She kept planting kisses on his face and lips as she slid down his body. Her weight pulled him over, and he dropped to his knees. He kicked the front door shut behind him and began kissing Loren's burning lips.

Marc frantically unzipped Loren's dress as his desire reached fever pitch. Meanwhile, Loren had stripped away his shirt to expose his chest. They urgently kissed each other's body while their clothing lay all about them.

Locked together at the lips, they stepped out of their discarded clothes and made their way to the bedroom, where they then fell onto Marc's double bed in an even more passionate embrace.

They each struggled to prevail over the other in an almost-frenzied effort to offer each other exquisite pleasures. Their passion was now almost unquenchable, and they came together in a flash of blinding light, exploding into each other in one heart-stopping moment.

All that night, they sampled each other's passion, and found themselves celebrating dawn's arrival fully sated and thoroughly exhausted. With the early morning light, they both reluctantly got out of bed and started to make breakfast. They were ravenous, and found themselves gnawing at unbuttered bread in an effort to get some sustenance while they waited impatiently for the toaster.

Loren looked wonderful in one of Marc's shirts. They smiled at each other as he poured her a cup of coffee, and vowed to spend many more such nights together.

Chapter Eight

The sun was shining warmly on Marc's face as he drove to the office the next day—his old optimism had returned, right on cue. He parked his car and opened up the office, first turning on the fluorescent lights, then the computers, and then every other gadget in the place before filling the coffee pot. He then checked the fax machine before settling down behind his desk.

The phone rang. "Good morning, Highmark Homes."

"Hello, sweetie. How are you?"

"Oh hi, Maddie," he said, his face brightening even more. Maddie and Robert had been married for just over a year now, and Marc always looked forward to their regular phone calls. "I'm good. How are you?"

"I'm fine, too. I'm glad I caught you in the office. Robert and I would like to pop in to see you this morning. We have something that we want to talk to you about."

"OK, It'll be great to see you two. What time will you be here?"

"Around eleven, if that's OK."

"Eleven's fine. How about we do lunch afterwards?"

"That would be really nice. I'm sure Robert would like that."

"Now, just what is it that you two want to ask me?" he fished.

"I haven't got time to go into detail right now, Marc, but I know you'll love it. It's just what you need right now, and, best of all, we'd be working together again."

"I already like the sound of it."

"Thought you would. See you at eleven, sweetie."

"Bye, Maddie." A broad smile lit up his face as he hung up the phone.

The day was looking up already. *Funny how quickly things can turn around*, he thought, pausing for a second before wading into the pile of paperwork that sat on his desk.

* * *

"Mr. and Mrs. LaPont are here to see you, Marc," his receptionist, Elle, said over the intercom. Her voice startled him, as he had been studying a file with deep concentration.

He sprung to his feet and reached his office door just in time to greet Maddie. They embraced, the force of her hug knocking Marc slightly off balance.

"Hello, Robert," Marc said, peering over Maddie's shoulder while trying to offer a hand to his brother-in-law.

"Hello, Marc. It's good to see you," Robert said, smiling at the siblings' closeness.

"Gee, it's good to see you two again. How are things going on the central coast these days?" Marc asked, guiding them to the lounge in the corner.

"We're at a new stage of the company's development," Maddie said, her face glowing with accomplishment.

"So, Maddie and I thought that it was time we spoke to you about an opportunity to become involved," Robert chimed in.

"OK, you've got my undivided attention."

"Well, where do I start?" Robert asked rhetorically.

"At the beginning, of course!" Marc replied, his interest piqued.

"OK. Maddie's convinced me that we should develop a retirement village on land that we own at a place called Charmers Beach, and we'd like you to build the whole thing for us."

"Wow, that sounds like some plan!" Marc said, struggling to take in the concept.

"There'll be around four hundred self-care units and one hundred full-care units, with all the usual retirement village facilities," Robert announced. "And they're all yours!"

"Marc, you can do this standing on your head!" Maddie said.

"I think you should consider starting up a new company," Robert suggested. "This would avoid any problems with the unions, who might otherwise try to use your involvement as leverage to damage your homebuilding operations. Apart from that, everything else should be straightforward." Apparently, Robert and Maddie had thought about all the pitfalls.

"The financing is in place with our bank, so you can count on being paid," Maddie said with a reassuring smile.

"The whole thing sounds fantastic," Marc said as the idea started to fire up his enthusiasm. "God knows I could do with a break right now."

"We thought so!" Maddie said, looking first at Robert and then at Marc.

After another forty-five minutes, Robert stood up and stretched, then said, "The finer details have yet to be worked out, so why don't we sort them out over that lunch you promised us?"

Marc was quickly warming to the prospect of adding medium-density building to his repertoire. The idea of developing a parallel building company that would complement Highmark Homes and add to its cash flow had real appeal, particularly after what he'd just been through with the conciliation.

As the opportunity to be part of this proposal sunk in, Marc felt a flash of excitement as he imagined what it must be like to preside over a successful group of companies. Had anyone else brought this proposal to him, he would have been very guarded, since many people used builders as a way of getting access to a cheap quoting or costing service. But with Maddie and Robert, he knew that it would be different. If they said that he had the job, then he did. He could trust them implicitly. They were not just his only real family but also his trusted friends, the sort of people he could rely on in a crisis—people of real character, people who would be there alongside him till the end.

*   *   *

"Where are we going for lunch?" Maddie asked as she climbed into the back seat of Marc's car.

"To that little Italian place in Monty Street; you know, Di Petro's," Marc replied.

"Oh, yes. Didn't it used to be owned by Sophia and her family?"

"It still is, *mia bella*," Marc said, with a mock Italian accent and a flourish of his hand.

"Robert, you'll love this place. It has the best homemade pasta and specializes in fresh seafood. Absolutely scrumptious!" Maddie said.

"Sounds good to me, honey. Just get me there!" Robert said as they all laughed.

Sophia was a round little woman with a big, happy face and full head of jet black, curly hair. She greeted Maddie and Marc with a big hug. They both tried several times to introduce Robert, but were instantly caught up in hugs and handshakes from all the family members who were on duty that day.

"I thought you said that this was a quiet little place!" Robert said to his brother-in-law out of the corner of his mouth as they were shown to their table.

Marc laughed. "It really is, once you get past the receiving line!"

After they were seated, Marc mused, "You know, there is a small problem about this proposal that might cause some difficulties."

"What's that?" Robert asked quizzically.

"Surely it isn't something that we can't overcome together," Maddie added.

"Well, you both know that I'm coming out of a bad batch of building contracts, and the expected losses will deplete my working capital. I'm a bit concerned that this could impair my ability to do your work."

"Do you want to tell him, Maddie, or should I?" Robert said with a cheesy grin.

"Best if you tell him, darling."

"No one knows your situation better than we do, Marc. That's why we're here. Payments in the medium-density business are a little different than what you've been accustomed to as a homebuilder."

"Oh?"

"A large, up-front payment will be made to you as soon as you establish a presence on site. In this case, it will be about $200,000. This should give you more than enough cash to kick off the job. The rest will take care of itself, once your building program gets under way and you start to generate regular progress payments," Robert said.

"Sounds almost too good to be true. Are you sure I'm worth all the trouble?" Marc asked humbly, as he realized the depth of their confidence.

"Nobody can build faster or better than you. This, coupled with your reliability and integrity, leave us little choice, old boy," Robert said.

"Now, let's order. I'm starved," Maddie said, calling a halt to all the talk about money.

* * *

By the end of lunch, everything was settled. Marc would start up a company—that they all agreed would be called Coastal Constructions—and it would be used to build the retirement village project only. The project was expected to take about two years to complete, and would be done in several stages.

Robert would supply Marc with the architectural plans and building approvals, and Marc would do all the structural engineering design. He also promised to get back to Robert with some firm building prices within the week.

During the following week, Marc had delivered his final estimates to Robert as promised. His price for the first stage and the estimates for subsequent stages were slightly below Robert's original budget. Robert told him that his bank had loaned him the money based on his budget, so Marc's cheaper prices made things a little easier for him.

This whole project already felt like a perfect arrangement: Robert and Maddie could get their retirement village built by the builder of their choice at a price less than their original budget, and Marc could have a steady stream of profitable work that would enable him to rebuild his operations.

Maddie obviously had Marc and his plight in mind when she and Robert had formulated the whole deal. *What would I do without my Maddie?* Marc asked himself. She was always there looking out for him, even though she had her hands full with her own life. The idea of seeing Maddie on a regular basis while working at Charmers Beach would be the icing on Marc's cake.

* * *

Loren, his new lady, was unimpressed by his lucky break. She saw the Charmers Beach job as an impediment to their relationship because of the site's distance from Sydney. When she told Marc about her concerns, he assured her he would see her as often as possible. After all, he told her, he would only be working an hour or so away, and would still be living in the same apartment.

"Oh, OK," she had said grudgingly. "I guess I can't have everything my way."

"Look, how about I take you up to see the site and introduce you to Maddie and Robert this weekend?"

"Yeah, I'd like that," she said.

Maddie met Loren over dinner on the following Saturday night at a quaint little restaurant nestled in the foothills above Charmers Beach. Marc had booked a room in a nearby motel, so that he and Loren would have a place to shower and change after spending the afternoon climbing all over the proposed building site. Marc was like a small boy as he excitedly pointed out all the features of the new site, and explained where everything would go in the finished project.

Maddie was her usual elegant self, and Robert, ever the gentleman, was charming to Loren. They all seemed to enjoy one another's company.

The conversation over dinner was friendly and varied. Maddie managed to ask Loren a few questions that showed Marc she was still looking out for him.

This time, it was he who wanted his sister's approval of his new partner, but he couldn't tell whether or not he had it. He would have to wait until he could get Maddie alone to find out what she really thought of Loren.

"Maddie, you look a little sad tonight," Marc said to his sister, sensing she had something else on her mind.

"Yes; we lost Yindy today," Robert replied.

"Lost? How do you mean *lost?*"

"He died this afternoon. Might've been bitten by something in the bush; he loved to roam. He just keeled over this afternoon," Robert said.

"Oh, Maddie, I'm so sorry. I know how much you loved that big old tomcat. He was such a character," Marc said sadly.

"Is there anything I can do?" Loren asked Maddie.

"No. He's gone," Maddie said softy.

"Please let me make him a coffin. I'll get a little box tomorrow and make him up a proper coffin. Let me do that," Loren implored. "It's the least I can do."

Early the next morning, Loren found a shoe store and a haberdashery, and got busy making a small coffin for Maddie's cat. Marc was surprised at the extent to which Loren was prepared to go, spending hours stitching the cushioned coffin lining together. She insisted that Marc drive her to Maddie's house so that she could be part of the late-morning burial ceremony.

Marc looked at Loren differently from that moment, and yet was still not quite sure what to make of her. *I've never noticed such compassion in her before,* he thought, trying to shut out his suspicion that she had just taken a golden opportunity to ingratiate herself with Maddie.

Chapter Nine

Marc quickly established a presence at the Charmers Beach site and set up a semi-permanent office to house his new operation. He decided to control the initial stages of the project himself, since he was well skilled in setting out buildings and roads with the help of surveyors. Each part of the retirement village was to be done in a separate stage, so that sales could be made progressively. The master plan envisioned the village's completion over ten stages. Although Marc took sole charge of the project, he still planned to hire a foreman to help him with the actual building once things really got under way.

Early on, Robert told him, "Marc, I've got a couple of important people from my bank dropping by early next week to see how things are going. I know you're only just getting started, but I would appreciate it if you could generate some real activity at the site that day."

"When are they coming?" Marc asked, as they entered his site office.

"On Tuesday. That gives you four working days."

"That'll be enough time. I'll get the dozers in to do some more site preparation, backhoes to dig more foundations, and the plumbers and concreters to do their work. That should create some dust!"

"Good on you, Marc! I knew I could count on you."

Marc grinned at his brother-in-law. "As they say, 'No worries, mate!' I'll see whom else I can find—the place'll be like a beehive by the time the bankers get here."

When Tuesday rolled around, things were humming. Robert proudly escorted the bank officers around a building site crawling with men and machines going in all directions.

The bankers said they were pleased that Robert and Maddie had employed a competent builder, and shook Marc's hand as he bid them goodbye. Robert gave Marc a wink of approval as they departed the scene.

"Brilliant!" was all Robert said when he returned from seeing the bankers off.

"I hope these guys don't come back tomorrow, Robert," Marc said as they drove away, "because the place will be almost deserted by comparison. I'm now a week ahead excavating the foundations, and I've got to give the concreters time to catch up!" They both laughed as Marc saw Robert to his car.

God, I only hope it doesn't rain and ruin all the work we did today, Marc thought as he locked up the sheds and headed for home.

* * *

The project involved the construction of a number of buildings on a single site, which kept Marc in one place for a while—thus eliminating the need to rove all over the countryside visiting several sites a day as he had done before. This aspect of the Charmers Beach job reminded him of his engineering days, when he was involved in large scale projects that required a fair amount of supervision and control. It also allowed him time to think things through properly without the need to rush off to the next job. Marc still maintained his Sydney office and left his receptionist to run most of the day-to-day matters, which were gradually scaling down as he completed each of his remaining housing contracts.

The freedom of working on another plane within the same industry seemed to agree with Marc, and he began to enjoy going to work each day. He started to lose the trapped feeling he had previously experienced, and quickly came to realize that the Charmers Beach project would not only help to heal him financially, but also emotionally. Added to this was the knowledge that he was genuinely helping Maddie and Robert establish themselves in their new enterprise.

There were all sorts of other unforeseen benefits to working on such a long-term project. One was the opportunity to work side by side with his favorite concreting team, led by Milo Lombardo, whom Marc had quickly put in charge of all the foundations. Milo had been there from the beginning; he had been the one constant in Highmark Homes. The nature of project home building, with its need to move tradesmen quickly from site to site, meant that they had not really worked side by side since those early Highmark Homes days, more than five years ago.

Marc had come to rely heavily on Milo over the years, particularly when he couldn't inspect some aspect of the foundations himself. On those occasions, he would have to take Milo's word that the work had been done properly, or that the supporting piers were founded on solid rock. And each time, Milo always had done exactly what he'd said. *Yes, Milo Lombardo is one of a rare breed indeed in the building industry*, Marc thought.

Marc got on well with the guys on site, and they had a lot of fun mixed with the serious side of doing the work. Their days were often filled with running gags as Milo and Marc displayed their wicked senses of humor for all to see. In this way, they kept the troops entertained, while strengthening their camaraderie.

*   *   *

In what seemed like no time, the Charmers Beach site took shape. All the internal access roads were in place, and it was easy to visualize the grand plan for the village from any of the higher vantage points around the site. Marc had assembled an experienced crew of excellent tradesmen, and everything really started to move along.

Each stage of the job flowed easily into the next, with no distinct separation between the stages, thus making it easy to plan and build continuously. Robert and Maddie had given Marc a dream job.

The job went along so smoothly that Marc had to check his calendar to remind himself that he had been on site for more than a year. In that time, the LaPonts had restored his faith in the building industry and humanity.

Marc also started getting inquiries from some of the bigger developers in Sydney, who wanted him to quote on some of their upcoming townhouse projects. He told Maddie and Robert about it, and they encouraged him to look into these offers. After all, they reasoned, Charmers Beach was going so well that it would probably be completed within six or seven months, about three months ahead of schedule, and it would take all of that time to quote, negotiate, and start another project anyway.

Marc didn't want to let the momentum at Charmers Beach slip while he was out looking for other work, so he appointed two supervisors to replace him and assist the foreman who had been with him since the early days of the project.

* * *

With his operation expanding, Marc divided his time between Charmers Beach and his office in Sydney. This left him little time for a social life, although he had been seeing Loren for more than a year now.

They both led busy lives, which made it difficult for them to find mutually convenient times to get together. This meant that their dates were often agreed upon only after several unsuccessful attempts, as other commitments got in the way. Whenever Marc found himself becoming frustrated with their schedule conflicts, he found himself thinking of the fragrance on Loren's lustrous skin, and the taste of her pillow-soft lips. Those memories never failed to arouse his senses, and drove him to persevere in arranging their next date.

Whenever they were apart, Marc always felt uneasy about her, based on the way they had met and some of the things she had let slip when they spoke. He naturally reasoned that anyone who could come on to him the way she had at the conciliation, without any provocation on his part, could easily do it again whenever another attractive male came along. He decided that it was time to air his suspicions.

"It's funny, Loren, but somehow I don't see you as the type of woman who would sit at home waiting for a man to come back from a hard day's work," Marc said over dinner that evening.

"Live life to the fullest and never look back; that's my motto. Who knows what tomorrow brings?" she replied with a reckless laugh.

"Your motto doesn't give me a lot of confidence, sweetheart," Marc shot back as his half-smile faded.

"What do you mean? Loren replied quizzically.

"I've called you several times at night, and you're never home."

"So what? Do you think I'm out with some other guy?"

Marc stared at the table for a minute before replying. "I don't know," he finally replied with a frown.

"Well, I'm not. I have to work for a living too, you know!" she said dismissively.

"There've been a couple of times when I wanted to get you, and I've called your number at work after getting no answer at home, " Marc said as he studied Loren's face.

Loren's face was expressionless. "Did anyone answer?" she asked in a flat voice.

"No."

"I'm not surprised, we generally don't take calls after six at the office," she expelled with an involuntary sigh. A look of relief briefly crossed her face, and Marc caught it. Her eyes darted away from his as she seemed to struggle to regain her composure, but within a moment she was back to her breezy, confident self again. "Anyway, why the third degree?" she asked with a smirk. Something in those green eyes, however, appeared to be taking notes.

"No reason; I just wondered."

"You're starting to sound like a stalker."

"Don't be silly—it's nothing like that. It's just that I'd like to think I'm the only man in your life."

"Isn't that obvious?" she said, curling her stocking foot around his calf under the table and shooting him a seductive look.

"Well, yeah," he found himself saying with a smile, but his instincts whispered something else.

Despite their limited opportunities and his lingering doubts, he and Loren still had a powerful relationship. When they were together, sparks always flew. It was clear they enjoyed each other's company, and always ended up breathless and in bed.

"I know I'm in lust with you," Loren purred as she cuddled up to him after they'd just had sex, "but I just can't tell if I'm in love with you."

"Oh well, you can't have everything," Marc mocked, trying to hide his dented ego.

Loren's pout smoothed into a contemplative gaze. "Don't you ever stop and wonder why we put ourselves out for the sake of sex?" As she rolled on her back, her flame-red tresses fanned behind her in the shape of a naughty halo.

"Who really knows?" Marc mused, smoothing her hair with his hand. "I know you joke about being in lust with me, but I think I'm becoming addicted to sex with you, sweetheart."

"And I can see no good reason to cure you such a wonderful addiction," she laughed as she rolled on top of him and started kissing him passionately.

Loren sizzled in bed, but he dared not ask her where she'd learned her sexual tricks, since he was almost certain he wouldn't like the answer. Nothing was taboo to Loren, and she had taught Marc quite a lot along the way.

She would often get little quirky looks on her face at the most intimate of times that would break Marc up. They would end up laughing so hard that they would unravel from whatever Kama Sutra position they were in before ending up on the floor, locked in an even more passionate embrace.

Loren was definitely unique, with an indomitable spirit. Nothing worried her; she seemed ten feet tall and bulletproof, and Marc liked that about her. When they were together, she made him feel as though they could survive any natural catastrophe known to man. The walls could collapse around them, and they would be left unscathed and still in bed, still holding on to their own brand of wonderful, wild, abandoned sex, with nary a care for the ruins around them, or their nakedness and exposure to the world.

*　　*　　*

After work one day, Robert asked Marc over to the house for dinner. It was a warm summer night, and after the meal, the two men went out on to the front verandah to enjoy the night air while Maddie made coffee in the kitchen.

"I love the smell of salt air," Robert told Marc as he breathed deeply. "It corrodes our cars and everything else in the place, but it's almost worth it be this close to the sea."

"I know what you mean," Marc said as he, too, filled his lungs.

Both men leaned against the verandah handrail, transfixed by the mixture of yellows that the full moon played upon the black, steady ocean.

Robert cast a sidelong glance at his brother-in-law. "I hope you don't mind me saying that you seem a little preoccupied these days, Marc," he began cautiously.

"Oh?"

"Yeah," Robert confirmed as he worked to keep his tone casual. "Everything all right between you and Loren?"

Marc quickly glanced back at Robert. *What's he getting at?* "Yeah, as well as can be expected, I guess," Marc replied with a hint of the same caution.

"What does that mean?" Robert asked with a curious half-smile.

"Oh, I don't know," Marc shrugged. "She's a hard woman to pin down."

"Is there a chance that she's taking your mind off what you're doing here?"

Oh, so that's it. Marc shook his head resolutely. "No, not a problem. Don't worry, Robert, I'll still get the village built on time."

Robert rubbed the back of his neck. "That's not my concern, Marc," he said with a sigh. "When we see you on Monday mornings, after you've been with Loren over the weekend, you seem somehow distant—it's as if you're wrestling with some underlying concern."

"It's not like that!" Marc fired back defensively.

After looking at Marc for a long moment, Robert turned his gaze back to the yellow moon. "Look, Marc. While most women—your sister included—are earth angels, there are some women out there who seem only to want to gobble up men; they like to take scalps. The harder the scalp is to get, the more they like to play the game, but it's still a game to them."

"You sound like you're speaking from experience," Marc commented with a smirk.

"I am," Robert replied soberly. "Not a lot, but enough. I think that women have a real advantage sometimes. We want to trust them with our feelings, and that can give them such power over us. Now, with someone like Maddie, that vulnerability is all part of a wonderful union that's as natural as breathing; but to a woman with some other motive, it can put you at a fatal disadvantage. These sorts of women take every bit of trust and exploit it to their own ends. They'd shatter your heart without even blinking." Robert shuddered. "They think nothing of the emotional damage they leave behind once their goals have been met and they move on. The more they hurt you, the more they think they're worth."

She's not like that! Marc wanted to shout back at his brother-in-law. Instead, he sighed.

"Maybe you're right," he admitted softly, his shoulders slumping under the weight of the accusations. "I just don't know anymore. I only hope that's not what Loren's all about. In the beginning, I tried not to allow myself to get too attached to her, and for a while that seemed to drive her to try even harder to hook me. But lately, as I've become more committed to her, she seems strangely distant at times. It's not something I can put my finger on, but something *has* changed between us." His fingers drummed a nervous rhythm on the verandah railing.

"All the more reason to stand back and take stock of the situation," Robert advised as his expression relaxed. "Trust your own instincts, and I'm sure you'll start to see what Maddie and I can see."

"Did Maddie put you up to this?" Marc inquired with a surprised smile.

"Of course not," Robert grinned. "It's just that we're both a little concerned about Loren. She seems OK on the surface, but we both get a sense that there's something else going on with her."

Marc turned and looked back through the living-room window to see his sister holding a tray with the coffee and cake, staring at them intently. When she noticed Marc looking back at her, she immediately turned away and began setting up the coffee table.

"You know I'm not always good at taking advice, but maybe there's something in what you say," Marc said quietly as he looked back out to sea, his inner peace suddenly disturbed. "I'll think about it."

Chapter Ten

Marc picked Loren up at her apartment at six on the following Saturday morning—a clear, crisp spring day full of promise. Loren had been talking about sailing on the last few occasions they had been together, and she had eventually convinced Marc that it would be a perfect way to spend the weekend.

"We'll cruise around the harbor and anchor in one of the quiet coves," she told him. "You'll see—we'll have a fabulous time

"I really can't afford the time," Marc protested. "I've got so much on at the moment..."

"Would you have me sail a two person yacht on my own? How can we have any fun if you're always working on the weekends?" Loren pouted. "Come on, Marc, I'll make it worth your while," she purred.

After finally chiding Marc into agreement, Loren set a date and arranged to rent a fully equipped sail boat from the Kirribilli Yacht Squadron.

"You can't rely on me," Marc warned Loren as they drove on to the marina. "I've never been out in a boat before. When I was a kid, the only water around our farm was the local swimming hole. We had plenty of trees though—I'm good with trees!" he joked.

"You don't have to worry about a thing," Loren declared with all the confidence of an old seafarer. "I'll show you the ropes. I'm a bit of a sailor; my father taught me."

"Oh, I didn't know he sailed. I'm surprised he can take the time, heading up a busy city practice and all. He's always too busy to meet me, that's for sure."

"He used to sail, but he doesn't get out very much these days," Loren replied, looking away.

* * *

At that moment, Loren thought back to her true sailing teacher: her law professor, James Shearer. She remembered the wood-paneled walls of his university-supplied apartment, his creaky four-poster bed, and how easily she had corrupted the youngest dean of law in the university's history.

James was a youthful-looking forty—a slight man whose longish, straight blond hair, combed across his right eye, gave him the look of a surfer. Loren seemed able to read James' mind, and knew just when to curve her supple body around his. How easily she could make him do anything she wished.

"Do you love me?" she remembered asking him one day after making love.

"I don't really know the answer to that question," he replied, caught a little off-guard. "I feel something pretty strong for you; that much I can tell you."

"Oh, and all the time I thought you loved me," Loren joked as if it didn't matter, even though she had given so much of herself to him that she felt entitled to expect him to be head over heels.

"So, what are you doing Saturday?" James asked, prudently changing the subject.

"Going sailing with you, aren't I?"

"Yes, that's right—you are. And you're the only person I take on board Libel."

James had named his boat after a course called "Defamation, Slander, & Libel," which he designed and had just finished teaching at the university a month before he bought the sleek white sloop.

"I like that. It makes me happy," Loren crooned as she started to kiss his body again, feeling she was valued after all. "Although sometimes I think you only want me as an unpaid deckhand," she muttered into his chest.

Professor Shearer was familiar with Colonial University's unwritten code about academic staff's liaisons with students—particularly with students within their own college. He had steadfastly avoided such involvements, even going so far as to avoid many of the campus functions in order to maintain that necessary distance. But Loren was different, and he was prepared to break a few rules for that privilege.

"What will we do if they find out about us?" he often asked her.

"You're my little secret, and no one's going to find out," she would always say reassuringly, which was enough to allay James's doubts. "I'll always be there for you."

Loren was so taken with Libel that she and James spent most of their weekends out on the water. She soon knew the difference between a mainsail and spinnaker, and a lot more than most people who manned their yachts on weekends. James trusted her enough to let her take the helm as they navigated out of the Heads and into the open sea. He had taught her well during their year together. She could now read all of the instruments, and was familiar with the satellite tracking and communication systems on board.

"My father used to take me sailing when I was young. He was a gifted sailor," she had told James on several occasions.

He readily accepted what she told him, since he had no real knowledge of her past. He was very much a here-and-now man, so Loren was free to spin any story she chose in their intimate moments together.

Their weekends consisted of cruising the ocean just off the coast, and spending their nights anchored in a sheltered bay. Loren would frolic nude above and below deck, exhibiting her considerable assets for anyone to see, knowing all the time that her only audience was James.

Whenever Loren strutted on the boat naked, she moved with all the grace of a sleek feline. She often pounced on her fellow shipmate playfully, triggering provocative foreplay that led easily into wild lovemaking. Loren gave freely of herself and didn't know how to live any other way, often ignoring James' sometimes reluctance to get too close.

* * *

Back in the present, Marc was warming up to the idea of sailing Sydney Harbour and its surroundings. He took the weekend's supplies down to the jetty while Loren finalized the rental arrangements and picked up the charts and sailing gear for their yacht.

Half an hour later, they were under way. Loren told Marc what ropes to untie and which sails to unfurl as they chugged sedately out of their berth and into the broad water.

It was everything that Loren had said it would be. The harbor glistened as the morning sun danced across its glassy surface. The bow of their yacht responded to Loren's experienced hands and cut a swath through the calm, blue water. The sights and sounds were foreign to Marc, who was now well into his crash course in sailing.

Loren spent most of her time at the helm, navigating past many of the sights dotting Sydney's magnificent harbor as Marc handled the sails. She gave him the wheel in the open water, and took it back whenever they ventured too close to shore or when a ferry or another yacht came near. He cuddled her from behind whenever he returned from completing the last task she had assigned to him.

Marc was getting to like spending time alone with Loren more and more. *I wonder if it would still be this idyllic if we got married?* he mused to himself. Loren certainly didn't seem like the marrying kind, but then, one never knew.

At around three o'clock, Loren eased the boat into the mouth of a wide cove and prepared to drop anchor. The yacht was about five hundred yards offshore—well away from the sea channels everybody else used. Loren told Marc that she liked to be naked when she was on the ocean, and started to pull her top off. She then started to unzip her shorts as she headed below deck, beckoning him to join her. Marc didn't need to be asked twice.

It was quite an experience, making love on the water. Marc had no idea what the boat was doing in response to the motions going on below deck, but imagined that the mast must be swaying from side to side in unison with their movements. The smell of the ocean provided a powerful aphrodisiac; the lovers indulged themselves for what seemed like hours.

Nearing exhaustion, Loren told Marc she needed a drink, and sent him to the galley to fetch one.

"Red, white, or beer?" he shouted as he bent over the small fridge, housed in the cabinet below the ship's sink.

"White, please. I think there's Chardonnay in there somewhere," Loren yelled back as she rolled over in the double bed.

"I see it," Marc said, grabbing the bottle and straightening up again.

In that same instant, something in the porthole above the sink caught his eye. He froze in panic, his mind instantly processing the image as the sharp white bow of another boat, headed right for them.

"Oh my God!" he shouted, dropping the bottle and sprinting into the forward cabin.

Before Marc could shout a warning to Loren, the crash propelled both of them against the hull. The collision cut the yacht cleanly in two, and for one terrible moment, Marc and Loren saw the white hull of the other boat pass by their cabin door.

For a moment, time seemed to stand still as they struggled to absorb what had happened. Only the cold water gushing in around their feet snapped them out of it. Marc then realized that the bed had slid during the collision, and now wedged Loren hard against the hull.

"Help me, Marc!" Loren screamed as she struggled to break free.

"It's all right, Loren—I'll get you out. Just keep calm!" he bellowed above the rush of seawater.

Marc started tugging at the bed, only to be engulfed by a torrent of frigid water. The water eventually caused the bed to float, making it easier to dislodge. Marc pulled Loren onto the bed, which acted like a raft for a few seconds as the water level rose.

He glanced at Loren, who was paralyzed on the bed next to him, her eyes filled with terror.

"We can get out of this, but only if you keep yourself together," he said as he squeezed her hand. "You're no good to either of us if you're going to panic—it'll just make everything worse."

"I don't want to die in a boat," she said as she started to cry.

"Who said anything about dying?" he retorted as the cabin filled with water. "We're going to get out of this together. Are you ready?"

They swam off the mattress and reached the door just as the boat hit bottom, its two halves colliding before coming to an unsteady halt. The halves reunited at a skew and ended up wedged together at deck level, leaving Marc and Loren with an escape path out of their watery tomb.

The two naked swimmers carefully eased their way out of the sunken yacht, and broke the surface a few seconds later. They could see no sign of their yacht or the boat that had hit them.

Loren started thrashing around as if she had forgotten how to swim. She was screaming and swallowing water, which only made her panic more.

"Calm down, Loren; I know you can swim!" Marc shouted as he tried to keep her afloat.

"Stop telling me to calm down, you bastard—I'm drowning!" she screamed hysterically, pushing Marc under the water in an effort to save herself.

Marc was fast realizing that Loren was not as mentally tough as she had made out. They were now in a life-or-death situation, and it looked like he had no choice but to be the tough one for both of them.

He pulled away from Loren and resurfaced close by. As she reflexively lunged toward him, he pulled back and smacked her hard across her face. "Now come on. You've got no choice but to swim for the shore," Marc told her.

"You hit me," Loren said with a look of disbelief.

"Would you rather I left you to drown?"

Loren's green eyes flashed indignantly. "No," she retorted, "but when we get to the shore, I'm going to hit you back."

She's going to be all right! Marc thought with a sigh of relief. "Good, just make sure you do!" he said, kicking off into the breaststroke with Loren in pursuit.

The tide was coming in, helping them cover the distance to the beach. They willed themselves to keep swimming, using a combination of breaststroke, freestyle, and sidestroke, and buoying their spirits with the thought that anyone seeing two naked people emerging from the water would immediately raise the alarm.

The melting muscles in their arms and legs begged them to find their feet as soon as they reached the shallows. They were totally exhausted when they reached the shoreline, and dragged themselves to their feet to find that they were standing knee-deep in water and naked to the world.

To their amazement, the dozens of people who were still on the beach this late afternoon were also naked. It suddenly dawned on them that they had landed on Lady Jane Beach, the only nude beach on the entire Sydney Harbour foreshore!

Marc looked at Loren's drained face, which held a quirky, bemused expression, and shook his head in amazement. They both fell to their knees and broke into a hysterical laughter.

*   *   *

After Marc and Loren walked sedately up to a group of bathers and tried to explain their plight, one of the group pulled out a cell phone and called the Water Police. The group then looked around for spare clothes, but only managed to come up with towels.

Thirty minutes later, a Sydney Water Police cruiser pulled up at the jetty, just off to the right of the beach. Sgt. Michael Palfrymen and Senior Constable Jennifer Vanner introduced themselves to everybody. Mandy and David, the two nudists who had volunteered to stay with the victims until the police arrived, had dressed for the occasion, leaving Marc and Loren looking like the only nature enthusiasts.

"We've got a couple of white overalls on board. They're not Armani, but they'll keep you warm and dry. That's if you nudists really want to cover up!" the sergeant said, tongue in cheek.

"Thanks," Marc replied somewhat curtly.

"Can you tell us what happened?" the senior constable asked.

"We don't really know," Loren said, shaking her head.

"We were minding our business, anchored in a quiet part of the harbor, when some maniac in a big white boat drove right through the middle of us!" Marc said.

"Did you get a look at the boat or the driver?" Palfrymen asked.

"All we saw was the bottom part of the hull when it drove straight through us. All I can tell you is that it was white. Did you see anything else, Loren?"

"No," she replied nervously. "It all happened too fast."

"Come on, let's get you two on board and into some dry clothes," Michael said. "We'll need to ask you a few more questions when we get back to headquarters."

*   *   *

After Chief Inspector Monroe, a big man with a constant, knowing smile, came in and introduced himself to Marc and Loren, he confessed that such boating accidents were very rare. "In fact," he stated, "I can recall only two such other mishaps in my twenty-two years on the harbor. And both of them happened when ferries had run over smaller craft that had tried to dart across their path at the last moment." He shook his head, mystified. "I've never heard of a stationary yacht being dissected by another craft while anchored. No one here has."

The chief inspector scratched his head as he pondered all the possibilities. After a series of routine questions yielded nothing, he shifted gears and began contemplating darker scenarios.

"Are you sure someone's not out to get you?" he asked.

Marc and Loren looked at each other blankly and slowly shook their heads.

"What do you both do for a living?"

"I'm in the construction business, and Loren's a lawyer," Marc said.

The chief inspector's eyebrows went up. "The construction business? Now that's often a can of worms."

"Well, I'm sure I've made some enemies over the years," Marc admitted, "but none I can think of who would lie in wait until I was on the harbor on this particular day. Anyway, those people would be too far back in my past. For the past year or so, I've been working on a site outside Sydney."

"Yours can be a particularly nasty industry," Chief Inspector Monroe noted somberly. "A lot of old European families seem to gravitate to it, and they have a special way of doing things. It wouldn't surprise me if there were a lot of their former enemies at the bottom of that harbor dressed only in concrete boots..."

"Come on," Loren interjected, finally finding her voice. "Surely that sort of thing doesn't happen nowadays!"

"Lady, not everything is settled politely in court," the chief inspector responded with a patronizing smile. "Many of these people's traditions run very deep indeed. Now, what about you? Do you have some disgruntled client who might be stalking you?"

"God, no!"

The chief inspector noted that the forcefulness of her reply was undermined by her nervousness as she fidgeted with her sleeve. "Well, there must be some reason for it," he continued. "An incident like this just doesn't happen out of the blue. If it were an accident, then there would usually be some evidence of it, like a runaway boat or some other very obvious link. Therefore, I can't rule out the possibility that this was a deliberate act."

"Honestly, we don't have a clue," Marc said.

"I suggest you both sleep on it and let us know in the morning if you come up with any leads. We'll obviously check all the repair shops, because the other boat must have been damaged. You can contact Sergeant Palfrymen or Senior Constable Vanner if you think of anything. Either way, they'll be in touch with you over the next few days after we retrieve the yacht. They'll take you both home now, if you like."

Marc then asked the senior constable if she thought the police divers would be able to recover their personal belongings from the wreck, and was told they would do their best. "Thank God, I keep a spare key under a loose tile near the doormat," Marc said quietly to Loren.

As they made their way out of the police station, flanked by the two officers, Marc and Loren were set upon by a gaggle of reporters who had already caught wind of the accident. They snapped photos and fired a barrage of questions while the television cameras caught the unsuspecting couple in their bright lights like two stunned jack rabbits.

Oh my God, Marc thought, *where did all these people come from?* Although he was always on the lookout for opportunities to spread the word about his business, this was the last sort of publicity he needed. He kept his head down and tried to keep moving through the crowd.

"Who did this?" one female reporter shouted at them.

"Why did you choose to anchor off Lady Jane Beach?" asked another.

"Do you have any enemies who would want to see you harmed?" asked a male reporter in the front of the pack. "What do you two do for a living? Has anything like this happened to you before?"

Marc and Loren were stunned by all the attention and didn't know how to respond. Sergeant Palfrymen, a burly cop who had been in the force for seventeen years, and had no such problems dealing with the press.

"We are continuing our investigations and cannot release any confidential information at this time. We are grateful for the assistance of this couple, but beyond that we have no comment to make. We will keep you advised of our progress," Palfyrmen told the reporters, whose heads dropped collectively as he finished speaking. The media pack parted as the two officers guided Marc and Loren to the waiting squad car.

Loren was strangely quiet on the way home, gripping Marc's hand tightly. Marc had never seen her this vulnerable before, and it evoked all of his protective instincts.

"It's going to be OK now, Loren," he murmured, and cuddled her closer to him as they were chauffeured home, courtesy of the police force.

*   *   *

Loren's mind wandered back to her professor and that fateful Monday morning—after one of their weekends on the water—when James was questioned by the vice chancellor, Ben Allsop, who had heard rumors that he was seeing one of his final-year law students. All this took place during the final examination period, while Loren was wrapped up in her last exam in the Great Hall. Afterwards, she and her classmates planned to hit the bars to celebrate their freedom.

James found his way to the Great Hall and positioned himself against the base of a large ghost-gum tree immediately opposite the main exit, looking worried and strangely distant. Loren saw him almost immediately, and was at his side within seconds. Elated having finished her final exam, she forgot herself and moved to kiss James' cheek. He recoiled and cast her a caustic glance that froze her in her tracks. Without a greeting or a question about her final exam, he launched into her.

"Look, someone's been going around telling the vice chancellor that I'm carrying on with a student."

Loren arched an eyebrow. "Well, aren't you?" she retorted as she felt the pain of rejection.

The professor's face flushed a brilliant red. "Yes of course," he admitted, "but I've always tried to be discreet. This could turn nasty if Allsop gets high-handed about things."

"Oh, I wouldn't worry about it. It'll all blow over."

"No, it won't; trust me. I've been around campuses long enough to know how it works."

"Well, you might have thought about all that before. Anyway, I'm off to the pub for a drink. I'm free of all of this now, and I mean to celebrate. Oh, and you're not invited!" she added flippantly before skipping off to join her classmates.

She remembered how her response had stunned him, and how he had stood there with his mouth open as she danced away. *Well, why not?* She concluded as the police car sped on. *He was just a man, like all other men...only interested in themselves. Why shouldn't I've gone out to celebrate on my own in spite of him?*

The next morning, James had apparently called Loren's number every ten minutes. After dozens of attempts, she finally picked up the phone at around eleven-thirty.

"Where the hell have you been?" he yelled into the phone.

Loren felt no desire to pander to someone so uncaring of her. "What do you mean? I've been here all the time." she said sullenly.

"Yeah, sure! I've been calling you for hours without any answer."

"Maybe my phone was off the hook. I did go out to the garden for a while."

"Don't insult my intelligence, Loren! You spent the night with someone else, didn't you?"

"No. I..."

"The least you can do is tell me the truth."

"Look, we're not married. I can do whatever I like. Anyway, I don't think you've ever told me that you love me, have you?"

"What possible difference would that make?"

"All the difference in the world to me!"

"Is that what all this is about? Me not telling you outright that I love you? What about the mess I'm now in because I dared to be your lover? Surely that's a sign of how I feel about you?"

"Look, this is *your* mess, not mine, and you should clean it up yourself."

"Thanks a lot. And what about what you said about always being there for me?"

"That's what you always say when you're sleeping with someone. Jeez...you really should get out more!"

"You really are pathetic, aren't you! You weasel your way into people's lives, create havoc, and then waltz out without a care in the world. The way you use up people is a crime. I hope that one day, it'll come back to smack you right across that deceitful face of yours. Good luck with the rest of your life. I'm sure you'll make an excellent lawyer. You've got all the right qualities," James shouted as he slammed the phone down.

"You sniveling coward, grow some backbone and don't blame me for everything," Loren remembered screaming at the dead phone. "I hate you for blaming me. I hate you!"

Marc's squeezed Loren's arm and pulled her back to the present. "Are you OK?" he asked her in the back of the police car.

"Yeah," she answered vacantly as she wondered if James Shearer had been out yachting that day.

* * *

Marc picked up the ringing phone as soon as he and Loren got though the front door.

"Marc, are you all right? We've been frantic ever since we heard about the accident on the news!" Maddie lamented.

"Yeah, we're both OK, Maddie. I've no idea what happened, but we're not hurt, and only lost our belongings."

"Thank God!" Maddie let out her relief with a whoosh, and it was clear that the tears were beginning to flow.

"Don't cry, Maddie. You know I can't handle it when you cry," Marc forced out past the lump in his throat. "Come on, buck up—I'm all right! Maybe I can I ring you back a little later? We need some time to get ourselves together—we're dressed only in the overalls that the police gave us, and we're starving."

"What on earth...?"

Maddie's fears quickly gave way to laughter, and the more Marc tried to explain, the louder the laughs became until he couldn't help joining in with her.

"Sounds like you've both had quite a day!" she finally got out when the hilarity subsided. "Now that I know you're OK, we can talk on Monday when you get back to work."

"OK, Maddie. See you Monday morning," Marc said as he hung up and joined Loren in the kitchen to prepare something to eat.

*   *   *

As soon as Marc arrived at his site office at Charmers Beach on Monday morning, he was met by Robert and Maddie, who still wore expressions of concern. After a long hug with his sister, Marc unlocked the office and showed the LaPonts inside. They sat themselves down while Marc unloaded the several files he was carrying on to his desk.

After Marc had filled them in on all the finer details about the boating accident, Robert and Maddie exchanged a knowing glance in the pause that followed. With an almost imperceptible nod to his wife, Robert cleared his throat.

"Marc, Maddie and I have been thinking a lot about what happened to you over the weekend, and we think that you'd better start watching your back a little more."

Marc smiled in spite of himself. "Sounds like you've been watching too many crime shows on television! Who could be out to get me?"

Maddie frowned in concentration as she prepared to speak. "Are you sure it's got nothing to do with Loren?" she asked quietly. "What do you really know about her past?"

Marc slammed his closed fist on his desk. "Come off it, Maddie. You're starting to become paranoid about Loren!" he shouted.

"I'm no such thing!" Maddie told her brother vehemently. "Before you met this woman, you never had people driving boats through the middle of you, did you?"

With the same tiny movements as before, Robert slowly shook his head at Maddie. "Come on, honey, let's not talk about it anymore," he said.

After exchanging another look with Robert, Maddie relented and changed the subject back to the progress of the Charmers Beach project.

The days soon passed into weeks, and the whole incident was forgotten as the police admitted to being no closer to finding the culprit. Time allowed both Marc and Loren to accept what had happened as some inexplicable phenomenon—almost as if it were something that they imagined. They were busy, practical people who had to get on with their lives. He had a business to run and she had a batch of briefs to prosecute, but that didn't stop them from constantly looking over their shoulder or peering up dark streets when they came home.

Chapter Eleven

A few weeks after the accident, Mark received several phone calls from John Hamilton—a manager within the huge Multi-Grid group of companies who seemed keen that Marc bid on work for the group.

When Marc met with him at the Multi-Grid Holdings head office, Hamilton—a short, thin, balding man in his mid-thirties who liked to power dress in pinstripe suits and matching waistcoats—introduced himself as the general manager of a new Multi-Grid subsidiary company called Multi-Build Pty. Ltd. This particular subsidiary had been recently set up to develop medium-density properties, and Hamilton thought that Marc's company would make the ideal builder for the group's new venture.

Hamilton was very persistent, and by the end of the meeting, Marc received the plans for a large townhouse project and was asked to quote on it as soon as possible. John told Marc that he had researched Coastal Constructions Pty. Ltd., and was very impressed with what he'd discovered. "If your price is right," he declared, "the job is yours."

Marc left that meeting feeling ten feet tall. He was pleased and quietly proud that word of his company's achievements had reached the dizzy heights of Multi-Grid.

All he knew about the chairman and founder of Multi-Grid, Martello Pressani, was that he was a self-made man and liked to use "Multi" somewhere in the title of all of the group's subsidiaries. Marc had heard rumors of Mafia connections in the early years, but nothing was ever proven. However, Martello always seemed able to win the important jobs from those early days onward. Over the years, he had built an enviable reputation, culminating in his being accepted as one of the founding fathers of the construction industry.

Marc had picked up most of what he knew about Pressani around the industry or from lunches with his friend, Jim Daniels. Whatever the truth was, Martello had made it, and now played in the big leagues. He had long since modified his behavior to suit, and was now a benefactor of the arts. Any of his "rough edges" had long ago been polished away by a succession of public relations experts.

Within a fortnight, Marc had delivered his tender price to Hamilton, who, after working his way through the figures, announced that Coastal Constructions had won the bid.

Contracts were prepared immediately for Marc's signature, and he was expected to start the project within the month. He had to sign a guarantee that he would complete this job within the twelve months stipulated in the contract, or else suffer a liquidated damages penalty. Marc was confident in his company's ability to deliver the job on time, so he happily agreed.

With everything signed, sealed, and delivered, the two men parted company with a handshake, and Marc went back to his office to set the necessary wheels in motion.

Within three months, Marc was working on two different fronts, and enjoying himself immensely. Maddie and Robert's Charmers Beach project was just about finished, and he was now free to pursue his other business ambitions. The cash flow generated from his new job was significant, giving him thoughts about expanding his operations. *Maybe I can emulate the Multi-Grid group in a smaller way*, he thought as he pondered the possibilities.

*   *   *

Before starting out in business, Marc had resolved not to acquire any formal management degrees. He figured this would allow him to evolve his own management techniques—free of the rigid constraints that are often a result of the university-course approach, with its formal and predetermined ideas. He believed that his engineering degree had already influenced his way of thinking, causing him to be logical and structured in almost everything he did.

In contrast, Marc always wanted his management style to be more a part of himself. He was satisfied that he had achieved this over the years when running his own businesses, and liked the idea of being a maverick in that part of his life. But if he had a special talent, it was his ability to spot the potential of any parcel of land. He could visualize a perfect house on the worst block of land, or conceptualize a finished office building on a lonely, vacant site.

He was also able to communicate his vision to others, quickly involving key people such as investors, bankers, and real estate agents—all of whom assisted him often in realizing his particular goals.

Marc's recent foray into medium-density building had given him some well-deserved time away from home building and the demanding clients that seemed to go hand in hand with that segment of the industry.

However, he had recently started to warm up to the idea of reentering the home building market, but only as a speculative builder of high-class homes. He reasoned that if he could buy land that no one else wanted and solve the various building problems, then he could deliver a quality home while also making a tidy profit.

What really appealed to him was the notion that he would no longer have to deal directly with individual owners. He would get all of his money this time, since the sales would be handled as part of a normal conveyance transaction, with everything paid at the time of settlement. His solicitors would handle everything, and this would separate him from the homeowners.

How could Marc ever forget some of his previous experiences, where some street-smart owner would hold back the final payment of $50,000 because he believed that the front door lock was too stiff, or something equally petty?

Over the course of his dealings, Marc had encountered many agents, but always seemed to gravitate toward one in particular—one who was fairly well connected and operated in the northwestern suburbs of Sydney, where land and houses fetched high prices.

Bruno Pinn prided himself on being the agent who set the market in that area, and his philosophy led him to deal with only a select group of builders. Bruno reasoned that if he sold a block of land to one of his builders who then built a home on it, which was in turn sold through his agency, then he would make two commissions. The second would often be more than twice the amount of the first, because of the increased value of the completed house and land package.

Bruno was a rotund man in his late fifties who always seemed to have an artificial zest for life. He had a habit of crushing clients' hands with his vice-like grip whenever he greeted them; whenever they inquired after his health, he inevitably told them that he was feeling "ab-so-lute-ly fan-tastic."

Bruno had often suggested to Marc that he become "one of his boys," and Marc was now seriously considering it. He liked Bruno, but thought that he was a sharp businessman who gave nothing away—the sort of person that made you want to count your fingers after shaking hands.

After a brief meeting, Marc announced his intention to join Bruno's exclusive group of builders. He commissioned Bruno to find some suitable land so that he could start building again, using Highmark Homes and its good reputation as his marketing vehicle.

* * *

Bruno took to the task with relish; in a matter of days, they were both tramping on vacant land all over northwest Sydney.

After looking at half a dozen subdivisions, Marc decided on a newly subdivided estate on which Bruno had exclusive marketing rights. Bruno assured Marc he could get favorable terms, particularly if Marc simultaneously bought several blocks. Marc immediately picked out ten blocks and gave Bruno the task of negotiating the terms.

"I can get delayed settlements on all of the blocks of land you picked out," Bruno said during his phone call the next day.

"That's good. What sort of terms are we talking about?"

"Very good ones! You'll have to pay for the first two blocks within the normal thirty-five day period. The next two can be delayed for three months, the two after that for six months, the following two for nine months, and the last two for twelve months."

"That sounds good to me, Bruno! That'll give me plenty of time to build before I have to pay for the next lot of land. It'll save me having to pay for a big land bank up front."

"Yeah, that's right. Needless to say, I couldn't get you any discount on the asking prices. The owners wouldn't agree to both delayed settlements and a discount. It was one or the other, so I figured that you would prefer the former."

"Yeah. I guess I can't have it both ways. You can tell your client they've got a deal. Why don't you send the contracts over to my solicitors so we can get the ball rolling?"

"Didn't you say that you'd changed solicitors lately, Marc?"

"Yes, I'm using a guy called Hamish Johnson, a suburban solicitor who promised me personalized service. I'll fax his contact details over to you."

"Great. You won't regret it, Marc. I know you'll make good money out of this arrangement."

Marc then got hold of the layouts for the first two blocks of land from the surveyor and set about designing homes. He had deliberately picked several of the cheaper blocks within the estate that had cross-falls on them, and planned to design homes with three garages underneath. He was also very careful with the landscape design, trying to accentuate the land's natural characteristics while also creating attractive, low-maintenance gardens. The final product was a high-quality, two-story home that looked more like an imposing, three-story mansion.

As soon as the building got under way, things rolled along smoothly. Marc's newfound freedom meant that he could make all of the decisions himself, thereby eliminating the potential for delays and conflicts during the various building stages.

His overall concept was to build these houses to include every possible feature. Carpet, curtains, light fittings, security alarms, air conditioning, open fireplaces, intercoms and, of course, landscaping were all standard inclusions. These houses were total "turn-key" projects, allowing an owner to pay for the house and move right in. The homes ranged in price from $600,000 to $1 million.

Marc also managed to set up a revolving line of credit with his bankers, who liked what he was doing and were prepared to finance all his projects.

The concept worked well, and within six months, Highmark Homes was completing two of these homes a month. They were selling so well that Highmark quickly gained a strong reputation for building individually designed, high-quality homes.

*   *   *

Finding enough land to meet the ongoing building program was always a problem for Marc. It was a matter of balancing the seller's asking prices with his ability to finance the purchase and the building costs to realize a profit. Many times, the seller wanted such a ridiculous price for his land that it left Marc no opportunity to make a profit after paying interest and construction costs.

True to form, he set about changing this by subdividing his own land. The first major subdivision opportunity he came across was on the property of a retired judge. None of the real estate agents in the area had been able to convince the old judge to sell and move away from his family home, but Marc thought, what have I got to lose?

Judge Harrington had once been a Supreme Court justice. During his days on the bench, he had gained a fearsome reputation for not suffering fools gladly, to which many lawyers could attest after feeling the lash of his sharp tongue.

Marc didn't know what to expect when he called on the judge unannounced late one afternoon. As he reached the front patio, he was taken aback by the lovely spread of purple flowers shed by the two Jacaranda trees overhanging the front porch. While the sea of color was stunningly beautiful, it was also treacherous, since it was easy to slip and fall on the harmless-looking petals, which melted underfoot. Marc rang the doorbell and waited for the judge's reaction to his intrusion.

"Hello, I'm Marcus Braddon of Highmark Homes. I'm sorry to call on you unannounced, but I hope that we might be able to talk about the possibility of me buying your property," Marc said with typical forthrightness.

"Well, young man, there have been many others who have come here to talk to me about that. They all ended up wasting my time, but then, they were real estate agents. I suppose it can't do any harm to talk to you. Come in. My name is Michael Harrington," the judge added, offering his hand. "Penelope," he shouted behind him, "this young man is from Highmark Homes. He wants to talk to us about selling."

It was obvious the old justice had lost none of his mental sharpness, although he and his wife looked old and somewhat frail. They had apparently been sitting around the fire before Marc's arrival. They rubbed their hands briskly as they stood in their doorway, even though it was a relatively warm day.

Marc was shown to a couch that faced the open fire. His eyes lingered over the walls, which were lined floor to ceiling with leather-bound books. Judge Harrington and his wife then sat in chairs positioned on either end of the couch, facing the fireplace. As a faint light globe and flickering firelight struggled to illuminate the room, Marc wondered what impression his fire-lit features were making on his hosts.

"Mr. and Mrs. Harrington, I was hoping you might be interested in selling your property to my company. If you are, I'm sure I can make you a very fair offer."

"Well, I'll tell you, Mr. Braddon," the judge said, looking across to his wife, "your timing is exquisite. Penelope and I have only just decided that this place is becoming too much for us. Our garden is too big for us to look after now, and we *have* been thinking of selling."

Great! Marc thought, mentally rubbing his hands in anticipation. "Do you have you a price in mind?" he inquired.

"Well, we have been approached by many agents over the years," the old judge replied, "but no one seems to think that we'll get the price we want."

"Tell me, what price do you want?"

"We want a million dollars!" they said simultaneously.

Gee, these people really know what they want, Marc thought. He knew that this would be his only opportunity to snare this deal because he currently had the initiative, which could easily be lost if the Harringtons listed their property with a real estate agent.

They spent the next half-hour discussing many things, including the couple's plans to move to the sea, the rare book collection on their shelves, the relative merits of French and Australian wines, and Highmark Homes and its operations. The general discussion had given Marc the time he needed to formulate a proper plan of approach.

Taking a deep breath, he began to outline the workings of his proposition. "I had a chance to do some calculations on this property before I came over today. If you are prepared to sign a six-month option, I will pay you upfront an option fee of $10,000, and I will also pay you an additional $900,000 for the property."

Marc then added: "This will save you from getting involved with an endless stream of real estate agents, and help you avoid all of the accompanying frustrations that often occur when dealing through them. They often try to haggle you down to a lower price once they've got your listing."

After a pregnant pause, the wily old judge said, "Mr. Braddon, if we enter into an option agreement with your company, you will save interest by not having to borrow the money needed to settle our purchase for another six months. I believe that this will save you about $100,000. We will agree to your six-month option if you agree to our million."

Marc was surprised at how quickly the old judge had summed up the situation. "That's a lot more than I expected to pay," he protested mildly.

"I don't think we can agree on anything less, and if we can't agree on a price, then we'll just have to put the place on the open market."

Judge Harrington was now moving in for the kill. He seemed to sense how badly Marc wanted the land, and had made it clear he would close the deal today, but only if he got his price.

Marc fixed his gaze at the fire and churned through the numbers in his head before nodding gently. "I think I can make my offer stretch to a million dollars," he said, "as long as we can close the deal here and now."

"Is our transaction to be conducted with or without an agent, Mr. Braddon?" asked the judge.

"Bruno Pinn's agency told me about your property, so I believe he's entitled to claim a commission."

"Yes, quite so, Mr. Braddon, quite so. Can I leave it to you to advise Mr. Pinn that I'm prepared to sign an agency agreement with him?"

"Yes, Mr. Harrington. Of course, you know that the $10,000 option fee is yours to spend as you like, once we've signed the option agreement. It's nonrefundable."

The old man cranked his head toward Marc and offered a little sardonic laugh. "Yes, I did know that. I used to be a judge, don't you know!"

Marc's flush of embarrassment was met with a relaxed smile from the judge, who had had his fun. "Yes, of course, Your Honor," Marc replied sheepishly. "Do we have a deal, then?"

"We do," the judge said, shaking Marc's hand enthusiastically.

After swapping their lawyers' phone numbers, the judge and his wife said their goodbyes to Marc, who smiled as he gingerly tiptoed across their flower-covered patio.

He was ecstatic about his day's work; he had bought one of the best properties in the northwestern suburbs for a very good price. He determined that the land could be subdivided into six blocks, each worth around $300,000. This would allow him to realize around $1.8 million less costs, and would give him an initial land profit of around $500,000. *Not a bad day's work!* he thought.

Everybody would get what they wanted out of this arrangement— the Harringtons would get their price, and Marc would get six excellent blocks of land at a discount. *This is what they call a win-win situation*, he figured as he looked back at the million-dollar property.

Chapter Twelve

Marc had little difficulty funding the Harrington purchase, and was able to start building on the land a few months after signing the option agreement. Realizing how much he had enjoyed the thrill of negotiating, Marc found himself searching for more subdividable land.

After letting all of the real estate agents in the area know he was on the lookout, Marc soon had as much as he could afford to own, quickly reaching the limit of his line of credit at the bank.

Another real estate agent, one with whom he'd had no previous dealings, called him, asking to meet him at a block of land at Huntley's Point that had just come on the market. It was Sydney Harbour waterfront land, which made it as rare as "rocking-horse poo," the agent assured him. Huntley's Point was only five miles from the Sydney commercial business district, located on a wide, deep-water part of the harbor where it met the Parramatta River.

It was love at first sight. *What a gorgeous piece of land*, Marc thought the moment he saw it, and its development potential hit him right between the eyes. He just had to have it. He immediately visualized subdividing the land into two waterfront blocks and one street frontage. If he built a jetty down to the water, he could create a prestige estate by enclosing the land behind a high stone fence.

The asking price for the whole thing was only $1 million, which made it a bargain, since he figured the three parcels would fetch between $4 and $5 million after they were subdivided.

Dollar signs danced before his eyes. The whole thing could be ready to market within four to six months. The profits would be spectacular, and would finally provide all the working capital he needed to properly finance his businesses. There was no way he was going to let this deal get away from him—not without one hell of a fight, anyway.

The trouble was, he now had no spare money, having fully drawn his line of credit. All his available funds were either tied up as working capital in his building operations or in his other land holdings.

Although tempted, Marc refused to ask Maddie and a Robert for a loan—that would mean breaking his golden rule about involving his family in speculative deals. He had learned to be fatalistic about these matters—if he couldn't fund it through his own means, then he figured it wasn't meant to happen.

How frustrating, Marc thought, thinking back to Shakespeare's King Henry crying out in vain when stranded in the middle of a blood-drenched battlefield: "A horse, a horse; my kingdom for a horse!" It seemed that Marc's horse was just as remote and would need to have a cool million dollars in its saddle.

He also couldn't help facing the fact that he would be stretching himself beyond his means and putting his other interests at great risk. Although the dangers tempered his impetuosity to begin with, ambition soon overcame his caution. *After all, if I'm going to grow my business, this is just a natural progression,* he rationalized. Marc wasn't going to let a little thing like money stop him.

He asked the agent to see what sort of deal the owner would consider. Would he accept an option, or take a smaller deposit on exchange of contracts? Could he delay settlement long enough for Marc to liberate some of his working capital?

The answers came back: no, no and no! If Marc wanted this land, he would have to have the $1 million ready and waiting now. The owner turned out to be a condominium developer who was hard up and needed to liberate the money pronto to meet his creditors' demands.

Think, Marc told himself. *Don't panic. Calm down. There must be a way around this.* Meanwhile, he tried to shut out the imagined stampede of his competitors, once they saw the potential he had spotted in this land.

Marc went to bed that night but stayed awake, his mind turning over every possibility of solving the problem. There had to be something that would give the owner what he wanted while allowing Marc time to get his finances in place to buy this outstanding property.

*   *   *

Over his years in the building business, Marc had dealt with many people from many walks of life. One of them was a man by the name of Reg Hanlon, who owned a lumberyard. Reg was a chain-smoking hulk of a man whose big red face always seemed to break into a ready smile whenever Marc called in to place an order at his lumberyard. Reg's company had supplied all of the timber frames and trusses for Highmark Homes since its inception.

In one of their casual conversations some months before, Reg had told Marc that he was retiring, and was going to sell his company to a major building materials conglomerate. Marc had since heard on the grapevine that Reg had gotten around $10 million when he finally sold the company a couple of months earlier.

Marc suddenly remembered all of this when he awoke the next day, and decided to contact Reg to see if he had any of that money lying around.

"Yeah, it's true enough, Marc. I got a packet for the company; so much that I've now got a tax problem," Reg Hanlon reported with a rueful laugh. "I've got $3 million tucked away in an interest-bearing account, awaiting a tax ruling on whether or not I'll have to pay capital gains tax on the proceeds from the sale."

"When do you expect to get that ruling?"

"Not for another a year at the outside."

Marc's face lifted. He decided to take a chance. "Would you like to make a profit on those funds between now and then?"

The pause took only a second. "Sure, why not? As long as it's safe, short term, and attractive."

Marc's hopes rose as he unintentionally clutched the phone receiver. "What do you need to see to be convinced? I'd be happy to set up a meeting."

"Well, it's not just me, you see. I have a partner, Dan White. We've been together since I started in business forty-four years ago, and we make all of the financial decisions together. I'd like him to come with me, if you don't mind."

"I've got no problem with that," Marc said with a smile.

They arranged to meet in Marc's office at eleven the next morning. That gave him a day to work out an attractive proposition—one that would get them as hooked on this unique Huntley's Point property as him.

I'd better do something about holding the land while I try to put the deal together, he thought.

The only way the agent would take the land off the market was if Marc paid him a deposit of a thousand dollars, and allowed the owner's solicitor to issue the contracts of sale to him.

"This will give you about two weeks to get yourself together. That's the best I can do without breaching my responsibilities to the client," the agent said.

Marc readily agreed to those terms, saying, "Beggars can't be choosers."

Reg had a heavily wrinkled face that was perennially red and sunburned. He drew labored, wheezy breaths between cigarettes and had a habit of closing his eyes for long spells when you were speaking to him, almost compelling you to nudge him back into the world of the living. If left to his own devices, Reg would stir back into life at a critical point in the presentation and ask a pertinent question. Although Marc had never seen Reg in a similar business situation, he felt sure that this was Reg's method of testing out the other person's knowledge and confidence. *If you know what you're talking about, then it should be easy to get past my closed eyes*, Marc thought.

Dan White was a different kettle of fish. Marc had never met him before, and knew only that he was a retired solicitor. Dan was short and stocky with snow-white hair, pale blue eyes, and a relatively unlined, tanned face. Like Reg, he was in his late sixties. His false teeth gave him a constant smile. It was hard for Marc to determine if Dan was smiling at him or cursing him from behind those clenched teeth, since his expression seldom changed.

Once they all got into conversation, it became obvious Dan was the business brain behind the operation. Reg instinctively took a back seat and held himself ready to chime in only if Dan signaled a need for his support.

"As Reg's already told you, Marc, we've got about $3 million to invest, pending a forthcoming tax decision. And yes, we could use this money if we found a highly profitable, short-term business venture; but it must be secure."

This was Marc's cue. "Gentlemen, I believe that I have just the project for you. I am looking for an equity partner, one who can finance the acquisition and development of a truly spectacular parcel of waterfront land I've just found." He went on to extol the virtues of the property, and his plan to subdivide it into three valuable lots.

Marc had prepared a spreadsheet and a summary, setting out all the development costs and potential profits. It all boiled down to the fact that, for a total cost of $1.5 million, including interest, they could jointly create $4 million worth of readily saleable land. The whole development would be completed within six months and would meet the chronic shortage of waterfront land in Sydney. *Surely these figures and the whole concept will whet their appetites*, Marc thought as he concluded his delivery.

"This looks quite good, Marc," Dan said, his interest clearly aroused.

"What sort of security will we have on our money?" Reg piped up.

"I propose that we do this as a joint venture," Marc replied smoothly. "I suggest we purchase a shelf company to buy the land, and split its shareholding in proportion with whatever percentage of the project each party will own. All the profits can flow back proportionately at the end of the venture."

"Yes, but what sort of security will we have?" Reg repeated.

Marc sensed a change in Reg's demeanor. Now that they were in the same room together hatching a deal, Reg seemed less amiable and more disposed to looking after number one. *Well, if that's the way he wants to play*, Marc thought as he couched his response with a similar degree of hard-nosed pragmatism.

Marc waited for Reg to open his eyes before giving an answer. "OK, Reg, here it is: You'll have a first mortgage on the property, plus a percentage of the ownership of the shelf company, whose only asset is the land itself."

Dan's eyes narrowed. "If we provide all the money, Marc, what do *you* do for your share of the profits?"

Marc was beginning to feel uncomfortable. These two men appeared to be trying to take over the meeting and the terms of the deal. *Time to reestablish the ground rules*, he decided. The tolerant half-smile that he had worn throughout the meeting faded to reveal a resolute jaw line.

"I have control over the land, and will be responsible for undertaking the actual subdivision. This part of the deal is critical, because unless it's done quickly and properly, all the profits could be frittered away in delays and interest costs. We could also end up missing the market if the economy changes in the meantime."

"Oh, yes; I can see that," Dan said, nodding thoughtfully.

Marc fixed both men with an intense gaze. "Not only is my part critical to the outcome of this project, but if I borrowed the money from a bank, they would only get interest and no part of the profit. Here, I am offering you both a much better arrangement, I think."

Reg's eyes were wide open now. "Don't get us wrong, Marc," he protested between wheezes. "We're interested, but what interest rate do you suggest? What's our share of the eventual profit?"

"Oh, I think that a 10 percent per annum flat interest rate and 20 percent of the final net profit would be fair," Marc replied.

"Ah, come on, Marc; surely that's a bit selfish of you!" Dan piped up.

Selfish! I let you two into the deal of lifetime and you tell me I'm bloody selfish! Marc wanted to shout back at the top of his lungs.

Instead, he measured his response. "I don't think so. You'd be getting a better interest rate than you're currently getting from the bank, plus first-mortgage security and partial ownership. What's wrong with that?"

Reg's eyes began to harbor a greedy glint. "We think we should have a little more."

"I can't believe this!" Marc exploded as he rocked back in his chair and looked Reg squarely in the eye. "Your share of the profits would be something like half a million dollars, and that's just for being involved!"

"It has to be worth our while to move the funds across and take the risk," Dan nonchalantly shrugged as he moved in for the kill. "I think you need to up the ante on our share of the profit."

Marc was fast beginning to realize that he had approached two men he really knew nothing about. On top of that, he was about to trust a large part of his future to two acquaintances who had just made it quite clear that they expected more than their pound of flesh out of this deal. After briefly reflecting on the prospect of losing out on this property, he resolved to persevere with them. *I've got to rise above all this and see if there's a deal in here,* Marc thought as he programmed himself to reenter the fray.

The three men finally reached an agreement: Reg and Dan would get a third of the profit on top of their interest payments. Marc would be paid by the joint venture for managing the subdivision and obtaining registration of the new land titles, which ensured he maintained control over the project. Getting paid for controlling of the project was just icing on the cake.

*   *   *

Marc worked closely with a solicitor who had done nearly all of his real estate legal work since he had started to buy land and build houses again. Hamish Johnson was a real stickler for detail, and had an annoying habit of going over every detail in the contract and reciting it back to Marc over and over again—a needless exercise, since Marc had often created most of the clauses himself. He tolerated it because going though this painstaking process ensured that nothing had been missed.

Marc got cranky with Hamish only if the lawyer tried to tell him that he couldn't do something that had already been agreed upon with the other party. On those occasions Marc would say, "Hamish, for God's sake, you're the bloody lawyer. Fix it!"

Hamish, following Marc's instructions, went to see Dan White a few days after the initial meeting so that he could sign the contracts.

"How did it go?" Marc asked when Hamish called him.

"Not too good!" Hamish replied.

Marc's face fell. "What do you mean?"

"Well, Mr. White said he went to see the land to make his own inspection before finally committing, and he didn't like the three large natural gas storage tanks on the other side of the river. He thinks they'll affect the marketability of the land after it's subdivided."

"What the hell would he know?" Marc exclaimed. "Those bloody things are about a mile away, and are due to be pulled down in a couple of years anyway!"

"I know, but he said that they've decided not to get involved in the project. They seem to think it's too risky," Hamish said sheepishly.

Marc looked away and shook his head in disgust. The sudden loss permeated his whole being, leaving him momentarily speechless.

After a short pause, he took a deep breath and collected himself. "I'm stunned, especially since we all shook hands on the deal. For God's sake, how can they renege now? Doesn't their word mean anything to them?"

"Dan said that he had made up his mind, and that it was no use you talking to either him or Reg, as you'd get the same answer."

"I can't believe it. There's got to be more to it. Someone like Dan White just doesn't go out to a site and decide he doesn't like it—not a site like this one, anyway. He's got to be up to something."

"Do you want me to check around?"

Marc thought about it for a second. He really wanted to find the real reason these two had backed out of the deal, but felt too beaten by Hamish's news to pursue the matter. He sucked in what seemed like all the available air around him, expelled it and repeated the process again until he felt able to continue.

"No, Hamish, there's no point," he said with a rueful sigh. "I've gambled on their word and not looked elsewhere for funding, so my time is up. It'd be suicidal to exchange contracts without a ready source of funds. I'll just have to let the property go. Maybe one day, we'll find out what all this was really about."

"I'm sorry, Marc."

"Hey, it's not your fault, Hamish. Just tell the other side that I can't go ahead. There's no point in messing them around, too."

*   *   *

The next day, Marc got a call from John Hamilton from Multi-Build Pty. Ltd., the company for which he was building one hundred and fifty townhouses at Abbotsleigh in the inner-city suburbs. Construction was ahead of schedule, and Marc expected to complete the project within the next few months.

"Marc, I wonder if you could pop into my office within the next couple of days. I have three new townhouse projects I'd like you to take a look at."

"Sure, John. Is tomorrow at ten OK?"

"Yeah, that'd be great. See you then."

When Marc arrived, John had his firm's next three projects neatly packaged and ready for perusal.

"We're so impressed with you that we'd like you to consider gearing up your operation to do all three jobs simultaneously," John told him.

Marc's eyebrows went up. "Simultaneously?"

"Sure! You can stagger the starts to suit your workforce, which means that you'll have to start the second and third projects a couple of months apart, but we're sure that you can handle it. We can work out the finer details later. We only want *you* to do the job, but we also want your best price!"

"OK, I'll look at these and get back to you in a couple of weeks or so," Marc said as he put the bundles of drawings and specifications under his arm.

He went back to his office and immediately started putting the estimate together. He involved several of his key people in that process, including Milo Lombardo, who was now his concreting supervisor.

"Marc, I'm a little worried about you putting all your eggs in one basket," his old friend confided. "What do you really know about Multi-Build?"

Marc shrugged. "Not a lot, I suppose. I know they've been good clients so far on the Abbotsleigh job. They pay well and they leave me alone."

"Look, I'm Italian, and I know how we think. It just seems strange to me that they'd give so much work to a relatively new kid on the block."

"Come on, Milo, you're being a bit paranoid, aren't you?"

"Maybe, but just remember that we Italians are very passionate—we can hate with as much passion as we love."

"I'll try to remember that," Marc said with a wry smile.

Three weeks later, he was sitting in Multi-Build's office, signing three separate contracts to build a total of five hundred townhouses for just over $32 million. All the contracts carried tough penalty clauses, but after his recent experience with the company and their professional approach, he was confident they would present no problem. It did mean, however, that he would have to watch his cash flow very carefully, as he would need all his available working capital to undertake the increased workload.

*　　*　　*

Some months later, Marc picked up a local paper from the Huntley's Point area and read about two blocks of waterfront land that had set record prices at a recent auction. Sure enough, they were the blocks he had planned to subdivide. They had sold at auction for $2.3 million each, while the third block that fronted the street had sold for $1.4 million—a total of $6 million for the lot, much higher than even he had imagined could be achieved.

Reading about it made him feel sick. *We would have made more than $4 million in less than six months, had we gone ahead with this deal. And my share would have been about $3 million*, he thought as he gritted his teeth.

Over the past few months, Marc had picked up on a rumor that Dan and Reg had tried to buy the land on their own after rejecting his scheme. Apparently, they had come unstuck when the land became public knowledge and the owner was swamped with offers. Marc couldn't resist the urge to tweak the conscience of his dropout partners.

Who knows, they may think a little differently in the future if ever they get another opportunity to invest in one of my schemes, he thought. So he cut out the article and sent it on to Dan White's Sydney address with a note.

Dan,

Here's some information that might interest you regarding that Huntley's Point site. This was an opportunity that knocked and went unanswered!

Regards,
Marc Braddon.

Chapter Thirteen

Marc was both disappointed and inspired by the Huntley's Point experience. He resolved to spend the rest of 1990 seeking out other development sites and lifting his focus beyond residential land developments. He set himself a regular schedule of actively looking for such opportunities, which eventually led him to a vacant site in Hillsford, a northwestern suburb of Sydney.

He spotted a large expanse of land right next to the railway station, and decided to explore its possibilities. Hillsford Railway Station was at the end of a spur line, and operated effectively only during peak hours. Train services were infrequent at other times, although Marc was aware of plans to make the line part of the main suburban grid, which would definitely change the underlying value of the site.

Marc had also noticed that another developer had just completed an "office park" complex in a neighboring suburb. After making discreet inquiries, he found out that this office park, which comprised two office buildings of three and four stories respectively, offered a whole host of extra features not usually available in commercial office space: a swimming pool, two tennis courts, changing rooms, and a multi-purpose center. It offered the tenants a new dimension of first-class recreational facilities, giving them an edge in attracting employees.

Marc realized that the basic premise of office parks was that they had to be located in areas relatively close to where the workforce lived. This meant that a tenant could cut down their employees' traveling time while also providing them with a working environment superior to anything available in the established central business districts. Marc foresaw this sort of development on the Hillsford site, and the proximity of the train station only made it more attractive.

He checked with Greensborough Council, the local authority, to identify the current owner and found that it was a publicly listed company. They had an approval in place for a smaller, less ambitious office building that barely utilized the site's potential.

During the course of conversation, Marc discovered that the Council owned the adjoining block of land, and immediately realized that he might also be able to buy this land and consolidate both blocks into a larger development that would dramatically increase the land value.

He called the property owner to see if it was on the market, and was told that it might be, if the price were right. After getting some idea of the asking price, he called Bruno Pinn's agency to arrange the purchase.

"Bruno, I've spotted some commercial land next to the railway station at Hillsford," he told his real estate agent. "A company called Integrated Developments Pty. Ltd., with offices in North Sydney, own it. I understand they'll sell it for about $2 million, and I'd like to buy it. I want to deal through your agency, so you'd better get your tail over there and list it!"

"OK, Marc, I'll get onto it straight away. I assume you know that the sales commission on commercial land is much higher than residential—about four percent—but the seller pays that, anyway."

"Yes, I know. This is probably the easiest eighty thousand bucks you'll ever make. All you have to do is sign them up on an exclusive listing on the basis that you already have a buyer!"

"Thanks, Marc; I won't forget this! I'll get back to you as soon as I've tidied up my end of things."

"OK, Bruno. Just get them to accept an exchange of contracts on five percent with a ninety-day delayed payment."

Bruno called back within a couple of hours to say that he had secured the listing and confirmed the $2 million price. Integrated Developments had also agreed to exchange contracts on five percent of the sale. They were anxious to sell, but happy to wait ninety days for a settlement. *Excellent!* Marc thought.

*   *   *

Loren didn't want to get out of the car. She hated the idea of getting grass all over her new black slacks, and knew that her high heels would sink into the soft earth.

"Come on, get out and walk over the site. That way, I can explain where everything is going to go," Marc told her.

"I can see just fine from here!" she said petulantly.

"You always say that you want to see what I do. Well, this is what I do!"

"I'm not going to get all muddy and dirty just to see a vacant block of land that I can see just fine from the footpath," she protested.

Marc smiled ruefully and shook his head. After a couple years of these kinds of scenes, Loren's reticence still frustrated him. He couldn't help comparing her to Maddie, who would gladly have dirtied her shoes to get a glimpse of one of his plans in the making.

"OK, OK." He sidled up next to her and waved his arms around as he described his plans for the block of land. Loren tried to act like she knew what he was talking about, but it was clearly all Greek to her. She could see only several acres of overgrown grass!

"Can we go home now?" she pleaded as soon as he'd finished his presentation.

"Yeah, sure," Marc said, accepting that Loren just didn't get it. She just couldn't see the magic in a virgin site or the value in a concept, preferring instead to be able to walk into a beautifully appointed, fully finished building.

If only Maddie were here! he wished. In that moment, he envied Maddie for being married to someone who understood the business and supported her dreams.

*   *   *

Marc had acquired a lot more liquidity in his companies since that ill-fated deal at Huntley's Point. He could now find the $100,000 deposit required to exchange the Hillsford land sale contracts without draining all his available cash. This was just as well, because in addition to the deposit, he had to cover the stamp duty on the contract, which was another $90,000—due forty-five days from the date of the exchange of contracts.

If Marc went ahead and exchanged contracts, he would secure the land, but without having a lender in place to provide the balance of the $2 million needed to complete the sale.

Although Marc was still worried about straining his working capital, he had decided he wasn't going to miss out on another deal by being faint-hearted. He was confident that the cash flow from his various companies was enough to allow him to grab this opportunity. He was also sure he could get a lender or a partner within the ninety days he had to complete the purchase, so he went ahead and exchanged contracts with Integrated Developments.

With the first property secured, he went to see Greensborough Council again, this time to determine if he could also wrap up the ownership of their land. To his delight, the town clerk received him warmly and said that the Council had been trying for years to get Integrated Developments interested in a joint development.

The Council was now prepared to sell the land for $1 million. This was non-negotiable, as they felt that any disadvantage in the price would be offset by their willingness to increase their planning limits to accommodate a much larger overall development. Marc negotiated a six-month option on the land on the basis that he needed the time to get a proper building design done for the larger, combined site.

Marc thought that this deal might suit Dan and Reg. He knew they had more than enough money sitting around to accomplish his objective, and figured that they would be easier to borrow from than a bank. *Money isn't their problem; the problem is getting those old buzzards to part with it*! he thought.

He also knew that Dan and Reg would want to get out as soon as they had realized a profit, and he could probably use this to his advantage to limit their involvement. He felt sure they wouldn't turn this opportunity down, not after the debacle they had caused by doubting his judgment on the Huntley's Point deal.

"Do you want to meet in my office at around eleven next Monday?" Marc asked Dan after briefly outlining his latest opportunity. There was no hint of urgency in Marc's voice, no hint of anxiety; only a quiet determination to play both men differently this time.

*   *   *

"It's good to see you again," Dan said, stretching out his hand to Marc.

"Yes, it's been a while," Reg added as he followed Dan into Marc's office.

Both men seemed a little ill at ease at first, but Marc's amiability seemed to break the ice and take away any hint of a lasting division between them.

After Dan and Reg settled down, they gave Marc the floor to explain his latest plan and make the pitch for their involvement. He was masterful, and held both men in the palm of his hand as he led them through his grand plan for the Hillsford site. Soon, they too were converted.

"We're very sorry about the way Huntley's Point turned out," Dan said rather sheepishly, "and we're now ready to follow your recommendation."

"Yes, and this project sounds brilliant!" Reg chimed in.

Marc had told them that the first property, which the joint venture had to buy for $2 million, could be worth as much as $3 million in the larger development, although he felt that it would be worth a lot more. Marc knew what sort of profit margin would be required to prick Dan's and Reg's interest; but he didn't want to raise their expectations too high, since he believed they would withdraw from the deal after less than twelve months. He needed to leave himself some room to buy them out at the appropriate time if need be.

The second property, on which he now held an option to purchase from the Council, would have to be settled in another seven or eight months down the road. Marc estimated that it would be worth at least $2 million then, as it was the key to the newer, enlarged development.

He told the two men that he was looking for a little over $3 million to settle the two properties, and offered them a fifty-fifty split of the profits once all the approvals were in place and the properties sold—provided, of course, that they put in all of the money required for settlement and fifty percent of the approval costs. They would also reimburse Marc half of the $200,000 he had already spent in deposits, option fees, and stamp duty.

"I tell you, Marc, we're keen to be involved," Dan said.

"But we still need to get out of this deal within twelve months," Reg piped up.

Surprise, surprise! "I believe we should be able to meet that timetable," Marc said.

"If we can do that, then we're definitely in!" Dan declared. "It seems to me that we would have the option of selling the site with its new approval to a larger developer who could actually afford to build the office park."

"Failing that, I'll just have to find another lender who will take out your interest, at a price, to allow you to achieve the desired profit," Marc added.

"Yes, that would also do it," Dan said while nodding to Reg.

Dan and Reg then instructed their solicitor to draw up the necessary papers. They always used the firm of Swanson, McMillan and Partners, who were known in the profession as "Swanson's." Michael Creighton, a middle-aged partner and well-experienced solicitor, always looked after Dan and Reg's interests.

Dan assured Marc that Michael Creighton would be in touch with Marc's solicitor, Hamish Johnson, in the morning to start the process of putting together the joint venture agreement.

As the meeting broke up, Marc said, "I hope that we can bring this deal to a speedy conclusion, gentlemen."

"Marc, I hope that you're not still stewing about that Huntley's Point deal. The timing and haste that surrounded it made it too difficult for us to participate. We now see what you can do, and really want to be involved," Dan reassured him.

"Yeah, thanks for offering us the opportunity to be involved in this deal," Reg added. "Commercial property suits us better than residential land—probably because we've always had offices in commercial premises and feel more comfortable being involved in something that we know!"

Oh, well, we'll see! Marc thought as he closed the door behind his new joint-venture partners.

*   *   *

The next few weeks saw a continual stream of communication between the lawyers. Marc got daily phone calls from Hamish Johnson, who sought his instructions on all the complicated legal points that arose during the drafting of the agreement. It appeared they were making real progress, and that the agreement would be in place long before the expected settlement date.

Then suddenly, when all of the basic clauses seemed to have been agreed upon, everything went quiet. Hamish and Marc found themselves waiting for the final draft of the agreement, and were starting to get edgy. Dan, Reg, and their lawyer, Michael Creighton, took turns reassuring Marc and his lawyer that they were just putting the finishing touches on the agreement. Meanwhile, the clock was ticking on the $2 million commitment.

When Hamish finally tracked Michael down after leaving several unreturned phone messages, Michael seemed unconcerned. "At worst, we'll have to use up the "Notice to Complete" time—you know, the extra two-week period at the end of the contract that allows us to settle after the expiration of the contracted settlement day," Michael had told him.

"But this isn't what I wanted," Marc fumed when Hamish relayed Michael's comments. "I thought we had given these guys and their bloody lawyers plenty of time to work out even the most complicated agreements!"

After pondering his options, Marc grudgingly accepted Hamish's news. "They've got the whip-hand. I suppose there isn't much we can do except wait."

The settlement day came and went, and on the next day, Hamish received the "Notice to Complete" from Integrated Development's solicitors, which meant that there was no room for error. The transaction had to be completed within the next fortnight, or Marc would forfeit his deposit and possibly be sued for everything that he had.

Marc finally reached Dan White, who assured him that everything was on track and that the settlement would take place in plenty of time—certainly before the last day allowed under the now extended sales contract. "We're just fine-tuning the joint venture agreement and tidying it up," Dan said. "We had to put our solicitor onto another urgent job, but not to worry. Everything's well in hand."

Marc circled the last day allowed for settlement on his desk calendar as an uneasy feeling permeated his bones. He dared not think about what might happen if those two let him down again. Their track record didn't fill him with confidence, but what could he do? They were now the only game in town.

The days leading up to settlement were pure agony. After watching the clock and standing over the phone for the whole week, Marc finally got news that the settlement would take place at 5 P.M. on Friday, the last possible moment allowed under the contract. He was also told that Michael Creighton would deliver the joint venture papers to his office for signature, and that they had to be signed before Dan and Reg would hand over the money required for the settlement to proceed.

One hour before the deadline on Friday, there was still no sign of Michael, who had phoned ahead some hours before to say that he was on his way. *Boy! Do these guys cut things close*, Marc thought as he paced around his office.

At 4:15 P.M., Michael finally walked into the foyer and was immediately ushered into Marc's office.

"How are we going to settle this deal if you're here and the settlement is supposed take place in North Sydney?" Marc asked Michael urgently.

"Don't worry. Reg is over at the other solicitor's office with the check in his hot little hand," Michael said as he sat down across the desk from Marc.

"Well, that's good! Let's look at the joint venture agreement, Michael. For a document that has been so hard to draft, you haven't really allowed me much time to read it, have you?"

Michael presented Marc with several documents comprising about two hundred pages.

"How can I possibly read these properly in less than forty-five minutes?" Marc said incredulously as Michael just shrugged.

He clearly didn't have time to read the whole agreement and could only scan it, quickly identifying the key parts as he went. He instinctively went to the part about the shareholding of the proposed joint venture company, and noticed that things had changed from the original understanding. The shareholdings in the company had been set up so that his shareholding had no voting rights and could be controlled by Dan and Reg on any issue. This would effectively give them control of the company and the development. Under this agreement, Marc could be booted out of his own development with little difficulty, if they so chose.

"You have to be kidding me, Michael!" he shouted. "This is not what we agreed!"

"Look, I'm only following instructions, Mr. Braddon. Either you sign the agreement with all the conditions intact, or you don't get the money. You'll lose the land and a good deal more, I dare say!"

"Well, thanks a lot! Your clients have had weeks to negotiate any changes. It's abundantly clear that they have set me up so that I would have no alternative but to sign anything that you put in front of me."

"I'm sorry, but these are my instructions."

"What sort of people are you working for, Michael?" he asked.

Michael's face flushed. "I can try to get Dan on the phone to see if he will amend the agreement, but that's all I can do."

"Please do that," Marc said. "You can use the phone in the next office."

Marc immediately called the solicitor acting for Integrated Developments and was put through to Jim Brent, the partner handling the matter. Thankfully, he was one of the principals and a decent fellow.

Marc hurriedly explained his predicament, "Look, my name is Marc Braddon, and I'm supposed to be settling a property at Hillsford, owned by your client, Integrated Developments. I have a major problem. I relied on joint venture partners to finance this purchase, and they have just turned up in my office at the last minute, asking me to sign a draconian agreement that will ruin me. I'm sure that if you look outside your office, you'll see a man with a check for $2 million. Can you grant me an extension of time?"

"How much time do you need, Mr. Braddon?"

"Another two weeks, if possible."

"I will get instructions, but I think that we can do that, provided that you are prepared to pay interest at, say, twenty percent for that time."

"I'd be happy to do that."

"Look, you wait on the phone while I try to get you an answer on the other line," Brent said. Marc started praying for some help from above.

After a five-minute wait, Jim confirmed that his client was prepared to grant a two-week extension. Marc thanked him and listened as Jim outlined his client's conditions. Toward the end of the conversation, Marc said, "I'll never forget this, Jim, and sometime I hope to be able to return the favor. Could you do me one more favor? Go out to your foyer and tell Reg Hanlon to go home and take his bloody check with him."

"I'm sure I can manage that, Mr. Braddon," Jim said with a chuckle.

Some people restore your faith in human nature! Marc thought, just as Michael came back into his office.

"I've spoken to Dan White, and he said that it was a 'take it or leave it' deal. No changes will be tolerated."

Marc just smiled and said, "Well, in that case, Michael, you can tell your clients that I'm leaving it!"

Michael's jaw dropped as he struggled to formulate a proper response. "What about the settlement?" Michael asked in dismay. "You'll lose the land and your money! What will I tell Dan and Reg?"

Marc's eyes narrowed. "Tell them that I have gained an extension of time and don't need them or their money. I'll find alternate financing by the time I have to settle. I have several other options, and will simply put one of them in place," Marc said, his voice quaking with anger as he vented his disgust.

The expression on Michael's face said it all. He quickly packed up his briefcase and left the office, realizing that his clients' master plan had just blown up in their faces. He now had to report back to them about his failed operation. *What a dreadful day*, Marc thought, as he packed up for the day. *I need some sympathetic company*. He dialed Loren's office number.

"Pick me up at six. I'll cook us a quick meal. That and my undivided attention will make your troubles go away," she said.

*   *   *

Marc climbed out of his car and walked around to the passenger side door to let Loren out. Her street was dark and secluded, but he couldn't shake the feeling that they were being watched. It had been nearly a year since their boating accident, but the whole thing still troubled him. He couldn't rule out that there was a connection between the accident and Loren, but no matter how hard he tried, he just couldn't put his finger on it.

He hesitated on the footpath for a minute, looking intently up the darkened street until he was brought back to the present by the sultry silkiness of Loren's voice.

"Relax; you're with me now."

"I'm relaxed," he said unconvincingly.

Although they had been seeing each other for more than two years, Marc could never really open up to Loren completely, even though she seemed somewhat committed to him. He couldn't help worrying that if he ever surrendered to her in earnest, she would simply get bored with him and move on to another challenge. Loren swore she would never lie to him about anything, but her need to reassure him only made him feel more uncomfortable.

Because Loren was a beautiful, desirable woman and turned heads wherever they went, Marc attributed his suspicions to his own underlying insecurities and told himself to get over it. He figured that since he was relatively new to long-term relationships, most of his insecure feelings were stemming from his inexperience. He knew that Loren had some problems, but the vulnerability he perceived in her the day of the boating accident just made him want to look after her.

Marc didn't really know what Loren's problems were, but figured that they went back to something in her childhood. Early in their relationship, she had told Marc that her father had ignored her when she was very young, shutting her out of his life until after she had become an adult. But this was inconsistent with some of the other stories that she had told him about how close she and father had been when she was a child. Somehow, Marc put more stock in her earlier version of events.

Loren never spoke of her mother, and Marc always wondered why. Whenever he would ask about her, Loren would quickly change the subject. Marc knew that there were only so many times he could ask the same question, and finally gave up trying. Not knowing whether she was a good or bad role model made it hard for him to understand what really motivated Loren in the things she did.

As soon as they entered her apartment, Loren took him by the hand and led him into her bedroom, pushing him onto the bed and devouring him on the spot.

"Loren, you're insatiable," he struggled to say under the force of her assault.

"I don't want to talk—I wanna make you moan!" she squeezed out.

In the middle of sex, she made little melting noises and breathlessly called out his name. But despite it all, Marc didn't believe she really loved him, not in the way he wanted to be loved, and the less he believed it, the more determined she became to prove it to him.

At the end of the day, Marc kept coming to the same conclusion: Although their relationship was unusual, it suited their busy business schedules—for the moment, at least. They made few demands on each other and provided one another with a physical release from all the stress that surrounded them in their jobs. Since his conversation with Maddie and Robert after the sailing accident, Marc hadn't discussed his confused feelings about his girlfriend with anyone. But he remembered Billy's words when confronted with difficult issues, and clung to them: "Time will sort things out, m'boy—just learn to be patient."

Chapter Fourteen

The next morning, Marc sat at his desk, paralyzed by the daunting task before him. *Where in God's name I am I going to find $2 million in the next fourteen days?* he kept asking himself.

He tried to confront his fears with logic, in an effort to pull himself together. Although he was living on a knife's edge of emotions, he wouldn't allow himself to admit the hopelessness of his task.

Marc then spent the next few days scouting around for financing, without luck. It looked like he was going to have to bank on Dan and Reg to come around, so he settled in to play the waiting game. He resolved to have absolutely no contact with the two men, allowing them to think that he didn't need them to settle the property. It was a dangerous game, but he had few other options. Marc began camping out by his phone, balancing his trepidation to answer it with his fear of missing a crucial call.

*   *   *

Three days after Dan and Reg had pulled their second stunt, Marc got an unexpected call from John Hamilton from Multi-Build. He sounded annoyed.

"Marc, we're very concerned about the progress on our three jobs. We've got a lot riding on you and your company."

"Why, what's the problem?" Marc asked in a perplexed tone.

"I'll tell you what the problem is!" Hamilton thundered down the line. "You're falling behind on the construction program!"

"I wasn't aware of that," Marc replied, trying to maintain his outer calm. "Everything's on schedule, as far as I'm concerned."

"Well, our schedules must be different, then! Look at the contract, and you'll see what I mean."

"Hang on a minute; I'll grab the files."

As Marc rifled through his filing cabinet, he tried to reconcile John Hamilton's threatening tone with all their previously cordial dealings. *What's all this about?* he asked himself. After checking the schedule of completion dates for the various stages of the work, Marc saw that he had not yet laid all of the concrete foundations.

"Can you now see what I mean?" John Hamilton demanded.

"Sure, John, but I already told you that we would attack the work differently than what your people envisioned," he urgently explained. "As long as we reach completion within the contracted time, then we're OK, right?"

"I don't remember you telling you that, or me agreeing to it, for that matter."

Marc felt as if his feet had been cut out from under him. He staggered in disbelief and fell back in his chair. *You liar! You can't get away with this!*

"Come on, John!" Marc argued desperately. "We discussed it in your office before I signed the contracts, remember? You told me that you didn't mind which way I performed the job, as long as it was finished on time. You *said* that!"

John's voice was now cold and irrefutable. "Look, Marc: It's no use arguing about it. You're in breach of contract, and that leaves us with few alternatives but to seek legal recourse."

Marc's stomach began to churn. "What? You must be joking! Is this an April fool's joke or something?"

"I can assure you this is no joke. Effectively immediately, we have frozen all your progress payments on the three jobs."

"That's something like three-quarters of a million dollars—money I've just spent over the past month or so on work that's now complete. What the hell do you think you're pulling here?"

"Maybe you should ask your lawyers. Oh, and take along the contracts when you go and see them!" John said before slamming down the phone.

Stunned, Marc sat with the phone in his hand for a full minute. He finally collected himself and began trying to digest the conversation he'd just had.

Everything about it was odd—the tone in John's voice, his attitude, and the hardball tactics of a company that Marc had always found to be very cooperative and professional. Something was going on here, and Marc was at a loss as to what it was. He leaned back in his black leather chair and gazed vacantly out the window.

A few minutes later, his receptionist, Elle, rushed into his office and said that a salesman from Hodginson Jaguar was on the phone, wanting to know when Marc wished to pick up his new Jaguar Sovereign. *Oh, shit!* Marc thought, *I forgot all about that!* It had been a long-term dream of his to own a new Jaguar, and he had placed an order for a dark blue one on the strength of the agreement he thought he'd reached with Dan and Reg.

Marc planned to lease the car through his group of companies rather than buying it outright, so he figured that the return of his capital would easily cover the lease payments. With everything in such a perilous state at the moment, rewarding himself for a job well done was the last thing he felt like doing, but he had no choice.

When Marc got to the dealer and took a look at the sleek lines of the shiny, brand new car, his mood began to lift. *I deserve this*, he thought as he drove it out of the showroom and admired its reflection in the shop windows. *It's only going to make me more determined to get through this entire trauma and keep this car!*

It was now mid-afternoon, and the opportunity to take his new car for a spin, coupled with his bad morning, spurred Marc to drive up to Charmers Beach. The Charmers Beach Retirement Village provided an opportunity for Marc to immerse himself in one of his recent successes, as well as an opportunity to see Maddie.

There was a heavy buildup of semis on the Sydney-Gosford freeway's two lanes. As the huge trucks struggled to negotiate a long, steep incline, they spewed thick, black diesel fumes into the air. Marc was forced to slow down and wait in a smoke-shrouded convoy as the trucks inched their way up the hill.

Why is it that semi-trailers always seem to want to block all of the available lanes on a steep incline? Marc wondered, resting his head on the steering wheel for a moment. The smell of diesel took his thoughts back to Charmers Beach and the newly started work on the retirement village site. *It all seemed so much easier then,* he lamented silently.

When Marc finally reached the retirement village, he was momentarily taken aback, having forgotten just how large it was. He admired his handiwork from the top of a nearby ridge before driving down to tour every street in the place. It filled him with a sense of hope. If he could create something this good, then he could conquer anything!

Marc then pulled up into the center's parking lot and went inside to spend a few minutes with Maddie and Robert as they worked.

"How are you?" Maddie asked, delighted at her brother's surprise appearance.

"Not too bad, Maddie," Marc lied reflexively.

His sister raised a disbelieving eyebrow.

"I see that Robert's car is not in the car park," Marc noted. "Is he in today?"

"No, he's in Sydney. Had to give a presentation at a seminar later today."

"That's a shame. I would have liked to catch up with him too, but it's you I really came to see."

"He'll be sorry that he missed you." Maddie paused to examine her troubled brother's face more deeply. "Now tell me, what's new? How's Loren?" she added instinctively.

"She's OK, I guess, but I've got a few more urgent problems on the work and finance fronts."

"Oh? Come and tell me all about it," Maddie said, directing him to the couch in her office.

After he told her about Dan and Reg and Multi-Build, Marc became dejected again. Maddie suggested they go out to dinner, since the day was quickly drawing to a close. It would be about six by the time they drove to the waterfront restaurant she had suggested on the Brisbane Waters at Gosford.

"It has such a wonderful view, it's bound to lift your spirits," Maddie assured him, locking up her offices. "Wow, is that your new car?" she added, when she spotted the gleaming new Jaguar.

"Yeah, well, that's another story," Marc said sheepishly.

* * *

The restaurant was everything Maddie had said it would be. It sat at the edge of a huge expanse of water that seemed to be the very lifeblood of the whole central coast. Small craft, ferries, and motorboats dotted the lake, making for a constantly changing landscape. As night rolled in, the houses that peppered the far shores lit up to provide a colorful backdrop to the happenings on the lake.

Marc smiled warmly and offered his hands across the table to his sister, who took hold of his fingertips.

"How are things between you and Robert?" he asked. "Is married life what thought it would be?"

Maddie's face appeared to glow from within. "It's more than I had hoped for," she answered softly. "Robert's wonderful in every way, and I'm so much more in love with him than the day we married. We seem to complement each other on so many planes—every day, we seem to grow a little closer." Her idyllic smile broke into a laugh. "It's probably nauseating for anyone else to listen to me go on about Robert, but what can I say? It's all true."

"Don't apologize, Sis. I'm delighted that you're sharing your life with someone who's on the same wavelength—someone who understands what's important to you," Marc said as a rueful expression passed crossed his face.

Before Maddie had a chance to ask her brother what was behind that look, Marc skillfully changed the subject.

"It's really hard to believe that you and I ended up here tonight. Of all the places in the world, here we are together on the central coast of Australia. We never imagined this place even existed when we were kids," Marc said thoughtfully.

Brother and sister reminisced about their childhood in Algiers, where they lived in a huge mansion that had belonged to an exiled multimillionaire. Their father, Richard, had somehow managed to secure the mansion for a peppercorn rent. It was so big, with its giant entry hall, massive marble stairways and gigantic rooms, that it made both Marc and Maddie feel very small and insignificant by comparison.

Maddie shook her head. "Do you remember how intimidating our bedrooms were, with their high ceilings and cold marble floors? At night, those bedrooms gave me such a strange, uneasy feeling that I used to sneak into your bed and huddle under the blankets until morning, remember?"

Marc chuckled. "How could I forget? You were there nearly every night, and you always brought those freezing cold feet of yours with you."

Their childhood home had two elevated courtyards adjoining the main living area on the second floor. At right angles to each other, they were about half the size of a football field. The section closest to the house was trellised with a sophisticated system of metal posts and beams to support the heavy, bountiful grapevines. The courtyards were just over three stories above street level.

The courtyard decks were sealed with black tar that would become soft and pliable in the hot North African sun. As children, Marc and Maddie loved to play in this black, gooey mess, finger-painting each other and anything else that moved.

A broad smile lit up Maddie's face. "Do you remember how Mum used to go off her head went she caught us playing in the tar?"

Marc smirked. "She was a classic, wasn't she? She used to give us such a hard time while she washed it off with kerosene and water."

"Then she'd calm down, only to get angry all over again whenever she found another splotch on one of us," Maddie giggled.

"Yeah, we had some good times together," Marc remarked with a laugh. "Just as well, because we didn't get to see much beyond the house and those courtyards—there were no other kids to play with."

Maddie's brown eyes grew serious. "I didn't like *all* the games we played," she said apprehensively.

"I suppose you're going to tell me again how much you hated my high-wire act," Marc said, rolling his eyes in mock exasperation.

"What do you think?" she retorted. "I still reckon it was cruel of you to make me watch you walk along sandstone coping three stories off the ground. That coping couldn't have been more than eighteen inches wide."

"Oh, it wasn't that bad," Marc mumbled.

"Wasn't that bad!" she echoed indignantly. "You always walked along the outer edge of the bloody coping while I was running beside you, begging you to get down!"

"Well, when you put it like that... " Marc smiled and shrugged.

Maddie smoothed her hair away from her face. "Honestly, Marc, I know you were only six, but where was your head in those days?" she said, laughing while Marc cringed in his seat. "I think that's where you got your taste for danger and the adrenaline rush it seems to give you!" she added.

"Maybe you're right, Maddie. I remember doing that high-wire act, but I also remember how relieved I was when I finally climbed back down. Yet the relief could never really replace the feeling I got from facing and beating danger every time I got up on that wall. That's what always brought me back—to try to cheat the odds once more."

"Well, that's where you are right now," Maddie told him with a wise look. "You're on top of that wall again, and you have to go along its full length before you can climb down to safety. You're challenged by a whole lot of things that you can control, and many you can't. You must find a way out of this situation; I know you can do it!" As dinner and their conversation wound down, Maddie invited Marc to stay the night at her house.

"Thanks, Maddie, but I need to get back to Sydney. I have to make an early start tomorrow. It's been fantastic to catch up with you. And so nice to talk about the old days," Marc said as they parted company outside the restaurant. "Thanks for all your encouragement."

"You know that I'm always here for you," Maddie told her brother as he started to climb into his car.

He stopped with his body half in the car and turned toward his sister and said, "When *you* say it, Maddie, I find it easy to believe."

She looked at him with a quizzical expression as he drove away.

* * *

Marc found himself still wide awake at three in the morning. He decided to get up and kill some time by showering and dressing. While in the shower, he realized that he could call Billy, as it was just after lunchtime in New York.

"There's something else worrying you, Marcy. I can hear it in your voice," Billy told him after they had finished discussing Marc's business problems.

"Yeah, I suppose so," Marc answered as he realized that he couldn't hide anything from Billy, even when he was on the other side of the world.

"Come then; out with it, m'boy."

"It's my girlfriend, Loren. I don't know, but there's something not quite right there. I get the sense that she's playing around, but I have no proof—just an uneasy feeling in my gut."

Billy cleared his throat awkwardly for a moment. "I make it my policy never to interfere with people's personal lives, but if you're worried about what's she up to, then why don't you change the times you call on her? Mix them up a little rather than going around when she expects you. That'll confirm what's really going on. It's only a suggestion, but..."

"I might do that, although if I find another problem with my life, I'll feel like ending it all."

"Don't even joke about that, Marc! You should never let anything get you to that point. Just keep that old Marc Braddon toughness going, and nothing will hurt you," Billy laughed.

"Lovely to talk to you again, Billy."

"Same here. Ring me anytime you need me, Marcy. I'm always here for you."

Marc froze for a second. "Thanks, Billy. Funny, Maddie said the same thing to me today."

"Well then, you're going to be all right, aren't you!"

* * *

Marc was ready for work before 5 A.M, and decided to follow his mentor's advice and call unannounced on Loren on his way to the office. He arrived just as dawn was breaking. The streetlights were still glowing, but the darkness around them was quickly fading.

As Marc pulled up to the curb in his new Jaguar, he noticed Loren's front door opening. Two silhouetted figures filled the threshold. At first, he didn't believe his eyes. There was his lover, kissing some other guy in her dressing gown, and it was obvious they had just spent the night together.

Loren appeared to be gazing directly at Marc's new car, but, never having seen it, she didn't recognize it. He felt his blood rise and his reason start to desert him; he clutched the steering wheel in an effort to prevent himself from rushing out to confront them both. As Loren's new lover got into a black Ferrari, Marc had the presence of mind to jot down his license number.

How could she do this to me? Marc asked himself disconsolately. He had suspected all along that Loren had a skewed moral code, but he had always be able to convince himself that their relationship was special and that Loren would draw the line at bringing another man into her life while professing her undying love for him. Marc was devastated when finally confronted by her duplicity.

Thankfully, the few extra minutes he gave himself in the car allowed him to regain his composure. He was now rational enough not make a scene—after all, he wasn't married to the woman, and she was free to see whomever she wanted. *But why would she go to so much trouble to convince me of her love, and then let someone else into her bed? What's happened to my world?* He sat there, deciding what to do next.

After a short while, he decided to take some positive action. He would tempt fate and challenge every obstacle that stood in his way, starting with the duplicitous Loren. He climbed out his car and knocked on her door. He noted how quickly she answered, opening the door without asking who was there.

There was a barely perceptible pause. *Surprise!* Marc thought smugly.

"Hi, there!" Loren finally said, in a sultry low voice that barely covered her surprise to see him at such an early hour.

"Hi right back at you," Marc said as he pecked her on the cheek and made his way inside. *Maybe you thought it was your new boyfriend again*, he thought as he glanced over his shoulder to try to catch an unguarded expression.

"Something wrong?" she asked innocently as she pulled at her dressing gown and overlapped it across her chest.

I would never have believed she was this deceitful if I didn't see it with my own eyes. "I suppose you could say that." He spun around and fixed her with a steely look. "Who were you with last night?" he asked evenly.

Her first reaction was to look down and to the side—a dead giveaway to anyone who understood body language, and the sure sign of someone who was about to tell a lie. A heartbeat later, she lifted her head and looked Marc squarely in the eye. "No one. I was here all night."

Well that's half true, I suppose. Marc shook his head incredulously. "Loren, I just pulled up in that blue Jag out there to see you in your dressing gown kissing some guy goodbye. Please don't insult my intelligence with your lies."

Her green eyes fluttered wide open. "Oh, was...was that you?" she stuttered.

"None other!" *Now let's see you talk your way out of this one*, Marc thought.

Her reaction surprised him. Rather than continue to make excuses, Loren arched her back and appeared to look right through him. "You shouldn't get so upset just because I'm sleeping with another man," she announced in her most matter-of-fact tone. "*You're* never around when I need you." A note of derision crept into her voice. "You and that stupid building company of yours—you try making love to *it*!"

For a moment, Marc could barely see through his veil of hurt and betrayal. "Well, thanks a bunch!" he stormed at her. "Don't you remember telling me that you loved me so deeply that you could hardly make it through the day without seeing me or being with me?"

"Well, that's just the sort of thing you say to someone when you're sleeping with them!" she said even more matter-of-factly.

"I thought that because you loved me, you'd be faithful!" Marc shouted. "That's the way it is for me. Why am I the only one who sees it this way?"

"I'm not going to lie to you anymore. Sometimes I feel like having sex, and you're not around, so I think nothing of picking someone up at a bar or somewhere else. It doesn't mean I *love* them."

An incredulous look crossed his face. "How's all this supposed to help me?" he asked angrily.

Loren's upper lip curled with disdain. "I think you need to get out a little more," she delivered with a cruel little smile.

"So I finally get the truth about Loren Wilmont. Your whole rotten attitude only confirms what I've always suspected—that you're reckless and take whatever you want, no matter who gets hurt."

"So why are you still with me?" she snarled.

Marc didn't have a good answer to that one, so he ignored it. "I'm convinced that you act the way you do because of some deep-seated emotional scars that you won't talk about."

"So when did you become a shrink?" Loren retorted sarcastically.

"Well then, what *is* it with you?"

Loren paused a second too long, and she seemed to know it. Her whole demeanor seemed to change. She looked strangely vulnerable again—just as she looked the day of the boating accident—and seemed to be working hard to get out the next thing she wanted to say. When she finally did, her voice sounded fragile and sad.

"I think it's you I really love, Marc," she murmured. "But I just can't abide by your strict interpretation of love and fidelity. I just can't be tied down that way; I don't think I'm cut out for anything conventional. I always seem to want my cake and eat it, too." Her eyes were fixed on the floor. "I kept meaning to tell you, but... "

This woman is crazy. How does she expect me to believe her? One minute she's coldhearted and totally indifferent, and the next she's cooing. This is one really mixed-up lady, Marc found himself thinking.

Loren continued, "I need a relationship based on strength, and I don't think that you can provide that for me. You're married to your work, and I'll always be second fiddle. I think I do love you, and I want you to always be in my life, but unless you're prepared to give me more of yourself, you should be prepared to share me with other men who will give me what you won't!"

Marc rubbed his eyes and sighed. "Look Loren, this all too much for me right now. I'm going. I need time to think this whole thing through—I'll see you later."

Ironically, before all of this had started, Marc had been toying with the idea of making theirs a lasting relationship. He wanted someone to share his life with, and liked the idea of looking after Loren. But now, he no longer trusted her. He knew that she didn't have the strength of character to stay with anyone through thick and thin. She was way too selfish and fickle to realize the value of a genuine relationship. Marc's eyes were finally open. *How did I ever get mixed up with this crazy bitch?* he asked himself as he spun the wheels of the Jag and made a quick getaway.

*   *   *

Things can't get much worse, Marc thought as he reached his office around ten that morning. Dan White had called to ask that Marc return his call as soon as possible. He looked at the message on his desk and dialed the number, not knowing what to expect.

"Look, Marc I don't know how it happened, but somehow we all got our wires crossed," Dan offered apologetically. "Can we meet to discuss our continued involvement?"

"I don't know, Dan; I'm still pretty upset at what you guys tried to pull," Marc replied cautiously.

"As I said, I'm sure that it was all a big misunderstanding. We can rework the whole arrangement, and we're open to doing this deal any way you want."

"OK, I guess it can't do any harm to talk," Marc said casually.

"It needs to be soon. We can all meet at my property in Upton Creek near Singleton. Can you come up here the day after tomorrow? You see, Reg's staying with me at the moment, so it'll work out well if you could come here."

"I'll see what I can do, but I can't promise anything right now. I'll have to see if I can change some meetings I had planned for that day." Marc bluffed. "Why don't you fax me some instructions on how to get to your place?"

"I'll do it right away. I'm sure that we can work things out, Marc. I really hope you can come up here. I'm sure it'll be worth your while. All we ask is that you give us a fair hearing, that's all!"

As Marc hung up, he breathed a sigh of relief. *Hmm. Well, at least that part of my "grand" plan is working,* Marc thought. *Now all I have to do is figure out what I really want from these guys. I've got to put aside my other problems in the meantime, because I really need to focus on this and play my hand carefully.*

Marc decided to keep Dan waiting for more than an hour before confirming he would be able to make the Upton Creek meeting. Dan assured him that Upton Creek was a comfortable three-hour drive from Sydney.

"It seems like a heck of a long way to go for a meeting, Dan!" Marc said, looking at the faxed directions and the map of the state.

"I know, Marc, but it's the only place we can meet, and next Thursday's the only day that we have available. After that, Reg and I are going overseas for a week, and we really want to sort this out as soon as possible."

"OK, then. If there's no other option, then I guess I'll see you next Thursday around noon."

Marc was aware that these fellows were trying to get him on their turf. *What the heck,* he thought, *I've got the upper hand now, even if I am perched at the edge of a steep cliff!*

In reality, Marc's position had never been so perilous, dangling over a long drop with one foot on the edge and the other in midair. These people effectively had him by one hand, and he was relying on them to pull him back in.

*   *   *

Marc rang his old friend, Jim Daniels, and asked if he knew anyone who could trace a car's license number. If anybody knew someone, it would be Jim.

"Sure, if it's important enough, Marc, but it might cost you a good bottle of Scotch for the policeman. They're not supposed to do that, you know!"

"Yeah, I know, Jim, but it's important to me."

"OK, I'll call you later today."

"Thanks, old mate. I knew that I could rely on you."

* * *

Later that day, Jim called him with the information. His voice bore a tone of concern. "I've got the owner's name. It's Antonio Pressani, Martello Pressani's son. Aren't you doing a lot of work for Multi-Build?"

"Yes, Jim, I am," Marc replied as he seethed with rage. "And I think I smell a rat!"

"Rumor has it that young Antonio's the apple of his father's eye. He works for the Multi-Grid Group as an executive general manager or something, but beyond that, no one knows much about him."

"Thanks a million, Jim—this is just the information I need. Seems I owe you another one!"

"Just look after yourself, Marc," Jim said, his voice underlying his concern.

Chapter Fifteen

Even during the fall, the large Liquid Amber trees lining Finnian's Wharf Road still looked majestic. The knotty bulges in their solid trunks reminded Marc of a garrison of well-muscled sentinels posted at regular intervals to guard the edges of The Appian Way. These trees stood impassively against the changing seasons, upper limbs stretching into an array of thinner branches, creating the skeleton of a perfectly formed canopy arching over the length of the road.

As Marc's Jaguar stirred the drying leaves into a flurry of color, the resulting image was almost surreal, forcing the solitary jogger who had just turned into the street to break his train of thought. As Marc passed the jogger, he detected a look of envy on the jogger's face—directed at him, far removed from the bite of the cold morning, cocooned in the luxury of the Jag.

Yet the aura of accomplishment and comfort the image portrayed to the jogger and the outside world belied the turmoil going on inside the driver's head. As Marc sped toward what probably was the most important meeting of his business life, he realized that in the next few hours, everything he had worked so hard to put in place—everything that had come to represent his life—could easily unravel.

What's to be said for all of this? Marc ruminated as the autumn scene flashed by him. *What the heck are we all doing here? Who really knows why we battle against such odds?* Marc couldn't readily answer for himself, let alone for the rest of humanity. All he knew was that today, he must travel a hundred and eighty miles to meet with Dan

White and Reg Hanlon at Dan's Upton Creek property to attempt to put the Hillsford deal back together.

Marc felt quietly confident that he now had the upper hand, but still recognized that he was in a very tight situation. In a little more than a week, he was committed to paying out $2 million for Hillsford, and he knew there was no other way of getting the money.

When Marc had secured the extension on the settlement date, which he'd needed to beat Reg and Dan at their own game, he had given the Hillsford property owner his solemn word that he'd find a way to settle. As a result, Marc now found himself faced with the added burden of making good on his word while saving his own financial hide. His current situation with Multi-Build also meant that he had to find some way of getting back the $200,000 he'd put into Hillsford in order to pay his pressing Coastal Construction's creditors for the work they had done.

I really don't know if I can pull this off. If I can't make it happen, everything I have spent the past seven or so years putting together is going to melt down before my very eyes, Marc fretted as he hurried along the lovely old street. He could almost sense the prospect of ruin shadowing him—a sense that was heightened by a continual barrage of light flickering in his eyes.

The pulses of light seemed to imply an urgency; the same urgency that made his chest feel tight. Marc leaned forward in his seat and looked up to discover that his tormentors were shafts of intermittent morning sunlight reflecting off the hood of his car after filtering through the naked canopy. Marc's mouth was parched as he flew past the rows of tree-sentinels lining the street, just managing to stay ahead of an imaginary shadowy banshee in hot pursuit.

Outwardly, Marc looked anything but threatened. Long ago, he had learned the art of looking cool under pressure, and believed that most of it was in the way one dressed. Today, he looked the very epitome of confidence and success in a brand new, charcoal gray Armani suit, matched by a crisp, cream-colored shirt. The outfit was set off to perfection by a Gucci silk tie patterned in small dark red and gray diamonds. He always wore pumps rather than the laced brogues everyone else was wearing. These were always highly polished, nearly always black, and of course, Italian.

Despite his cosmopolitan image, Marc still felt like an old warhorse readying itself for yet another battle.

*   *   *

Soon after clearing the city outskirts, Marc found himself engulfed in a constant dark green landscape that, while beautiful in its own right, seemed strangely forbidding. The bush seemed to swallow him up, only to occasionally release him into an opening of cleared farmland before gathering him in again. This scene kept repeating itself as he drove further inland.

After an hour on the road, Marc felt as though he was no closer to his destination. In this limbo state, he had plenty of time to think about the people and incidents that had helped to define his life.

He summoned an image of his parents—his father as a thin, finely muscled man in his early thirties, and his mother, the obedient army officer's wife in her knitted twin sets and tartan skirts—the way Marc remembered them when he was young boy.

I think they loved me, Marc concluded. He had always perceived his parent's disinterest in him as something that related to his behavior, but had now come accept that they were just busy people who saw him as a complete human unit rather than a needy little boy. *I'm all right; I'm still here and going strong—so I must be made of sterner stuff and I guess I have them to thank for that.*

Marc's thoughts then turned to Maddie. As he relived all their experiences together and gave thanks for the bond that had developed between them—which was stronger today than ever—his face relaxed into a smile and a rush of warmth pulsed through him. *She's truly an earth angel,* he marveled.

These sweet memories of his sister soon triggered images of her polar opposite. As Loren's flame-red hair and sultry green eyes washed over his mind, he felt another stab of pain at how she had let him down. *I probably had no right to expect anything else from her,* he concluded, expelling a solemn breath.

Next, Marc quietly thanked God for sending him Billy, who had looked after him so well after he left home as a kid. Marc could hardly believe that he had come so far since those days—he had come from being a snotty-nose apprentice to a serious businessman, complete with all the heartaches and headaches that went with the territory. *Billy, Billy, why didn't you tell how hard all this would seem on my worst days?* Marc smiled ruefully as his thoughts returned to the task that lay ahead of him.

Marc checked the clock on his console and saw that he had been driving for more than two hours. His thirsty Jaguar was registering just over a quarter of a tank of gas, and his legs were in need of a stretch, so he decided to make a pit stop. He still had another twenty miles to go before reaching Upton Creek, and wasn't sure if there were any gas stations in the sleepy little hollow where Dan White lived.

He saw signs that told him that Singleton was another two miles further on. It was a reasonably large country town that, according to Dan's directions, was about a half-hour's drive from his final destination. It was nearly eleven, and Marc was making good time. After his hour of reflection, it now felt like he had a car full of friends and family supporting him in his cause, and he felt more relaxed about the meeting's implications. Now, he was just wishing that it were over and done with.

As he drove into the main street of Singleton, he was immediately struck by the familiarity of the place; surprised by its similarity to so many other large Australian country towns he had visited in his travels over the years. The whole town seemed to be centered around one long, wide main street. All the cars were parked with either their noses to the curb, or in the parking bays that straddled the middle section of the road.

Nearly every shop had a two-story street frontage, and was protected from the elements by its own bull-nosed, corrugated iron awning. At first glance, these awnings seemed continuous as they stretched along on both sides of the street as far as the eye could see. Uniquely Australian in design, they extended from the shop front to the edge of the sandstone curb, where sturdy timber posts supported them. Each post was set in its own sandstone-capped brick pier, which rose from the edge of the curb. Almost every awning sheet was painted in alternating bands of green and gold or green and silver.

The monotonous color scheme seemed to freeze these buildings in Australia's federation period, when the six separate colony states of

New South Wales, Victoria, Queensland, South Australia, Tasmania, and Western Australia joined to become the Commonwealth of Australia in 1901. Only the odd major building—like the town hall or the moving-picture theater—punctuated the continuity of the federation streetscape, although they, too, had been built in the same style as the multitude of shops.

As Marc drove down the main street, he noted that the only appreciable break in this uniquely indigenous façade was the small community park, with a cenotaph that commemorated the townsfolk claimed by the great wars. He had little trouble imagining the locals gathering around it each April for their Anzac Day service in honor of the flower of Australian and New Zealand youth, who went bravely to their slaughter on the Turkish shores of Gallipoli at the behest of Mother England during the First World War.

Settling on a gas station at the far end of town, Marc guided his car alongside a pump and was greeted by a cheerful attendant. "Fill her up, sir? Can I check your oil and water, too?"

Driveway service? Now that's something I haven't seen for years. "Yes please," Marc smiled, marveling at how country life always seemed unaffected by the ravages of economic rationalism so evident in city life.

Marc climbed out of the car and stretched his aching back, simultaneously surveying the place for restrooms. The cold autumn morning had given way to clear blue skies and mild temperatures; the gentle breeze whispering through the service station kept the mercury steady at around seventy degrees, making it a very pleasant morning to be alive.

In an hour's time, I'll be in another battle royale, Marc thought as he sat alone in the service station's café with a cup of coffee in front of him. *I wonder if Dan and Reg have really softened their stance—I pray that I'm reading this situation correctly. If I'm wrong, this could be the shortest and most spectacular career in this history of the Australian building industry.*

*   *   *

Marc recognized the landmarks from Dan's faxed directions, and knew that he would be on time for the noon meeting. Calmness fell upon him as he approached the house, and he felt strangely detached from the upcoming proceedings. He felt sure that he would be able to handle anything that Dan and Reg threw at him today. On the way up, he had hatched a basic game plan that would allow him to use their greed against them; he just hoped that it would work.

The area reminded him of Evan's Vale, his hometown in the southwest part of the State. The hardpan, orange clay roads and the white fence posts seemed to fit his memory of some of the farms around that town. He looked in the rear-view mirror to see the Jag's bellowing cloud of dust as he drove up the unpaved country road.

Marc remembered how he and Maddie would sometimes ride on the tailgate of their father's old station wagon when they returned from the village's general store or post office. They would let their legs trail off the tailgate and compete to see who could get the most caked-on dust on their shoes and socks. Those same clouds of dust rose behind his Jaguar today, but the circumstances were a lot different. He suddenly longed for the security he felt as child, before he was forced to grow up and become part of an unforgiving and uncaring world. *How much simpler things are when we're young,* Marc reflected wistfully.

Upon entering Dan White's main gates, Marc felt himself stiffen as he saw Dan and Reg waiting at the top of the driveway to greet him. Both men were standing with their arms folded across their chests. They didn't look like two men ready to roll over and give him what he wanted.

I'm not going to let anything throw me. I'm simply going to play hardball to get from these guys what I need—anything less simply won't be enough to get me out of trouble, Marc reminded himself as he approached the waiting men. *There's no way that I'm going to let these two guys deprive me of my future; not after everything I've been through to get this far—not for all the tea in China.*

178

Chapter Sixteen

As Marc entered the main hallway of Dan's two-story homestead, he marveled at the skillful restoration efforts undertaken to preserve the century-old home. The timber skirting boards were high and ornate, the twelve-foot ceilings edged with wide, elaborate cornices, and the ceiling light points decorated with fancy, circular plaster patterns. The solid brick walls were smoothly plastered and painted in dark, Victorian-era colors. Closely striped red, white, and beige wallpaper extended from the floor to about four feet up the wall. At the top of the striped wallpaper, a three-inch-wide floral wallpaper stencil set off the painted walls beautifully. The light fittings on the walls and ceilings all seemed to blend to create a wonderful ambience, a perfect marriage of the old and the new.

"Please take a seat," Dan said as he ushered Marc and Reg into his drawing room.

"How many acres do you have, Dan?" Marc asked, politely making conversation.

"I've just purchased an adjoining property last month, and that brings it to 11,800 acres," Dan said proudly.

"Wow, that's quite a spread!" Marc exclaimed.

"If you like, and time permits, I can show you around the place later," Dan offered.

"That'd be nice, but we might be pressed for time. I've got to get back to Sydney tonight, and it's a three-hour journey, as you know."

"Well, let's get down to business then, shall we?" Reg suggested.

"Yes, Marc; what's your situation with the Hillsford property?" Dan asked.

"Look, I don't want to rake over old coals, but your actions the other day have made me very wary about dealing with you fellows." Marc paused just long enough for the two men to start squirming. "As it is, I have just about put in place another source of funding to complete the purchase of Hillsford," he added coolly, "so I'm not sure just where you would fit in at this point."

Marc knew that these men weren't stupid; they knew he wouldn't have driven all the way to see them if he didn't need them. But the fact that they called a meeting at all could only mean that they were hungry to get back into the deal, too. Somehow, Marc sensed that he had them. To test his theory, he decided to keep the bluff going.

Dan shot a furtive look across to Reg, who seemed to nod slightly. "As I told you over the phone, Marc, we want to deal with you," he said. "We would very much like to put the dealings of the other day behind us, and we want to know what sort of arrangement you'd consider to resurrect our original deal."

"Well, as I just said, I honestly don't think I need you guys for this one," Marc replied with a poker-face, hoping to panic them by mentally separating them from what they rightly saw as a pot of gold.

Dan leaned toward him. "Marc, we're really not like that!" he protested.

"There must be some sort of a deal that would suit you better than the one you've put in place with these other people," Reg whined. "Tell us what that is, Marc."

"Well, for a start, they want a lot less than you do, and they haven't let me down twice, as you have!" Marc chastised sternly. "Besides, what guarantee do I have you'd keep any bargain that we might make?"

Reg looked across at Dan—with a tiny raise of the eyebrows, he seemed to will his ally to up the ante.

"If we can agree on something here today, we'll show our good faith by settling on the land without signing anything," Dan said. "We'll only require the normal mortgages. You can appoint us as directors and fix up the voting rights later, when we sign the final joint-venture documents. How's that for blind faith, Marc?"

Marc settled back into his chair as if he had all the time in the world. "That's a hell of a change from where we left off."

"Come on, then, Marc," Reg blurted again. "Tell us what you want!"

Marc leaned forward again. "OK. These other people are prepared to put in all the money for the acquisition and development stages at five-percent interest for the initial twelve months. They are also prepared to extend this, if required. They'll do all of this in return for a one-third share of ownership and a one-third share of the profit."

"Goodness me, that does sound like a very generous arrangement!" Reg said, looking at Dan incredulously.

"Perhaps," Marc replied with an enigmatic smile. "Maybe, based on your newfound faith in me, we can find deal in here somewhere. I would want the same interest rate arrangements and terms as these other guys are offering. And for that, I would give you a twenty-five percent ownership in the property."

The disappointed silence in the room was almost palpable. Dan was the first to break it. "Marc, aren't you being a little tough? Only last week, you agreed that we'd be fifty-fifty partners!"

"I hate to have to keep reminding you fellows, but a lot has happened since last week!"

"Surely we can negotiate a higher percentage," Reg said hopefully.

With that, Marc's casual politeness vanished—in its place was the ironclad toughness of the warhorse. "I don't want someone who knows nothing about the development telling me what to do," Marc said bluntly. "You asked me what it would take to get back in, and I'm telling you."

Dan appeared to be losing his zest for the battle. It was as though he had bounced off Marc's tough exterior and hit the floor. By contrast, Reg was suddenly more focused—as he leaned toward Dan, he seemed to mentally will his old business partner to get up and back into the battle again.

Dan's tired eyes found Reg's face and read his determined expression. He looked around the room, took a deep breath and suddenly seemed ready to get back into the fight.

"Well, all right," Dan said with a sigh. "We're prepared to become minority partners, but before we determine the size of the shareholdings, we'd like to find out what else we can do to sweeten the pot."

Marc rubbed his chin thoughtfully. "Well, you could reimburse me all of the money I have laid out to date on this project, which comes to a little over $200,000. I would also want you to pay all of the architect's fees for a suitable set of plans to allow me to lodge a new development application, along with all of the related costs. This will probably cost another $100,000," Marc added, watching them mentally add up the figures.

Dan rocked back in his chair, unable to conceal his surprise. He finally managed to choke out a question: "Are your other people paying all these fees?"

"I haven't asked them for the architect's fees, or those other costs," Marc said, finally being honest.

Dan smiled knowingly. "We're certainly prepared to put the extra couple of hundred thousand into the venture. Is there anything else that we should consider, Marc?"

"Well, there's the purchase of the second block of land, the one currently owned by the local council, within the next six months. I'd want an assurance that you'll advance the whole $1 million, along with all the legal costs of about $50,000. Oh, and I would like reimbursement of the option fee I paid to secure this land." The length of Marc's wish list was starting to embarrass even him.

"All these things are possible," Dan said, smiling wryly. "Is there anything that you've forgotten?"

"I don't think so."

"We need to talk about the ownership issue, because we really need more than twenty-five percent, particularly if we pay all these extra costs." Marc didn't want to make it too easy for them. *Let them fight me for more!* "I'm not too keen to increase my offer of twenty-five percent," he said firmly.

"Look," Dan blurted, "if we meet all of your demands, then I believe we will exceed any other offer you may have. That being the case, we should be in for at least a third of the overall ownership." Reg quietly nodded his head in agreement.

"Well…" Marc tried hard to hide the growing sense of euphoria that was welling up inside of him. *Hold it together—don't blow it now. Just keep it going...* "If we can put all this down in an agreement here and now and sign it, then I'll agree to give you a one-third interest in the development. You'll have to agree to settle with Integrated within two working days, on the basis of the non-voting shareholding that we spoke about. I'll give you a first mortgage over the whole property in return for the advance of the $2 million."

"That will do us just fine, Marc!" Dan said, jumping out of his chair to shake Marc's hand. Reg gave him a big, cheesy grin and offered a hand as big as a bear's mitt.

*　　*　　*

After the basic details of the agreement were written down and signed by all parties, Marc and his new partners had a beer to celebrate.

Although Marc appeared calm and collected on the outside, he was relieved that he had been correct in his assessment that Dan and Reg were desperate not miss out on another windfall profit by again doubting his ability. He had created a powerful desire in his "robber baron" associates, and had used this against them beautifully. *Maybe I'm finally starting to learn about the psychology of a deal*, he thought. *But I've got to stop living so dangerously, or I'll be old before my time!*

Owning two-thirds of a property that would to be worth two or three times its original cost wasn't bad, particularly when it ended up costing him nothing. The prospect of his potential profit almost made Marc light-headed.

Meanwhile, the other two couldn't help congratulating themselves.

"We've been watching you, Marc, and we really think you're a good person to deal with," Dan said. "No one has ever made it so hard for us before. You're strong-minded, and you know how to deal with tough situations. Both Reg and I believe you've got the Midas touch when it comes to property. We're only sorry that we didn't trust your judgment earlier with those waterfront blocks. We know we missed the boat with that deal, and we didn't want to do it again."

"You don't know how close you came to losing this opportunity," Marc said, reinforcing the scope of their victory in their minds.

"That became abundantly clear to us over the past few days. I guess we took some bad advice," Reg said.

"It's a sad fact of life that the field of property is littered with so-called 'experts' who often know little about development, or the development potential of properties," Marc commented. "These same experts are always around to give advice, but rarely have the guts to get involved themselves. Most won't put their money where their mouths are. They're voyeurs, watching others take the risks as they look on from a safe distance."

"Ain't that the truth," Reg agreed.

* * *

After a couple of drinks, Marc realized it was now nearly three-thirty, and told his new partners he really had to go. Both men came out to see him off.

Dan shook his hand and said, "We're putting a lot of faith in you, Marc, and we're equally sure that you will make us all plenty of money. We had to test you, you know. I'm sure you understand—it's only business."

"I only hope that our other dealings aren't as rough!" Marc replied with a wry smile.

Dan and Reg laughed as Marc climbed into his car to head back to Sydney. He promised to visit Dan's property some other time, and Dan assured him that he would have plenty of other opportunities to do so.

As soon as he was out of sight, Marc let out the bottled-up feeling of victory that was now ready to erupt inside of him. "Yahoo! I did it. I did it!" he shouted out as the rush took hold.

The magnitude of what he'd done today was slowly sinking in, gradually replacing his uncertain future with a reality that he had only dared dream about up to this point. He had been to the very edge of his world, looked over into his own particular abyss, and come face to face with his personal demons. He had met them, faced them, and bested them—all on the battlefield of their own choosing.

* * *

Marc found Maddie's office number in his car phone's memory and hit the automatic dial feature. "Hi, Maddie. How are you?"

"I'm fine, but more to the point, how are *you*, Marc? Did you have your meeting with those horrible men yet?"

"Yes. And I got everything that I wanted out of the snakes, plus more!"

"Oh, that's brilliant, Marc! Come on, then; tell me everything!"

Marc told Maddie what had transpired.

"My, you have done well! It sounds like you put the fear of God into those poor guys."

"I think the worst part was finding enough courage to walk into the meeting in the first place. To my amazement, they wanted in on the deal even more than I had realized."

"I'm so glad that it worked out that way. Isn't that great!" Maddie said.

"It was one of those once-in-a-lifetime things—you know, Maddie, when everything goes just right. It went better than I could've ever planned. I feel on top of the world right now."

"I'm so happy for you, Marc. Listen, why don't you come by the house on the way back? I'd love you to stay the night. You must be really tired, and Robert and I would love to see you. We could all have dinner together to celebrate."

"Sounds terrific. Why didn't I think of it?"

"Can I take that as a yes?"

"It's a yes."

"Good! If you need to change your shirt or anything else, I'm sure that Robert can help out. Do you remember that friend of mine, Elisa, the archaeologist? She's staying with us at the moment, and I am sure that she'd love to go with us to dinner."

"Maddie! What are you up to?" Marc asked with a raised eyebrow. "I told you about my little episode with Loren—you know I'm sworn off women at the moment!"

"I know, Marc. It's just a happy coincidence that Elisa's here. She just finished a two-year dig in Crete, and can tell you some pretty interesting stories about the place. I promise you that she's nothing like Loren—I wouldn't wish someone like her on my worst enemy!" she declared passionately.

"OK, Maddie, I think I can cope," Marc replied, laughing at how quickly and vehemently his sister put up her defenses on his behalf.

"I'll see you around six. A shower and shave will wash off the road grime, and I can't think of anyone else I'd rather be with tonight."

"All right, then, it's settled. I'll let Robert and Elisa know. See you around six, sweetie."

Maddie was the one person who could always brighten up his life with just a word. He always felt so good whenever he spoke to her, and was now looking forward to going out to celebrate with her and Robert. That hot shower sounded pretty good, too!

Marc suddenly realized that he would now be able to afford the Jaguar. There would be enough money in the company to easily meet the lease payments. *Hey, I can probably afford to buy the thing outright if I really wanted to!* That thought rekindled the happy feelings all over again.

Tomorrow, the next day, or the day after that would give him more than enough time to redefine his next targets. Today, with all of its special joys, was for savoring without dilution! Marc wasn't going to let practicality smother the elation he was still experiencing from his great victory. He soaked up wave after wave of euphoria as he headed toward Maddie and Robert's house.

Chapter Seventeen

As Marc pulled into the LaPonts' driveway, he saw their porch lights blazing. It was just before six, and the late-afternoon shadows had given way to a premature darkness. He got out of his car just as Maddie was opening her front door. Smiling broadly as she walked toward her brother, she chanted, "Mar-cy! Mar-cy! Mar-cy!" and jabbed the air with her right fist.

Marc laughed out loud as he walked quickly into her open arms.

"How was your trip, sweetie?" she asked from inside their embrace.

"Fine, Maddie. Is everybody home?"

"Robert's on his way, and should be here in about half an hour. Elisa's taking a bath."

"I'm looking forward to that hot shower, Maddie. Do you remember those dusty old roads around Evans Vale? Well, the same sorts of roads are all around Dan White's property. I came away feeling grimy; maybe it's a leftover from those times we rode on Dad's tailgate!"

"Yes, I remember," Maddie said with a knowing laugh. "Let's have a cup of coffee, shall we? I've just brewed a fresh pot, and we can chat before you get into your shower. You can tell me all about your day."

"I'd love a coffee," he said as they made their way to the kitchen. "The smell's just reminded me that I missed lunch today. I forgot about it in all of the excitement!"

"Let me make you a snack then; you must be starved!"

"No, honestly, Maddie; I'm really past that point. I'll wait for dinner."

"You should take better care of yourself!" his sister gently scolded.

* * *

Marc always felt strange using other people's bathrooms, particularly when he had to borrow Robert's shaving gear to scrape the day's growth off his face. He thought nothing more of it, diving into the shower before the shaving cream had a chance to dry. The endless stream of hot water seemed to pour new energy into Marc's battle-weary body, and allowed him a momentary reflection on the day's events. He wanted to stay there forever, enjoying the wonderful feeling; it seemed like such a fitting reward for what he had been through today. Unfortunately, Multi-Build flashed across his mind, and he realized that reality would soon come crashing back and that this was just another step along the rocky road of life.

After helping himself to Robert's after-shave, deodorant, and one of his tailor-made shirts, Marc went down to the living room, where everyone had gathered for a pre-dinner drink.

Robert greeted Marc warmly and immediately introduced him to Elisa, whose natural beauty struck him immediately. She was a slender brunette with deep blue eyes, and her five-foot-eight height gave her a willowy appearance. She wore little makeup, yet her inner beauty shone through her eyes and her radiant smile. Her short, dark hair was beautifully styled and accentuated her classic European features. Marc couldn't help thinking that she must have just stepped off the cover of *Vogue*. But there was something else about her that he couldn't put his finger on—maybe it was the sharp intellect and keen curiosity in her eyes, or the warmth and friendliness in her manner.

Marc immediately began kicking himself mentally for not taking up Maddie's earlier invitation to meet Elisa. He looked over at his sister's knowing smile, which clearly said, *See? I knew you'd like her!*

* * *

Everything about the evening seemed to flow beautifully—the restaurant, the décor, the food, the wine, the service and, of course, the company. Marc found dinner with Robert, Maddie, and Elisa to be an engrossing experience—one that seemed to have him on the edge of his seat as he came in and out of the various conversations. Everybody was in top form, and the many topics they discussed allowed Marc to get a further insight into Elisa's intellect and her strong-minded approach to life. Elisa told marvelous stories about her recent experiences in exotic countries. She was passionate about her work, and her ability to easily communicate knowledge about her fascinating profession made her stories all the more interesting.

A couple of hours and three glasses of wine later, Elisa was entertaining them with another story from her stint in Crete.

"And when the local police arrested half my archeological team one night in a sleazy bar because they were in the wrong place at the wrong time, the rest of us had to scrounge together all of our pennies and valuables to put up enough surety for them to make bail," Elisa recounted merrily. "I had to act as our lawyer because no one else could speak the language, and we didn't have a cent to bless ourselves with, let alone to hire a local. The local magistrate was a crusty old codger who sat behind a high desk and always seemed to be trying to look down my blouse."

She barely finished before joining in the contagious peals of laughter. Wiping her eyes, she managed to continue. "So there I was at my legal best, with almost no idea of protocols and niceties, trying to get my team back on the job. The judge ended up fining them all the money we had collected for bail, but agreed not to record convictions against them for drunk and disorderly behavior. He also agreed to return our cameras and watches, so I suppose I had my first win as a lawyer anywhere in the world!"

As her friends started clapping, a change seemed to come over Elisa. "Oh, look at me. I seem to have done all the talking tonight," Elisa said with some embarrassment.

"No, no, no!" Maddie said with a reassuring wave of her hand, confirming what they all thought. "We all love your stories."

"Oh, yes; please don't stop," Marc added.

"Archaeology is a fascinating subject, and not something we hear a great deal about up here at Whitefeather Cove. It makes for far more interesting conversation than stuffy old property deals!" Robert commented, grinning at his brother-in-law.

"Absolutely!" Marc shot back. "I'm riveted by your stories, Elisa. I could sit here all night listening to you."

Marc quickly reached the conclusion that Elisa had an incredibly positive attitude toward life and her work, tempered by an awareness of the cruel realities that often lurk beneath the surface. She also seemed unaffected by the cynicism and jealousy in her particular field of academia, and seemed able to rise above such basic flytraps of human frailty with natural elegance. Marc was quickly coming to the realization that he had never met another woman remotely like Elisa.

"Marc! You're staring!" Maddie said, chiding him back to the present.

"Oh, am I?" he inquired as everyone broke into unbridled laughter. Elisa didn't seem to mind. She just smiled with a delightfully bashful expression and looked away.

Marc noted her reaction. *She may be adventurous and opinionated in her work,* he thought, *but maybe she's a little shy when it comes to romance. Maybe she doesn't meet the type of men she'd go out with in academia or on her expeditions.*

As the wine began to take hold of him, Robert waxed sentimental. "Elisa, do you remember the first time we met?" he asked.

Elisa's face lit up with a smile. "Yes, of course I do, Robert. It was at the university's biennial conference."

"That's right." He turned to Marc. "A few years ago, Maddie insisted that I take her to hear Elisa speak at the International Society of Archaeologists' Conference. Here I was, expecting a starchy academic, and out she walked—looking more like a runway model who had never gotten her hands dirty." He looked back toward Elisa. "Although I didn't know anything much about archaeology, I actually understood everything you said that day," he said with a chuckle.

Elisa cast Robert a broad smile. "Well at least I managed to change your view of archaeologists, didn't I?"

"You did. I now think they're all highly intelligent, good-looking people with wonderful senses of humor—but then again, you're still the only one I've met," Robert joked. "Maybe if we keeping inviting you to stay with us, we'll all become knowledgeable enough in the subject to carry a spade on one of your many digs!"

Elisa's mouth wrinkled into a smirk. "Maybe, but in *my* business, you need several degrees just to shovel dirt—we like to think that we produce the world's most qualified laborers." She grinned. "Anyway, you're already too overqualified—I think you've moved more dirt around making your land subdivisions than all the archaeologists on the planet put together," she shot back as the table erupted into laughter.

"You two are always pulling each other's leg," Maddie said in mock exasperation. "Don't worry, Marc; these two are the best of friends. They just can't get by without their daily fix of levity."

"So tell me, Elisa, what did you have to go through to become a world authority in archaeology?" Marc asked as he captured her eyes.

Elisa looked down at the table for a moment as she gathered her thoughts. "Let's see…after graduating with first-class honors at twenty-one, I immediately undertook my doctorate and finished it before I turned twenty-four. That was nearly six years ago. Since then, I've traipsed all over the world with my spade and bucket. I've either been on, or have led, expeditions to Egypt, Israel, and most recently, to Crete."

"Amazing," Marc murmured. "It's good to know that there are people like you are out there, still trying to push the frontiers of knowledge a little farther."

Everything that Elisa had said and done at dinner made Marc realize just how different she was from Loren. He was still trying to assimilate the fact that this lady had been under his nose for the past few years and they had not met. *You really are an idiot sometimes, Marc Braddon*, he told himself.

* * *

After the group returned home, Marc suggested that they all go for a walk on the LaPonts' secluded beach.

"We're really beat, Marc. I think we'll turn in and have an early night," Maddie told him. After an appropriate pause, she suggested, "Why don't you and Elisa take a walk? It's such a beautiful—more like a balmy summer's night that an autumn night. You can be Elisa's white knight, should she need your protection."

"A white knight for a fair maiden—now that's something I could be good at," Marc said as he turned to Elisa with a disarming grin.

"I'd love to get some sea air. If you're going to protect me, how can I refuse?" Elisa joked back, wearing a smile that flooded her face with warm radiance.

After bidding Robert and Maddie good night, Marc and Elisa found their way down the narrow path to the edge of the sand, where Elisa took off her high heels.

They sat on one of the smooth, exposed rocks that dotted the white sand and watched as the waves ebbed and flowed onto the foreshore. As the tide slowly rose, the waves inched farther and farther up the dry reaches of beach, making small gains as they wet and smoothed out the wind-roughened sand, slowly eradicating all evidence of their trek across the beach.

As he looked at the waves that were washing against the shore, Marc gradually found himself telling Elisa about what was important in his life, and how different experiences had impacted him, and other things he had thought he would never tell another living soul.

"When I look back on my childhood, I think of a lonely kid trapped in a deep forest. It seemed to me that I'd be trapped there forever—one day seemed to run into the next, and there appeared to be no escape," he said with a haunted stare. "No matter how many trees I chain-sawed or how much wood I chopped, my dad expected me to go out the next day and do it all over again—or at least that's how it seemed. It was a soul-destroying time in my life."

"What a terrible experience," Elisa murmured softly as a concerned expression ran across her face. "How did you cope?"

Even though it was dark out, Marc's eyes flickered with steely resolve. "Well, I knew that it was going to either make or break me, so I made my mind up to use it as a character-building exercise. Every day, when I went into the bush, I convinced myself that I was taking one step closer toward gathering the skills and toughness I needed to take on the world. So, I ended up using the whole experience to make me mentally tougher."

"It's amazing how our childhood experiences affect the way we live our lives," Elisa said with a supporting squeeze of his hand.

After a long pause, Marc tried to shake himself out of his memories. "Look at me, Elisa. You were keeping us all in stitches at dinner, and now I'm bringing you down with all these childhood issues. Let's talk about you again. Tell me about your parents and your background. Where did you grow up?"

"So it's my turn again, is it?" A knowing smile ran across Elisa's face as she accepted Marc's prompt to change the course of their conversation. "Well, let me see." She paused for a moment. "My parents are Russian. Their families lived in Harbin after the Russian Revolution. Both came from very wealthy families, and wanted for nothing. But they had to leave most of their possessions and wealth behind when they fled the Bolsheviks in the early 1900s. Otherwise, I'd be on guard duty at the Kremlin and you probably wouldn't understand a word I was saying right now." She grinned.

"Although both sides of my family abandoned everything and moved to China," Elisa continued, "they were able to regain some of their wealth through businesses they started up there to serve other Russian ex-patriots who had also fled communism. My mother never did a day's housework in her life. As a young girl, she couldn't even boil water. Both she and my father had servants to wait on them hand and foot, and lived very privileged and sheltered lives."

Marc couldn't help interrupting. "I can't help thinking how different your life as an archaeologist must be from the privileged and pampered life that your family had," he remarked. "What made you decide on something as demanding as archaeology for a career?"

Elisa shook her head with a wry smile. "I never had much of an opportunity to be rich and pampered, because when communism came to China, my mother's and father's families were uprooted once again to Shanghai: a beautiful seaport city that was known as 'The Paris of the Far East.' My parents met and married there, and that's where I was born, although I don't remember anything about the place."

The smile slowly faded from Elisa's moonlit face as she seemed to steel herself for what she needed to say next.

"They lived in Shanghai for four years or so, until once again, they were forced to abandon everything they owned one frightening night when a massive communist uprising threatened all our lives. I was only about three, but my parents told me about how they packed whatever they could into three suitcases and ran for the docks. We waited there for three days before we could board the first overcrowded ship that would take us. The final destination was not important, as long we got away from the turmoil and danger that became communist Shanghai. That ship took us to Cyprus, where we subsisted without any money for about a year before finally migrating to Australia in the late 1950s.

"My mother and father really had it tough. Their old lives had given them almost no training in survival skills. I have a lot of respect for them because of the way they started all over again, using only raw intellect and common sense to carve out a new life for us.

"Do you know that my mother couldn't speak a word of English when she came here? And she certainly couldn't cook." Elisa looked down at the white sand and smiled. "My father always reminds her about her first attempt at making chicken stew. Believe it or not, she cooked the chicken whole, feathers and all, with its gizzards still inside. I'll never forget that concoction—a stew of potatoes and other vegetables mixed in with floating chicken feathers. The poor chicken was drowned with its head still intact. It made an amazing sight with its limp neck and boiled eyes hanging over the edge of the pot. Just the thought of it. Yuk!" Elisa said with a shudder as Marc nearly fell off the rock laughing.

"My mother is now a fantastic cook, one of those gifted people who can create a superb meal out of almost anything. She still doesn't speak perfect English, but she has incredible smarts and an uncanny intuition that gives her the ability to read any situation accurately. I love them both very much," Elisa said, her voice quivering with emotion. "They are my real heroes."

Spellbound, Marc shook his head and replied, "Anyone who would abandon everything they had for the safety and the happiness of their young daughter must indeed be remarkable people. I'd very much like to meet them one day."

Elisa just smiled. "Why do I have the feeling that you will? You know, Marc, I think you're a bit like them. Maddie always talks about you and what you're doing, and from what she's told me, you've always been prepared to change yourself for the better, even though you could have easily rested on your laurels. I guess that's what makes you so special. Most people have to cling to a safety blanket while you just fling yours away, no matter how comfortable it is. I really like that in you!"

"Coming from you, I take that as a high compliment indeed," he said with a smile, but he was genuinely moved. "I really don't want tonight to end, Elisa," he confided. "I somehow feel that today is a turning point in my life."

"Me, too," Elisa said as she looked into Marc's eyes. The moonlight gave her face a softness that Marc found inviting. *No, I'm not going to jump right in.* Marc thought in an effort to stop himself. *I don't want to spoil tonight by allowing myself to get carried away; there's no way I want to repeat the whole Loren saga again.*

They came within a few inches of each other's lips, but hesitated. Instead, they smiled broadly at each other and began to climb down from their rock.

As they wandered back up the narrow track to the house, neither of them had much to say. One thing was for sure: They had formed a bond on the beach that definitely held possibilities for friendship, and perhaps a great deal more.

Chapter Eighteen

At breakfast, Maddie and Robert asked Marc all about the preceding night before Elisa came down to join them.

"Oh, Marc, it's so hard to get anything out of you!" Maddie blurted in exasperation. "Come on; tell us how you two got along. We're both dying to know."

"If you two got on as well as you did at dinner, it's a wonder you're still here," Robert said jokingly. "I almost expected a note on kitchen table telling us that you two had eloped and were halfway to some honeymooner's paradise by now."

Marc flashed a broad smile and sniggered. "Well, I would normally get after you for that kind of disparaging remark, Robert. Instead, I just want to thank you for introducing me to the most captivating, gorgeous, intelligent, and wonderful lady I've ever met!"

"Whoa, don't hold back on our account, old chap," Robert quipped.

"Yes!" Maddie let out a triumphant shout, and the two men grinned. "I'm so glad," she said enthusiastically. "Elisa is a very special person, just like my big brother." Arching a tactful eyebrow, she ventured, "She's quite different from Loren, isn't she?"

"Yes, she is, all right. And I'm glad you're happy," Marc said with an impish grin as he scraped his butter-filled knife across his toast. "So you *did* have something in mind when you invited me to stay over last night," he added knowingly.

"Who, me? Don't be silly," Maddie dismissed with a mischievous smirk as Elisa entered the room, wearing a warm smile.

"Good morning," she sang cheerfully. Her face lit up as her eyes met Marc's, and she transferred that smile to Maddie and Robert as if they all shared the remnants of some funny story. Showered and dressed in a pair of faded denim jeans and a long-sleeved cream shirt, she looked fresh and full of energy for the day ahead.

"What?" she inquired of Maddie, who was smiling like a Cheshire cat.

"Oh, nothing," Maddie answered breezily. "I'm just pleased that you enjoyed the sea air so much last night."

"Yes, there's a lot to be said for a stroll in the night air around here," Elisa replied tongue-in-cheek as she looked into Marc's smiling face.

While everyone ate and talked, Marc considered lingering for a little longer at Whitefeather Cove, since there was nothing much he could do in the city. He still hadn't quite worked out how to handle the Multi-Build dispute, but couldn't help but speculate if Loren and Pressani were mixed up in it somehow. He decided to let time take care of matters, and was keeping his men on all the sites in order to avoid further grounds for complaint. All of the negotiations with Dan and Reg were now behind him; only the legal documents needed to be put in place, ready for the settlement of the Hillsford property, on Monday. This would be done over the course of the day, whether he sat behind his office desk or not.

As Marc observed Robert leaving to prepare for a busy Friday, he made up his mind: *Why not take a day or so for myself?*

When Marc announced his intention to stay as he poured both women another cup of coffee, he could almost see the gears in Maddie's head turning as she worked out a way to go out for the day and leave her brother and her best friend to get better acquainted.

"You work too hard, Marc," she remarked. "You should take more time off and pamper yourself a little." She paused for just the right amount of time before suggesting, "Why don't you and Elisa go for a walk down to the Binalong Caves at the other end of the property? They're only forty-five minutes away, and there are some fantastic rock formations down there. It's something I have been meaning to show Elisa for some time, but unfortunately, I have to go to the office today to finish up some paperwork," Maddie said with a match-maker's smile.

"Sounds good to me!" Marc responded with an even bigger smile. "You've been telling me about these caves for ages, so maybe it's time I took a look, too." After another pregnant pause, he looked over at Elisa. "Would you like to go there with me this morning?"

Elisa's eyes lit up. "Yes, as a matter of fact, I'd like that very much."

"How about we leave around eleven?"

"OK, I'll be ready," she said eagerly. "I'll pack us a picnic lunch."

"I'll take care of the beverages," Marc offered. "I'm sure Robert won't mind if we raid his cellar for a nice bottle of white wine, would he, Sis?"

Maddie gave her assent, her eyes sparkling with excitement.

* * *

The Binalong Caves were set in deep bushland, a backdrop that was in complete contrast to the serene white beach at the homestead end of Maddie and Robert's property. Since Marc had grown up in the bush, he was able to point out many of the species of native flora to Elisa, who had spent little time in the country.

"This all looks so familiar to me," Marc said with some surprise. "The tree line reminds me of the property that Maddie and I grew up on."

"Well then, you can be my tour guide for the day," Elisa said with a nervous laugh.

As they walked across a wide expanse of golden, wild grass toward the forest of eucalyptus trees that bordered the knee-high grassy meadow, Elisa was awed by the deep greens, soft yellows, and light crimsons of the tree line.

Elisa seemed slightly hesitant as they were about to enter the forest. "The 'bush' looks spectacular, but it's a little forbidding for a city girl."

"Don't worry, Elisa; there's nothing in there that can hurt you. I'll see to that," Marc told her as he took her hand.

"As long as you don't say 'trust me'. Whenever anybody says that to me, I tend to run the other way," Elisa grimaced as she tiptoed through the carpet of golden, dried eucalyptus leaves that covered the forest floor.

"I promise I won't ever say that to you," Marc smiled as he made a mental note.

As they journeyed deeper into the bush, Marc found himself recounting many first-hand experiences. Everything he saw seemed to remind him of some long-ago happening, and he enjoyed having Elisa beside him to share those memories as they came flooding back.

"You see that big dead ghost gum over there?" Marc asked as he pointed to a gigantic old tree in a small clearing. "When I was a kid, I used to have to drop a trees like that on my own."

Elisa looked at him, then back to the tree. "My God, however did you manage?" she asked with a look of disbelief.

Marc puffed his chest out in jest. "Well, when you're a kid on property, you have to do all sorts of Herculean things every day. It's just part of the survival process."

Elisa's blue eyes grew wider. "But that tree must weigh tons!" she argued animatedly. "Isn't it dangerous?"

Marc thought about his father, and suddenly felt deflated. "Yeah, it's dangerous all right," he said ruefully.

Elisa moved closer to him as they ventured deeper into the forest.

As the next few minutes went by, it began to dawn on Marc that this was the first time he had been in the bush since the accident that had killed his father. Elisa's comment had reawakened the last remnants of guilt he still carried around with him. *There's nothing I can do about that,* he told himself resolutely. *My father would approve of Elisa and would want me to get on with my life, so that's what I'm going to do!*

When the forest floor suddenly changed from a carpet of leaves, wild grass, and a collection of flowering shrubs to barren, rocky terrain, they knew they had reached the caves. Within a few more steps they found themselves looking over the edge of a gorge that seemed a hundred foot deep.

"Wow, it's a long way down," Elisa said, as she hung onto a nearby tree and peered over the edge.

"You're not kidding," Marc said. He was less adventurous, and stayed back behind the edge of the gorge.

Elisa glanced behind her and flashed a smile. "A builder who doesn't like heights—now that's something I didn't expect," she joked.

"Not these sort of heights, Elisa," Marc admitted with a modest chuckle. "I can climb anything I'm building, but I'm not too keen on looking over cliffs on slippery slopes. I don't know—it's a little hard to explain. When I was a kid, it felt like I could do anything; now, I seem more concerned about my own mortality," he said, feeling awkward.

Elisa's eyes shone with compassion. "I think I know what you mean," she said softly. "Let's see if we can find a way down, shall we?" she suggested as the expedition leader in her took over.

They spent considerable time looking through the ancient rock formations, which fascinated Elisa. She found all sorts of Aborigine relics on the cave floors, and used the torch they had brought along to discover some hidden ancient tribal paintings in several of the lower caves.

Marc marveled at the way Elisa instinctively knew where to look for relics and cave paintings. It seemed to him that she was guided by some sixth sense. *What else would I expect?* he mused. *This lady is in her element. What better place to bring an archaeologist?*

"This place ought to be listed by the archaeological society!" she declared as they peered around their tenth cave of the morning.

"I'm not sure Maddie and Robert would want the whole world traipsing all over their property," Marc protested.

Elisa shot Marc an incredulous look and waved away his objection with a sweep of her hand. "Don't be silly! Something like this has to be made part of our national heritage. I'm sure Robert and Maddie would want it that way."

Marc shook his head and smiled knowingly. "Maybe so, Elisa, but I'll leave that to you, shall I? I only hope that Robert meant what he said the other night about his interest in archaeology."

They climbed back up to the top of the gorge and sat on top of the high rocks that overlooked the valley—a perfect picnic spot, they decided.

Lunch was washed down with a couple of glasses of white burgundy as they sat looking into the magnificent valley that lay before them. Marc noticed that Elisa had become thoughtful and silent.

"A penny for your thoughts, pretty lady," Marc said invitingly.

"Oh, it's nothing," Elisa said without conviction.

"Come on, what better time to bear your soul? There's only me and trees out here, and we can both keep a secret."

Elisa's mouth softened into a smile as she turned to look at Marc. "I was just thinking about the other part of the story I told you last night, and how similar our lives really were when we were young."

Marc hoped his smile would disguise his curiosity. "Oh?"

"You know, last night, when you talked about how lonely your life was when you were a kid? Well, my saddest memory was when I was separated from my parents. I was only four; it was terrible, and not something that I can easily forget!

"We had just arrived in Australia, and couldn't find a place to live that accepted children. My parents were forced to put me in some sort of boarding school. I remember that it was a school farm with cows and chickens, but to me, it was more like a concentration camp. I had to get up at dawn and help milk the cows—me, who had never even seen a cow close up before! They were about twenty times bigger than I was, and these huge beasts with their big eyes struck every imaginable terror in me at first. I quickly came to realize that they were really very gentle creatures, and I spent most of the milking sessions patting their faces."

"That's amazing! I had no idea places like that existed," Marc said with surprise.

"Unfortunately, they do. Or they did, at any rate." Elisa looked at the sky and shook her head. "I still remember the way we all had to parade every morning at dawn, with our milk pails, aprons, and rubber boots. My boots were too big for me, covering all of my legs and ending right up under my little skirt. How anyone could expect a four-year-old girl to milk a cow is still beyond me!

"Feeding the chickens was even worse. Those sharp beaks chased me all over the yard until I finished scattering their food on the ground. Those bloody birds used to harass me and scare me to death!"

Marc let out a muffled snigger, but understood the hopelessness that Elisa must have felt.

She accepted his compassionate expression and continued. "I hated it and couldn't understand why my parents had forsaken me. The headmistress was a strict disciplinarian who expected everyone to do their share of farm work, no matter how old they were. She picked on me all the time. I was so miserable.

"One day I decided to extract my revenge: I snuck into her office, took her prized marquisette watch, and flushed it down the toilet."

"Fantastic," Marc shouted as they both broke into a hearty laugh.

"Unfortunately," Elisa continued as the mirth bubbled across her lips, "I didn't have the makings of a master criminal, and told all the other kids what I had done. They eventually squealed on me when the old dragon of a headmistress breathed fire down their necks. Thankfully, my parents came to fetch me just in the nick of time, but they had to pay for that blessed watch, so my revenge came at a price!" Elisa finished as Marc laughed out loud again.

After a few moments, a look of sadness came over her face. "I know it sounds funny now, but it wasn't funny then," Elisa said ruefully. "It's amazing that I can still vividly remember what happened to me as a four-year-old. That horrible feeling of being abandoned still stays with me, even after all this time. Sometimes I think that I became an archaeologist to prove to myself that I could endure long periods on my own, cut off from other people, especially those I love, but don't quote me on that because I still don't know the real reason why I do what I do."

As Elisa turned toward Marc, the tears that had suddenly welled in her deep blue eyes told him even more eloquently of her pain. He instinctively put his arm around her, and she leaned on his shoulder for several minutes before they decided it was time to head back.

Marc marveled at the similarities in their backgrounds. Elisa, like him, had struggled with the feelings of hopelessness that came from being trapped in a situation over which she had no control. *There's much more about this lady than meets the eye,* he thought as they walked back through the bush, hand in hand. Marc decided to take a chance and confide in her.

"Elisa, when I told you about my times on my own in the bush, I never mentioned my one secret desire, which was to meet a girl who truly understood me—someone who had been through similar experiences in her life, someone who would recognize me instantly because we were kindred spirits."

Marc suddenly felt vulnerable. He was not used to admitting his deeper feelings to anybody. Business had trained him to always hold back information about himself and what he was really thinking. Suddenly, he had just bared his innermost feelings to a girl he had only just met. Now, he feared her reaction.

Elisa's eyes shone again in a knowing sidelong glance. "It's funny, Marc, because when you told me your story yesterday, I was there. I felt the loneliness of your long days in the bush," she said, her face full of understanding and concern. "Maybe we *are* kindred spirits."

Marc looked at her lovely face and beamed back a relieved smile. He had never met anyone with whom he could share those sad, lonely times in his own personal wilderness. Loren was not the sort of person who would stop long enough to have a meaningful conversation: She was too shallow, lacked real compassion and was only really interested in being entertained. *Elisa makes me feel like I can overcome any obstacle in my path,* Marc noted with growing excitement.

In Elisa, he had found the person who instinctively understood the desperation of those days. She also seemed to understand his need to test the strength of his character in that most unforgiving environment. Maybe it was the similarities in her own life while on those remote digs that allowed her an insight into his days in his own personal purgatory.

The warmth in Elisa's eyes somehow softened the time-toughened memories of that part of his life, and only confirmed his theory about why all those things had happened to him—it was so he and she would recognize each other when they finally met.

"You know, Marc, I really like what I've seen in you today—this unique mixture of strength and vulnerability," she told him. "On one hand, you're the master of this strange and dangerous environment, chainsaw and axe in hand, and on the other, this lone figure trapped in the depths of the forest."

Deeply moved, Marc blinked hard at the horizon for a few moments before looking back at Elisa. "Well, I like what I've seen today: a caring, empathetic lady who can still find her way, even when she is whisked away from her natural habitat," he answered lightly as he planted a delicate kiss on her forehead.

When they got back to the homestead Marc excused himself. "If I'm going to stay for the weekend I had better get back to my apartment and get a fresh change of clothes," he said as he prepared to drive off.

"Hurry back," Elisa cooed as she waved him away.

* * *

Marc and Elisa dined with Maddie and Robert that night, and then decided to have a quiet dinner on their own on Saturday night.

"It's your first date, so everything needs to be just right," Maddie advised her brother. "Leave all the details to me."

Sure enough, everything was very cozy at the romantic little restaurant Maddie had recommended. She knew the owners and had made the reservation herself, ensuring that Marc and Elisa got her favorite table in the corner.

After sitting down, Marc and Elisa seemed strangely ill at ease as they both seemed to realize that this was their first real date. For the first few minutes, Elisa watched Marc nervously rearrange the silverware and the position of the glasses in front of him. With a glint of mischief in her blue eyes, she began mimicking his moves exactly until their eyes met and they exploded in laughter. As the evening moved along, Marc and Elisa relaxed in each other's company and were absorbed in conversation. Marc decided it was time to tell Elisa about his near-death experience in Sydney Harbour and his unsuccessful attempts to get to the bottom of it.

"I feel something is missing from my memory, just outside my reach," he agonized. "It's like having something on the tip of your tongue."

"Our minds are amazing," Elisa responded. "They can retain an extraordinary level of detail…"

A light suddenly went on for Marc. "Yes! That's it, Elisa!" he cried.

A curious expression ran across Elisa's face. "Glad to help. But what'd I say?"

"You gave me the clue I think I needed to solve my little conundrum."

"Oh, good!" a puzzled Elisa replied. "Mind sharing it with me?"

Marc smiled. "All in good time, m'dear; all in good time."

* * *

The weekend flew by, and Marc bid everyone goodbye as he headed back to his office the following Monday morning. Elisa had told him she would be based at her university for the next few months, which meant that they could see each other regularly. On that basis, he arranged to meet her on the following Friday for dinner at a city restaurant they both knew and claimed as one of their favorites.

Marc drove away from Elisa with the realization that he finally had to sort out his private life—something he had never been motivated to do before because that was the one aspect of his life that he had let ride. He and Loren had not spoken since that morning last week, and he still wasn't inclined to make the first contact. But even though he felt Loren didn't really deserve the courtesy, Marc still felt compelled to end their relationship face to face before getting more involved with Elisa.

In the meantime, Marc also had to handle the other matters at hand, such as ensuring that the Hillsford property settled on time and managing the other aspects of his building and development businesses. He also needed to find a solution to his current impasse with Multi-Build, and do so without getting involved in litigation.

As he drove across the Peats Ferry Bridge on the Hawkesbury River, Marc realized that he had drifted farther and farther away from Loren over the last week. *Who knows why I've kept on with her and her cruel, black-widow way of loving,* he thought. In the context of what he now knew, Loren's rantings about undying love sounded hollow, and bruised his soul. In contrast, the weekend he spent with Elisa at Maddie's had suddenly changed his view of the world. He sensed he had met the first woman he could really trust, besides Maddie. Elisa had given him a new sense of hope. She reinvigorated his sagging expectations of love and made him believe again in the possibilities of life.

*   *   *

Upon his return to the city, Marc got a call from his solicitor confirming that the Hillsford property had finally settled that morning, enabling him to mentally mark that item off his list. Marc then arranged to meet Loren at her house on Wednesday evening at seven. He wasn't looking forward to it.

He also made an appointment with Dr. Williamson, who agreed to see him on short notice when Marc said there was something of great importance he needed to find out about his immediate past.

*   *   *

Dr. Williamson began the routine with which Marc had become familiar a few years earlier. Having spent a considerable time asking Marc about the period in his life that he was trying to revisit, Williamson darkened the room and hypnotized his subject.

As Marc gradually relaxed to the warm, melodic tones of the doctor's voice, he hoped for a breakthrough. *I hope this works*, he thought as he drifted over the edge into a subconscious state.

Time was standing still for Marc now, and Dr. Williamson's voice seemed to come from everywhere at once.

"Can you picture that day on the yacht?" the doctor asked. "Lift your right index finger if the answer is yes."

Marc's felt his right index finger lift up.

"Are you now anchored in the harbor?"

Marc again lifted the same finger.

"You are now at the fridge in the galley, bending down to select a bottle of wine," the voice calmly informed him. "You will soon stand up and glance out of the porthole, but not yet! You will answer my next question by speaking. The sound of your own voice will soothe you and drag you down deeper into hypnosis, and you will remain calm, very calm, and hypnotized while you're speaking. Now, as you stand up, glance out of the porthole and read out loud the name on the bow of the boat you see coming toward you."

"*Multitude*," Marc said immediately.

*   *   *

Armed with this new information, Marc spent Tuesday making some inquiries. The people he called at the Maritime Services Board were very helpful, they told him the boat was registered to the Multi-Grid Group. Marc also found out it was moored at Church Point, and wrote down the name of the marina before thanking the lady on the other end of the phone. "That's OK," she told him. "It's public information, and we're happy to help."

Marc jumped in his car and headed for Church Point and the Cavendish Marina, located high on the north side of Sydney. He was in no mood to admire the bright blue skies above, or the magnificent view offered to those crossing the Sydney Harbour Bridge. He was oblivious to everything as he started to fit the puzzle together, hoping that the marina's records would confirm his suspicions.

"Hello, my name is Matthew Pittman. I'm with the Maritime Division of AMP Insurance, and I'd like to inspect the logbooks for a boat owned by the Multi-Grid Group called *Multitude*. I believe it's moored here," Marc said convincingly.

He was in luck. A casual employee, unaware of the marina's strict confidentiality policy, was staffing the marina. Marc could tell that "Jim," as his name tag read, would cooperate by the way that he jumped to his feet when "Matthew" spoke to him authoritatively.

"I have the logbooks right here, sir," Jim said, as he pulled a set of books out of the four-drawer filing cabinet that sat in the corner of the office.

"May I?" Marc thumbed through the various entries. After a few minutes, he asked Jim if he could have some photocopies. Jim offered to make them immediately. "Matthew" then thanked the young man for his cooperation and assured him everything was in order with the insurance cover as he left the dock.

*   *   *

Marc placed a call to Antonio Pressani at the Multi-Grid Group's head office. Antonio came on the line.

"Mr. Braddon, you don't want me. You want the general manager of Multi-Build, John … "

"No, I want you, Antonio. I have several things I want to discuss with you. Seems we have a lot in common, you and I. For one thing, we apparently like the same kind of women, and we both love being on the harbor. I want to see you alone at five this afternoon. I'll even come to your office."

There was a pregnant pause on the line. "If you want me to get involved in a contract dispute with one of our companies, you're mistaken."

"I think you're involved right up to your neck, so stop fooling around!"

"If you want to waste your time, go right ahead, but I don't have time for this of sort nonsense," Antonio said offhandedly

Marc lost his patience. "Look, Antonio, do we meet, or do I go to the police?"

There was another pause. "I'll meet you, but I still say you're wasting your time."

*   *   *

Antonio had a huge corner office in the Group's Milsons Point headquarters on the north side of the harbor next to the Harbour Bridge. It had a spectacular view of the Sydney skyline, which Marc found odd, since the usual view from most of the city skyscrapers looked to the north out toward the Heads.

Antonio Pressani was a tall man with an athletic build, handsome, and clearly of southern Italian descent. With a stone-faced expression that revealed nothing, he guided Marc to a seat in the far section of his office where they could talk freely.

The two men couldn't be more different. Although they were about the same age, Antonio had clearly been brought up with the best of everything and was used to having anything that he wanted, while Marc had earned what he had the hard way.

I reckon this guy's not a man who's easily denied, Marc noted to himself. *Something tells me the way he's pursuing Loren shows that she's probably the one person he can't readily possess.*

"That's what all this is about, isn't it?" Marc started.

"All what's about?" Antonio said aggressively.

"Please, let's get real, here! I'm talking about your relationship with Loren Wilmont," Marc said, cutting to the chase.

Antonio cocked an arrogant eyebrow. "I don't know what you mean."

"Look, Antonio, I saw you and Loren at her front door last week. You know, after you spent the night together," Marc explained matter-of-factly. "You drive a black Ferrari, license number ANT 001, and unless you're in the habit of letting your twin brother drive your car, it was you!"

Resignation began to creep into Antonio's poker-faced expression. "OK, so it was me," he exploded defensively. "You don't own her. So what!"

Marc parried Antonio's attempt to dismiss him with a steely glare. "Well, so far, it suggests only that you and I were dating the same girl at the same time. But when you add up all of the other coincidences, you get a different picture. In the past eighteen months, my life has been upended. I've been cut in two while on the harbor, won an amazing amount of building work from your group, and now find myself threatened with financial ruin in a half-baked contract dispute with one of your companies."

Antonio sat up in his chair and returned Marc's glare. "I hope you're not inferring that any of this has anything to do with me."

"Oh for God's sake, wake up, Antonio! I wouldn't be here if I didn't have proof," Marc said confidently. "Here's a copy of the log from your boat, *Multitude*, showing that you were out on the harbor on Saturday, October 12, last year—the day that your boat sliced the yacht Loren and I had hired in two."

A menacing expression filled Marc's face as his pent-up feelings erupted. He wanted to grind his finger into Antonio's breastbone. "You nearly killed us, you jerk," he snarled, "and the police are still looking for you! How do you think they'll react if I pass this bit of information on to them?"

Antonio held up his hands in wide-eyed innocence. "It wasn't me. Why would I risk the life of the woman I love?"

"I can't answer that for you. I have no idea how your mind works; maybe you just lost control when you saw that Loren and I had gone down below, and figured that if you couldn't have her, nobody could!"

A determined expression ran across Antonio's face. "You can't prove it was me!"

"Don't put me to the test, or you might end up behind bars!" Marc shot back. "Then there's the other coincidence," he continued, "where I get invited to quote on all of this work that Multi-Build suddenly has available. The first quote came about just after the boating accident. Tell me, Antonio, did you finally realize this wasn't 1935 Sicily and that the police here are much better at catching Mafiosi crooks? Is that what made you decide to catch me in your web, getting me in deeper and deeper financially before bankrupting me as a way of turning Loren off me? I must admit it's a much subtler plan, but your mistake was going for the old method first. It blew your cover and left a clear trail leading straight back to you!"

The two men exchanged a long, hateful stare. Finally, Antonio slouched in his chair and rubbed his eyes—the posture of defeat.

"So, where do we go from here?" he muttered quietly.

Marc sat back in his chair and straightened his shoulders. "We need to understand what each of us wants out of all of this."

Antonio's eyes flashed with resolve. "For me, that's easy. I want Loren."

"And I want a simple life, free of phony contract disputes and people stalking me. And I don't really *want* Loren."

Antonio sat back in disbelief. A puzzled look danced across his face. "What?"

"Had you simply asked me instead of trying to kill me, we could have saved each other a lot of grief," Marc said quietly.

Antonio puffed up his cheeks and blew out the stale air, along with the futility of all his efforts. He looked at Marc, and both men shared an ironic snigger.

Chapter Nineteen

As Wednesday came around, Marc found it hard to concentrate after winning his required concessions from Antonio Pressani. He was back in business and should have been doing cartwheels, but instead, he was preoccupied with sorting out his love life.

As seven o'clock rolled around, he approached Loren's door with some misgivings. *I just hope she doesn't loose her cool*, Marc prayed to the steel gray skies above. Loren answered the door still dressed in the clothes she had worn to work. She had discarded her jacket, but still wore the cream blouse and navy skirt from her business suit. She also wore an apprehensive expression as she welcomed him with a hug.

"I've been waiting for you," she said as they walked to the living room, where a bottle of red wine and two glasses waited on the coffee table.

Marc had to clear his voice before asking, "How are you, Loren?"

Loren smiled a little too wide and tugged nervously at her blouse. "Very busy, you know, with all the preparations for a big case that starts next week."

"I know what you mean. I've been doing a lot of running around myself."

"Yeah, I haven't seen you for a while, Marc." She narrowed her eyes in suspicion. "Have you been hiding from me?"

"No such luck. You'd find me even if I hid under a rock!"

"Only if I wanted to!" she replied with her quirky little laugh.

Marc decided to cut to the chase. "I've got something I want to talk to you about, Loren," he said as she finished pouring the wine.

Loren dropped her gaze. "Why do I get a sense of impending doom?"

"Come on, Loren…we both know we'd destroy each other if our relationship became serious."

Her emerald green eyes looked piercingly into his. "What are you trying to tell me?"

Marc fidgeted as he began delivering the speech he'd been composing in his head that day. "That our basic differences are far too great for us to overcome, and we'd both benefit from a fresh start with someone else," he said as diplomatically as he could. "Maybe we can learn from the mistakes we made with each other."

The temperature in the apartment suddenly seemed to plunge into the single digits. Loren's eyes narrowed again—this time in rage.

"You lousy jerk!" she shrieked, picking up a glass of wine and throwing it in his face.

As the wine rolled down the contours of his face and dripped freely onto his cream sports shirt and denim jeans, Marc's expression hardened with contempt. Remembering why he was there, he fought hard to regain his balance.

"How could you think that I'd ever give you up when I've given you so much of myself?" Loren told him in between ragged sobs.

Marc blinked in amazement, much as if he'd just woken up on the dark side of the moon. "What? You mean the way you've led me on while you slept around with every Tom, Dick, and Harry? Get real, Loren! No matter which way you package it, you're little more than a whore."

"And you're too adolescent to make any sort of commitment!" Loren hissed.

"Only an adolescent would start throwing around glasses of wine during an argument," Marc retorted. Looking down, he noted with satisfaction that the wine had also stained her couch.

"Well, I'd rather be an adolescent than a weak-willed sissy, which is all you turned out to be, Marc Braddon!"

"Listen, you stupid little girl, nobody in their right mind would marry someone like you," he shouted. "Who needs a tramp for a wife!"

"Get out!" Loren screamed. "Get out of my house!"

"With pleasure," Marc snarled as he got to his feet.

But before he had taken four steps, Loren began to sob again. "I knew we were doomed from the moment you found out about the other men in my life. I ruin everything good in my life with my own special brand of stupidity. There's no one I care about as much as you—you have to believe me!" she pleaded with the desperation of a five-year-old as she cried into her hands. "How am I going to get by without you?"

She's trying to pull me back in, but it won't work, Marc thought resolutely. *But I can't just leave her crying...*

Softening, Marc returned to where she was sitting. "You'll be OK, Loren. You'll never be alone." *That's for sure,* he cynically noted to himself.

As she looked up at him, her green eyes rimmed with red and her mascara starting to run, Marc couldn't help but think that Loren had never looked more genuine than she did now.

"Look," she appealed quietly, "I've got a talent for making the difficult work; please let me try."

"No, Loren, it's no use," he said gently. "Surely one of your...other men can give you what you want."

"Maybe..." she responded ambiguously. "I do have this one guy who wants to marry me." Her eyes lit up as an idea flashed into her mind. "I could marry him and be your mistress..."

"That's not going to work either, Loren," Marc said dismissively.

Loren took a balled-up tissue from her pocket and wiped her eyes. "Let's not talk about it any more right now, Marc." She looked up at him again beseechingly. "I would still like us to remain friends. Do you think we can manage that, at least?"

Marc felt nothing more than pity for her now, and wanted to let her down as easily as he could. *If she needs me to tell her what she wants to hear, then why not?*

"Of course we can," he answered, almost wishing he hadn't said the things he had.

"I suppose we'll eventually get over each other, but it's going to take me a long time," she said, as tears filled her eyes once more.

The deep-seated anger Marc felt for the wrongs Loren had committed seemed to melt away. He now felt genuinely empathetic toward her as they embraced and kissed each other goodbye.

On his way out, Marc looked back over his shoulder one last time at Loren on her sofa, looking thoughtfully into the wine glass she was holding. He couldn't help wondering if she saw the glass as half full or half empty.

*   *   *

The next few days passed very slowly, and Marc found himself counting the moments until he saw Elisa again. For some reason, he was nervous about meeting her again; perhaps because he wasn't sure if she'd feel the same way toward him when they met up again in the city as she had at Whitefeather Cove.

When Elisa walked up to his table and sat down, all his doubts evaporated: her face said it all. *Who was it who said a single smile could light up the whole world?* he wondered. Marc knew he could never put a price on the warmth that radiated from her when she beamed that bright, genuine smile of hers.

"Hello, beautiful lady. I hope you still like the Henscke Mount Edeleston," Marc said, pouring Elisa a glass of the ruby-red wine as she joined him.

"I've been known to change my preferences, but not in wines. Well, not in the space of a week, anyway!" she said with a chuckle. "I am impressed that you remembered."

Marc put on his most debonair expression. "How could I forget?" he boomed in his deepest tone. "After last weekend, its incredible softness typifies so much of what I like about you."

"Why, kind sir, you say the *nicest* things," Elisa replied in her best southern-belle accent.

"So, what sort of a week did you have, Elisa?"

"Both hectic and terrific." She inclined her head toward him with an inviting look. "Thank God, I had that time at Whitefeather Cove to recharge my batteries. Otherwise, I don't know how I could have coped."

Marc leaned in closer and smiled. "Well, I certainly enjoyed my time there."

"So did I. Maddie and Robert are such a marvelous couple. They made me feel so at home. And I met this fabulous man up there!" she added with a wink.

"I think it was providence that made me go there so that I could meet you," he said.

She flashed him another radiant smile. "I've got some wonderful news to share with you, and I wanted you to be the first to know!" she said, struggling to contain her excitement.

"OK. You've got my undivided attention."

"This afternoon, the vice chancellor called me into his office and told me I've been short-listed for an associate professorship in my department, based on the quality of my field work and the international papers I have been publishing," she said, beaming.

"Wow! That's absolutely brilliant! Congratulations, Elisa. Professor Elisa Zubreroff; now that has a nice ring about it! I know they'll pick you for the job. That's wonderful!"

"And another thing: The university's exhausted its exploration budget for the next twelve months or so, which means that I'll have to stay put for a while. Funny, but I don't seem to mind too much."

"This is sounding better and better all the time! We have so much to celebrate tonight—your new job, my Hillsford settlement, the solution to my contract dispute, and us being together. Oh, and our first anniversary. Do you realize it's been a whole week since we first met?"

"My, doesn't time fly!" she said cheekily. Then her face grew thoughtful again. "Oh, Marc, I hope I get that promotion."

"You will, don't worry. Who are you up against?"

"I don't really know. I think that Jeremy Close from my department will be interviewed, and maybe someone else from the outside, but it's hard to say for sure. I'm already starting to get nervous."

"You'll be fine. I'll bet you're way ahead of the pack."

"Thanks for your vote of confidence," she said resolutely. "You know, I am so exhausted. When I get back after a long dig, there are dozens of meetings and debriefings to attend. All of the crates have to be unpacked, and every item has to be properly catalogued. That's what I like the least about the job, but it's all done now," she said as a relieved expression ran across her pretty face. "Now, I'm ready to relax!"

"I've had a pretty amazing week, too," Marc told her. "I can hardly believe what I've been able to accomplish this week. I've sorted out my whole life in the five days since I last saw you, and feel like I need a holiday!"

"I've been meaning to ask you, Marc, if you had anyone else in your life," Elisa said in a way that suggested that it was a well-rehearsed question.

"No, Elisa; only you," he said with a disarming smile. "I was in a relationship but that's now ended—we weren't right for each other."

"Speaking of holidays," Elisa said, deftly changing the subject, "I'd love a real holiday, but the university thinks I've been on holiday by being overseas on a dig. I can't get a break for a few more months—not until this semester ends, anyway."

"You know, it's funny. When I think back to my university days, I always get this image of academics lolling around the staff room, sipping tea and chatting about lofty subjects," Marc said ruefully.

"It's not been like that for me, I can promise you! I seem to spend all my time either digging for buried treasure, cataloguing my finds, or writing papers for international conferences. And that doesn't take into account my lecture load. It's all go if you want to succeed in today's universities."

"In truth, I was never close enough to the academic staff to know how it all worked. You're first real-life academic I've really known."

"Well I promise I won't mark you down because of that," Elisa joked.

"Forgive me; you must be starved, Elisa. Shall we order?" Marc said, motioning to the waiter who was hovering on the other side of the room.

They spent the whole evening oblivious to everyone else as they toasted and enjoyed each other's company. They were the last couple to leave the restaurant; as the owners and their staff ushered them into the night, they gave the couple knowing looks.

"I have a special surprise for you," Marc said, his eyes twinkling with a hint of mystery.

"Oh, and will you still respect me in the morning?" Elisa joked.

"I'll always respect you, Elisa, no matter what," Marc said with a conviction that was somewhat out of context with the lightness of their conversation. Smiling, he returned to his jovial mood. "I want to show you my favorite spot in the entire world. I have never shared it with anyone before."

Elisa wore an intrigued expression as she approached Marc's parked car. "OK, I'm game. Lead the way, McDuff."

Marc drove through a maze of streets in the eastern suburbs of Sydney until he reached a park with a panoramic view of the city. He escorted Elisa to a park bench, and they sat in silent wonder as they drank in the magnificent view.

"I've never seen the city from this perspective before," Elisa marveled. "It looks close enough to touch, yet we must be at least five miles away."

"Yeah, I love the way the bridge seems to cut through the lights from the buildings on both sides of the harbor. You can see why it's such an important part of the city."

"The Opera House looks spectacular from up here. You were right; it truly is a unique place—and it's free for anybody to enjoy."

"They just have to find it. Now promise me you won't tell all your friends about it," Marc said with a look of mock pleading, "or we'll never be able to get this close to a park bench again!"

They sat there watching the lights of the ferries and small craft wind their way up the harbor toward the bridge, giving the otherwise static scene a degree of animation. The mixture of colored lights from the buildings and structures on both sides of the harbor, set against a dark night sky and reflected in the calm waters that dominated the foreground, seemed to hold them in wonder.

He looked into her eyes and instinctively found himself kissing Elisa's lips before he knew what he'd done. She responded by pressing her lips into his. Marc didn't need any more—just that unspoken confirmation she, too, felt something quite special.

"Come on, my beautiful lady, your chariot awaits. I'm don't want to keep you from your beauty sleep—not that I think you really need it," he added hastily.

"That's not always how I feel in the morning," Elisa quipped as they walked arm in arm toward the car.

They sat in the car outside Elisa's parents' house for another hour talking about all sorts of things. Every time Elisa bid Marc "good night," it would start off another round of kissing that kept them together until they started talking all over again. After the third unsuccessful attempt to break away from each other, Elisa finally mustered up the resolve to open the car door.

"Good night, my sweet prince. You must allow me to go before I turn back into a pumpkin," she joked.

"That only makes me want to hold on to you a little longer to see if you do," Marc joked back as he leaned forward.

"No, no, no, we girls must have our secrets," Elisa laughed as she slipped out of his grasp. "Good night, sweetie; ring me in the morning," she whispered before making her way to the front door and closing it behind her.

Chapter Twenty

Marc's personal life was more settled now than it had been for a very long time. He finally had a relationship with someone he knew he could really trust, eliminating the nagging uncertainty and associated worries that Loren had often created for him.

Having settled the Hillsford property, Marc now gave some thought to putting together a plan to take Dan and Reg out of the deal. The first step in this process was to agree on a proper basis for the development with Greensborough Municipal Council, which was still the owner of the adjacent property he had optioned. The new development application was to include the Council's property as part of its overall scheme.

Marc went to see the general manager, Jock Stanley—a big man with a larger-than-life face who had been with the Council for most of his working life and had worked his way up to the top job through sheer determination and persistence. He knew the workings of this particular political machine better than anyone.

"Well, Jock, what sort of development do you think the Council will approve on this commercial site?" Marc asked.

"I know we're keen to have a landmark commercial building in that area, so anything you suggest will get a proper hearing," Jock said.

"I'm looking at a three-building office park development, which means that I'll probably need to get approval to increase the floor space ratio from one-to-one to about two-to-one. That'll give me a good-sized development with the proper scale to be a landmark development."

"Good," Jock replied with a nod. "Even though this is going to require the Council to rezone the site, if I know the local councilors, they'll want something significant to establish that part of their electorate. I just hope that the neighbors don't kick up too much fuss."

"Do you feel it would be safe for me to instruct my architects to design something based on a floor space ratio of two-to-one?" Marc asked hopefully.

"Yes, I do. I feel certain that if the finished design has appeal and is imposing enough, I'll be able to get it through the approval stages. Don't worry about that!"

"That's good enough for me, Jock. I'll get in touch with my architect first thing tomorrow morning."

* * *

The following Saturday night, Marc and Elisa were back at the same restaurant they had visited on their first "city" date. The place seemed even more intimate than they remembered, and they became intoxicated by each other.

Drawn to the sound of his deep, low voice, Elisa unconsciously leaned closer and closer to Marc as he talked. Dimly aware of the relationship at work, Marc felt his voice gradually drop down what seemed like a couple of octaves as he, strived to entice his lady love a little closer.

"Oh, what a beautiful evening," Elisa said as they made their way to Marc's car, parked in a well-lit side street.

"Oh yeah, I feel *so* alive. Is it the wonderful weather, or just being with you?"

"Me, of course," Elisa smiled suggestively.

As Marc opened the passenger side door, Elisa spun around to encircle Marc in an embrace. They kissed passionately for a few long minutes in full view, as if to announce to the world that they were a couple.

When Elisa had coyly mentioned during dinner that her parents were away visiting friends in Melbourne for the weekend, Marc knew he didn't have to ask her what she wanted to happen next—he instinctively knew to drive her straight to his place.

As soon as they entered Marc's apartment, he put on some soft music and dimmed the lights. They sat on his couch and began kissing—first softly, and then passionately. They could resist their mutual physical attraction no longer; it was as if nature herself were bringing two unstoppable forces together.

They were quickly transported into a heightened state of passion. Every kiss was more urgent than the last. It was a heady cocktail, this mixture of desire and trapped emotions, and it was being unleashed with every potent kiss.

Marc drew back his head for a moment. "Is this OK?" he asked her urgently.

Elisa guided his mouth back to hers for the answer.

They kicked off their shoes and stepped out of their unwanted clothes, leaving them in a pile in front of the couch as they hurried into Marc's bedroom to begin yet another series of passionate kisses. Elisa looked virginal in her white-laced lingerie, and Marc was taken aback momentarily by her magnificent form. That thought was swamped by the powerful emotions that surged through him when their lips met again.

They took turns to offer each other pleasure, lovingly kissing and caressing each other's body as they climbed further into each other's souls.

Their desire for each other was now all-consuming. It easily carried them past the awkwardness of a first encounter, making their union seem both natural and exquisite. As Marc hovered over Elisa, they both savored every sensation until they could no longer contain themselves and burst into each other with a rush that pushed their heartbeats to the very limits of tolerance.

They both collapsed into each other's arms in complete, but temporary, exhaustion; they couldn't get enough of each other, and eagerly journeyed together up several mountains that night. They were totally exhausted by dawn, and slept in each other's arms until midmorning.

When they finally awoke, Elisa said, "I never believed myself capable of such passion. I can't believe that I somehow knew what to do—it's not an area in which I have volumes of experience," she said with a little awkwardness.

"After what we experienced together last night, all of my 'experience' adds up to nothing," Marc replied tenderly.

"I've never known anything like that before," she confided. "Is it always going to be that good?"

"Nope," Marc replied bluntly.

As Elisa's eyes widened and she searched for a pillow to pelt him with, he pulled her onto his bare chest and finished his thought. "It's going to be even better."

The intensity and depth of his feelings for this wonderful woman stunned him. The breathless feeling she gave him was worth waiting half a lifetime to finally experience. He knew instinctively he had found the woman he wanted to marry and spend the rest of his life with, but he wasn't going to spoil it by telling her that right now like some lovesick fool. He would keep quiet until he was absolutely sure she felt the same way.

*   *   *

Jeremy Close came out of the interview room and told Elisa that the panel now wished to see her. She was their last interview, which indicated her seniority among the applicants.

"Please take a seat, Elisa," Campbell McIntosh, the dean of her faculty and current boss, told her as she entered his large timber-paneled office.

Three other deans assisted McIntosh to make the selection: one each from the engineering, mathematics, and arts faculties. All sat around a large oak table. Elisa took a seat facing the panel.

McIntosh began the interview. "Your credentials are impeccable, and we all agree that your field work and the papers you have written are first-rate. Still, I feel I must ask how would you cope with the administrative aspects of an associate professorship where you'll be expected to assist the dean in the day-to-day running of the department?"

"It's not a role I've had, but one I'm looking forward to," Elisa replied confidently. "I feel that I can quickly adapt. As a senior lecturer, I now take part in aspects of the administration already."

The dean of engineering took his turn next. "Do you feel that being a young woman—a very attractive young woman—will in any way inhibit your credibility with the students?"

Are you kidding? You can't ask that, she thought incredulously. "I honestly can't see how it could," she replied as diplomatically as she could manage. "I interact with them in my present role, and feel that I have a good relationship with them."

During the ninety-minute interview, many of their questions centered on the fact that Elisa had spent a lot of time away from the university on her many trips. It suggested to her that that, her youth and her attractiveness were weighing against her. Although they later made all the right noises, Elisa was growing concerned about her chances.

* * *

Brunno Pinn, Marc's real estate agent, had introduced him to Kenneth Carlisle, an architect and British expatriate who had lived in Sydney for the past twenty-three years. He was a dapper little man who loved to wear tweed suits and colorful bowties. He was three times married and divorced, and hit the scotch pretty hard at every social opportunity.

After Marc decided to engage Kenneth, the architect suggested that they meet for lunch at his club. Going to lunch with Kenneth was a real experience, a test of one's survival instincts, as Marc soon found out to the detriment of his liver.

They met at the club around noon on the following day. It was the type of old-world club that exists for businessmen in big cities all over the world: The carpet was a thick, plush pile, woven especially for the club with its insignia integrated into the weave. The period armchairs, with their green, padded-leather upholstery, were arranged into congenial clusters throughout. Priceless Australian art adorned the walls, filling every available space of the conservatively colored walls.

Kenneth insisted that they have a drink or two at the bar before going upstairs to the dining room. The usual small talk followed, and Marc was introduced to all the club members who approached them as they stood at the bar. Contrary to his preference, Marc found himself chatting about absolutely nothing with people he didn't know from a bar of soap. It was all a bit ingenuous, like a politician working a room.

He and Kenneth were finally ushered to the dining area, another grand room with even more art hanging on the walls and just enough tables to make the place look exclusive.

Two staff members seated Marc and Kenneth at a table in the corner, where a bottle of the club's white wine awaited. Their waitress then served the wine before finally leaving Kenneth and Marc alone.

After a short while, Marc spelled out his vision for the Hillsford site amid occasional interruptions from Kenneth, who peppered him with questions. Which direction did the site face? How much slope was present? What sort of buildings surrounded the site? Marc tried to answer Kenneth's questions while continuing his detailed briefing.

"Look, Kenneth," he concluded, "I've cleared the way with Greensborough Council to increase the floor-space ratio, and would like you to design an office park with real presence."

Kenneth shot Marc a slightly disbelieving look. He sat back in his seat and cranked his neck to put his head off center with Marc's, as if to exaggerate his doubt about Marc's last statement. "Are you sure, old boy? We don't want you spending all your money on a design that Council won't ultimately approve because it's outside their current zoning requirements."

"The general manager has given me his personal assurance that he will see the rezoning through all the approval stages," Marc said emphatically. "If he can't do it, then no one can!"

Pursing his lips, Kenneth waved away his concern with a flourish of his right hand. "Well, it's your money, Marc. I'm a mere servant of your will," he said as he downed another glass of wine.

"I've always been prepared to take a calculated risk. That's the only way I know to make money and get ahead of the rest of the pack."

"You're a marvel," Kenneth said with a smile.

"Not so marvelous, really," Marc deflected with a modest grin. "In this case, the risk is minimal because I am in the driver's seat, and Council can deal only with me. I don't see it as much of a risk, although I *do* like the thrill of the deal!"

"Shall we order?" Kenneth suggested. "The club does a wonderful filet mignon if you like that sort of thing. And the veal is simply splendid."

The wine kept flowing freely as they discussed Marc's requirements and waited for lunch. When the entrée arrived, so did another bottle of white. Marc also noticed a bottle of red wine awaiting them on the adjacent serving table. *Surely all this wine isn't just for the two of us?* he thought. Marc was starting to feel the effects of the first bottle, and the prospect of two more made him realize that he had better hurry up and convey everything he intended to say to Kenneth while he still could.

"This site is a cracker. It's right on top of a railway station and just off an arterial road. It'll be a wonderful landmark development, and should set the scene for a small commercial strip," Marc said. "I visualize a three-building office park with a swimming pool and tennis courts as part of the development. The surrounding area will be heavily landscaped, and should be an asset to the neighborhood."

"I think I know what you mean," Kenneth replied after swallowing another of his succulent Sydney rock oysters. "We did several other office parks, a couple of them on the riverbank in Brisbane. They can be quite spectacular."

"That's why I came to your firm, Kenneth. I'm looking for the spectacular."

"I'll do some preliminary sketches, and we'll get together early next week to see if you like my ideas and how they might work on your site."

"Sounds good. I want to get the plans done as quickly as possible so that I can lodge the development application with my friends at Greensborough Council. While I need to have the job done quickly, I also want it to be good."

"I understand. You know, Marc, every other Council I have dealt with has been really slow at approving commercial developments. I hope you don't have to wait too long for this one."

"As I said earlier, I was assured it'd go through as smoothly and quickly as possible. I can't do any better than that, can I, Kenneth?"

"No, I suppose not," Kenneth replied with a shrug. "It's just a pet peeve of mine: turning myself inside out to get a job done quickly, only to find that it sits in Council waiting for approval for a further six months!"

"I guess that makes me the optimist at this table," Marc remarked, laughing.

They were now well into their meals and the bottle of red. Marc was glad to have gotten most of his instructions across to Kenneth, because everything started to change fast for him. He had to work harder at focusing, pushing back in his chair every time he looked up from his plate. Kenneth must have noticed it, because he kept asking him if he was all right.

Marc excused himself and headed for the toilet, working hard to control his gait in order to disguise his state of inebriation. He felt as if he'd taken over someone else's body. *God knows what I look like to the sober people around the place,* he thought, hoping that the other diners were either too immersed in their meals or conversations to notice, or half-sloshed themselves.

It was an unreal experience for Marc, standing at the urinal and rocking on the balls of his feet as he tried to stand upright. He tried to convince himself that the mere act of urinating was sobering him up. The notion that he was somehow still in control was an absurdity only a drunken man could contemplate.

When Marc finally returned to the table, he saw that Kenneth had ordered yet another bottle of red. His glass had been topped in his absence. He then resolved give up on the rest of the day and take a hotel room for the night.

The luncheon crowd left the dining room as Kenneth and Marc made their unsteady way downstairs to enjoy a game of billiards, a cigar, and a few more drinks.

Marc wasn't worried about anything anymore. *Why not relax and enjoy myself?* he thought as he gave into the wonderful, floating feeling. He was used to the stuff in small doses, but Kenneth was a true master of the art. Marc could only watch in awe at Kenneth's capacity to drink while still appearing sober. Or at least that's how it looked to Marc who, at this point in time, was no great judge of sobriety.

*   *   *

As he tried to lift his pounding head off his hotel pillow the next morning, Marc realized that putting his body on the line wasn't really for him. He resolved to ensure that Kenneth didn't put him in that position again. He would arrange from now on to have their meetings take place in either Kenneth's office or his own, where copious quantities of coffee, tea, or water could be consumed with total impunity.

Over time, Kenneth had looked at all aspects of the proposed office-park development and came up with some excellent concepts. He had designed each floor so as to maximize the area of useable office space, which in turn increased the final value of the whole office park.

After several meetings over the next three weeks, the plans were ready for filing with the Council, which Kenneth did on Marc's behalf so that Marc wouldn't immediately be identified as the developer. Kenneth's firm also undertook to act as the first point of contact for any resultant resident inquiries or dissent. Marc was happy with this approach, because his friends at Council knew where the application was really coming from.

With the plans now filed, Marc could settle back and take care of his other business interests and devote more time to Elisa, who was still fretting about her prospects for promotion.

"It's only been a few weeks. These things often take a month or two to be decided," Marc told Elisa over dinner.

"The rumor mill has it that I'm running neck and neck with Jeremy, who is far less qualified and has only been at the university for five minutes. It's that bloody 'glass ceiling' thing again, isn't it?"

"Look, honey, whichever way it comes out, you'll still be who you are. No one can take that away; you're the best archaeologist in the place, and everyone knows it."

Elisa's blue eyes deepened with love and gratitude. "You're my strength," she told him as she took his hand across the table.

*   *   *

Marc's medium-density building company was making good progress with the three Multi-Build jobs. He had picked up another large medium-density project that was to be done in several stages, and this ongoing work gave him a steady base workload.

Coastal Constructions Pty. Ltd. had an almost-full schedule and was faring pretty well, although it had started to attract the attention of the building unions. Marc had been lucky up until now, and had not had any real trouble with the unions before.

The company had just started a staged development in Chippendale within the inner suburbs of Sydney. Within two weeks, Marc had met Willie Adams, the local organizer from the BTU, the Building Trades' Union. Willie was a short, slight man with a manner that reminded Marc of a Jack Russell terrier. He could swear like a trooper, and had no fear when it came to facing down his enemies. No matter how unreasonable his position, he'd fight tooth and nail to prevail.

Marc and his staff would spend the whole day trying to reason with Willie, only to have him revert to his original unreasonable position by the end of the meeting.

Like all good unions, the BTU picked on bogus safety issues. Most of their criticisms centered on building practices that had been in force for years on just about every building site in the country. They would then blow a tiny aspect of that practice out of proportion and dig their heels in until they prevailed and builders did things their way.

Ironically, their own members, who were also Marc's subcontractors, didn't want to do things the way that the union dictated. His company would then be blamed when the unions came back to find their demands ignored.

Once the unions swooped down on him, what Marc had previously seen as a nice little area of the building game developed into a true minefield. Stop-work meetings were followed by a show of muscle by Adams, who would then drag the men off the job.

These strikes became weekly occurrences, and Marc was becoming frustrated by the futility of it all. He had to find a way to deal with Willie.

"We can't go on like this," Marc told him one day.

"Well, if you weren't so bloody well preoccupied with the almighty dollar, maybe you'd make sure that things got done properly around here!" was Willie's hackneyed reply.

"There's a limit to what we can do. It's up to the men to work safely. We can't hold their bloody hands, you know."

"Look, if I see any of our members breaking the safety codes, I'll personally authorize you to boot them off the job!"

"I'm going to hold you to that, Willie," Marc said, grudgingly giving him the benefit of the doubt one more time.

But the very next week, the union members were back on strike over a safety issue when the men refused to follow union safety procedures. Of course, Willie insisted that it was all Marc's fault. *So much for the assurance of a self-appointed despot!* Marc thought after Willie delivered his predictable verdict on who was to blame.

Marc then instructed his site managers to placate the unions by personally supervising the construction of all the safety-related structures. And after a relatively steep learning curve, they got much better at dealing with Willie and his union. They cut down the lost time due to strikes to half a day per month—a remarkable achievement for a group of industrial-relations novices.

Once Willie became aware of Coastal Constructions Pty. Ltd., he started visiting all their sites as well. *Thank God I've finished Robert and Maddie's job. Their finances wouldn't have stretched to cover this sort of union guerrilla warfare. At least they're well out of it,* Marc thought, even if he was now knee deep in it. Strangely enough, Willie caused little trouble on the Multi-Build sites. *Maybe the Pressani family is better known in union circles,* Marc thought, smiling cynically to himself.

Thankfully, Marc's home-building operations were exempt from union interference. This protocol had been established some years earlier as part of an expensive government inquiry into the efficiency of the cottage building industry. The study had concluded that this segment of the building industry should be left wholly to market forces, as it was already very efficient. But in spite of this well-entrenched protocol and its ongoing support from all levels of government, the unions still tried to infiltrate this last bastion at every opportunity.

It was a daily battle to keep them from establishing a beachhead in cottage building. The unions targeted builders who had operations in both the union and non-union areas of the industry. Their strategy was to force concessions from builders on union-affected sites and translate these across to their cottage-building sites. Any individual successes they achieved would then be heralded as a precedent and held up so that the rest of the cottage builders would take heed.

Fortunately, the vast majority of home or cottage builders were renegades themselves, and averse to being told what to do—especially by some hothead from a union. They played off the union's attempts to penetrate their sector of the industry by treating them with complete and utter disdain.

They were always hard of hearing whenever the union representatives called, often turning their backs on them in midsentence. This contempt exasperated the unions, who were then forced to beat an undignified and hasty retreat when a piece of heavy, earth-moving equipment came their way.

Who wants to be a builder? Marc wondered. *What with the unions, difficult clients, unreliable subcontractors, the vagaries of the weather, and the economy, it's got to be a dog's life.*

Chapter Twenty-one

By the early part of 1991, the federal government was starting to show signs of reverting to its usual "paralysis by analysis" approach to managing the economy. The Prime Minister was telling anyone who would listen that a recession might be inevitable—things were going too well, and the country might have to cool its overheating economy for a while.

Marc shook his head as he watched a typical morning news report. *I love living in Australia; it's a truly magnificent country, but our politicians and industry leaders need a swift kick in the pants*, he thought with a grimace. *They panic way too easily about hiccups in the economy. What happened to our famous pioneer spirit, the can-do attitude that made Australia one of the wealthiest nations in the world at the beginning of the century?*

Most of Marc's profits had been poured back into his companies in an effort to make them recession-proof. In recent years, he had tried to wrest back as much of the control and decision making as possible from the people that normally dictated the terms under which most builders operated. First, he only built spec houses that did not rely on building contracts with owners; and in order to limit the affect of real estate agents—who indirectly controlled the number of projects a spec builder could undertake by selectively selling land to whichever builder they felt offered them the greatest opportunity to make a resale of the finished house and land package—Marc recently began buying and developing his own subdivisions for his home-building operations.

As a result, Marc was the one in control of his cottage building and land development company workloads, and was consequently responsible for finding every opportunity for these companies. This freedom also carried a financial risk, as he had to borrow heavily to build his spec houses. His land development company also relied on borrowed funds for its continued operation.

But things hadn't gone bad yet, which gave him some time to plan for a downturn. At times like these, Marc counted even the smallest blessings; prior warning of a recession meant he could plan ahead for a rainy day.

His biggest concern was his medium-density operation, which did rely on outside contracts for its survival and had a looming hole in its future work schedule that would manifest in less than a year. He knew that he couldn't look to Multi-Build for any more work, because they had recently informed him that they were leaving this part of the industry.

I think the real truth is that Antonio Pressani only set up that division in the first place to trap me and win Loren by default, Marc mused. *Now that Pressani finally has Loren in his grasp—literally,* he noted with a grimace—*he certainly doesn't want me or my company anywhere within a mile of either of them. It's a shame,* Marc reflected ruefully, *because I could have done with a big client like them.*

Marc scoured the newspaper and his network of contacts in search of more contract work for his company. There was no immediate urgency at first, but although he found and quoted work, Marc soon realized that all his competitors were doing likewise. Suddenly, building prices started falling to ridiculously low levels. *I can get work if I'm prepared to work for nothing, but who needs that?* Marc thought. So he kept looking.

*   *   *

Elisa had introduced Marc to her parents soon after they started going out together. Marc had hit it off with them immediately, and was taken aback by their genuine concern and interest in him. It was a complete contrast to Loren's parents, whom Marc had never met in the two years or so that he and Loren were together.

Marc started visiting their house for lunch on Sundays and, as the weeks passed, he enjoyed being part of Elisa's family, even if only as an honorary member.

Everything Elisa had told Marc about her parents on the night they met at Whitefeather Cove was true. Her mother, Alexandra, was an extraordinarily attractive woman with classical Russian features; although she was in her early fifties, her short, neatly cut, jet black hair did not house a single gray hair, and her olive skin was soft and wrinkle free. She was an aristocratic-looking woman, and her straight posture made her look taller than her five-feet, five inches. Her indomitable spirit sat nicely with her warm, welcoming heart.

Elisa's father, Peter Zubreroff, was an equally impressive man whose family was related to the Czars. He was nearly six feet tall, slender and straight, with dark brown hair graying at the temples. After many years in business in Russia and China, he was now content to make a living from owning and running a small group of dry-cleaning shops specializing in valet services. Peter exuded a youthful enthusiasm whenever he talked about his favorite subjects: fishing, travel, business, and politics.

Whenever Elisa's parents spoke with Marc about his business interests, it was almost as if they were willing him on to better things. Like Elisa, they gave him the feeling they were on his side and provided him with moral support in everything that he did.

Taking time out on the weekend to see Elisa's parents was very pleasant, and allowed Marc a momentary escape from the pressures of business. The Zubreroffs were cultured world travelers, which made for stimulating conversation around the dining table after one of Alexandra's sumptuous meals. Marc would often use such occasions to discuss an idea or concept he had been mulling over in his mind, figuring that four good heads were better than two.

"This is just a another stage in the never-ending cycle that's symptomatic of business all over the world, Marc," Peter said when Marc told him of his concerns about the current recession. "I've been through this type of cycle many times before—you'll get through it. You just have to approach your problem from another angle to find a solution."

"You also need to give yourself time to find that solution," Alexandra offered.

"Yes, I agree with Alexandra; things will become clearer if you allow them to unfold," Peter added. "Don't panic, because that often stops you from being receptive to new ideas and opportunities."

"You've always found solutions to your problems, Marc," Elisa said with supreme confidence. "You're a winner! And you'll find a way around your current problem. Proven winners like you always make it to the finishing post. Just keep the faith, honey."

*   *   *

In the meantime, Greensborough Council had approved the development application for the Hillsford site. Dan and Reg called frequently to ascertain the progress on this land. Dan had hinted that he and Reg wanted to "cut and run" if a half-decent profit could be realized on their investment—no doubt as a result of the changes looming in the economy.

This gave Marc an idea: *Maybe I should arrange to have Hillsford reappraised, now that its new rezoning has been approved.* He figured that the land value had increased but was not sure by how much. Maybe it was enough to enable him to refinance the site and remove Dan and Reg from ownership. *If the valuation is high enough, I might even be able to refinance my whole operation as a way of battening down the hatches for this recession.*

Marc decided to call his solicitor, Hamish Johnson.

"Hamish, didn't you tell me once that you had a senior contact in one of the regional banks?"

"Yeah, his name's Michael Dunne."

"How 'senior' is he?"

"I think he can approve up to $10 million."

"He sounds like the man I need to meet!"

"I can set it up. When do you want to meet?"

"Yesterday!"

At his initial meeting with Michael Dunne, Marc spoke only about the appraisal and agreed to pay Michael's bank a fee to determine the current value of the Hillsford site. This particular bank was reputed to have the meanest, tightest appraisers in the land, so he reasoned that any valuation they came up with could be relied upon by them or any other financier he might approach.

Marc spent the next couple of days preparing the information required to facilitate the appraisal. Hamish then set up a luncheon meeting with Michael, and Michael's assistant manager, Graham Tse, to enable Marc to personally hand over the information to the bank.

Hamish and Marc had an ulterior motive: to explore the possibility of borrowing the necessary funds for Marc's proposed refinancing package from Michael's bank.

Michael Dunne was about six feet tall, with straight black hair, a tanned complexion, and small intense eyes. He was quite lean, and said that his hobby was running. He mentioned twice in a few minutes that he had just run his first marathon. The thought of all that exertion made Marc draw a longer sip of his chilled white wine.

Before too long, Marc knew that Michael represented everything he disliked in bankers. If first impressions were anything to go on, Michael was two-dimensional and transparent; appeared to have little personality or empathy; and was focused only on his desire to secure a new account without taking any risks.

Whenever Marc dealt with two-dimensional people like Michael, he always had to work harder at being open and friendly. "It must take a long time to build your body up enough to run a marathon," he said flatteringly. "How many times a week do you run?"

"Every day."

"Every *day*?"

"Fifteen to twenty-five miles each time," Michael said proudly.

"That's amazing. You must have fantastic willpower."

Marc's time-honored approach seemed to work, because by the end of lunch, Marc and Michael were quite friendly. Michael told Marc that his bank was on the lookout for bright new businesses to back. "From what I know of you and your operations, you're precisely the sort of person our bank wants to deal with," Michael concluded with a toothy grin.

"Thank you, Michael. So I take it that your bank is willing to undertake an independent appraisal of my Hillsford property?"

"Yes, I think we'd be happy to do that for you." In a measured way, Michael continued, "We would also welcome the chance to refinance this property and all your other operations after the appraisal is done, if that's what you would like."

"I think that might be a distinct possibility," Marc told the banker with a smile.

Michael seemed noticeably more confident as he offered his next suggestion: "It would be easier for me to consider financing the Hillsford site if you and all your companies were customers of the bank."

Marc hesitated. "That's quite a task, Michael, changing all of my checking accounts and other banking facilities."

Michael made a reassuring wave of his right hand. "Graham will look after all the details; won't you, Graham?"

Graham Tse, a small man of Southeast Asian descent, smiled at the ease with which his boss had delegated the complicated task. "Sure— it's just a matter of doing all the paperwork."

Michael turned back to Marc. "There. All you need to do is give Graham your details and he will take care of the rest."

"I'll think about it," Marc promised.

Shifting all my banking arrangements wasn't in my plans, Marc thought as he walked out of the restaurant behind his luncheon guests, *but if I can get hold of the additional funds I need to pay off my Hillsford partners and recapitalize my other companies, then maybe there's something to it.*

The next few weeks passed quickly, punctuated only by the occasional telephone call from the appraiser as he tried to gather the necessary pieces of information needed to complete his task. Marc had supplied him with all the drawings for the proposed office-park complex, along with his construction estimates.

The whole process was aimed at establishing the residual land value—the finished value of the office-park complex less its construction and financing costs.

When the appraisal finally arrived, it was more than Marc had hoped for—it was a whopping $13 million. *Wow! It's hard to believe that a bit of vision and raw determination can turn a $3 million* *purchase into a $13 million property within six months*, Marc thought, reading and rereading the one-inch-thick valuation report.

* * *

Marc's thoughts then turned to the fate of Dan and Reg. He had some pangs of conscience about taking them out of the deal without mentioning the massive increase in the land value, but he reasoned that they wouldn't have done him any favors if they were in the same position: They had already proven it by trying to ambush him earlier.

After searching his conscience, Marc decided that it would be best to ask Dan and Reg what they wanted for their share. He called Dan and arranged a meeting to discuss a buyout. After all, Marc reasoned, if he bought them out now, they wouldn't have to find the $1 million that was soon required to purchase the council land and complete the Hillsford site consolidation.

"Have you found a buyer for our share?" Dan asked.

"I think I may have something. I'll fill you in next Tuesday. Is eleven all right for you, Dan?"

"Yes, I'll be there. I'll see if Reg can make it. If not, don't worry—I'll come alone."

On the following Tuesday morning, Dan and Reg were shown into Marc's office.

"Well, gentlemen, I may be in a position to give you a way out of your short-term investment," Marc said.

"We've said all along that we were looking only for a short-term investment, eh, Reg?" Dan said.

"Yeah," Reg concurred enthusiastically. "Now would be a good time to cash in, particularly with the settlement of the council land nearly upon us. If we get out now, we can avoid putting in the extra million needed to complete that purchase."

"What were you able to put together, Marc?" Dan asked, trying to contain his anticipation.

"I don't have anything firm yet, but I felt we needed to meet so that I could understand exactly what it is you fellows want out of this deal," Marc replied.

"Reg and I have discussed this before," Dan replied quickly. "We feel that anything more than a twenty percent return on the funds that we put in would be a good return."

Marc raised his eyebrows. "Twenty percent of $2.5 million over six months?" he shot Dan an incredulous look. "That's forty percent on an annualized basis. I'd say that'd be a brilliant return!"

"That's on top of the interest that we're charging on the money we lent, of course," Dan said with a flash of his pearly white false teeth.

"Oh, of course," Marc smiled back.

"Tell us about this buy-out arrangement you have, Marc," Reg asked.

"I think I may have another backer: one whom I believe will finance me into ownership of the whole property."

"Why would that be advantageous to you?" Dan quizzed.

"Well, for one thing, they would take you out of the deal, since all you wanted was a profitable short-term arrangement. They would do that while also allowing me to refinance some of my other operations before the money market gets any tougher."

"I can see where you're coming from," Dan said. "I always like to know what the other fellow's motivation is. It gives me a comfort factor," he said with another flash of dentures.

So far, so good, Marc rejoiced as he prepared to take the final step. "On this basis, I'd like you to put something in writing to formalize your expectations of a pay-out," he told the two men. "I'll need it to convince the incoming financier of the need to draw those funds out of any new monies I may borrow."

"We can do that. We'll fix a figure that'll hold for, say, a month," Dan offered. "Is that OK with you, Marc?"

"Yes, but as I'm borrowing from someone else to pay you off earlier than expected, I believe you should be prepared to accept a lump sum of half a million dollars as full and final payment. This'll end up giving you a forty percent return on the funds you loaned me less than six months ago," Marc said.

"You love to deal, don't you?" Reg said with a smirk and a shake of his head.

Dan cleared his throat and shot a dismissive look at Reg before turning to face Marc. "We don't really have a problem with that, Marc.

If you can swing the deal, it'll work out well for us. Don't you agree, Reg?"

"Yeah, I'm happy with that," Reg replied in a suitably chaste tone. "With some luck, we'll soon have our money back in the bank, tucked away in a safe term deposit. That'd make me very comfortable."

They all rose and shook hands. As he showed them out, Marc confirmed that Dan would send him a fax summing up their discussion.

Marc was pleased with the meeting. He had been able to find out exactly what these men wanted out of the Hillsford deal without telling them too much about the increased value of the land.

His conscience was now clear. *I reckon if I'm going to take the risk and borrow against the land to pay my partners out, while also giving them the guaranteed profit they want, then I can't be accused of any wrongdoing*, he reasoned to himself.

Because Marc also knew that land values could change with the economy, or one's ability to actually produce the planned development, he realized that his partners may well end up better off than him if he couldn't make the Hillsford development a reality.

*　*　*

Marc decided to contact Michael Dunne two days later.

"Hello, Michael. I was wondering where you were with my restructuring package?"

Silence reigned on the line. "Was I supposed to do something on that?"

So much for banker's promises, Marc thought with a grimace. "Don't you remember?" he urged. "At lunch the other week, you said you'd put a proposal together for me."

"Oh, did I?" Michael inquired innocently. "I'm sorry; I've been snowed under. Can you put something together for me to consider?"

"Sure, Michael." *Why didn't you bloody-well say so in the first place instead of causing me to lose two weeks?* he silently fumed.

Luckily, Marc had already prepared a draft submission, and only needed to tidy it up before sending it. Some days later, he rang Michael to see if he'd had time to consider the submission.

"Yes, it looks very positive," Michael pronounced. "It seems to fit the bank's lending criteria."

"How long will it take to get approval?"

"A few weeks. I'll have to present it to my superiors to smooth the path."

Marc then heard nothing for another two weeks and called him again.

"Things are moving forward, Marc. I'd like you to prepare a set of consolidated financial figures for all the companies within your group with cash flow predictions for the next six months."

Marc began to sense that he was just getting the runaround. "I'm happy to do that, Michael, but I need to know if this loan application is going to succeed!" he replied.

"This loan approval is within my discretion, and I can approve it pretty much without anyone else," Michael assured him. "However, I do need to be satisfied about several aspects of your group's capacity to pay off the loan."

Well, if it's within your discretion, why have you stuffed me around for so long, you bloody clown? Marc wanted to scream.

Instead, Marc took a deep breath and said, "OK, I'll arrange for my accountant to produce these figures as soon as possible."

Within three days, Marc had sent the information to Michael. After waiting for another week, he called again to check on the progress of his loan. After a lot of small talk, Michael asked for yet more information. Marc took another deep breath and duly obliged, accepting the banker's assurances that things were progressing nicely.

A week later he pressed the issue again, reminding Michael of his need to settle with his partners on the Hillsford site. "These things take time," was the best that Michael could offer. After another week without answer, Marc wanted to call Michael again, but found it increasingly difficult to come up with new excuses that would allow him to do so without appearing desperate.

Finally, at the end of the following week, Marc got a call from Michael's assistant, Graham Tse, who asked for a detailed disbursement schedule of the funds that he had requested from the bank. Marc happily ran through them with him on the phone: $3 million to refinance the mortgages on the Hillsford site and pay out

Dan and Reg; $1.1 million to settle the adjacent Council land and pay all the legal costs; $1 million to fund future land acquisitions for speculative building; $600,000 to fund a year's interest on these borrowings; $300,000 to recapitalize companies within the group, giving them additional cash to trade. In short, he needed $6 million.

Graham readily agreed that it seemed a safe bet for the bank to lend that against a primary security of $13 million. "I'll pass these figures on to Michael," he said. "I'm sure that he'll call you shortly. I don't think the bank can lose on this deal, and I know Michael would like to have this loan in his portfolio to build up his monthly figures."

Graham was certainly right about Michael calling back. He was on the phone within about fifteen minutes. Marc expected that Michael wanted to complain about his wanting to borrow a million dollars to speculate on property, but his complaint was about Marc's request to borrow $300,000 to recapitalize the operating companies within his group.

"This suggests an inherent weakness in your trading position," Michael said. "I'd like you to give me specific information on the trading outlook for the companies within your group to explain why you need this money."

"I do foresee some small losses in Coastal Constructions Pty. Ltd. as a result of the tough trading conditions we're starting to experience," Marc said without guile.

"Losses!" Michael exclaimed. "You never said anything about losses. I'm not sure I can advance monies to your group if you're making losses!"

With that, Marc exploded. "You've got to be kidding me, Michael! I am putting up security that, based on your own valuation, is worth $13 million, and proposing to pay the first year's interest in advance, and you're balking at diverting a lousy $300,000 into working capital? Tell me you're joking!"

"No, I'm not joking. I'll have to look very closely at this deal. I'll get back to you," Michael said before hanging up the phone.

Marc sat at his end of the phone, a look of amazement on his face, trying to assimilate the conversation.

Marc never received another call from Michael. In fact, Michael had to be cornered into taking Marc's call on the fourth try when Marc, several days later, had finally given up waiting.

As Michael paused, Marc sensed the weasel squirming in his chair as he choked out the words he'd been trying to avoid. "Look, Marc, I'm not comfortable with this loan application, and I don't think that I can recommend it to the bank for approval."

Marc's face went ashen as he struggled to find the right response. "Well, that's just wonderful, isn't it?" he said sarcastically. "You've wasted four weeks of my time, and might well have cost me the opportunity to buy out my partners. Yet you insisted on making all the right noises to keep me from looking at another bank for finance. And all you can say is that you're 'not comfortable?'"

"I'm sorry, but I have to sign off on the deal, and I'll be the one held accountable. I can't really say any more. Maybe if you hadn't told me about your impending losses, I might have carried on with this deal."

"Surely you're joking! This is a total contradiction. If I tell you the truth, I'm not worthy of the risk, but if I lie to you, I am?"

"That's often how it comes out," Michael said sheepishly.

"Little wonder people like me can't understand you bankers," Marc spat. "Most of you have an undecipherable logic all your own!"

"Maybe we do," Michael admitted with a sigh. "I can only suggest that you avoid telling other lenders about these impending losses; it puts them off."

"Thanks for the advice," Marc replied bitterly.

*   *   *

Meanwhile, Elisa fought ambivalent emotions as Campbell McIntosh struggled to explain the selection panel's decision, which had taken nearly two months to be announced. After ten minutes of small talk, she was still waiting to hear why she had been overlooked for the associate professorship she'd been all but promised several weeks earlier.

"It's really nothing to do with your abilities...we really had the most difficult time...this in no way affects the way the university sees you..."

As an incredulous look ran across Elisa's face, her eyes began to darken. "How would you expect me to take it, Campbell? It's the very thing I've being striving for all these years!"

"Elisa, I just *told* you that this in no way reflects badly on you," McIntosh said in a chiding tone.

"If four mature, intelligent men won't pick me over some less qualified Johnny-come-lately, then how do you *think* it'll look?" she shot back with a dangerous glint in her eyes.

McIntosh suddenly appeared concerned. "I need to know that you'll remain professional and work with Jeremy."

Elisa slowly raised her gaze and looked McIntosh squarely in the eye. "Oh, I'll be professional all right, Campbell—you can depend on it! But what I *can't* guarantee is that I'll be working with him for very long."

With that she stood up, turned on her heels, and left Campbell McIntosh's office.

Chapter Twenty-two

Back to square one, Marc thought, licking his wounds as the outcome of his dealings with Michael Dunne's bank sank in. He decided to phone Elisa at the university to tell her about his latest debacle, and to hopefully receive her good news about the associate professorship.

Minutes later, he'd reached a teary Elisa, telling him how she had missed out on the job.

"Ah, honey, don't cry; we both know how unfair it is," Marc soothed into the phone. "I don't even work at that bloody university of yours, and I know you're the best archaeologist in the place."

"Thanks, sweetie, but unfortunately, you don't count around here," Elisa sniffled. "You're not a misogynist."

"Listen: Why don't I pick you up in half an hour and we can go somewhere nice for lunch, like Doyle's at Watson Bay? I'm sure that under the circumstances, one of your friends would cover your classes for the afternoon."

"Luckily, I don't have any classes—just a staff meeting that I'd rather not go to," she noted with a dark smirk.

"Then it's settled. I'll pick you up out in front of your department and we can lick our wounds together." he said reassuringly. "A panoramic view of the city and the sparkling harbor, some of Doyles' famous beer-battered John Dory, and an icy bottle of Brokenwood Semillon will be a good way to recharge both our batteries!"

"Is everything OK with you?" Elisa asked as she picked up on the unusual tone in his voice.

"Nothing we can't handle together," Marc hedged. "I'll tell you all about my day when I see you, but not until we get you turned around and perky again."

* * *

Over the next week, Marc spent several evenings holding Elisa's hand and acting as her sounding board, allowing her to work through her anger at being denied her rightful reward for all her hard work. Eventually, with his help, she began to accept the reality of the situation.

"I'm going to make the best of a bad lot," Elisa told Marc. "But I'm still determined about looking for another position at a different university."

"I'm with you all the way," Marc replied tenderly. "Just don't take a job *too* far away, will you?"

Meanwhile, Marc had brought Elisa up to speed about his financial problems, and she kept coming up with positive suggestions and encouragement. Marc appreciated her efforts, and told her so over dinner the following weekend.

"You're always right there in my corner no matter what, and I can't tell you how much that means to me," Marc confided as a radiant smile lit up Elisa's face. "Your loyalty amazes me, because it's not a quality I've been able to attribute to many of the women I've known. Maddie, of course, is the one outstanding exception, but that's not quite the same thing," he noted with a chuckle.

"I should think not!" Elisa agreed with a hearty laugh.

Marc's eyes shone with an inner light as the merry moment gave way to seriousness again. "Whenever I'm with you, Elisa, I come away convinced that I can take on the world."

Elisa took Marc's hand, looked deeply into his eyes and beamed compassionately. "I see you as a man with a mission—someone who must succeed for the good of us all. Don't ask me why, but I really do see you that way."

Marc was blown away. "Really?" he managed.

"Yes," Elisa said forcefully, her eyes glowing with the same inner light. "And what's more, I believe that you're destined to succeed."

*   *   *

After contemplating his financing options, Marc decided to contact Andrew Innes, his old banker from the days when he had first started building. Over the past six years, Marc had moved away from Andrew's bank when his operations began to demand more flexibility. Andrew had since moved up the promotion ladder, which came as no surprise to Marc because he was a "good operator." His most recent promotion had made him general manager of commercial accounts, and he now operated out of headquarters in the center of the Sydney CBD.

Marc made an appointment to see Andrew, who, although very busy, agreed to see him the next day.

Andrew was tall man in his fifties, who was still full of enthusiasm for someone whom he felt was genuine. He seemed to understand just how far Marc had come since they last had dealt with each other, and stretched out his hand with an unusually welcoming smile for a banker.

"Hello, Marc; it's been a long time since we dealt with each other. What is it, about three years?"

"Yes, I guess it has been that long. I am pleased to see that you're doing so well in the bank," Marc said, reinforcing their handshake by covering Andrew's hand with his free left hand.

"Well, you know what it's like in large organizations. One always needs to appear to be doing the right thing. The bank has odd ways of measuring performance, but I seem to be working my way through the corporate obstacles," he remarked with a chuckle. "Anyway, how can I help you?"

"I have a piece of commercial land at Hillsford that's been appraised at $13 million. I'd like to borrow about $6 million against it so that I can purchase it from my current partners and do a few other things. Do you think you can help me?"

Andrew nodded with a knowing smile as he showed Marc to a seat on the couch in the office. "That doesn't sound too difficult, particularly since I know you and how you operate."

"I've taken the liberty of preparing a submission that sets out everything. I hope it gives you what you need to assess my proposal."

"Still the same old Marc, I see," Andrew observed, cracking a grin as he accepted the file.

As he spent the next hour going through the proposal, Andrew recognized from the figures Marc had given him that the companies had grown considerably in financial strength since the days of their initial dealings.

"I like the look of this, Marc. I'm sure the bank would like to renew its old association with you, and that alone should provide sufficient motivation for us to do the deal," Andrew said as he walked Marc to the elevator.

It's amazing how different two bankers can be! Marc thought as he left Andrew's bank.

He was right. Within two weeks, and after only two short meetings, Andrew's bank had approved the necessary finance. Marc now could pay off Dan and Reg and have all the additional working capital he needed to fund his operations for the next year or so.

Having worked so hard to close the deal, Marc's mind now turned to the financial burden he had just taken on. Although he had made provisions for the next twelve months of interest in the initial loan, he knew he would have to generate a larger cash flow or develop Hillsford into an income-producing property in order to service the debt.

A fortnight later, right after Marc's solicitors had confirmed that the final part of the loan had been advanced, he called Elisa. "I think that it's time for us to celebrate another small victory. How about I drop by at about seven and take you out to our little Italian place tonight?"

"Sounds marvelous, sweetie!" she replied happily. "I love it when you're in your 'I just conquered a small part of the planet' mood. I wouldn't miss it for the world."

"Believe me, you're the only person I want next to me at times like this," Marc replied tenderly. "So, what sort of a day are you having today?

"Thankfully, my life is a bit saner than yours. Everything's going well around here at the moment, although it's always hectic as we approach the end of the semester."

"You can handle that job of yours standing on your head...now there's a thought. My mind boggles at the prospect."

"Don't be naughty, Marc! There'll be plenty of time for that sort of thing later. You never know who's listening in around here," she whispered. "See you at seven. Oh, and should I pack my toothbrush, too?"

"I love the way you read my thoughts! See you, honey."

As he put down the phone, Marc recognized that his life had changed for the better almost from the moment he met Elisa. The longer he knew her, the more in awe he became of her simple, yet unique character traits. She was always cheerful and rejoiced in her own special way about being alive. Nothing was a problem to her; she saw only solutions.

Marc had grown to trust her completely, and knew that she would always be on his side through thick or thin. Apart from Maddie, Robert, and Billy, no one had ever shown him that sort of loyalty before.

*　*　*

As the next few months passed, Marc really enjoyed having someone special in his life. He and Elisa could talk for hours about any subject, and never lost interest with each other's daily trials and tribulations. Somehow, their conversation was always fresh and interesting.

He had been able to talk to Loren, of course, but somehow it always seemed as though they talked as a way of filling in time or deflecting the conversation away from some new problem between them that neither of them had wanted to deal with. *How can two women be so different?* Marc found himself asking more and more.

All he could really conclude was that he had fallen for Elisa in a big way, and could no longer imagine his life without her.

Their six-month anniversary had just come around, and Marc was more committed to her than he could have ever imagined. *Maybe it's time to start thinking about a more permanent arrangement*, he thought as he lay in bed alone in his apartment.

After tossing and turning for an hour, he finally decided to ring Billy in New York for some sage advice.

"So nice to hear your voice again, Marc," Billy greeted him warmly. "I was hoping you'd call. I've got doctors' appointments over the next few days, and was worried I'd miss you."

"What's wrong, Billy?" Marc asked as he held the receiver a little tighter.

"Old man's disease," Billy replied with a rueful chuckle.

Marc felt like he'd just been kicked in the stomach. "What?"

"Prostate problems. I just can't pee like I used to," Billy stated with his usual frankness. "I'm going to have a series of tests to see what's causing it,"

"Good God, Billy, I hope it's not serious."

"No, Marcy—the doctors think I might just need a 're-bore.' They don't think I've got the big C."

"Thank God." Marc sighed with relief.

"Now, enough about peeing; it's all I've been hearing about for days on end. Tell me what's happening with you."

"My problems pale into insignificance against yours, Billy. Maybe I should call back later, when you're out of the woods."

"Don't be silly, Marcy!" Billy bellowed, forcing Marc to back the phone away from his ear. "I told you that I'm OK. Now tell me what's on your mind."

"Well," Marc ventured, "I've told you about Elisa…"

"Ah, yes, the lovely archaeologist lady. From the pictures you sent me a while ago, I can see she's a smashing-looking lady. Half your luck, lad!"

"Yeah," Marc replied, imagining Billy's eyes lighting up thousands of miles away. "But there's a lot more to her than good looks. I know she's the one, and I'm thinking of proposing to her."

"Congratulations!" Billy said heartily.

"Thanks," Marc said somewhat apprehensively. "But…"

Billy let loose with an exasperated sigh. "With you, there's always a 'but', isn't there? Come on then, out with it."

"Well, the only thing is, I'm not sure how she'll respond."

"Well, she loves you, doesn't she?"

"Yeah, I think so."

"Then you've got it made."

"But Billy," Marc persisted, "I'm worried that she might see being married as limiting her career prospects; and my financial situation is never what you'd call brilliant. I'm always hanging over the edge of a cliff somewhere. What have I really got to offer her?"

Billy answered immediately. "Yourself! And if she's the right one, she'll snap you up."

"You think so?"

"I *know* so! I knew that my Mavis and I were meant for each other almost from the first moment we met. I proposed to her in the middle of the Great Depression. I had no money, no job, and few prospects, but she took me on anyway—don't ask me why," he noted with a chuckle. "We made a good life together. Mark my words, Marcy, if Elisa's the lady for you, she'll have known about it long before you did!"

As Marc looked out his bedroom window at the darkened facades of the houses opposite, a smile broke across his face. "Billy, what would I ever do without you?"

"Just don't ask me to solve any of your high-powered business problems," Billy joked. "I was only a simple tradesman, remember."

"There's nothing simple about you, Billy. You're a wonder! Just keep yourself well, old mate; you just might have a wedding to go to 'down under'."

"Don't worry about me, Marcy, I'll be there," Billy laughed into the phone.

"I'll hold you to that!" Marc shot back.

*   *   *

Later that morning, Marc rang his sister to get the woman's point of view.

"That is absolutely fantastic news!" Maddie squealed with delight. "I'm going to love having Elisa for a sister!"

"Don't break out the bubbly yet, Maddie. I've still got a few things to puzzle through. I mean, take my perilous financial situation…"

"*What* financial situation? You're a long way from broke."

"But Maddie…"

"Marc, I promise you that Elisa wouldn't lose sleep over money," Maddie replied firmly. "She's seen hard times, and they've made her— not broken her."

"But don't you think marriage might conflict with Elisa's archaeology ambitions?" Marc fretted. "Let's face it: You don't see too many archaeologists doubling as wives and mothers."

"No, you don't," Maddie conceded. "But if anyone's going to buck that trend, it'll be Elisa. When it comes down to it, she's like the rest of our breed; we can juggle several things at once throughout our lives. It's you men who seem to be able to handle only one thing at a time!" she teased.

"Point taken, Sis," Marc replied with a smirk. "But what about the fact that I spend so much of my time at work?"

"I'm quite sure that Elisa's job will keep her busy at work, too. Marc, you're *thinking* too much," Maddie chided. "This is something we're supposed to do with our *hearts*!"

Suddenly, Marc was decided. "You know, I think that you and Billy are right. I'm going to do it!" he declared.

"That's the spirit, Marc!" Maddie cheered. "Remember, Marc, I want to be the first to know, so promise me you'll call as soon as she says yes."

"I wish I had your confidence, Maddie," Marc replied wryly.

* * *

Marc invited Elisa out to dinner on the following Saturday night, and even though he had been to the same little Italian restaurant in Surrey Hills many times before meeting her, it now seemed different. It had sparkle: It seemed as though Elisa somehow lit up the whole place with her smile and her warm, melodic laugh.

"You're in a particularly good mood tonight," Marc told Elisa after they had finished their entrée and consumed a glass of red wine.

"Why not? I'm out with you aren't I, and you always end up making me laugh. I just *love* hearing about all the quirky people you've built for. Come on," Elisa implored, "tell me another one of your funny building stories!"

"Oh, all right," Marc conceded with an amiable chuckle. "Have I ever told you the one about Mrs. Steinfel?"

"Who's Mrs. Steinfel?"

Marc closed his eyes. "Probably my worst nightmare."

"This sounds like a good one!"

"OK. Eva Steinfel was a Hungarian Jewish princess, and a real lesson in self-control. She had this old house that stood on top of a hill overlooking the harbor, and she wanted to renovate it. Her husband had passed away some years before, leaving her with a respectable bank account and too much time on her hands. I thought Eva was a little strange from our first meeting, and as time went on, I just accepted that she was a bit eccentric."

A look of intrigue passed over Elisa's face. "She sounds like a real dousey."

"Yeah, you could say that. Anyway, I was pleased when she selected Highmark Homes to do her building work. Little did I know then how determined she was to get her pound of flesh out of me. She called me three or four times every day to ask questions about every aspect of her renovation, long before I'd even set foot on her site.

"As soon as the building started, I got a barrage of complaints—the workmen had trampled on her flowers; dust was getting into the house; the carpenters made too much noise with their hammering. Couldn't they just be a little quieter?

"She insisted that I ferry her all over town in order to choose tiles for the new upstairs bathroom or anything else that she could fit in, including the odd bit of grocery shopping. I went along with her because I just wanted to see the back of her.

"When the day came to strip off her old roof to make way for the new first-floor addition, she stood on the front lawn, arms folded, supervising every aspect of the job. Luckily, everything went like clockwork, and by day's end, a heavy waterproof sheet covered the entire roof area. It was large enough to hang down the walls on all sides, and was tied off flush with the walls to keep out the weather.

"After spending the whole day on site with Mrs. Steinfel, who seemed to enjoy barking instructions at 'her' tradesmen and anyone else who came within her sight, I settled down at home to enjoy a quiet evening alone."

"How many scotches did you have that night? Elisa asked with a pert smile.

"I'm not saying," Marc said with a grin, "but I do remember falling into bed exhausted."

"Isn't the right expression 'tired and emotional?" Elisa sniggered.

"Elisa, how I am I going to tell this story if you keeping butting in?"

"OK, I'll keep quiet—I promise."

Marc smiled at Elisa's playfulness and continued. "I hadn't noticed a storm blowing in from the southwest until a crack of lighting lit up my bedroom. Then the clap of thunder sounded like an explosion and sprung me out of bed. After gathering my wits, I opened the blinds and looked down my street to see sheet after sheet of heavy, wind-driven rain surging toward me. It was a horrible night, so I drew the curtains and tried to settle back into my warm bed.

"The phone rang at eleven, just as I was dozing off again. Sure enough, it was Mrs. Steinfel. I had an unlisted number and she still managed to get it, God knows how. She told me she could see two wet spots in her bedroom ceiling where rainwater was building up, and according to her, they were getting bigger all the time. I told her I couldn't do anything about it at that hour, and that if it did drip, to just catch the water in a bucket or a pan until I could fix it in the morning.

"After another two phone calls within ten minutes of each other, she rang me again in a complete panic. She now had dozens of leaks in her ceiling and her bedclothes were getting wet. 'Mr. Braddon, you get yourself over here this very instant!' she commanded. I had long since given up the idea of getting any sleep anyway, so I went.

"When I arrived at her house, all of the lights were on and the front door was wide open. I closed it behind me and gingerly entered the lion's den, calling out her name as I walked along her hallway. 'I'm in my bedroom,' she shouted. As I entered, she yelled, 'Will you just look at this mess?'

"I felt so sorry for her. Her hair was wet and matted, and her damp nightgown clung to her small bones while the ceiling dripped all around her. Realizing that the source of her aggravation had arrived, she went into overdrive and began thrashing around the bed, screaming at me like a demented banshee.

"Just when her performance had reached its crescendo, a large crack appeared directly above her head, suddenly quadrupling the flow of the drips that were raining down on her. We both looked up simultaneously to see the plaster ceiling stretch as it strained to hold back the rainwater that had built up during the night. In the next instant, the ceiling collapsed along the length of the crack, causing an avalanche of rainwater and plaster to drench Eva's thin body. She squatted in bed, spitting out the mixture with a stunned daze. Finally, she was lost for words!"

Elisa tried to suppress a hysterical laugh, nearly spitting out the mouthful of wine she had just taken in the process. Marc couldn't help reacting to the runs of red wine that managed to escape and trickle over Elisa's lips as she reached urgently for her napkin.

"I love it!" Elisa said as she rocked back in her chair, laughing with gusto.

"Yeah, well, what can I say—I sure can pick 'em," Marc said with a good-natured grin.

"You sure can, my darling," Elisa said, shaking her head as the mirth fluttered across her lips.

"I know I've told you this before, Elisa, but when I spend an evening with you, I always come away feeling terrific."

"You make me feel the same way too, honey. I love being with you. You invigorate me."

"Well then..." he hesitated for a second before taking the plunge. "How about marrying me?"

Marc thought that Elisa had never looked lovelier than she did in the next instant, when she immediately answered, "I'd love to!"

He instinctively threw his hands in the air and shouted, "Brilliant! Absolutely brilliant!" Coming down to earth again for a second, he took her soft hands in his and said, "You know, Elisa, I love you very much. I can't imagine what life would be like without you."

Elisa's eyes had become large and luminous. "I know," she murmured tenderly. "Me, too. Had you asked me to marry you that day at Binalong Caves, I probably would have said yes. Even then, I knew you were the one, my darling."

As Marc slid a sparkling diamond ring onto Elisa's finger, he said, "I know we'll be good for each other; we'll build a life with us at its center. We'll be fantastic together!"

Marc walked around the table and pulled Elisa to her feet. They stood near their table, locked in a tight embrace, kissing deeply. Suddenly, they became aware that they were the center of attraction, silhouetted as they were against the dimly lit walls of the restaurant. As the people at the nearby tables began to applaud, Marc and Elisa just returned bashful smiles and left the table to go to the dance floor.

As they moved together to the strains of Chicago's *"If You Leave Me Now,"* they felt certain everybody else in the place knew this was a significant moment for them because everyone looked upon them so warmly.

"There are hundreds of things to plan," Elisa whispered into his ear. "The date, the church, the reception..."

"We've got plenty of time to work those details out," Marc said as they hugged. A moment later, he drew his head back. "Now, be honest with me—are you sure that being married to me isn't going to affect your being an archaeologist?"

"As opposed to being married to someone else, you mean?" Elisa quipped.

"No," Marc laughed. "You know what I mean!"

Elisa ran her fingers through Marc's hair as she considered her answer. Finally, she said, "Being an archaeologist is just one of the things I do—loving you is something I do all the time, no matter what else I'm doing."

Marc drew back from their embrace and smiled lovingly at his fiancée. She had just answered all his questions with a few words.

Marc took his fiancée back to his apartment. He opened a bottle of Bollinger champagne, put on some soft music, dimmed the lights and lit the aromatic candles that Maddie had given him for such an occasion.

"My, you do know how to seduce a lady," Elisa purred as she melted into the mood.

"Not just any lady," Marc murmured as he nuzzled her ear.

Their lovemaking was sensational and only got better each time they were together. There was more power, more breathless anticipation every time they touched each other. Marc found himself aching to be with her in such a way. Their passion seemed endless, and they made love for what seemed like minutes but were really hours.

At the end of their lovemaking session, Elisa sat up in bed, her tousled hair spilling over her shoulders. "You know, I think we should get married in the middle of next year, during my midyear break," she mused. "That way, I can be a June bride. It'll take me nine months to plan everything, anyway."

"You sound just like Maddie," Marc remarked with a laugh.

"Well we *are* going to be sisters, you know," she joked.

"I really want to marry you tomorrow, but I understand that women must plan that special day to perfection," Marc said in resignation. "I can live with that, as long as you keep coming home to me. I couldn't live without you being here."

"What's that song say, 'ain't no mountain high enough.'"

"Good, then it's settled," Marc declared with an ear-to-ear grin. "Let's move in together!"

Elisa's expression instantly changed from ecstasy to sheer terror. "Oh, Marc, you know I can't do that!" she cried. "My parents would die if I lived with you before we married; I'm already dealing with their paranoia just because I'm looking for an apartment. They're staunchly old-fashioned about how a woman should behave before she gets married. I don't totally agree with them, but I would never do anything to hurt them. When it comes down to it, I must respect their wishes and the traditions of my Russian heritage," Elisa concluded earnestly. "It's the one thing about loving me that you will have to live with."

Marc laughed as he rolled on to his back. "I knew you were too good to be true!"

"We have to be realistic, that's all," Elisa soothed. "We're both practical people, and we can't change that on a moment's notice. We can't live together before we're married, but I do promise to visit you regularly," she said, grinning as they both slid back under the sheets again.

*   *   *

The next day, as he opened the mail, Marc made a conscious decision to start all over again with the renewed vigor and responsibility of a soon-to-be-married man.

He came across a square envelope and thought that he recognized the handwriting. Sure enough, it was a wedding invitation from Loren. She and Antonio Pressani were to be married in three months. Across the embossed printing, she had written, "I'm getting married and you're *not* invited. I'm sure you'll understand. Wish me luck! Loren."

Marc smirked at Loren's cheek, expecting no less from her. Still, he held no ill feelings, and hoped that she would settle down with Antonio and find true happiness.

He buzzed his secretary, Elle, and asked her to get him the number for Interflora. He sent six white carnations to Loren's office with a card that simply said, "Pleased to get your great news. I hope it all works out for you, Marc."

He then ordered three dozen red roses, and had them delivered to Elisa at the university. The note said: "Thank you for making me the happiest man in a hard hat! I'll love you always, Marc."

* * *

Elisa was delighted to receive Marc's flowers and phoned him as soon as she read the card. "You're so kind, but…three dozen roses! Where I am going to put them all? My office is going to look and smell like a flower shop!"

"They'll just have to give you a bigger office; that's all there is to it!" Marc shot back with a laugh.

"Anyway, thank you for giving me such a nice problem to solve. You've made my day again."

"My pleasure."

"Marc," Elisa began after a slight pause, "there's something I wanted to talk to you about—I really think that it would be nice if you asked my father's permission to marry me."

"What!" Marc sputtered incredulously. "This is the nineties, Elisa; people don't do that sort of thing anymore, do they? Oh, it's the traditional Russian thing again, isn't it?" Marc resolved before Elisa could respond.

"Will you do it for me, sweetie?" Elisa asked in a little girl's voice.

"Yes of course, honey," Marc assured her. "There's nothing I wouldn't do to make you my wife." Suddenly, his whole body tensed with worry. "But what if your father says 'no' after you've said 'yes'?"

"My parents love you—that won't happen," Elisa soothed.

Later that afternoon, Marc and Elisa were standing outside Elisa's parents' house. Elisa took her engagement ring off and gave it to Marc. "You can put it back on my finger after my parents give us their blessing," she said tenderly.

"*If* they give us their blessing," Marc added dubiously.

"Buck up, my little buckaroo," Elisa delivered with a winning smile. "You won *me* over, didn't you? How hard can it be to convince my parents that they should let you marry me?"

"The things I do for you..." Marc replied with a rueful grin as he knocked on the front door.

Within a second or two, the door swung open and Peter Zubreroff appeared in the doorway engulfing his daughter in a warm hug. As Peter extended a hearty handshake to Marc, Marc noted that he seemed unusually happy, and wondered if he somehow knew what was planned.

Peter sat down in his favorite lounge chair with his wife, Alexandra, by his side in the other single armchair. Marc and Elisa sat on the couch opposite her parents. All four engaged in a good fifteen minutes of small talk as Marc tried to prime himself to pop the question.

Marc finally decided it was time. He looked across at Elisa, who was becoming slightly impatient with his procrastination and giving him a look that clearly told him to get on with it.

God, I hope you say yes, Marc thought as he looked into Peter's face and cleared his throat.

"Mr. and Mrs. Zubreroff," Marc said, looking nervously at both parents, "I love your daughter very much."

Marc paused for a moment and tried to gauge Peter's reaction. Peter was poker-faced, giving no hint about how he felt about what Marc had just told him. Marc took a deep breath and forced himself to continue.

"I know Elisa loves me, too, and...I would like to ask you for her hand in marriage."

Peter looked across to his wife. Alexandra offered an almost imperceptible smile and nod. Peter seemed almost overcome for a moment before a smile ran across his lips. As he spoke, his voice quivered with emotion.

"Marc, Alexandra and I bless your marriage to Elisa, and we are very pleased to have you as our son."

At a loss for words, Alexandra stood and spontaneously embraced Marc, kissing him on both cheeks before turning her attention to her daughter. Peter got to his feet and swallowed up his future son-in-law in a massive hug before giving him the same ceremonial kiss on both cheeks. Marc could see tears of pure joy in Peter's eyes.

"Elisa is everything we have in the world," Peter told Marc. "She is very important in our lives, and we want only that which will make her happy. We know that you two will be very happy together. This is all we dreamed about when we fled Shanghai all those years ago to allow our daughter to have a chance at happiness and a proper life."

Alexandra steered Elisa into a tight circle with the men and they all shared a group hug, smiling and kissing each other as they all savored the moment.

"This calls for a celebratory drink," Peter declared, moving toward his small bar in the corner of the living room.

After pouring a neat scotch for Marc and himself, Peter poured the women a sweet sherry. As Peter put the drinks in each person's hand, he said, "To Marc and Elisa, and Elisa and Marc; may you both enjoy a long and happy life together in married bliss."

After the toast, Marc pulled Elisa's engagement ring from his pocket and slid it back onto her finger as her parents looked on lovingly. Elisa shot him a look that clearly said: *See, I told you there was nothing to worry about!*

A few weeks after announcing their engagement, Elisa moved out of her parents' home into a smart, two-bedroom apartment on the northern side of the city overlooking the harbor. Still the dutiful daughter, she visited her parents at least twice a week for dinner, dispelling any doubts her parents might have had that she would forsake them once she was living on her own.

Chapter Twenty-three

Loren stood in front of the altar at St Mary's Cathedral resplendent in her virgin-white wedding gown. A trail of bridesmaids and flower girls attended her while several generations of the Pressani family fidgeted in the pews. Loren's mother, Margaret, and her latest man occupied the first pew on the right, standing alongside Loren's father and his second wife. Margaret and her former husband ignored each other as the priest asked the congregation to be seated.

The full wedding mass seemed to go on forever, and Loren's mind began to wander as the priest droned on. *I wonder what he's doing now. I'll bet he's not really happy.*

Tilting her head to look into her future husband's urgent gray eyes, she was jolted back to the moment.

"Are you all right?" Antonio whispered.

"Yes."

"OK?"

"OK."

She straightened her shoulders.

After another fifteen minutes, she found herself drifting away again. *I'll get him back; he's the only man who's ever left me. I'll find a way to convince him that this'll work if it's the last thing I do!*

There was a sudden silence, and the priest was nodding at her. Antonio looked on anxiously, willing her to speak and mouthing, "I do."

She'd missed that bit and took a chance by saying, "I do," out loud. The congregation let out a collective sigh of relief.

*   *   *

It was early 1992, and the obligatory recession was biting deeply into just about every area of business. Overnight, the economy had turned from being a hotpot of activity and enterprise into a quagmire of despair and uncertainty. Whole areas of commercial endeavor were suddenly no longer viable; businesses were closing and offices vacated every day. Yes, this recession was different, all right—it was downright vicious!

Marc knew he needed a strong and steady cash flow in this environment. In the past, he had been able to rely on contract building to provide this for him, but this sort of work was also becoming hard to find and even harder to win as the competition for work became more fierce everyday.

Paradoxically, if Marc had won any of the dozens of bids he was forced to submit, he would have feared he had made a monumental mistake somewhere in his calculations and had quoted too low a price.

He had to be very focused, particularly since he and Elisa would be married in about six months. He didn't want them to struggle as he'd always done for the sake of his businesses. He wanted to be free of that sort of worry so that they could enjoy each other.

The initial injection of cash from the loan had really steadied his ship, so to speak, but another interest payment of $500,000 was falling due soon after they planned to marry. The recession had forced Marc to gear down his building operations, and the idea of paying an annual interest bill of $500,000 from a reduced cash flow was not very appealing.

Marc had most to fear from the sudden exodus of lenders from commercial property development, who had also realized this recession was causing many businesses to close their doors, creating an abundance of vacant office space in commercial business districts around town. As luck would have it, Marc's biggest asset was a vacant parcel of commercial land whose value depended upon someone wanting to build yet another office development.

He surveyed the carnage all about him and surmised, *this rotten recession is certainly different from any of the others that I've been through. It seems to have struck at the very heart of every enterprise and has caused people to lose confidence in themselves.*

* * *

When Marc returned to work on the following Monday morning, he reminded himself that it was now time to be creative and get back to some solid basics.

He had become aware of a well-established builder who was trying to sell his business and retire. The recession was hurting his operation as well, apparently giving him an added motivation. Marc's old friend, Jim Daniels, who had since been promoted to general manager of his building supply company, knew the builder's operation and suggested that Marc check out this opportunity.

The name of this group of companies was the Vanity Homes Group Pty. Ltd., and as luck would have it, the owner, Myles Vanity, was an old chum of Jim Daniels. Jim told Marc that Myles was a man from the old school: his word was his bond. "If you make a deal with Myles and he shakes your hand, then you know you've got a deal," Jim stressed on several occasions.

At first, Marc could only see problems when Jim suggested that he take over Vanity. He was wary of company takeovers, considering what he had heard and read about their unforeseen and inevitable difficulties, and thought it was a bit like buying a second-hand car.

Almost against his better judgment, Marc asked for all of the financial information on this group of companies in order to take a proper look. He set himself no timeline to indicate his interest to Vanity, as he wanted plenty of time to sleep on the idea.

"That's all right, Marc," Jim said as he dropped off Vanity's books for Marc's inspection. "Just look at the companies with an open mind; that's all I ask. If I'm any judge, you'll like what you see!"

* * *

Elisa's Monday was a little different.

Jeremy Close knocked only once as he flew into her office. He was a short, brash young man with nondescript features and a superior demeanor, unbearable since his promotion and happy to upset anybody under him.

"Elisa, how about you take my eleven o'clock class?" he told her. "I have to run some errands."

Elisa looked at him with disbelief. "Jeremy, I have to prepare for my own lecture at two. I need the time to research today's topic."

"You can wing it; you'll be fine."

A determined look settled on Elisa's face. "You can't just fly in here and give me your class on fifteen minutes' notice!"

Jeremy placed both hands on Elisa's desk, bending down to look her squarely in the eye. "I'm your boss; I can do anything I bloody-well please!"

Elisa shot back a caustic look that froze him to the spot. "Then maybe you should bloody-well find someone else to cover for you," she delivered firmly.

Jeremy's face turned pale with anger. "Don't make me go to the dean," he threatened.

"Go see whomever you like, because I'm not covering for you!" Elisa retorted. "Just because you made associate professor doesn't mean you can dump your lecture load on the rest of us. Had you asked me nicely, I might have considered it, but as it is, I think you should get lost, or go to the dean's office, or wherever else you want."

Jeremy's shocked expression deepened into resentment. "I won't forget this, Elisa," he snarled as he turned on his heels.

"See that you don't!" she said forcefully as he reached her office door.

* * *

Marc reluctantly opened the files Jim had brought him, having resigned himself to the fact there would be nothing in them of interest. However, as he poured over the financial figures and projections, he started to see some real possibilities with this operation.

There are some obvious synergies between my operation and Vanity's. Although our building operations are in different parts of the market, they seem to complement each other, he observed. As Marc delved deeper into the Vanity Group's operations, it became clear that he could readily merge the two groups and that they would dovetail together very nicely.

This group had a sizeable market share, giving it a critical mass in its marketplace, which was something Marc had sought several years earlier. It seemed that Vanity had started to piece together a vertically integrated business by manufacturing a number of the components they used in their building operation.

Some years earlier, they had acquired a well-known kitchen cabinet manufacturer and made all of their own timber frames and roof trusses. He could see new product lines evolving from these related activities, and foresaw the development of even more manufacturing operations to augment the building works. *I'll need to quickly decide if I want to do anything with this group before someone else spots its potential!* he told himself.

The financial figures showed a group turnover of around $150 million per annum, which looked like more than enough to save his bacon. Better yet was the fact that Myles Vanity operated all of his companies with high level of overhead, and this soaked up almost all of the profits. Marc reasoned that if he could streamline these costs, then he should be able to produce a solid profit on the current turnover while also capturing the strong cash flow he so badly needed.

Marc called Jim, told him of his interest, and arranged to meet with him.

*   *   *

They met on the following Monday at a Chinese restaurant handy to Jim's office. Jim was dressed in a smart business suit and seemed well suited to his new role as general manager of his firm's building hardware division.

"I'm pleased that you're thinking of taking this on, Marc," Jim said as they both sipped their long glasses of cold lager. "I reckon that Vanity is the ideal vehicle to get you into the big league."

"Are you looking after this deal for Myles Vanity, Jim?"

"Well, I suppose you could say I'm his unofficial broker. He asked me to check out potential buyers without making it known to the industry at large that he wanted to sell."

"Yeah, I suppose he wouldn't want it to get around," Marc said as he cast an eye over the menu.

"Apart from anything else, it might panic Vanity's trade creditors, creating a cash flow and confidence crises for his day-to-day operations."

"I can see that," Marc said, nodding discreetly.

"For my part, I'll introduce you to Myles and allow you two to get down to working out if there's a deal that'll work for you both."

"Sure; it's all very well for us to speculate, but you never know if you've got a deal until you talk to the man himself."

Jim nodded and undertook to arrange a meeting for later that week, promising to confirm the details with Marc sometime the next day. "Now, I strongly recommend the salt and pepper lobster. I have it nearly every time I come here," Jim admitted.

"I'm in your hands, Jim. I always seem to be in your hands, don't I?" Marc smiled.

Chapter Twenty-four

The following Thursday morning, Marc arrived at Vanity's office and met Jim in the parking lot. Jim looked a giant as he stood next to his late-model Ford sedan. They greeted each other with a warm handshake.

"Pleased to see that you could make it today," Jim said with a wide smile.

Marc threw his friend a sideways glance. "Are you kidding, Jim? I wouldn't miss this for the world!"

Myles Vanity was a respected pioneer and a well-known figure in the cottage building industry. Vanity's headquarters were in Silverwater, an industrial suburb in the geographical center of Sydney, and its operations housed in a modern complex that combined a plush front office with a practical adjoining factory.

Vanity's offices had a modern, well-to-do look about them with their neat, charcoal marble façade and dark-tinted glass windows. The parking lot was beautifully landscaped with a myriad of green, orange, and red flowering plants filling the extensive gardens between the parking bays. *This place certainly makes a good first impression,* Marc thought as he and Jim made their way to the entry foyer.

The reception area was no less opulent and professional. A circular marble staircase wound its way up to the first floor. The curved reception desk, fashioned out of the same marble was designed to fit the curved theme of the opulent foyer, created a striking image. *This place just gets better and better,* Marc marveled as he and Jim took a seat on the black leather couches nearby.

Moments after Jim announced their arrival to the receptionist, Marc and Jim were asked to meet Mr. Vanity, who would be greeting them at the top of the circular staircase.

As they stood up, Jim turned to Marc and whispered, "Myles is a man of quality. He may look like everybody's grandfather, but below the surface, he's tough as an old boot. In all of our dealings, he's been straight as a gun barrel. I know that he's not negotiating with anyone else at the moment because he gave me his word that he would give anyone I introduced first bite of the cherry."

As they went up the stairs, they saw a stout little man with a big smile—a Santa Claus look-alike without the big red suit and the long white beard. A shock of tightly curled white hair and a close-cropped white beard set off his round, jovial face.

"Welcome to the Vanity Homes Group, gentlemen! Good to see you, Jim!" he boomed. "Ah, and this must be Mr. Braddon!"

"It certainly is," Jim answered with a quick sidelong grin at Marc. "Marc Braddon, I'd like you to meet Myles Vanity," he said as they neared the top of the circular staircase.

The two men shook hands.

"Pleased to meet you, Mr. Vanity. I've heard quite a lot about you," Marc said.

Myles rolled back a little on his heels, as if he were sizing Marc up. "I hope it wasn't all bad; please call me Myles. Come into my office, won't you?"

Soon, the men were sitting on another black leather sofa with matching armchairs. Myles sat on one of the lounge chairs directly opposite them, engaging his guests in small talk until the coffee and tea arrived.

"So, Jim tells me that you have an interest in acquiring my group of companies," Myles stated, moving to the edge of his chair.

This guy doesn't mess around, does he, Marc mused as he gathered he thoughts. "Well, yes, I do, and my interest was heightened when I analyzed your financial figures and projections," Marc said.

Myles nodded sagely as he rubbed his white beard. "I think the company's got a glorious future. The only problem is that I'm getting too old for this game," he admitted with a rueful smile. "I have no successor to hand the reins to, and although I'd like to stay on, my wife thinks I have worked hard enough. She keeps telling me I should retire and enjoy what's left of my life," he stated candidly. "After much consideration, I've come to agree with her."

Marc's face relaxed. "I'm glad to hear you say that, Myles, because I was wondering why you wanted to sell. Building companies are notoriously hard to sell, and anyone buying into such a company would need the cooperation and support of the seller to successfully complete the sale."

"Oh, Myles knows that, Marc." Jim chimed in. "He and I have talked about the difficulties, and I'm sure I speak for him when I say that he is motivated to sell."

Marc took a deep breath. "Well then, Myles, I want to explore the possibility of buying your group of companies. I came here today to look into a number of specific areas I have highlighted in the reports I was given."

Myles widened his eyes and sat more upright. "I have as much time set aside as you need. Tell you what, Marc—why don't we adjourn to the boardroom next door? There's a lot more room to spread ourselves about, and I'll get my financial controller involved, too."

"I think this is an ideal time for me to leave," Jim said with a knowing smile as the other two men rose to shift the meeting into the boardroom. "I'll call back later to see how things are progressing."

Marc was immediately struck by the warmth of Vanity's boardroom: Its plastered walls were painted a deep, rich creamy color, contrasting dramatically with the dark-stained Tasmanian Oak table that stood imposingly at its center. Twelve high-backed swivel chairs, neatly upholstered in dark tanned leather, were positioned around its perimeter. The table's polished surface reflected the soft light filtering through the tinted floor-to-ceiling windows. The overall effect was a welcoming place conducive to great thoughts and ideas. *I'd love to have an office like this someday,* Marc thought as he took up a position around the boardroom table.

Myles brought in his financial controller. "Marc Braddon, let me introduce you to Stephen James. Stephen has been with the company for seven years, and is my right-hand man," Myles added with a friendly pat on Stephen's back.

Stephen struck Marc immediately as a confident fellow. He was a tall, solidly built man who appeared to be in his mid-thirties, although he was graying prematurely around the temples.

"Stephen will assist us," Myles continued, "and if you have any specific questions about the business beyond our meeting today, he has my authority to deal directly with you." Myles opened his copy of the documents Marc had been given. "So, where shall we start?" he asked.

"I was very interested in your last five years' results," Marc replied. "They seem to suggest a steady operation, but one without much growth."

Myles let out a snigger and looked across at Stephen. "Well, that's me, I suppose!"

Looking back at Marc, he spoke frankly. "I have been trying to consolidate the operations over that period. I guess someone as young as you might see that as a conservative approach, but I haven't wanted to put myself under too much financial pressure. We are trading quite well, but quite honestly, we've felt this recession a little deeper than I thought we would."

Stephen cleared his throat. "We've talked often about expansion into new and related businesses, but Myles feels that things should be paced to ensure our long-term stability," he explained diplomatically. "After all, the company has been the leader in the field for over twenty-five years."

Marc sensed that Stephen was pro-expansion but had been bridled by Myles, who wanted a trouble-free life in a trouble-filled business. He decided to keep an eye on Stephen as someone who might be able to help him to run the businesses if he decided to buy. *Who better to give the job to than a man with intimate inside knowledge of the operation?* he thought.

"These figures also show that the group has gained a benefit from some old but rather large tax losses," Marc observed. "These losses are just about used up and won't be available to me, should I purchase the group, so there's no advantage there."

"That's right," Myles said. "We paid dearly for the experience when we started making our own windows, trusses, and kitchens. There's a big difference between building houses with subcontractor labor and controlling a manufacturing process. Anyhow, that's all behind us now. We've been profitable in all areas for the past two years."

Stephen nodded, looking as if he felt compelled to better explain his boss's comments. "We were forced into manufacturing our own building materials as a result of the last building boom," he said with a grimace. "No one would or could supply us, and we nearly went under, all because we couldn't build the hundreds of homes we had on the books. This strangled our cash flow, and we spent nearly all of our time meeting with our bankers, trying to convince them of our viability."

"What an experience that was," Myles said as he rolled his eyes. "I wouldn't be there again for quids!"

"Yeah, I can empathize with that," Marc chimed in. "The building business has plenty of highs, but far too many lows."

Stephen shook his head. "There's nothing more frustrating than nearly going out of business when you have more work on the books than you can handle, and all because you can't get the materials to do the work and earn your progress payments. After that, we decided we were too big to be dependent on outside manufacturers, and that's when we started making our own key building elements."

"It's taken time, but I now think that we're on top of things, and starting to reap the rewards," Myles said confidently.

Marc agreed with him. It was the vertical integration of Vanity's various activities that had pricked his interest in the first place. He recognized that Myles had created a unique home-building business: one that could be used as a sound basis for further expansion by someone with the foresight to expand it and the other manufacturing-related businesses. *The more I delve into this business, the more I like what I see,* Marc thought as he absorbed all he had been told.

After analyzing the financial data further, the three men adjourned to inspect the adjacent factory, which manufactured all of Vanity's timber frames and trusses. A few hours later, Marc had seen everything except the kitchen and window manufacturing operation, which was located on the other side of the city. He arranged to visit it with Stephen the next day.

Returning to the boardroom, the three men again sat down to a freshly brewed pot of coffee and started discussing future cash flow predictions as a prelude to fixing a purchase price.

"How can I be sure of these projected cash flow and profit figures?" Marc asked.

Myles shrugged and looked across at Stephen before turning back to Marc. "I can't give you any guarantees, Mr. Braddon," Myles said. "You'll just have to use your own judgment. But I can give you my word that these are the same figures we're working with right now. They've not been manufactured for the purposes of selling the companies."

Marc's initial observations, coupled with Jim's glowing recommendations of Myles's character, made him somewhat accepting of Myles's claims. *Somehow, I believe the old bugger,* Marc thought. *Still, I have to make sure that I'm not seduced by his charm to the point of forgetting to ask the right questions.*

They had worked around the issue of the price long enough, and were now nearing the end of a long, grueling day. The boardroom table was cluttered with many empty coffee cups, making it time to discuss price.

Myles' Santa Claus-like benevolence evaporated. He paused for a moment and looked across to Stephen before fixing a steely, determined look toward Marc. "I want $45 million for the whole operation. And I think that's a fair price," he said, projecting a firm and resolute chin.

That's about what Jim told me he'd want, Marc remembered as he pinched his bottom lip with his thumb and forefinger. "That's a big price, Myles!" he countered. "I'll probably need your cooperation to convince a group of financiers to lend me the money."

Myles' face spread into an expansive smile as his munificence returned. "That's not a problem. I've developed a good relationship with my bank over the years, and they have benefited from nearly every house sale I've ever made," he explained. "As a result, they've ended up with customers who'll usually take out a twenty-five year mortgage, a credit card, and a series of personal loans over the years for house improvements, pools, and cars. And all without lifting a finger. I'm sure they wouldn't want to lose the guaranteed business they get without spending a cent on advertising."

Marc was pleased that Myles so readily accepted his suggestion. "That's what I meant when I said you needed to be motivated to sell. Your assistance with the bank could prove invaluable."

"If we can agree on a deal, I assure you you'll have my help to make it work," Myles said reassuringly.

Marc was surprised at how quickly Myles had made the transition back to an obliging old coot, once all the tough stuff has been dealt with.

Marc sat back in his chair and rubbed his chin thoughtfully. He then smiled at both Myles and Stephen and said, "I'd like to take away everything you've given me today and study it carefully, but I must say I'm very interested. After I see the other manufacturing operation tomorrow, I should have an answer for you by the end of next week." Marc then turned to Stephen. "I'll see you at Vanity Kitchens at ten tomorrow morning."

"It was a pleasure to meet you, Marc!" Myles said as the two men shook hands. "I'm sure that Stephen will look after you tomorrow and show you everything you want to see."

"Anything you want, Mr. Braddon!" Stephen said dutifully.

Chapter Twenty-five

A bright, sunny morning greeted Marc as he approached Vanity's kitchen factory at Five Dock. Stephen, who had arrived a few minutes earlier to clear the way for Marc's visit at the security guard's gatehouse, was waiting at the gate to guide Marc into his designated visitor's parking spot.

The factory was quite modern and covered a huge area. Marc noticed that there were no windows in the light gray concrete walls and surmised that the design relied heavily on translucent roof sheeting for natural light.

Upon entering the factory, they were handed safety glasses and earplugs. As they put them on, Marc looked around the vast workshop in amazement. *Look at the size of this place!* he thought, trying to assimilate the massive scale of Vanity's kitchen manufacturing operation.

There were dozens of computer-controlled machines cutting and shaping long sections of laminated particleboard. Another group of machines was pressing veneers onto these boards to create the kitchen bench tops. The finished pieces were then polished by yet other machines before being carted off to one of several pre-delivery assembly areas dotting the workshop floor.

Bathroom vanity units were made in another part of the factory. These, too, were made from scratch. In that section, Marc was astonished to see acres of four-story-high vertical shelving and racking that stored all manner of hardware items, which were retrieved by special manned lifts that ran up and down the aisles. *I've never seen anything like this before,* Marc marveled as he stood transfixed, watching the tiny manned lifts shoot up toward the roof, pick out an item from the racks, and return to the ground with their cargo on board.

After watching several cycles with Marc, Stephen said, "There's a lot more we need to see, Mr. Braddon. We make all our shower screens and windows in here as well."

"Yes...yes, of course," Marc replied, almost as if overwhelmed, as he prepared to move on.

They inspected the area where the aluminum windows, shower screens, and other glass-based items were made. This section was partitioned from the rest of the factory by a brick wall that isolated one operation from the other to eliminate any risk of cross-contamination from the chemicals used in the respective manufacturing processes. The place was a beehive of activity, and Marc was beginning to realize just how big the Vanity Homes operation really was.

Any builder who can utilize all the output from a place this size has to be a force to be reckoned with in the marketplace! Marc thought, even before Stephen told him that Vanity Homes utilized about eighty percent of the output from this factory. The balance was sold through various outlets to small builders and trades people who made their living renovating kitchens and bathrooms.

"I reckon this factory has the ability to increase production by at least another fifty percent over its current output," Stephen shouted above the factory noise. "It's only a matter of developing a few new markets to fuel that growth. I'm sure that would better utilize the investment Vanity has in the place, while reducing the group's overhead by spreading costs across a broader manufacturing base."

This concept was certainly not lost on Marc, since it had been the underlying reason for his initial interest in the Vanity Homes group. *A picture is worth a thousand words,* he thought as he witnessed the strength of the group first-hand, rather than relying on figures on a balance sheet.

Marc spent the rest of the morning in the factory office with Stephen, pouring over a myriad of production figures and capacities. No one else from the Vanity Group was involved, as Myles wanted the negotiations to remain secret. Marc asked Stephen many questions regarding the group's current operations and markets, and was pleased with the answers.

There certainly is enough here to sweeten the pot if I decide to proceed with this acquisition, particularly as the quality of these products is so high, Marc noted to himself. *They could readily be marketed to any number of additional users.*

Marc also liked the way Stephen James handled himself. He was helpful, and Marc sensed that he was keen to see a new owner take over the companies. Maybe Stephen saw an opportunity for advancement. Marc hoped so, because he knew he would need some help to run the place if he proceeded with the acquisition.

* * *

With lunchtime fast approaching, Marc offered to take Stephen out to a restaurant, figuring they needed a change of scenery. He wanted an opportunity to obtain some more first-hand information about Vanity, and to observe Stephen in another environment.

They went to a local Greek place that Stephen and Myles frequented whenever they visited the factory on their audits. "I'm sure you'll like this place," Stephen told Marc. "It's cozy and private, and the food is renowned."

"Tell me about your background, Stephen," Marc asked as the waiter opened and poured a bottle of a South Australian Cabinet Sauvignon into the glasses set before them. "How did you get into this business?"

Stephen looked away for few moments while he gathered his thoughts. Once he had assimilated his response, he looked back at Marc and appeared slightly apprehensive. "Well, after I got my accounting degree, I started looking around for an industry that would allow me to specialize. I answered an ad, and Myles interviewed me himself. I guess we just hit it off. He offered me the job, and we've been together ever since. Sounds almost like the sort of explanation you might get from an old married couple, don't you think?" Stephen said with a nervous chuckle.

Marc raised his glass to Stephen and said, "Cheers." Both men took a sip and nodded their approval of the wine selection.

"I understand that you two have been through a lot together," Marc casually observed. "I sense a closeness that only comes when there's mutual respect; the sort of thing that happens when you go through a tough campaign and come out the other end together."

Stephen nodded and shifted slightly in his chair. "Myles is a terrific fellow. I would never do or say anything to hurt him, but I must say that I'm glad he's talking to you about selling the company. Over the past couple of years, I've sensed he's had enough. He's taken the business just about as far as he can, and I think now he's just treading water."

So you are *keen to see a change in ownership,* Marc noted with satisfaction.

"I hope I'm not making you feel uncomfortable," he said with a disarming smile. "Sometimes I feel that I ask too many questions!"

"Oh, no!" Stephen replied reassuringly. "My job is to answer all your questions. Truth be known, I probably have a stronger allegiance to the business than to Myles. I honestly think the business would benefit from some new thinking."

"You sound like someone with a number of his own ideas," Marc said, nodding thoughtfully.

"I suppose you could say that." Stephen eyes lit up as he leaned forward in his chair. "Myles and I have had many discussions about expansion, but his lack of vision always seems to get in the way of the opportunities. It can be frustrating, especially if you're the one who has to deal with negative results of his indecisiveness," Stephen said with a slight frown.

Marc smiled knowingly, remembering his frustrations during his time as an employee. "I think I know what you mean. A long time ago, when I worked for a group of consulting engineers, I experienced the same frustration. I had to abide by the partner's decisions, even when I often felt I was closer to the problem and could therefore offer a better solution. Unfortunately, this always seems to come with being an employee, no matter how senior, but I think it's good to care about the company that employs you."

"I'm glad to hear you say that, Marc, because I could end up working for *you!*" Stephen said with another nervous laugh.

Marc liked the way Stephen was handling himself. Pouring him another glass of wine, Marc offered Stephen a supportive smile and asked, "So, tell me, Stephen, do you think that the Vanity Group could be run more efficiently?"

Stephen pursed his lips as he pondered the question. "In a word, yes! Our overhead is way too high for the size of the operation."

"How would you go about cutting it down to acceptable levels?"

Stephen shifted again and looked a little guilty as he began to disclose more information. "You have to recognize that over time, Myles has allowed the business to become a vehicle to provide employment for his family. Three of his children work for Vanity, as well as a number of nephews and nieces. If I were to be honest about their worth, I'd say that none of them is worth feeding!"

Marc's eyebrows shot up in surprise. "I hadn't picked that up anywhere in your information pack."

"Of course not—how could you?" Stephen leaned back and rubbed the back of his neck with a tired smile. "Myles assumes that anyone buying the companies would want to put their own people in place. And I believe he'll give his children some of the money from the sale of the business. This will leave them free to go off and start their own enterprises. I think he accepted long ago that none of them could ever run the company. They just don't have the business acumen, and would destroy the place!"

"Hmm. That explains the inordinately high overhead I picked up when I analyzed your figures at the outset," Marc observed. "So what dollar value would you put on these extra overheads?"

Stephen paused as he added the figures in his head. "I'd say at least a million dollars is going to this group in direct wages. If you add indirect costs for things like pension contributions, cars, holidays, etc., then you'd easily get that figure up to one and a half million a year."

Marc fell back in his chair. "Wow!" he blurted. After a moment to collect his thoughts, he continued. "Any other areas where costs can be cut without affecting the overall performance of the companies?"

Stephen nodded. "I think that our whole marketing area needs to be reviewed. We have arrangements with our marketing and sales people that are overly generous. It pays them too well for too little effort, and ends up giving them no real incentive to sell. A number of other areas in the operation would fit into this category."

"Do you believe these things could be easily remedied?"

"Yes! It just takes someone with the will. Myles seems to have gotten himself into a frame of mind where he doesn't want to upset anybody or anything."

"As I said, when I first looked at your figures, it seemed to me that your manufacturing costs were a little out of kilter with your level of production."

"You can say that again!" Stephen said with a wry smile. "I have been telling Myles that for ages, but it falls on deaf ears. Maybe it's because we had such a difficult time establishing the manufacturing operations, but for whatever reason, he doesn't want to expand that part of the business. As I think he admitted to you the other day, we were not manufacturers when we started out, but simple builders. As you well know, today's project builders are only really managers of subcontract labor. It's a big jump to become a manager of a manufacturing process, with all the direct labor issues and problems."

Marc just nodded. "So would you now feel brave enough to make the changes necessary to bring things back into balance in these areas?"

"Oh, yes; just give me the chance! I reckon that I could shave about $3 million a year off our overhead in the first year. I also think these savings would actually help the organization by making things run that much better."

I like the way this fellow thinks, Marc assessed silently. *I also like the way he seems to put his loyalty to the company ahead of his fondness for Myles. I think I could use a man like this to help me set the place up properly.*

*   *   *

Back at his office, Marc attended to several matters before calling Elisa, who had just returned to her office after delivering her morning lectures.

"How did it go?" she asked with concern.

"Pretty good. I think I have a good idea of what their operation is all about. I like their financial controller, a guy called Stephen James. I think he might be someone I could work with."

"That's great."

"I've invited Robert and Maddie down for dinner tonight. I'd like you to come along so that I can bounce some thoughts off you, too."

"Sounds like a plan!" Elisa responded warmly. "I'd love to help. I have a staff meeting that's going to run until about seven-thirty. If you pick me up at the university, I'll leave my car here and we can go in one car—that'll save us parking two cars in town. You can drop me back after dinner, if that's OK."

"Yeah, that's no problem. I'll be there at seven-thirty. I'll park at the side entrance of your department. Can you clear it with the security guard at the front gates so that I can get into the place?"

"I'll do that as soon as you hang up. See you then, sweetie."

*　*　*

Robert and Maddie met Marc and Elisa at a restaurant in Kent Street, in the southern part of the city. During dinner, Marc was able to discuss the whole scenario with them all.

Maddie focused on helping to solve her brother's most immediate problem. "Will these companies give you what you are looking for in terms of a bigger cash flow and turnover?" she asked.

"I'm sure they will," Marc replied quickly. "Their combined turnover is so large that it swamps anything I can produce with my current operations. The cash flow in the group has got to be ten times what I currently generate!"

Robert leaned forward. "It sounds like a bargain to me, Marc, particularly if what you say about the growth potential is true."

"I know I'm not a businessperson, but I can't see any flaws in your logic," Elisa said encouragingly. "I'm sure you'll find a way to take over the group. You'll succeed because you don't know how to fail!"

"That's our Marcy!" Maddie chirped as the rest of them laughed.

Marc topped up all their glasses again. "So, you all think I'm on the right track?"

"Yeah," Maddie replied. "I like your idea about making the group run more smoothly and profitably—like a public company rather than the private family company it has been—before listing it on the stock exchange."

Two down, one to go, Marc thought as he looked questioningly at his brother-in-law.

"I agree with Maddie," Robert told him. "I also agree that it will probably take two or three years to change the public's perception that Vanity is no longer a family-run company, because shareholders are traditionally suspicious of 'Mum-and-Dad' companies, or those which run solely on the energy of the founder," he added.

Marc nodded. "Yeah, I know the whole country's still in the grip of a recession, and market sentiment has been negative for the past two years, but it just *has* to turn around eventually! I know that nothing is certain in this world, but I do feel that the share market and the economy will return to good health over the next two to three years."

"We all agree with you, Marc, and think that you're right on the money!" Maddie said with a broad, supportive smile.

"Now all you have to do is to go out and find a way to buy the company," Elisa chimed in.

Robert lifted his glass and said with a cheesy smile, "To Marc and his noble quest to find his Holy Grail—may he find true happiness and fulfillment in the acquisition of Vanity Homes!"

Everyone laughed and lifted their glasses to celebrate Robert's toast.

*   *   *

As Marc drove Elisa back to her university to collect her car, he was struggling with mixed emotions. He relished the support he had received, but for the first time in his life, he found himself questioning his motives and wondering out loud if being so driven was the right way to live.

"Don't get me wrong, honey," he told Elisa. "I still need to do this deal to survive. It's just that having you next to me has made me start to consider other aspects of my life. Maybe business shouldn't be everything." He glanced at his fiancé and searched her face. "Do you think I'm so driven that I can't see anything else, Elisa?"

After looking out the window thoughtfully for a moment, Elisa looked back at Marc. "You *are* a driven man, Marc, but that's just a fact of life. I suppose it's a habit you've developed over the years in order to achieve what you have. Now it's probably so ingrained in you that you can't do it any other way."

Marc shook his head slowly. "I am starting to feel that I'd like to change some parts of my life; I feel I'd like to slow down a little so that I can discover myself." He looked into Elisa's blue eyes and said, "I think you're probably the only person who can help me to do that."

A compassionate smile filled Elisa's pretty face. "You know I'll gladly help you, but only if you ask. I'm not going to change you into some other person just for my sake, because there are so many things about the way you are that make me love you."

"No, I don't want to force a change of character either. It's just that I think there must be lots of things I've missed out on by my single-minded obsession to succeed," Marc said thoughtfully. "I don't want to do anything radical. I guess I'll just have to allow time to take its course and help me to decide what's best for me."

Chapter Twenty-six

When Marc arrived back at his office the next day, he did so with renewed vigor and enthusiasm. The next piece of the puzzle required him to put his lenders in place.

He had heard of a relatively new merchant bank that had been involved in a lot of deals around the city: Whitney, Whyte & Partners, or simply Whitney Whyte, apparently specialized in takeover finance. Marc didn't go into specifics over the phone with Adam Boyd, the senior partner, preferring to give only a basic outline of his proposal. The last thing he wanted was for anyone to find out about the opportunity he had uncovered, reminding himself of that old wartime saying, *"Loose lips sink ships."* He would go into detail only after he had a signed confidentiality agreement in his hot little hand.

Adam Boyd met him in the reception area. He was a solidly built man who appeared to be in his late forties and liked to power dress. He wore a blue pinstriped shirt, red tie, and red and blue striped braces, but still emitted a friendly persona.

They moved into their boardroom, and Marc was offered tea, coffee, or mineral water. The latter was novel, he thought. No one else had ever offered it before in a business meeting! As it was a hot day, and he was a parched from his walk across the city to their offices, so he opted for the water. He was left alone in their boardroom while Adam went off to order the refreshments and fetch one his assistants.

Whitney Whyte's boardroom was impressive by any standard. Looking around the room, Marc recognized several pieces of valuable and renowned Australian art hanging on the soft-blue walls. The ceiling was created by a very elaborate plasterboard design that utilized several layers of false ceilings placed at varying angles, making it a modern work of art in its own right.

When Adam returned, he introduced his assistant, Jennifer Watkins. She handed Marc her card, which stated she had a bachelor of business degree with majors in banking and marketing. She certainly looked the part of a young professional in a tailored, navy blue business suit and a high-neck, cream-colored blouse.

"My first order of business is to ensure the confidentiality of the information I must impart to you both during this briefing," Marc stated. "Does your firm have a standard confidentiality agreement you are prepared to sign in situations like these?"

"Yes, we do," Adam answered. "However, it's not really necessary since once you become our client we are required to maintain the confidentiality of any information between us, somewhat akin to the relationship that exists between doctor and patient."

"I understand that, Adam," Marc responded cautiously, "but at this stage, we're just talking. I have yet to engage your firm, and I would prefer you both to sign a confidentiality agreement before I proceed."

"Very well," Adam said amiably, opening a folder and passing Marc a copy of his firm's standard agreement.

"Yes, this will do," Marc decided after reading the two short paragraphs.

All three signed both copies of the agreement, and Marc was given an executed copy for his records. As he placed it in his briefcase, he withdrew two copies of the papers he had prepared for the meeting and slid them across to Adam and Jennifer, who by now were quite curious.

"The group of companies I am interested in operates under the name of the Vanity Homes Group Pty. Ltd. The parent company has a number of subsidiaries whose operations are based in the project or model home building market here in New South Wales. Most of the companies in the group are vertically integrated, in that they manufacture or provide many of the building products used by the other companies in the group.

"This particular builder has been established for some twenty-five years. For most of that time, he has occupied the number-one position as the largest builder in the state. The group has a combined turnover of around $150 million a year, and last year made a net profit of $4.8 million," Marc said.

"Hmm. Sounds very interesting, Marc. I take it you have checked out their operations and can verify all of the statements in your submission?"

Marc nodded.

"That being the case, what price have you agreed to pay for this operation?" Adam asked.

"That hasn't been finalized yet, but I'll probably have to pay around $45 million to secure the whole thing."

"And that's where we come in, I presume?" Alan nodded.

"I'm not looking to borrow the whole amount. I expect that after I negotiate the immediate resale of a number of unwanted assets, I'll need to borrow around $32 million to complete the sale and inject some much-needed working capital into their operations."

"How do you propose to sell these assets on settlement to reduce your borrowings?" Jennifer asked.

"I have been through Vanity's balance sheet and asset register, and have identified several large landholdings that are superfluous to its current home building operations. I propose to sell these back to the current owner as part of the overall deal." Marc paused to gauge their reaction.

James turned to Jennifer and cast her an inquisitive look. He then turned back to Marc and said, "You've certainly got our attention, Marc; tell us more."

"I'm going to suggest Myles Vanity build custom-built mansions on this land to give him something to do in retirement," Marc continued. "Vanity Homes would never be able to build its normal project homes on this land; the land is too upmarket for that and would represent an unnecessary financial risk for the company."

"You're reasonably sure of the value of these landholdings?" Adam asked.

"I'm working on values that are pretty well established and based on recent sales in those areas. Anyway, it'll be part of the overall arrangement, and in that context, the value of these assets will be agreed upon beforehand as part of the final deal."

Adam nodded. "OK. Let's move on, then. Do you have an overall plan for the group after acquisition?"

"Yes. I propose to overhaul the entire operation to dramatically reduce the overhead and streamline production. I'll do this by introducing new management techniques that will create a pseudo-public company culture in preparation for a public offering in two to three years time."

"Interesting," Adam said, leaning forward in his chair. "We may also be able to help you there, too, as public offerings are another of our specialties."

Marc smiled. "I'm aware of that, but my purpose here today is to gauge your interest in my overall proposal, as well as your ability to help me secure the necessary funding."

"From what you have told us, I think we can assure you that we would like to be involved," Adam replied with a smile of his own. "I would like your permission to take away all the details you have provided in order to work up a proposed acquisition timetable, as well as a schedule of our fees." Turning to Jennifer, Adam asked, "Jenny, how long will we need to put all of this together?"

"Forty-eight hours," was Jennifer's immediate response. "We could schedule another meeting two days from today."

"Is that satisfactory, Marc?" Adam asked.

"Yes. I'm very keen to get on with things."

"We never seem to come across anyone who isn't," Adam said as they all laughed.

*   *   *

Jennifer and Adam called Marc several times over the next two days to qualify some of the information they needed for her submission. They were back in the boardroom in what seemed like no time at all, by the time they met again, they were almost like old friends.

"Based on the figures and projections you gave us," Adam said, "we have produced our own spreadsheets on the group's value, pre- and post-takeover. We have accepted your assumptions in compiling our figures, and I have to say that it looks as if you have unearthed a real gem here," he concluded with a smile.

"Yes, the earnings before interest and taxation show that you can easily manage a loan of up to $40 million, even on a five-year principal and interest repayment schedule," Jennifer added. "Provided you're confident you can effect the changes in the group's overhead and turnover that you've set out in your papers, you'll have little trouble making the payments."

"I'm happy with my projections," Marc stated. "I've based them only on what the group is actually doing right now in the middle of a recession. Things can only get better as the economy picks up," he reasoned.

"You're preaching to the choir," Adam joked.

"Well, where do we go from here?" Marc asked.

"We'll give you a draft copy of our investor's report, once we produce it, so that you can look it over and make any comments you feel are appropriate before we take it to the market. In the meantime, I have something else for you to look at," Adam said, handing Marc a two-page document. "This is our fee agreement. It sets out our charges for procuring the finance for this project. You'll note that it has a requirement for an up-front fee of $50,000. This is payable as soon as you retain us, and is part of our overall fee of one percent of the funds procured."

"Wow; that's around $320,000 on the amount I plan to borrow!" Marc gasped.

"Well, that's our fee," Adam said offhandedly.

"Surely this is a fairly easy deal to place with a lender," Marc said. "Any big bank would love to get their hands on the potential pool of borrowers that Vanity produces—around two thousand homeowners a year, at the last count."

"Well, maybe, but you know what banks are like. They have to be spoon-fed a deal to understand it. If we take this deal on, then we guarantee you that we can access the funds you need, and that's what you pay for—the ability to complete your end of the deal. If you look at it that way, Marc, I'm sure you'll see we're not expensive."

How can anyone in my position disagree? he thought. "OK. You've got a deal, but I need you two to work on this matter straightaway, as I'll be under a lot of pressure next week to make a commitment to Myles Vanity."

"Pressure is what we do best," Jennifer said reassuringly.

"You can rely on us, Marc," Adam chimed in. "I guarantee you that we'll be there at the end."

This was all Adam felt he had to say to close their agreement, and he was right. Marc was confident that Adam and Jennifer had just made a commitment to join him in overcoming whatever obstacles were going to be thrown in their paths. This meant that they, like Marc, would have to work ridiculous hours as they juggled their other commitments. Somehow, they would all have to make the time to attend meetings on short notice, take the dozens of urgent phone calls that had to be answered, and generally do whatever else it would take to get this deal to where it could be put to a trading bank.

That was what Marc really wanted from them—their commitment and support, based upon their belief in him and the quality of the deal he had brought to the table. He was sure he really needed Whitney Whyte and Partners, as he couldn't afford to take risks with this takeover bid.

Chapter Twenty-seven

Marc's next meeting with Myles Vanity took place at Vanity's home, in the suburb of West Pennant Hills in northwest Sydney. Several years earlier, Myles had purchased a five-acre property in what was then Sydney's last rural enclave—an 'oasis,' as he described it to Marc—in the middle of quarter-acre suburbia. It took a number of years before he could actually afford to build his family's dream home on the property.

Everybody should be entitled to a dream like this! Marc thought as he turned into the wide driveway and peered through the gates at the huge white house with its perfectly manicured lawns and gardens. Myles's gates were large and forbidding, painted in a glossy black accentuated by a gold trim. Family crests were proudly displayed on the center of each leaf and painted gold with black trimmings, as were the speared tips of the black bars that carried through the top rails of these gigantic gates.

How civilized! Marc marveled as he pulled up to the illuminated intercom box, which was built into one of the gate's brick columns, and depressed the button to announce his arrival.

Like magic, the intercom crackled with a voice. "Hello. Can I help you?"

"My name's Marc Braddon. I am here to see Mr. Vanity."

"Oh yes, Mr. Braddon. Mr. Vanity is expecting you. Please drive up to the front doors. I'll make sure the dogs are secured, so please come straight in," the voice said through the intercom as the huge gates swung open.

Dogs! Marc thought with a start. *Myles didn't say anything about dogs!* Driving up to the house, he envisioned a pack of snarling German Shepherds circling his car and baying for blood.

The vicious canines receded into Marc's imagination as Vanity's gates swung completely open to reveal his immaculate grounds. The long black driveway contrasted sharply with the ash-white concrete curb, and the road surface was finished to a perfect smoothness unlike anything seen on a public thoroughfare.

The edges of the driveway were bordered by continuous flowerbeds whose delicate colors made for a striking show as one meandered up the long drive toward the house. The lawns were mowed in patterns typically seen in the fine old English country gardens in movies or magazines.

The whole place dripped money and made an unmistakable statement that nothing of inferior quality had ever been considered when this house was built. The house had clearly been designed to replicate the federation period, circa 1900—a popular style of architecture in that part of Sydney. It was a rambling, two-story house, although the feature windows in its roof area made it look as if it were really three stories. *It looks bigger that it really is, if that's possible,* Marc observed.

As Marc's car neared the front doors, he cautiously checked for any sign of vicious dogs, putting him momentarily in mind of the "Hound of the Baskervilles." But if the house and grounds were anything to go by, the dogs were more likely well-groomed pedigrees that obediently mustered at their kennels on a whistled command.

The front doors opened just as Marc drove under the portico. Myles, who was waiting to greet him, seemed to have taken on the look of the "Lord of the Manor" rather than the jovial Santa caricature Marc had become used to at their last meeting.

Myles stood next to another fellow Marc took to be his butler. He was a tall man in his fifties, graying at the temples—unmistakably an ex-army man, from his ramrod-straight posture. He was dressed in gray striped trousers, a somber waistcoat and a black bowtie.

The butler immediately asked if he could take Marc's coat. He then ushered Myles and Marc into a sitting room off the grand entry foyer before closing the double doors and departing in silence.

This place is even more amazing on the inside, Marc thought as he sat down in one of a group of chairs set around a large coffee table, which appeared to be made from ancient dark oak. The room had high, raked ceilings and was overlooked by a series of scalloped gallery balconies that extended off the first-floor hallway. There was a huge open fireplace with a massive brick hearth and an equally wide chimney, concealed behind a two-story sandstone brick wall. Not surprisingly, a portrait of Myles Vanity hung above the mantelpiece. After studying it, Marc concluded that the only things missing from Myles' portrait were his mythical hounds or his trusty old steed.

"My, this is a very impressive house," Marc said as Myles settled down in the chair opposite him.

Myles widened his eyes and smiled. "Yes. It's the product of a lifetime of hard work. Nothing here came easy!"

"Just how big is it?"

Myles stopped and thought for a moment. "I forget. I used to know. Um...about sixteen thousand square feet, seventeen hundred square metres."

"That's a huge house!" Marc said, overwhelmed.

Myles huffed out a little laugh that seemed to indicate a family joke. "We felt we needed to build it at the time. You know, as fulfillment of a lifelong ambition. We planned it for years before we could actually afford it, and then we just seemed to follow through with the building. It's really way too big for the family nowadays, but we've all gotten used to the luxury of the space."

"You seem to have taken a great deal of care with every aspect of it. It's a very impressive house, and the grounds are absolutely flawless!"

"Thank you," Myles replied as he twisted in his seat to make himself more comfortable. "Funny, but we don't have that many visitors. We've just become used to the old place, I guess."

I think we've exhausted the small talk, Marc concluded. Straightening his posture, he suggested, "Let's get down to business, shall we?"

Myles sat up. "Yes. Well, when we left off at our last meeting, you were going to come back if you were genuinely interested in buying my companies. I know you told Stephen that you were keen to do business. So tell me, what is your offer?"

You're a bit quick off the mark. I was hoping we could take a few minutes to get to the money! Marc thought as cleared his throat. He fixed Myles with a serious look and projected his determined chin.

"It's not that straightforward, Myles. I am very interested, but how I structure my offer depends upon how you want to exit the company."

A bemused expression ran over Myles's face as he sat back in his armchair. "Oh! I hadn't given that a lot of thought, I must admit."

"It's important for me to know if you want to retire completely or semi-retire and keep on building. On this basis, I can structure a deal that should suit us both."

Myles looked even more puzzled. "I don't follow, Marc. How does that vary your offer?"

"I've been looking at the companies' assets, and if you are looking at the semi-retirement option, I believe it would be in both our interests if you retained the land the company has in its land bank. I don't think that Vanity Homes can build on this land—it's too upscale for the sort of contract homes it builds. On the other hand, *you* could use it to build speculative houses at your leisure before selling off the completed products to the public."

The confusion in Myles' eyes seemed to clear. "I see what you mean. I really think I would choose the semi-retirement option. It isn't good for a man who's worked hard all his life to just stop dead. All the people I know who've done that *have* dropped dead!" he noted with a rueful chuckle.

"Well, if you choose this option," Marc said, "then the price will change to reflect the value of the assets you will take out of the deal." He moved toward the edge of his seat. "There are several other aspects of our arrangement I would want you to consider…"

"What are they?" Myles asked suspiciously.

"Nothing sinister!" Marc assured him. "It's just that we need to agree on how to manage the sale, particularly after it's all been finalized."

Myles seemed somewhat surprised by the detail of Marc's thought processes. He allowed a good-natured smile to escape from his lips. "OK, just how do you see things operating after the sale?"

So far so good, Marc thought. "I think it's important for the companies to retain the various Vanity Homes names, as these are valuable trademarks that are immediately recognizable in the marketplace. I would want the right to trade under these names, and I need to know that you are not going to use any of them in your new enterprises."

Myles considered the implications of what he was being asked, and after thinking it over for a moment, nodded. "That would be agreed. I must say that I'm very conscious of my good name; and it's important to me that nothing is done to harm it, so I need to be comfortable with your ongoing plans for the company."

Marc sat back and smiled. "Myles, I am even more conscious of your good name, because it's a big attraction in this deal. I assure you that I don't plan to damage such a valuable asset. I foresee keeping you on as a consultant for, say, two years after the sale, and I would want the right to use you as the public face of the group in any advertising. I would pay you a separate annual fee for the right to do that, depending on the number of campaigns we run."

Myles' eyes did a tour of the room as he pondered Marc's offer. "That sounds OK to me," he said finally.

"I also want to set up a contingency fund out of a small part of the purchase price to cover any unforeseen liabilities that might crop up within, say, two years of the sale," Marc added. "If I move quickly on this deal, I won't really have time to determine what ongoing liabilities, if any, are in these companies. Therefore, I think it's only fair that a sum of around $3 million be set aside to cover any contingent liabilities that might come up during the first two years. The money could be put into an account in your name so that you would get the interest on the money, with both of us as signatories so that we must both agree on any amount to be paid out of this fund. This would protect us both."

"I suppose that's fair enough," Myles said with a nod. "What's your next problem?"

Marc smiled as he mentally ticked off the items in his wish list. "I'll probably want to set up a set of parallel shelf companies and take over all the Vanity Homes contracts upon the closing of the purchase. This way, your old companies and their various taxation structures will remain in your hands."

Myles slid back in his armchair and offered Marc an openhanded gesture. "Nothing you've said so far presents a problem, Marc. Tell me, what sort of time frame are we talking about? When do you think you'll be able to pay over the monies to complete the purchase?"

"According to my financial advisers, I should be in position to do that within three to six months."

Myles frowned. "Hmm. Six months is a little longer than I had hoped for. Is there anything I could do to speed things up?"

OK, here goes. Marc moved back to the edge of his chair. "If you really want to help, you could introduce me to your bank. That might make it easier to get the necessary funds, since they know and understand your operation. I know you've already offered to do that, and I believe they'd give the whole matter far more consideration if you sponsored the approach. As you said at our last meeting, your companies give the bank millions of dollars in business every year, and they won't underestimate Vanity's value in that regard."

Myles threw his head back and laughed. "Oh, is that all? Consider it done, Marc. When you give me a firm offer we both can agree on, I'll have a talk with my manager on your behalf. He also happens to be the bank's chief commercial manager, so he should be able to assist you."

"I have retained a merchant bank to help me put the financing package together, but your bank could short-cut the whole process and speed things up immeasurably."

"Now, how much money are you talking about?" Myles said, finally asking the question he had obviously been trying to get to all evening.

Marc paused for a moment before leaning a little closer to Myles. "I am able to offer you the $45 million you want, but I can only do this if you take back the land bank that you've created in the company at closure for an agreed value of $12 million," he said firmly.

Myles's quick mind summarized the essential elements of the deal. "This means I can walk away with $30 million in cash and have $3 million tied up in that contingency fund for two years, plus all the vacant land I have acquired." A satisfied look ran over Myles's face. I like it! OK, you've got a deal."

Marc's eyes lit up with enthusiasm. Both he and Myles stood up and crossed the small space between them to shake hands on their agreement.

"That's marvelous, Myles!" Marc said. "I'll draw up a basic agreement for your signature and fax it to you tonight! Once that's executed, we can finalize the other matters between us. I'll try to settle this purchase as soon as I can—I believe I can do it well within the six-month time frame I mentioned, although that's what we'll have to put into our agreement as a safeguard."

They had a scotch to consummate their deal. After their second round, Myles gave Marc a tour of his fabulous home. It made Marc wish he had one just like it, but for now, it was enough he was buying Myles' company.

*　　*　　*

The next day, Marc reported to his merchant bankers that he had signed an agreement with Myles for the purchase of all his companies. He said that Vanity had not only agreed the price, but also the other key issues affecting the sale.

"You've done marvelously well, Marc!" Adam Boyd said as he perused the document containing Myles Vanity's signature. "You prepared this yourself?" he asked with sneaking look of admiration.

"Yes—I didn't want to give Myles time to change his mind," Marc replied. "It was important to get this deal nailed down, and I didn't want his legal advisers crawling all over the terms and creating unnecessary friction between us. This way, we now have our terms defined, which means that the legal eagles only have to prepare a set of legally correct contract documents."

"I suppose I have to agree with you." Adam said with a chuckle. "It's just so refreshing to see someone who's game enough to commit to a deal of this size without a battery of solicitors in tow. Well done, I say!"

"But now, I do need a good firm of commercial lawyers to do all of the necessary legal work to complete this deal. The firm I've been dealing with would be out of their depth in this type of deal."

Adam pondered the question for a moment and suddenly appeared to have the answer. "I can recommend an excellent firm, if you'd like. They're a city firm: small enough to personalize their service while still large enough to have real clout. Their name is Arness and Company, and they're in the building next door."

"I suppose it would make sense for you to work with someone you know," Marc mused, "and having them close by would have its advantages."

"Shall I set up a meeting with the senior partner?"

"Sure, why not? I'm available at a moment's notice if it will help to speed this deal through."

Chapter Twenty-eight

When Marc and Adam met with Mary Arness in her offices the next morning, Mary's professionalism was immediately apparent: She spoke with authority and clarity, dressed in a smartly tailored business suit. Her black hair was neatly styled and showed no signs of graying, although she must have been in her mid-forties and lived in a high-powered world.

Marc started out by outlining his needs. "I feel I need a high-powered city firm to represent my interests in this matter," he told Mary.

"I told Marc that we had worked together on many projects," Adam chimed in, "and that we have closed every deal we've done together. "

Mary had listened intently throughout their meeting and said very little. Now, she suddenly came to life as she quickly began outlining some of the pitfalls she had typically encountered in these sorts of takeover deals. "I think that you *will* need a firm capable of dealing with some of the hard-nosed players that you're going to encounter in a deal like this," she told Marc. "And after you take over a company the size of Vanity Homes, you will also need to have good representation, because you're bound to encounter a brand-new set of problems at almost every hurdle until things eventually settle down. It's important that you always end up in the best position that the circumstances will allow."

"And that's where your firm comes in," Marc said with a smile.

Mary acknowledged him with a nod. "We really only deal with a select clientele. That's because we need to be able to provide each of our clients with our full attention in their moments of need."

As the meeting drew to an end, Marc stood up. "I would like to engage your firm, Mary, on the proviso that you personally are involved in my matters," he said.

Mary readily agreed. As he left the room, Marc was pleased. *Now I've got team in place that'll allow me to put this deal to bed*, he thought.

*   *   *

Ben Allsop, Colonial University's vice chancellor, had summoned Elisa for a private meeting. As Elisa made her way through the university's manicured grounds toward the chancellor's wing, she wondered if she was about to be chastised for her run-ins with Jeremy Close. *If that's what this is about, then I'll give Ben a piece of my mind*, she decided as she approached his door.

"Elisa! Please come in," Ben said warmly.

Elisa forced out a smile. "How are you, Mr. Allsop?"

"Fine. But please call me Ben. More to the point, how are *you*, Elisa?"

What's he getting at? Elisa measured her response. "OK, I guess."

Ben shook his head contritely. "I wanted to apologize to you for what happened with that bloody associate professorship. I've deliberately left the subject alone for several months to allow you time to let off some steam." He let a smile escape as he added, "And it's just as well, from what I hear."

A defiant expression ran across Elisa's face as she folded her arms. "You're not going to support Jeremy too, are you?"

Ben reeled back in horror. "Absolutely not!"

Well, that's something, anyway, she noted grudgingly as Ben leaned forward to continue.

"Elisa, what happened to you is a travesty. I made it clear to our esteemed deans that you were the best qualified candidate and my choice for the post." He lowered his voice. "Between you and me, I think they tried to send me a message at your expense."

Elisa cocked a suspicious eyebrow. "Oh?"

"I also think they couldn't stomach the thought of a woman being able to tell a man what to do." Ben shook his head ruefully at his colleagues' stupidity before offering Elisa a supportive smile. "Elisa, I want you to know that that job should have been yours. And I'm going to put things right!"

Elisa shot Ben an incredulous look. "How?" she managed.

Ben rubbed his hands together in thought. "I might arrange a little sideways 'promotion' for our Jeremy," he mused. "Whatever happens, I want you know that you're by far the best person in your entire department. In fact, I would be delighted if you were the dean, so please don't let this sorry incident sour your view of the university."

Elisa let out a sigh of relief as she began to relax in the vice chancellor's company. "Thank you, Ben. I must admit I was becoming disillusioned, and was beginning to think I must've done something monumentally wrong."

"No, no, no, Elisa. It seems that we both have to turn the tide. Will you give me the opportunity to try?"

A broad smile flooded Elisa's face. "Yes, Ben—of course I will."

*   *   *

On the way back to the Whitney Whyte's offices, Marc reminded to Adam and Jennifer that he had previously secured Myles Vanity's word that he would assist him to raise the necessary funds from his bank if needed.

"That'll definitely be an option we'd want to explore," Adam replied. "But first, we need to finalize our briefing papers so that we can properly define our needs and the scope of this transaction before we approach any banks."

"It wouldn't hurt for Myles to tell his bankers about the sale and make them aware that Marc is the buyer," Jennifer said to Adam. "It might well bring them to us!"

"I agree, Jenny. If they want to keep the business they currently have, then they'll have to deal with us. That should have them hopping around trying to get into this new arrangement," Adam said with a laugh.

"All right, then; I'll ask Myles to put out some feelers," Marc said.

* * *

Marc phoned Elisa and asked, "Can I come around to your place tonight? I have some good news."

"Yes, of course, honey. You must be telepathic—I was just about to call you to ask you over to share *my* news."

"Do you want to tell me now?"

"God, no—not if you're coming around. I want to see the look on your face!"

"It must be good. Let me guess...now, let's see...could it be..."

"I'll go by the butcher's shop on the way home and grab us some stir-fry or something, if you'll get the red wine."

"Is seven OK?"

"Perfect."

It was always pleasant to sit out on Elisa's balcony and talk as the city lights sparkled across the magnificent waterway. Even the largest, most insurmountable problems seemed insignificant when painted onto this expansive living canvas.

A few hours later, they were sitting there, pleased with each other's news and satisfied that events were finally turning in their favor.

"I really like sitting out here watching the lights and ferries go by," Marc told Elisa as he reached for her hand.

"I'm starting to wonder if it's me or the view that brings you over here!" she joked.

After a couple of glasses of wine, they found themselves melting into the landscape, their thoughts washed away by the ebbing of the harbor tide. Elisa's balcony was becoming their favorite spot to sort out all the problems of the world, as well as their own.

* * *

The following day, Marc put in a call to Myles Vanity. "Myles, I wonder if you could now introduce the idea of me buying your companies to your bankers?"

"Yes, of course. I'd be happy to. Can I give them your name and contact details?"

"Yes, please."

"Unless I'm a very bad judge, they'll soon want to talk to you, Marc," Myles said with a laugh before asking, "How's everything going?"

"Very well. I met with my team yesterday, and we have almost finalized all of paperwork on the finance side. I also engaged a firm of commercial lawyers to handle the agreements, and they should be in touch with your lawyers today, so things are moving along nicely."

"I'm pleased to hear that. If there's anything else I can do, please let me know."

"Thanks, Myles, but getting your bank involved is a big help already."

Marc's next task was to brief Mary Arness and her people, and he went through all of his files on the takeover to sort out what was relevant to her. After a couple of hours of sifting and copying, he had a complete and up-to-date set of documents, ready for an express courier.

He then called Mary to let her know the papers were on their way. She would peruse and digest them overnight before contacting him in the morning to discuss her proposed strategy regarding the legal side of the takeover.

The next day, Mary told him she had a taxation specialist on her team who could advise Marc on the best structure to adopt after he completed the takeover. "This," she said, "will save you a fortune both now and later, and will avoid problems in the future."

Marc agreed. Mary's positive attitude and her obvious competence were a great source of comfort to him as he ventured farther into the big end of town.

* * *

Two days later, Marc was sitting in his office when his receptionist announced that Kenneth Carlisle, the architect on his Hillsford project, was on the phone.

"Hello, Kenneth. How are you?"

"Excellent, Marc!"

"That's good. Now what can I do for you on this fine day?"

"It's what I can do for *you!* I'm with a fellow by the name of Larry Symes, a freelance business development manager who's connected with Civil Holdings. He'd like to talk to you about fully developing the Hillsford site's potential."

Marc positioned the phone closer to his ear, his interest piqued. "OK, you've got my attention, Kenneth."

"It'd be a lot better if we could come over and talk to you face to face. You really need to meet Larry. Can you see us this morning?"

"Sure. When can you get here?"

"In about forty minutes."

"OK, I'll see you two then!"

Larry was a man in his early thirties who had been around developers and developments all his life. He had cut his teeth in the industry while working for a couple of legendary entrepreneurs who had developed some of the most notable buildings around the country. He came across as a real "can-do" person: someone used to climbing over obstacles every day on the way to fulfilling his goals.

"Marc Braddon, may I introduce Larry Symes," Kenneth said after he and Larry were shown into Marc's office. "Larry has a proposition that should interest you," he added as Marc shook Larry's hand before motioning both men to sit in the two chairs that faced his desk.

"I believe I can come up with an arrangement that'll allow you to fully develop your Hillsford site into an income-producing commercial property without the need for you to inject anymore cash," Larry told Marc.

"Sounds very interesting, Larry. Tell me more!"

"The sizes of the three proposed buildings being four, five, and six stories, together with the decentralized location of the site, make it very attractive to a number of national firms who are looking for cheaper premises in this recession. With the advent of computerization, they're also looking to decentralize their operations while seeking a location closer to their white-collar employees' homes. Were they able to find such an office, they could cut down on a lot of other costs associated with bringing their staff into the Sydney CBD every day."

Marc nodded. "I see that. It was the logic behind my acquisition of the site in the first place."

"Well," Larry continued, "I believe I can introduce at least three major companies who'll take all the available space. That will allow us to develop the basic financial model you'll need to put the necessary funding in place for the full development of your office park complex."

"How exactly?"

Larry grinned. "As you know, I have a connection with Civil Holdings, undoubtedly the largest commercial builder in the country. With their size and track record, they can give any bank a guaranteed construction price and time to complete the work. They also have a balance sheet of about $10 billion to back up their guarantee. I can get like guarantees from the prospective tenants, and therein lies the secret!"

After more questions and answers, Marc saw the full picture. "So, you're able to use the Civil Holding's guarantee to lock in a construction lender who's happy to lend on the strength of the builder's balance sheet and track record because he knows that a second lender will pay him upon completion of the buildings. This second lender is guaranteed that his loan will be serviced because of the quality of the eventual tenants." Marc shook his head with a smile. "This plan is brilliant in its simplicity; it relies upon the ability of incoming tenants to guarantee that not only will they take office space in the completed buildings, but they also have enough financial strength to commit to a long-term lease."

"I thought Larry was supposed to be the one explaining how the whole thing works!" Kenneth said with a broad smile.

"OK, Larry, I'll play. If you can put all this together, I'll gladly go ahead with the development. We'll obviously have to talk more to sort out the finer details, but I like your scheme. The fact that Kenneth has worked with you before only adds to my comfort level."

Marc shook hands with both men and showed them out, agreeing to meet again as soon as Larry had something more definite to report.

*   *   *

The rest of the week flew by, and Marc had almost forgotten about asking Myles to call his bank until his receptionist told him that a David Rhodes from the Commercial Banking Corporation was on the line. He immediately recognized the name of the bank as the one that the Vanity Group used.

"Hello, Marc Braddon here."

"My name is Rhodes, David Rhodes, and I'm the Chief Commercial Manager with the Commercial Bank. Myles Vanity spoke to me about your arrangements and asked if I was interested in talking to you."

"Oh yes, Mr. Rhodes."

"Please call me David. May I call you Marc?"

"Yes, of course."

"I wonder if we could meet, Marc. I'm in our head office, which is located in Martin Place. I suggest that we meet here, provided it also suits you."

"Yes, I'm often in that part of the city these days, and could arrange to see you without too much difficulty. When would you like to meet?"

"As soon as possible. Is eleven o'clock Monday too soon for you?"

"No. Eleven o'clock Monday's fine."

"I'll see you then, Marc. If you give me your fax number, I'll ask my secretary to send you my contact details and our office address."

After making some discreet inquiries, Marc discovered that Rhodes was the second-most senior officer of the Commercial Bank, and would certainly have the authority to approve a loan of thirty-odd million almost on the spot. *We'll see*, Marc thought as he entered his appointment with David Rhodes on his desk calendar.

Chapter Twenty-nine

When Marc arrived at the Commercial Bank's headquarters at the Macquarie Street end of Martin Place, he stepped onto a floor designed by a minimalist architect. Large amounts of open space separated the sparse art deco furniture that decorated the reception area. All this underutilized and expensive office space seemed to convey an image of sophistication and control, and only made Marc more aware of just how much money banks really made.

The view from the reception area was breathtaking, and Marc drank it in as he waited for someone to fetch him. From that magnificent vantage point, he could see the entire harbor and its foreshores and beyond the Heads. *What a great place to work*, he thought as David Rhodes intruded into his vagaries.

David Rhodes was a fit-looking man in his fifties, about six feet tall and of medium build. He looked like the outdoors type, from his craggy face's deep tan. He wore the typical banker's attire: a white shirt with widely spaced red stripes and plain white collar and cuffs. He balanced this with a red tie, colorful floral suspenders, and gold cufflinks. *These city-banker types are so predictable*, Marc thought as he sized David up. *They all seem to want to power-dress in the same sort of uniform.*

"Pleased to meet you, Marc," David said as he offered his hand.

"It's good to meet you too, David."

"Come into the boardroom. A couple of my colleagues would like to meet you," David said, his voice echoing in the emptiness of the reception area.

Their boardroom was the biggest Marc had seen. It was enormous, and its table seemed to stretch forever. At least fifty chairs were placed around it. The décor was just as opulent. The best of everything had been used, with no expenses spared.

At one end of the table, two other men waited. David introduced them to Marc, and after shaking hands, they all exchanged business cards. Marc noticed that one of them was a fellow called Kevin Morisset, whom he recognized from the financial papers as the bank's CEO. The other man, Brian Cavendish, was also a general manager and operated in the bank's corporate governance area.

After all the formal introductions were concluded, David told Marc of his bank's keen interest in the takeover plans that were in process with the Vanity Homes Group, emphasizing to Marc the importance of this group to his bank.

"We've had a long and valuable association with Myles Vanity and his companies," David said.

"Yes, it hasn't always been easy," Kevin added. "But Myles has always come through, and we now see his group as one of our most valued customers; we value the business very highly."

"Banking is all about relationships," David told Marc. "We stood alongside Myles when he needed us, and he has returned the favor over the years by maintaining his banking loyalty."

All right guys, I get the message, Marc thought as he fall back in his chair under the two pronged barrage from the bankers.

"We'd certainly like to maintain this relationship with anyone who might take over the operation. That's why we'd like to talk to you about any plans you might have in that regard," Kevin said.

Marc nodded his head to acknowledge his understanding and prepared to respond. "Well, it's no secret, at least in some circles, that I am in the process of acquiring the operations of the Vanity Group," he began. "I'm still looking for the necessary funding to take over these companies. As part of this arrangement, I'd also like to provide some additional working capital for the group."

David leaned forward, an accommodating smile flashing across his face. "Can we be of assistance in that regard?"

"Possibly. I've engaged a firm of merchant bankers to assist me in putting together a proper proposal that will outline my needs and plans for Vanity."

"May we ask who that is?" David inquired.

"Whitney, Whyte and Partners. I'm dealing with Adam Boyd, the senior partner."

David nodded. "Oh, yes. We know Adam and the firm, and have had a number of dealings with them over the years. In fact, I think we've just concluded a rather large deal with them, underwriting a public share float they promoted, I believe."

"Yes, that's right," Brian Cavendish said, joining the conversation.

"We know the Vanity businesses fairly well," Kevin asserted, "and have taken the liberty of projecting some figures on its possible value and capital needs in anticipation of our meeting today. As we said at the outset, we are keen to continue our involvement with the group, even if there is a change in ownership."

Marc felt that he was being asked to put his management credentials on the table. He paused for a moment to get everybody's attention before delivering his vision for Vanity. *I'd better make this good,* he thought as he sucked in a deep breath. "In a nutshell, gentlemen, I believe I can rationalize this group by reducing its overhead dramatically while increasing its overall efficiency. In addition, I believe there are a number of excellent opportunities for this group to expand its market share by better developing the current markets it and its subsidiaries currently enjoy."

"That'll require a good deal of experience and managerial knowledge," Brian Cavendish observed.

"I'm confident that we'll have that expertise, particularly as I intend to retain a number of the current key people at Vanity," Marc replied. "With my guidance, we can set up a culture that'll allow this group to be run more like a public company."

"We find that interesting, Marc. We've always wanted Myles to run the place a little more, shall we say, at arms' length," David confided with a wry chuckle, appearing to share an inside joke with his colleagues. "We have also had a lot a dealings with Myles' right-hand man, Stephen James, and have found him to be an asset to the group."

Marc nodded. "Yes, I feel the same way. He figures highly in my plans. In fact, I plan to promote him to general manager after the takeover."

"That's very good to know," David said with a smile. He looked down at the file in front of him and started flipping through papers as he prepared for his next question. "Have you determined your borrowing needs yet?"

Marc had decided in advance to set the figure higher than he needed in order to gauge their reaction and get a feel for how keen the bank was to deal with him. "I'll need to borrow something like $35 million to conclude this deal and properly capitalize the post-takeover group," Marc said, projecting his determined chin.

Kevin didn't flinch. "May we ask how much you're paying for the group?"

"$45 million for everything."

David seemed to drop out of the meeting for a few moments as he did some mental arithmetic. A troubled expression ran over his face.

"Assuming that the value of the companies is as you believe, this gearing appears a little high for such a risky loan," he objected. "Thirty-five million dollars divided by $45 million would have you geared to about eighty percent!"

"I have other assets which I'll bring into the new group, such as commercial property in which I currently have about $7 million worth of equity," Marc offered. "And this will increase when I fully develop it. At the same time, I'll take other non-core assets out of the group upon settlement. I feel the gearing should level out at between sixty-five to seventy percent when the new entity is reappraised after the takeover," Marc added to show that he, too, was on the ball.

The CEO waved away any concerns with a flourish of his right hand. "Those gearing levels don't scare us away, particularly if you have a good business plan. We'd like to see that and any other post-takeover projections you might have, but we want you to know we are very interested in continuing the relationship that we currently have with the Vanity Group," Kevin confirmed.

Great! Marc inwardly celebrated as he worked to hold his exterior reaction in check. "I'm pleased to hear you say that. I'll have to discuss it with my people at Whitney Whyte's to see what they think," Marc said in a noncommittal way.

"We place a considerable premium on the value of the business that Vanity Homes brings to this bank. It is a valuable resource for a lot of home loans and associated finance for us. With that in mind, I can assure you that we'll look favorably at any deal that you might put to us," Kevin assured him.

"Kevin, I'm sure that your bank will have an opportunity to be involved in this process. When that happens, I'd like you to move with haste. I want your best terms, so please don't make me drag them out of you. I hate getting into 'Dutch auctions,' and if that happens, I often find myself walking away from those who expect several bites of the same cherry!" Marc said with a note of warning in his voice.

Kevin straightened his posture and looked suitably concerned. "We hear you, Marc. And we can assure you we'll do the right thing!"

* * *

That was a good meeting; I wonder what my advisors will make of it? Marc thought as he walked toward Whitney Whyte's Martin Place offices.

Realizing that he had a few spare minutes, Marc checked his watch and noted that Elisa was on her lunch break. He pulled his mobile phone from his coat pocket and rang her at work.

"I'm so pleased that everything went well with Vanity's bankers," she told him in response to his news.

"Yeah; if I'm any judge, they're keen to get in on this deal," he replied as he neared the building. "I really can't talk now, Elisa, because I've arranged to go straight over to Whitney Whyte's offices to report on the outcome of the meeting. How about we get together tonight?"

"OK...why don't you come over to my place at around seven? I'll cook us dinner."

"Great." Knowing that Elisa was as fabulous a cook as her mother, Marc grinned from ear to ear at this news. "See you then, honey."

Marc popped his phone back into his jacket pocket. Catching his reflection in a ground floor shop window in Whitney White's building, he tidied up the line of his coat.

As Marc entered the revolving doors in Whitney White's grand foyer, he remembered how positive the bank had been. *If the bankers are true to their word, then they could make the whole job of financing this takeover very easy*, he thought as he smiled to himself. *If it gets too easy, I may have to ask Whitney Whyte and Partners for a discount on their usual fee*!

*   *   *

"How did it go?" Adam Boyd asked, while showing Marc into his office.

"Pretty good, as a matter of fact."

"Wait—I'll get Jennifer so she can hear what you've got say. No sense in repeating everything, is there?"

Jennifer Watkins, with whom Marc had had more daily contact than anyone else, came into Adam's office. After a brief hello, she listened intently as Marc told them about his meeting with Vanity's bankers.

"That certainly sounds encouraging, doesn't it, Jenny?" Adam said afterwards.

"Yes, it does," she replied brightly. "To tell you the truth, Marc, we've been having a bit of trouble matching your financing needs with the criteria of some of the banks we usually deal with."

Marc cocked an eyebrow. "Why's that?"

"Your gearing is a little too high for most lenders," Adam explained, "and that's a problem. I still think we can do the deal, but it's going to take quite a lot of explaining, and we might end up with a lender who wants more than their pound of flesh just to be involved," Adam finished with a slight grimace.

Marc shot Adam a look of horror—this was the first he had heard of any difficulties. "How do you mean?" he asked.

"If you want to fit into some of these bank's criteria, you may have to reduce the size of your proposed loan," Adam stated. "This may then cause you difficulties in that it will restrict the amount of working capital you can bring into the group. It may also stop you from doing the things you need to do to make the new group operate efficiently."

Marc took a moment to digest this sobering information. *There's always something blocking my way,* he thought as he solemnly shook his head.

"On the other hand," Adam continued, "if we go to a non-institutional lender, they may want some equity in the group to make their risk more palatable. This could mean giving them a shareholding, which you would then have to buy back later or that they would realize if you eventually floated the new group on the stock exchange. Either way, they'll want interest on any money they lend you, as well as a share of the action."

Marc looked at Adam and Jenny in dazed disillusionment. "God, I didn't figure on any of these outcomes!" he said exasperatedly. "I thought that you people guaranteed you could do the deal when you accepted your up-front fee! Now you're telling me how hard it all is."

"We still believe that we can place the loan, Marc," Adam said soothingly. "It's just that it may not be with a *bank*, that's all."

Back to square one, Marc thought bitterly as he put his head in his hands for a moment.

"What happens if I arrange for all or part of my funding needs myself?" he asked. "Do I still have to pay your full fee, or do I only pay a percentage based on the amount of money that you find?"

"The way we operate is that we get paid our full fee regardless of who finds the money or which lender advances the funds," Adam said emphatically. "It's based on the successful completion of the original deal."

Marc raised his head to give Adam a dismissive look. "Not a bad business, eh, Adam?" he noted sarcastically. "Someone engages your firm, then finds himself doing all of the work to secure the funds and still ends up paying you for the privilege of doing your job! It's a bit like having a dog and doing your own barking, isn't it?"

Adam looked away sheepishly for a moment. When he turned back to face Marc, he sat up a little straighter and looked his client in the eyes.

"I'm afraid so, Marc, but it won't come to that. We have to prepare many documents to facilitate any loan, and that's one of our main tasks.

We really do know what these lenders want to see and how to present this information," he assured his client.

Marc sighed. "I made a deal with you, and I'll stick by it, even if it turns out that I end up raising all of the funds through Vanity's current bankers. I just think it's a little rough, that's all!"

"We really will be a valuable part of the process," Jennifer said, feeling it was now safe for her to reenter the conversation.

"I hope so," said a dejected Marc. "I have to get my money's worth somehow!"

"I've drawn up a list of the additional information I'll need from you to complete the submission for funds," Jennifer said.

"Fine," Marc said, accepting the piece of paper Jennifer handed him. "I also want you to increase the amount to be borrowed from $32 million to $35 million."

Adam shook his head. "This'll only make the job more difficult!" he said.

"I've spoken to the people at the Commercial Bank, and this is what they're expecting to see in our submission," Marc argued. "If I'm any judge, they won't balk at this figure. They're more interested in my future business plans for the group than in imposing a rigid lending ratio based solely on stodgy, fixed assets."

Adam threw up his hands. "OK, Marc, you're the boss. If you think they'll go for it, then that's the way we'll present it," he said somewhat grudgingly.

"They'll go for it," Marc assured him. "We all know how these banks work. My latest projections indicate that I'll need a little more money than I originally planned to run Vanity. I can't go back and ask them for more later on, so we'd better get what we need from them the first time around."

"You're putting a lot of faith in your ability to read these guys," Adam said warily.

"Maybe so, but I believe they'll do the deal at this higher level, particularly when I put all my other assets into the new consolidated group," Marc replied. "These alone will bring down the gearing levels within a range that should be acceptable even to the most conservative bank."

"Will you give us all the final details for the submission?" Jennifer asked.

"Yes, of course. I'll fax it to you first thing in the morning," Marc said as he got to his feet.

Chapter Thirty

Arriving early, Marc used his key to let himself into Elisa's apartment, hoping that time alone on her balcony would allow him to get things back into perspective. It had been the sort of day where he couldn't decide if he'd won or lost. He knew Elisa would help him regain his equilibrium.

Elisa came home, aglow and smiling like a Cheshire cat. She could hardly contain herself.

"What is it, honey?" Marc asked.

Her smile stretched a little wider. "Can't you guess?"

Marc's mouth dropped open. "The professorship?" he gasped.

"Yes! I got it! Ben called me in just after you rang to give me the news."

"Fan-bloody-tastic!"

They hugged, kissed, and danced around Elisa's balcony.

"Ben Allsop was true to his word. That jerk, Jeremy, has been transferred to the university's annex in Armidale in the middle of nowhere, and I've been appointed to his post."

"How did your boss take it?"

"Who cares? Campbell will be retiring in a couple of years, so what he thinks doesn't matter."

Marc put his arms around Elisa. "I'm so glad you finally got your big break, honey. You really deserve it!"

"Oh, I must call Mum and Dad. They've had a huge celebratory dinner planned for ages, and they'll be relieved to finally be able to stage it. Must ring Maddie and Robert and invite them along as well," Elisa said, rushing back inside.

By the time the sun rose again over the harbor city, both Marc and Elisa felt reinvigorated. As they ate breakfast out on Elisa's balcony, Marc was able to see the harbor from a different perspective. From early in the day, this unique, picturesque waterway became a hive of activity. Ferries trundled across the expanse of water, arriving at the main quay from all points up and down the harbor. As water taxis sped across its glassy surface as they picked up and delivered their fares to the most convenient wharf, and sailors pointed their yachts out to sea for a day's leisure in the salty air, Marc recalled the day he and Loren were nearly killed on the harbor. He thought about how differently things could have turned out, and gave silent thanks for the life he now had.

Marc turned toward Elisa with a smile. "The sight of all of this humanity on the move really gets you going, doesn't it?" he observed. "It has the opposite effect you might think it'd have. Instead of wanting to sit back and watch this whole scene play out before lazy eyes, you find yourself wanting to jump into it so that you can be a part of it all!"

"Well then, what are we waiting for?" Elisa said as she sprang up from the table and went inside to grab her bag.

By the time Marc dropped Elisa off at the university and arrived at his office, he was raring to go. His first task was to quickly put together the additional information Jennifer had requested. He revised the numbers to match his increased borrowings before faxing everything off to her by midmorning as promised.

He was now free to tend to some of his other, less pressing building problems. There was still staff to instruct and manage, progress payment claims to process for his various jobs, and checks to be drawn and signed to pay his company's creditors.

Life isn't all about high finance and takeover bids, he reminded himself. It takes a lot of oil to make the wheels of industry turn, and he had found out a long time ago that he often had to be that oil.

This whole sequence of events had made Marc more philosophical than usual, and he found himself talking to his young receptionist, Elle Majors, in the quiet of his reception area. Elle was efficient, dedicated, and loyal, and had never given him reason to complain about any aspect of her performance. She was attractive and dressed smartly, making an excellent first impression to anyone who visited the office.

Today, she listened attentively as Marc waxed lyrical about the pressures of being in business. Elle was used to this. Having worked for him for the past three years and grown up with his business, she had been thoroughly trained in his way of doing things.

"Tell me, boss, do I still have a job?" Elle asked, smiling when he paused.

"Yes, of course," Marc responded with an incredulous laugh. "What makes you ask that?"

Elle shrugged. "It's just that you sound like you're going to throw in the towel."

"I guess I'm just complaining out loud. Don't worry about it, Elle."

I really need this takeover to succeed, he thought as he returned to his office. *I long to be free of hunting down enough money to pay the bills every month. I just want to be able to focus on something more, something that would give my life more meaning.*

* * *

The fax machine in his office rang just as he was preparing to leave for the day. Marc wondered who would be faxing him at eight-thirty at night. It was a twenty-six-page fax from Jennifer Watkins sending him a draft copy of the main submission for the Vanity takeover.

After collecting the last page, he returned to his office, settled back down behind his desk, and started to carefully go through the document. It read well, and covered every aspect of the proposal. After reading through it again, Marc decided to call Jennifer to see if she was still in the office. Somehow, he knew she would be.

"Hello, Whitney Whyte and Partners," Jennifer said, her voice sounding a little wooden at the end of another long day.

"Are you *still* there?" Marc asked, pretending to scold her.

"Yes, I am!" she shot back. "And it has something to do with you and that document I just faxed you!"

"You need to get a life, Jennifer. You know what they say about 'all work.'"

"Oh? What *do* they say about 'all work,' Mr. Braddon? I'll bet you're calling me from work right now, aren't you?"

"Yes," he admitted with a chuckle. "I'm probably the world's worst workaholic."

"I agree," Jennifer delivered smugly. "Anyway, I'd be happy to get a life once this and the other dozen deals I'm working on are all put to bed. I hope you called to tell me you like the submission."

"Actually, yes, I did. I can't see that you've missed anything, and I like the way you reworked the numbers around my higher loan requirements. I'd like to sleep on your report and get back to you in the morning with any comments, but it looks terrific."

"Great. Once you've signed off on the submission, we can get it printed and bound, and submit it to our target lenders and institutions."

"Who do you have in mind besides the Commercial Bank?"

"Quite a few banks, but we don't want to shop this deal all over town. If we take it to too many people, it might have a detrimental effect on the whole deal. We'll want to meet with you again to decide which of these banks you're prepared to deal with."

"I suppose that's a big consideration. I don't want to get into bed with someone who'll make my life miserable after they've got themselves involved with the company."

"That's why we see it as such an important consideration. We want you to succeed after we get the money in place for the takeover. It's not in our best interests either to see our clients hit the wall because of poor planning or bad choices on our part."

"That's comforting," Marc said with a laugh. "It's good to see that you guys are earning your fee."

"If you remember, I told you we would do that," Jennifer chided good-naturedly. "I'll wait to hear from you tomorrow with any changes you might have. We can also set a time for our next meeting then."

"I need to thank you for putting the proposal together so quickly, Jennifer. Maybe we should make our next meeting a business lunch. That way, I can thank you personally and we can discuss how you're going to get a life!"

"OK. Lunch with a non-threatening male would be a nice change, but I'll have to take a rain check. I'm snowed under at the moment."

"That's why we need to talk," Marc said with an admonishing lilt in his voice. "Good night, and thanks for all of your hard work."

Now that he saw his takeover submission in print on someone else's stationery, he was starting to feel more confident about the future. *Funny that*, he thought as he switched the office lights off.

One thing was certain; Marc was now closing in on his destiny. It was now only a matter of time before he would know whether he was going on to bigger and better things, or whether he would be stuck chasing the same sort of clients for money to pay his accounts in a continuous replay of the previous month's events.

Chapter Thirty-one

Almost a fortnight had passed since Marc sent back his comments on the Whitney Whyte's draft. During that time, Marc seemed only to be running from meeting to meeting as he made himself available to his consultants to discuss the different aspects of the eventual submission. This was the pivotal document, upon which the banks would decide whether or not to lend him the money he needed for the takeover. He had met with Adam, Jennifer, Mary and several of their support staff on numerous occasions to thrash out a final strategy, and he was about to meet with them again today.

These people had done this sort of thing many times before, and their main goal was to entice the selected banks into a bidding war so they would fight one another to secure the business. Marc's team was well versed in the psychology of business banking, and knew they had to put these bankers in a highly charged, competitive situation if they were to have any chance of achieving a quick, favorable, and binding commitment.

Marc had accepted Whitney Whyte's recommendation to limit his approach to only four banks. He had also accepted the fact that he had to acquire this loan on the first round, as he couldn't expect to succeed if he had to take his deal to a second tier of banks. He knew from personal experience that bankers were an incredibly fickle lot—no lender wanted to be part of a stale proposal that his competitors had already turned down.

Marc went about his life while trying to take the next few weeks in his stride. He dared not think about the prospect of failure—the catastrophic effect this would have on his life was too horrific to contemplate.

He had resolved to leave things in the hands of his advisers, and was determined to wait for them to contact him. Yet he paced the floor, isolated by his thoughts and fears, hanging on each incoming phone call.

Just when Marc thought the stress was getting unbearable, his receptionist buzzed and asked him if he wanted to speak to a Loren Wilmont, who had insisted she was a personal friend.

What does she want? he puzzled before saying, "Sure, Elle, put her through."

After a short pause, Loren's sultry voice resonated down the line. "Hello, Marc. How are you these days?"

"Good, Loren," he replied politely. "How's married life treating you?"

"Well… " she sighed.

Uh-oh, Marc thought, his senses put on alert. "I see you're not using your married name," he ventured.

"I am, but I thought you might think it was my husband's mother if I didn't use a code!" She giggled nervously.

"Fair enough." There was something about this conversation that wouldn't let him relax. *What's she up to?* he wondered. After an awkward pause, he managed, "Well, this is quite a surprise."

"You know I could find you even if you hid under a rock!" Loren smirked as she repeated her favorite line.

"Yeah, I guess so," he responded with an uneasy laugh. *What's she up to?* he wondered as he hung on her next word.

Loren's voice dropped to a husky murmur. "I do miss you, you know. It's not the same."

Here it comes, Marc thought with a grimace. "Well, of course it's not the same, Loren…"

"I really miss you."

"Yeah, we had some great times together. But…"

"Can we get together for a coffee today? There's something really important I need to talk to you about."

"I don't think…"

"Look, you always said you'd be there for me if ever I needed you and, well, I need you."

I knew I was going to regret those words, Marc thought as he bit his lip. "OK, OK," he relented. "But let's do it tomorrow instead. How about we meet at that café down at the Quay…you know, the one where we used to go."

"Michael's?"

"Yeah, that's it. I can be there at three. Is that OK?"

"I'll meet you there. Oh, and thanks, Marc."

Marc slid back in his chair and pondered her call for a few minutes. *What have I just done?* he wondered.

*   *   *

Elisa was there for him every night to bolster him up after he had suffered through the torment of another day without news. Ironically, Elisa's working life was now going along beautifully. She had taken to her new professorship like a duck to water.

Even with all of her support, Marc still found himself standing alone on her balcony at three in the morning, looking across the harbor to the city with its partially lit high-rise offices crowned by neon signs.

He now had the added pressure of his upcoming meeting with Loren to further cloud his thinking. He had considered telling Elisa all about Loren, but rationalized that it would serve no useful purpose and would only worry her unnecessarily. After all, he was only going to provide a sympathetic shoulder for an old friend, and he didn't want to risk Elisa getting the wrong idea about it.

With all these thoughts added to the primary burden of his financial survival, Marc stared dully into the vacant high-rises, contemplating what lay ahead if this loan didn't materialize. He found himself peering into a dark, forbidding abyss and shuddered with icy fear. He instinctively grabbed onto the verandah handrail before switching his thoughts to a more positive outlook, like a pilot pulling his plane out of a fatal dive at the last minute. *No! I'm not allowing myself to drop into a chasm of self-doubt; not after coming this far!*

He had the presence of mind to remind himself that he could be only days away from actually succeeding, since he had not heard either way from anyone. Things could be progressing beautifully behind the scenes, and as far as he knew, his people might just be holding up on telling him too much too soon.

Yes, that's got to be it, he thought. He closed the glass balcony door and reentered the warm, safe confines of Elisa's bed.

*　　*　　*

Loren's face lit up as she spotted Marc from her vantage point outside the cafe. As she rushed up to him and planted a kiss on his cheek, Marc smiled a little uncertainly, a little reluctant to reciprocate—knowing from experience that such affectionate gestures of Loren's were often designed to swamp her prey with a warm feeling of how much she cared.

Almost as soon as they sat down at their old table in Michael's café, Loren started complaining about married life.

"It's not all it's cracked up to be," she told Marc when he felt compelled to ask her how she was enjoying being married.

"I'm sorry to hear that. What's it been, six months?"

"Five months and twenty-three days, but who's counting! It's a bit like being in jail."

Is that what this is all about? Marc wondered. "I don't know about that, Loren. It can't be that bad," he said, in an attempt to sidestep the issue. "Now, what did we come here to talk about?"

As Loren pursed her ruby lips and blew across the top of her cappuccino, Marc was suddenly ambushed by a rush of his old desire. *What's wrong with you!* he reprimanded himself. *Elisa would die if she knew you were anywhere near a vixen like Loren. You've got to get control. Loren will always be trouble. It's Elisa you really want, not Loren, so start acting like it!*

Loren expertly translated the look. She leaned forward, her eyes deepening into forest-green pools. "Surely you miss me?" she whispered.

Still stunned, Marc hesitated too long to disagree with her. "Yes, I suppose I do. But I don't miss you in *that* way," he continued hurriedly as a smile began to steal across Loren's face. "That's all behind us...we're just friends now..."

She reached for his hand, her face betraying a hunger that was getting more difficult for her to hide. "I miss you too, Marc," she murmured.

I should've known, Marc mentally flagellated as he took his hand back and started to recite his brush-off speech. "Loren, you're a great person..."

Loren wasn't listening as she unfastened the top button of her blouse, never taking her eyes off him. "If you miss me, and I miss you, then maybe we should get back together."

Marc hastened to break the spell that she was beginning to cast. "But Loren, I didn't come here to ..."

Loren unfastened the next button with a sexy smirk. "Do you want to get a room and play?"

This was too much. "What?" he exploded, causing people at nearby tables to look at them. He lowered his voice to a discreet hiss. "You're married and I'm engaged!"

Loren's hand did a sudden jerk, slopping some of her coffee on to the table. "Engaged?" Her eyes narrowed in hurt surprise. "When were you going to tell me?"

Marc threw up his hands. "Does it matter? Anyway, aren't you concerned your husband will have you tailed?"

"Oh, him! He's a pussycat."

Marc thought about Loren's "pussycat" and how he must have lain in wait for them for months before driving his boat through the middle of theirs. He had sworn never to tell Loren it had been Antonio as part of their truce to settle the Multi-Build fiasco, but today he was sorely tempted to break his word.

"Loren, please be careful," he warned. "Your husband and his family aren't very broadminded when it comes to adultery."

Her face lit up with a smile that reminded Marc of a cat that had just eaten a canary. "Oh, they'll never find out! I'm much too careful for that."

This woman hasn't changed a bit. She's just as devious and self-centered as ever, Marc thought as memories of all the pain of her infidelity came rushing back. In an instant, Marc's resolve hardened.

"Well, I'm not going to test your theory because, unlike you, I'm blissfully happy with my partner!"

The sexy smirk was back on Loren's face, but her eyes were growing deadly serious. "I bet I could change your mind!"

Marc's jaw grew more determined. "You'll never get the chance."

"She can't be as good as I was!" she declared emphatically, her eyes now revealing a hint of desperation.

"No, Loren. She's better."

She reacted as if he had struck her, but still wouldn't give up.

"I want you to fantasize about me licking you from head to toe," she said feverishly as her foot came out of her high-heeled shoe to rub Marc's ankle. "Think about what it would be like to have a woman who wants you to do anything to her, someone who would…"

"That's enough, Loren!" Marc bellowed. "I came here because I thought you needed me."

She appeared to crumble as her eyes filled with tears. "But I do, Marc! I need you so bad."

"I'll get the bill!" he said as he stood, leaving her at the table.

Why did I get myself back into this? Marc wondered, shaking his head as he stood at the cash register waiting for his change. *One thing's for certain,* he promised himself: *There's no way I'm going to let this crazy woman anywhere near my life again.*

* * *

After two weeks of agonized waiting, Marc finally received a call from Adam Boyd summoning him to Whitney Whyte's boardroom, where Adam, Jennifer, and Mary, together with their respective assistants, awaited him.

"Well, we think we've got some good news for you, Marc!" Adam announced. "We have solid offers from three out of the four banks we approached. The fourth has been too slow in getting back to us, so we've decided to move forward with what we've got."

"That's encouraging!" Marc responded, relief flooding his whole being. "Is Vanity's bank among the three?"

"Oh, yes; the Commercial Bank was the first to respond late last week," Jennifer replied. "We told them we would need a week or two to consider their offer in detail. We also told them we had to await the other bank's responses before we could get back to them with a clearer indication of our position."

Adam rubbed his chin for a moment. "I suppose they have a distinct advantage over the others in that they know the business," he observed. "We felt it would be good to make them wait while we got the other offers together. We don't want anyone to think that we're too eager by accepting the first offer that comes along, do we?"

"I suppose not," Marc replied, shaking his head wearily. "But I don't mind telling you it's given me a good deal of heartburn to have to wait until now to find out what you were up to!"

"We're sorry about that, Marc," Mary offered, "but we had to check out the various legal ramifications and other implications of the offers to ensure that we were in position to properly advise you."

"Fair enough. Well, what is on the table?"

"The most favorable offer is from the Commercial Bank, as you might expect, but we still think we can get them to do a little better," Adam said.

"Yes, they're quite keen to keep the business," Jennifer chimed in, "and we figure we can get them to shave another half percent off their interest rate while allowing you a slightly more flexible plan in the way they propose to take their securities for the loan."

"Marc," Mary began, "we're concerned that you maintain a position that will allow you maximum flexibility with your available assets in order to have as many as possible available to you, should you ever need to mortgage them to raise additional capital. Flexibility is the key to survival, as you know."

"To that end, we think we can get a slightly better deal out of Commercial," Adam advised him. "We all want you to succeed, and experience has taught us to negotiate everything at the front end of the deal."

"Yes, you can never successfully negotiate with anybody, particularly a bank, if you have your back to the wall. It really is a matter of who's holding all the cards," Mary added.

"I agree with all of that, and I'm glad I hired you all," Marc said, grinning. "I just don't want to lose the loan along the way."

"Neither do we," Adam replied with a chuckle. "I suggest that you let us gauge the reactions of the bankers as we go; we can then set our requirements accordingly."

"I'm more than prepared to do that. Just keep me up to date with your negotiations on a daily basis," Marc pleaded. "I can't stand sitting in my office staring at the walls and wondering what you're doing on my behalf!"

Adam nodded compassionately. "I hear you, Marc. Jennifer will talk to you regularly to keep you right up to speed on everything that's happening."

"There's another matter I need to discuss with you, Marc," Mary said. "It's about all the legal documents I'll have to produce to tie up the whole Vanity purchase. I haven't wanted to spend thousands of dollars of your money so far to produce reams of paper to consummate a deal that might not happen. Now, if you're confident we're going to be able to firm up the financial side of things, you should instruct me to finalize the legal documentation."

"I think we should go ahead and get that tidied up without further delay, Mary," Marc replied, smiling. "I want to be ready to move as soon as everything is in place with the bank! I'll take the risk on spending the money because I've got every confidence in my team's ability to put this together." A good feeling permeated the room.

* * *

He rushed over to the university to tell Elisa the news. She put the papers she was grading for the next lecture aside for a moment to hug him in a spontaneous outpouring of relief and joy.

"Now I really have to get through these papers before my next lecture, Marc," she told him, "but you can stay here as long as you're a good boy and don't interrupt me!"

"OK, I'll be good," he said in his most obedient schoolboy voice as he sat down on the end of her desk. "I promise."

Elisa then left Marc to his own devices, which meant that he had to keep himself occupied while resisting his urge to toy with her as she tried to concentrate on her work.

Looking around the room, Marc realized that this was the first time he had *really* looked at Elisa's office because, up till now, he had just accepted it for what it was—Elisa's office. On closer examination, he saw that it was an interesting, very personalized room. It reflected part of her character, a side of her that he was seeing for the first time.

Every available shelf was filled to capacity with artifacts and figurines that she and her students had dug up over the years. The objects filled every corner of her office, making it a kind of inner sanctum.

The walls, like those in the other offices, were lined with imitation mahogany veneer. Only a small single window facing one of the courtyards eased the claustrophobic feeling emitting from the dark paneled walls. Where possible, Elisa had covered them with bright posters depicting everything from archaeological displays at different museums around the world to the showing of movies like *Casablanca* to be held at some obscure, middle-eastern theatre.

In her inimitable way, Elisa had created a neatly stacked library of black, hard-backed binders and arranged them in perfect order, using dig locations whose significance and importance were known only to her as the criteria for their order. This was immediately contradicted by papers sitting in disarray on every other available flat surface in the room. Only she knew the location and content of these stacks, and perish anyone silly enough to mess with her meticulously organized mess.

"Well, I suppose I'd better get back to the office and get on with things!" Marc said as Elisa raised her head from a paper she was marking.

"I'm sorry I can't go with you for a celebratory drink, but duty calls," she said, looking at the rest of the papers ruefully.

"That's all right. I didn't expect to bolt in here and drag you out on a whim. How about dinner tonight at our favorite little Spanish place?"

Elisa's face lit up in anticipation. "I'd love that. You can tell me about your meeting over a glass of nice Sangre De Toro—I'll look forward to that. Shall I meet you there at around seven-thirty, or do you want to pick me up here?"

"No, I'll collect you, my love. I don't want you running around the city alone in the dark."

Elisa smiled appreciatively. "Ever my shining knight," she murmured as she stood up and hugged him.

As Marc left, Elisa's smile took on a different quality—it was as if she knew something. She looked over at the picture of Marc on her desk. "You're truly on your way now," she said tenderly.

* * *

The next morning, Marc sat in Mary Arness' office, listening intently to what she had to say.

"I know you have a binding agreement in place with Myles, but we'll need something much more substantial to lock this deal up to the satisfaction of a lender," Mary said.

"Up till now, I've been satisfied that Myles is a man of his word. But," he said with a shrug, "as you say, we can't afford to slip up once we get the approvals in place."

"That's right, we need to have a tight set of documents signed, sealed, and delivered as soon as possible. What do you think of these?" Mary laid out a set of papers across the meeting room table. "There is an agreement, a memorandum of understanding, and several other ancillary documents tying up the deal as you've explained it to me. Everything in these documents will allow you to take over and operate the companies from day one."

"I see you picked up on the provision for the simultaneous settlement of the land assets I'm giving back to Myles. And the deed he must sign to guarantee me the use of his name and image for the new group of companies," Marc said as he flicked through the documents.

"Everything should be there, Marc, but I think you should take a copy with you and quietly read through it. Let me know if you need any changes or find something I've missed. Once you're happy, I'll send a set over to Vanity's solicitors."

"I'll call you tomorrow, Mary. I'm pretty keen to bring everything to completion as soon as possible, so I don't want to be the one holding things up!"

Within a couple of days of giving Mary the OK to send all the papers to Vanity's solicitors, Marc was again summoned to a meeting with his advisers. He knew there were now firm offers on the table from all four banks. All of the details had been worked out, and it was now up to his advisers to submit their recommendations for acceptance. The meeting was to be held in Mary's offices, since a number of documents had to be executed in order to go forward with whichever loan Marc decided to accept.

At the end of the presentation, a discussion ensued about the relative merits of each proposition. No matter which way they looked at the other proposals, the one from Commercial Bank always came out on top. Finally, after everybody had had his or her say, Marc decided he would go with the offer from Commercial. He was ultimately swayed by this bank's offer to provide all the funds to settle the transaction within four weeks from the acceptance of their letter of offer.

Marc had to sign a copy of this letter to signify his acceptance of the loan and its various conditions. He also had to execute a whole lot of related bank documents to activate the loan.

Mary and her people had checked everything, so Marc had no difficulty signing on the dotted line, signing both on his own behalf and on behalf of his various companies by affixing the company seal in the appropriate places.

If Marc had reason to complain about how slowly things had moved up to this point, he now had to contend with the opposite situation. Everything started happening at once, and he was now more grateful than ever that he had a team of expert advisers to look after his interests. There were documents and minute arrangements being hatched by the hour, and so much activity that his head was spinning as he struggled to keep up. *I feel as though I'm being challenged to stay ahead of all this paper,* Marc thought as he signed yet another batch of documents.

He was nearing exhaustion as he tried to run his existing businesses while also trying to attend to every new detail that kept cropping up as everyone tried to keep the takeover on track. No sooner had he met the latest requirement identified by his bankers or solicitors than something else would loom as critical. Although everything had to be attended to and his advisers were doing everything sequentially, the sheer volume of paper generated on both sides of the transaction was mind-boggling.

Finally, there was a lull: Marc had a week until his next meeting was scheduled to occur, during which the whole transaction was to be settled. Marc had been invited to this settlement, which was somewhat unusual, since such meetings were usually the province of lawyers and bankers. This time, the meeting would be held in the large boardroom at Whitney Whyte's city offices—probably the only boardroom in the entire Sydney CBD Marc had not yet visited.

As this meeting was somewhat ceremonial, Marc asked if he could invite Elisa to witness its conclusion. "Yes, of course," was Mary's immediate response. "She's most welcome."

* * *

In recent months, Marc had told Elisa about his tour of Sydney's most grandiose boardrooms. All of them seemed to have one thing in common: their size and grandeur was such that it made one wonder how they could fit within the limited space of a high-rise office building.

But as they entered the large boardroom at Whitney Whyte's city offices, they were both taken aback by its opulence.

"Does *everyone* in this city have grand boardrooms that reek of success and money?" Elisa asked him under her breath.

Marc smiled at Elisa and said, "I think they're all making too much money."

This room was accessed via heavy double wooden doors positioned at its center. Immediately to the right was a huge, ancient wood table surrounded by forty heavy chairs upholstered in a tasteful period print. The table took up about half of the room.

At the other end was a massive bar set against the far wall, similar to what one might expect in some of the world's better hotels, and it was carved out of a dark wood similar to that of the boardroom table. A white-jacketed barman behind the bar was polishing glasses and setting up quietly. Facing the bar were lounge chairs and small tables arranged in convivial patterns like an exclusive gentleman's club.

Marc and Elisa were shown to their seats next to Mary Arness, Adam Boyd, Jennifer Watkins, and their assistants. Marc spotted the fellows from the Commercial Bank at the end of the table and introduced Elisa to David Rhodes, who then introduced her and Marc to his team of bank representatives and solicitors. Everybody then settled down to await the arrival of Myles Vanity and his team.

Well, we finally made it, Marc thought as he smiled at Elisa and made himself comfortable in his seat. The settlement was arranged for exactly eleven, and each group readied itself by rechecking all the various documents they needed to complete the transaction.

No one seemed too concerned that Myles had not turned up by 11:05, and most put it down to a last-minute traffic hitch or something similar. At 11:10, the various groups started to murmur between themselves. At 11:15, Marc was starting to become concerned that Myles had changed his mind.

At 11:23, the boardroom doors swung open and in rushed Myles and his entourage, all stressed and out of breath.

"I'm terribly sorry," Myles said in between gasps. "Our taxi got caught in a cross-town traffic jam, and after waiting in the cab for fifteen minutes without going anywhere, we decided to walk the last four blocks ourselves."

Everybody understood and accepted Myles' apology. Marc let out a quiet sigh as he dared to relax.

After all the proper introductions were made, Marc and Elisa sat back while the legal people went through their routine. Documents were checked and double-checked for signatures as parts of the transaction were completed. First, there were the papers regarding the purchase of the Vanity Group's assets. Then the property within the deal had to be dealt with and its ownership transferred, and finally, the various deeds of agreement had to be signed and exchanged.

The Commercial Bank then provided checks to meet to the various payments. David Rhodes, who already knew Myles from their banking dealings, ceremonially handed over to him the biggest check for $30 million. Marc was asked to join David and Myles, and the three men all shook hands and held the check up for a photographer.

David then handed over a series of other checks and finally put one for nearly $2 million into Marc's hand to cover the additional working capital he had requested. It would immediately be deposited in his new Commercial Bank account.

"Well, ladies and gentlemen," Adam suggested after all business was concluded, "shall we retire to the bar for a drink to seal our dealings?" Elisa beamed, all her confidence in Marc justified. "You did it!" she whispered into his ear as she squeezed his hand.

"Yes," Marc replied, almost in disbelief. "I did, didn't I?"

Chapter Thirty-two

After enjoying two celebratory drinks with the party of bankers and advisers, and accepting all of their hearty congratulations and good wishes, Marc and Elisa bid farewell to everyone and left to plan their own celebration. They felt like screaming for joy in the middle of Martin Place, but held off as dozens of somber, business-suited men and women milled about the busy plaza, bringing back a sense of time and place.

Marc still had to pinch himself to believe that in the last few hours, he had fulfilled a plan that, up until today, he had only dared dream about. Marcus Braddon was now the owner of the Vanity Group of companies, and could make his dreams come true with impunity.

"Your place or mine?" Marc asked, as the cab he had hailed pulled up at the curb.

"Your place, I think. If I know you, you'll become restless when you start thinking about how you're going to handle things at Vanity in the morning, so it's best if we stay at your place."

A knowing smile passed across Marc's lips. "God, I knew there was a reason why I decided to marry you! You really do think of everything, don't you, beautiful?"

Elisa raised an approving eyebrow. "That's because I know you so well. If you're too far away from all of your bits and pieces, you start to get fidgety. This way, you can break off at any time to prepare yourself for your big day tomorrow."

"OK, my place then." He gave the driver his address before settling into the back seat of the cab with Elisa.

Marc's had chosen his apartment in Glebe for its proximity to his offices, which were located on the southern fringe of the Sydney CBD in the suburb of Strawberry Hills. He preferred to live close to the city, and enjoyed the freedom of being able to get anything he needed whenever he needed it through the array of twenty-four-hour services available. He realized that if he moved his headquarters to Vanity's offices in Silverwater, it would add half an hour to his daily commute between home and office, but that was a small price to pay for the continued advantages of city living, not to mention financial survival.

As soon they arrived, Marc called Maddie and Robert to tell them his good news. They were delighted, and confirmed they would be coming to his celebration dinner that evening. "We'll meet you here at seven-thirty then," Marc told his sister.

"Is everything OK?" Elisa asked as she dialed her mother's number.

"Yup. They'll meet us here at seven-thirty. That'll give us plenty of time to pick up your parents. I've booked Don Quixote's for eight," Marc said with a jovial smile. "Somehow, it seemed appropriate for a man who also likes tilting at windmills!"

After spending fifteen minutes on the phone to relate the day's events to her parents and tell them about the dinner arrangements, Elisa looked at Marc, who had been busily calling his friends and associates on his mobile phone at the other end of the apartment.

"What do you want to do now?" she asked, after going to the refrigerator to fetch a bottle of their favorite white wine. Marc placed two long-stemmed glasses on the kitchen table before rummaging through the drawers for the corkscrew.

Marc's eyes were full of suggestion as they met Elisa's. "At times like this, when we achieve a truly great moment, I just want to make passionate love to you before collapsing in your arms and letting the warmth of your lovely naked body rejuvenate my battle-weary soul."

Elisa cocked her head and shot Marc an approving smile. "I was thinking exactly the same thing! This time, though, I'll be making out with a soon-to-be very rich young man, which makes it all even more exciting."

Marc threw Elisa a look of mock surprise. "Oh? And here I was thinking you were such a nice girl, so unaffected by wealth and all that stuff!"

Elisa smiled broadly and threw up her right hand, as if to stop Marc in his tracks. "Hey, give me a break! I'm only human, you know," she responded with a laugh. "Anyway, I'm curious to see if your newfound success has changed your performance in bed. Not that I've had anything to complain about so far."

Marc raised his eyebrows. "Hmmm. Daring me to be great again, are you? Let's see if we can light your fire," he said, chasing her into the bedroom and causing her to spill most of her wine as she laughed and scampered ahead of him.

* * *

"Wow, oh wow!" Elisa said with a sigh. "We've made love before, but I think this bordered on indecent! I won't try to put a name on it, but it was great! Do you think your successes will always have such an impact?" she inquired with an impish grin.

"I hope so. It *was* terrific, wasn't it?" Marc said as he slid under the sheets and beckoned Elisa to join him. "Let's just stay here for a couple of hours. We'll snuggle up and let the world pass us by. Who knows, we might even be able to do it all over again!"

"Sounds like a plan," Elisa said with a mischievous glimmer in her eyes.

Marc's mood began to change as they lay together. Looking into Elisa's deep blue eyes, he allowed himself to show his vulnerable side for a moment. "You know, sometimes I see myself as a selfish person, consumed by my problems and focused only on business. And I worry about not supporting you as much as I'd like in the things that are important to you."

A puzzled expression crossed Elisa's face. "You're anything but selfish, my love. You're probably the kindest man I know, and I love you for that. It's OK for you to look out for your business interests. It's what makes you function. I'm lucky to be able to tap into the other parts of you, and I love doing that!"

Marc smiled warmly at his fiancée. "When I'm with you, I feel whole—complete, somehow. You make it natural for me to be the way I want to be, if only the whole bloody world would stop getting in the way!"

Elisa propped herself up on her elbow and kissed Marc softly on his forehead before settling back down next to him. "I think I know what you mean. It must just be part of the magic between us, I guess." After a moment's pause, she added, "I get a lot from you, too, you know. When I needed to defend myself against that horrible Jeremy person and the other chauvinists in the university, I drew on some of what you taught me about your battles. That's probably why we're so good together—we complement each other."

Marc's smile stretched the corners of his mouth as he looked upon Elisa with wonder. "Why are you women so smart? Seems to me you had this whole thing figured long ago while here I am, still struggling to find the right questions to ask."

"Shush, my darling," Elisa said, resting his head on her soft bosom. "I intend to take the rest of our lives to try to explain it to you."

* * *

The two owners of Don Quixote's had recognized Marc's name on the reservation list, and were now on hand to show him and his party of six to their table.

Peter Zubreroff immediately linked the choice of restaurant to Marc's exploits, and proposed a toast: "To Marc and all the other noble Quixotes in the world."

Robert, Maddie, Alexandra, Elisa, and Marc all laughed out loud and happily joined the toast.

"It's mind-boggling just how far you have come," Maddie said, her brown eyes shining with admiration of her brother. "It seems like only yesterday that you that turned up at my place after you won those concessions from the two men who tried to exploit your skills for their benefit. What were their names again: Vic and Bruno, wasn't it?"

"Vic and *Alan*," Marc corrected.

"Close enough," Maddie replied with a smirk. "I wonder what ever became of them?"

"You know, I haven't heard of either of them for years," Marc said with some surprise.

"I'll bet they'll choke on their cornflakes when they read the morning papers!" Robert joked.

Alexandra beamed proudly at her future son-in-law. "Are you ready for your big day tomorrow, Marc?" she asked.

"We picked out a new suit for Marc to wear when he makes his grand entrance," Elisa answered.

"I couldn't say no," Marc said sheepishly as his sister shot him a bewildered look. "You know what they say: 'Clothes maketh the man,' or something like that."

"It's only partially true, Marc," Peter corrected with an approving smile. "After all, there has to *something* of quality inside all those fancy clothes."

"And you've proven you can go the distance, Marc," Robert chimed in.

Marc felt himself blushing at all the compliments from the people who were closest to him. As he looked into their joyful faces, he took a moment to master the emotions that threatened his composure. He raised his wine glass.

"Now, let *me* propose a toast: To the most important people in my life. Each of you in your own way has made an immeasurable difference, and I thank and salute each of you." The whole group responded with wide smiles as they raised their glasses in response.

With that, the high-spirited group settled down to spend a memorable night together celebrating Marc's remarkable rise to the top of the business world.

Chapter Thirty-three

Marc's first day as the new owner of the Vanity Homes Group didn't start off with a triumphant entry into their Silverwater offices. His first order of business was to visit his old offices to set up a workable communications system, now that he would be based in Vanity's palatial offices. *No sense in keeping two sets of offices*, Marc thought, particularly since he planned to integrate his existing operations to increase the overall size of Vanity and to take advantage of the economies available through this merger.

He left his secretary, Elle, to hold the fort. She would field all calls and convey that everything was business as usual with his existing operations. This would allow Marc enough time to inform his clients of his relocation, and to assure them that his new business arrangements would not adversely affect them.

While he was in his old office, a call came in from Larry Symes, with whom he had spoken on several occasions since their initial meeting.

"How are you doing?" Marc asked.

"Just about there, Marc! I've got written expressions of interest from three major organizations. Each one wants to take one complete building, and I now have a firm price and construction time from Civil Holdings."

"That's great!"

"Yeah; we need to meet soon to devise a plan of attack to tie up the financial and contractual sides of this project. As I told you before, we can probably use the banks you currently deal with to stitch this whole thing up. When can we meet?"

"I don't have any time right now; I need a few days to sort things out at my new operation..."

"Yeah, congratulations about Vanity Homes—its all over the morning papers," Larry interrupted. "It sounds like a terrific buy."

"Thanks, Larry. How about I call you tomorrow, and we get together later in the week?"

Marc jumped in his car and started out for Silverwater. He had phoned earlier to tell the Vanity receptionist that he would be there at eleven.

He also asked that she tell Stephen James he wanted to see him as soon as he got in. *I hope that doesn't put the fear of God into him,* Marc thought as he drove along Victoria Road. He imagined what it would be like, were he in Stephen's position and his new boss said he wanted to see him even before arriving in the office.

As he drove into Vanity's parking lot, Marc was besieged by a gaggle of reporters who had obviously been tipped off about his arrival. They fired a barrage of questions as he climbed out of his car.

"What plans do you have for the Vanity Homes Group, now that you're the owner?"

"Will you be breaking up the group so you can sell it off separately?"

"Will Myles Vanity have any part of the new arrangements?"

As the reporters descended upon him, Marc held his hands up as if to hold them off. "Steady on, fellas. This is my first day on the job, and I haven't even made it into the foyer yet! I think you're expecting too much from me. I'll be happy to talk to you once I've had time to get a feel for the place," Marc said.

"Can you at least tell us of your immediate plans for the building companies?" one of the reporters asked. "There are a lot of people out there who're in the process of getting a Vanity home built. They must be worried by this takeover."

Marc delivered a confident smile. "I can only say that my takeover will strengthen the companies. I am injecting additional capital into the group, and with my other activities, the Vanity companies will become an even stronger force in the industry," he answered smoothly.

"What sort of additional capital are you injecting?" another reporter asked.

The nerve! An incredulous look passed over Marc's face, but rather than bite the reporter's head off, he composed himself to deliver a calm reply. "Vanity's a private group. You know you're not privy to that sort of information," he said in a chiding tone. "Ladies and gentlemen, I haven't even put my feet under my new desk yet. I'd be happy to give any of you an interview by appointment once I've settled in. Until then," Marc concluded with a disarming smile, "I ask you to let me go inside without the escort you've all so kindly provided for me."

They slowly dispersed, the financial press with their notebooks safely tucked away while the evening news crews checked to ensure that they had enough material before heading back to polish the raw footage for the six o'clock news.

As Marc walked into the front doors, the receptionist smiled. "You handled that very well. Mr. Braddon," she said as she stuck out her hand. "I was here when you first came to see Mr. Vanity, but we were never formally introduced, I'm Sally Johnson."

Marc smiled as he shook her hand. "Pleased to meet you, Sally. I wonder how these people knew when I would arrive?" he asked aloud, searching her face for any clues.

"I really don't know, Mr. Braddon," Sally answered with wide-eyed innocence. She looked down at her switchboard that had conveniently lit up again.

Marc smiled knowingly. "Never mind. No harm done," he said as he headed up Vanity's foyer stairs toward his new office.

At the head of the stairs, Myles's old secretary, Margaret Struthers, was waiting to show him to his new office. "Myles cleaned out everything over the weekend," she said. "All his keys and other security items are in the top left drawer of the desk."

Marc put his briefcase down and surveyed the office as he slid into Myles's old chair. Margaret smiled at the ease with which he assumed control and offered him a cup of tea. "You take your tea white with no sugar, don't you? I remember from your first visit."

"Yes, that's right," he replied with an appreciative grin. "Could you please ask Stephen to come into my office and ask him if he wants a cup of something, too?"

A few moments before the tea arrived, there was a hesitant knock on Marc's door. "Come in," Marc told Stephen, and motioned him to one of the two chairs facing his desk.

Margaret followed Stephen in with their cups of tea and asked if she should close the door on her way out. Marc nodded.

Marc slouched in his chair and let out a relieved sigh. "Well, Stephen, it's finally happened! Here we are, the new regime fully ensconced in the palace. I suppose you're wondering what happens next?"

"Yes, I am," Stephen answered a little nervously.

"As I said when we first discussed Vanity, I want to make this company grow and establish itself as an even greater force in the industry. I want it to be the first choice for homebuyers when they think of building a home. When we integrate the activities of my building and land development operations into the Vanity companies, we should end up with a much better balanced group of companies. Once everything is integrated, we should be able to embark on an expansionary program that will allow us to quickly grow the overall group."

Stephen nodded. "I think that's just what the doctor ordered, Marc."

"I suppose you're wondering if you're going to be part of my program or a casualty of it, aren't you?" Marc said with a wry smile.

Stephen looked decidedly sheepish as he prepared to respond. "Well yes, I guess I am."

Marc's expression transformed to reflect his serious focus. "When I took over this group, I decided to follow a particular path. I believe one must understand everything about an operation before effectively changing it for the better. If I were to do this alone, it would take me more time than I can afford, and that's where you come in. I'm impressed with your knowledge of Vanity and your dedication to it."

"Thank you." Stephen said modestly.

"Your work with Myles and the group has given you a unique opportunity to get a handle on every aspect of the current operation. It puts you in an ideal position to advise and manage the integration and growth processes of the new group, now and in the future. In short, Stephen, I'd like to appoint you general manager of the whole operation effective immediately, at a new salary fifty percent higher than your current one. What do you say to that?"

Stephen jaw dropped open. "I say that's absolutely wonderful!"

A broad smile covered Marc's face. "I take it that's a yes?"

Stephen's eyes were wide open as he rushed to respond. "Oh yes, absolutely, yes! I've always wanted to be part of an operation that's really going somewhere, and what better than being able to do it with one I already know so intimately?"

"While I believe we should develop a strategic plan in place for our new integrated operation, I don't want to delay any other plans that you might have, for fear of a new competitor coming on the scene."

Stephen leaned forward enthusiastically in his chair, as if he were beginning to feel he was on safe ground. "To hear you say that is music to my ears, Marc. I've been bound by Myles's lack of vision for too long. I have dozens of ideas for change and growth. Many of these can be implemented immediately. I'd like to run them past you as soon as possible."

Marc grinned at his new right-hand man. "Well, I'll be here most of the time from now on, as I'll have to take a hand in most aspects of the initial integration myself. Tell you what: Go and develop your ideas into a master plan for the group over the next few weeks. Then we'll sit down again to discuss it in detail. In the meantime, we can discuss and implement the immediate changes that need to be made as we go."

As Stephen prepared to leave, a sober expression filled his face. "Thank you for this opportunity, Marc. I won't let you down, and I know you won't be sorry."

In Stephen, Marc had secured a key person who could help him accelerate his plans to turn his new group into a more powerful and profitable building entity. That in itself was a good day's work, but there were still a lot of things to be done on his first day.

Next, Marc had to allay his new employees' fears about their future employment. Before taking over the group, he had resolved not to make any decisions regarding retirements or lay-offs for at least three months, giving Vanity's current employees every opportunity to prove themselves. He had made this decision knowing that his newer, expanded group would be able to use every employee that was worth keeping.

His decision not to sack anybody immediately was made easier by the resignation of all of Myles Vanity's immediate family members upon the completion of the takeover. That had been a condition of the deal, and had been brokered by Mary Arness and her legal team. He was pleased that Mary had insisted on this provision, as it simplified his life no end.

"Mr. Braddon, Stephen said you wanted to see me," Margaret said as she reentered his office.

"Please call me Marc, Margaret. If you want to call me Mr. Braddon, you can do it in front of visitors. Otherwise, it's Marc."

Margaret smiled at her new boss. "OK, Marc."

"I wanted to talk to you about your future here. I want to know if you're comfortable with the change in ownership and if you still see a future for yourself here, beyond your loyalty and the work you did for Myles."

Margaret's expression changed to one of earnestness. "Yes, I hope there's a future for me here. I'm getting along in years and have thought about retirement, but I don't want to go just yet. I'd like to keep on working for a while longer, if you'll have me."

Marc shot Margaret a friendly smile. "I have no problem with that. I'd like you to stay on and become my private secretary. I think you'll be invaluable. I'll wager that you hold a huge chunk of the corporate memory of this group of companies. For a while, it's going to look as if I'm picking your brains, but it's a process I have to go through."

Margaret was suddenly at ease. "I understand. I'd love to become your private secretary. And thank you for the vote of confidence, Mr. Braddon...I mean, Marc."

"Good. I'll need you to coordinate with my current secretary, Elle Majors. She and I will need to spend some time together to nail down a number of my current matters, and she'll work with you initially as part of the handover."

"I'm sure we can share you without getting into a fight!" Margaret said with a wry smile.

* * *

Marc spent the rest of the day meeting his new employees at the Silverwater office and warehouse facility. Stephen introduced him to every employee, explaining his or her functions and departments along the way. By day's end, Marc realized that he had over three hundred direct employees and about nine hundred subcontractors working for him.

How am I going to meet their salaries? he wondered as the scope of his new operation gave rise to a moment of panic. When he asked Stephen about what cash flow difficulties he might expect in that regard, Stephen laughed and said that the incoming cash flow, which was often over $3 million a week from the group's building and manufacturing activities, was very steady and generally took care of payroll without difficulty.

OK, it's obviously too early for me to be questioning the workings of the place? he thought, resolving to see how things worked out before getting overly concerned. Controlling a giant cash flow was going to be a novel experience for him, particularly after being used to managing cash flows less than a twentieth of what Vanity generated.

Marc had to get used to the scale of his new empire, so he decided to busy himself by integrating his present activities into the Vanity operations. He also had to organize the development of his Hillsford office park complex, and figured that by the time he had done all this, enough time would have elapsed for him to accept his new, expanded world.

He was sitting behind his desk in his huge new office, still trying to take in the events of the day, when Elisa called at about six-thirty.

"I just saw you on the six o'clock news," she gushed excitedly. "Apparently you were on all three channels. Mum and Dad saw you on two channels, and I saw you on the other. We all agreed that you looked very handsome and business-like. Rather the Svengali, aren't you!"

"Give me a break, honey!" he pleaded with a laugh. "I just got here. If I appeared calm, I can assure you that I was like the proverbial duck: calm on top of the water while paddling like mad below."

"We all have great faith in you, Marc. It's bound take a while to get the feel of the place, but once you do, there'll be no stopping you. You'll see."

Marc looked over at Elisa's photograph on his new desk and smiled. "I appreciate the vote of confidence. You know, I've already seen how the big end of business works. These sorts of businesses are so strong; they don't worry about such mundane things as making the weekly payroll. It's a given in a business of this size. They seem to be focused on the big picture instead. "

"Isn't that what you wanted, honey? You've always felt trapped by the size of your other businesses."

Marc sniggered. "Yeah, that's right. I think I'm going to enjoy this part of the business world."

"So, on to more pressing matters: Will I be seeing you sometime tonight?"

"Yes, after I finish up a few more things," he answered with a grin. "I should be at your place by about eight, if that's all right. Do you want to go out for dinner?"

"Not tonight. I wanted to prepare us a special dinner to celebrate the end of your first day as the new owner of Vanity. Eight o'clock is fine, and you can tell me all about your day then."

Marc's grin widened, reflecting his immediate appeal at the prospect of a quiet meal with his lady. "Sounds great!"

"Bye, now," Elisa cooed as she hung up the phone.

What a great day! Everything went so well, Marc thought as he put down the phone. Yet he realized the size of the challenges that lay ahead. At least now his future was in his own hands, and he knew he wouldn't allow anything or anyone to wrest control of that situation away from him.

Chapter Thirty-four

Sally Johnson, Vanity's receptionist, told Marc that Larry Symes had arrived for their eleven o'clock meeting and was waiting in the foyer. He ushered Larry Symes into Vanity's impressive boardroom. Although he had been in charge of Vanity for only a fortnight, Marc now had the run of the place.

"Right Larry, what have you got for me?"

"I've now got letters from all the potential tenants and a firm price from the builder. This should allow us to put the construction funding arrangements together because we've eliminated most of the risk for the lender," he said enthusiastically as he handed Marc the letters.

"I think this'll do it," Marc said, scanning the letters.

"Good. Do you have a bank in mind?"

"Yeah, I think I'll approach my current lender on this property. Leave it with me, Larry; I should be able to get an answer within a fortnight or so."

Andrew Innes's bank still held a mortgage on the land, so it made sense to ask him to provide the construction funding. Once the complex was completed and starting to generate income, he would invite Vanity's main banker, Commercial Bank, to provide the take-out funding for Andrew's bank. In this fashion, all his debt would end up in one neat pile. This arrangement would also allow him to use the equity in the finished complex to underwrite Vanity's future needs for additional working capital.

Marc knew that Andrew Innes and his bank were only interested in solid, well-defined commercial property deals and would be happy to participate as the construction financier, provided another bank was standing by to take them out of project at completion. They would be happy to receive the significant fees that this part of the transaction would generate.

* * *

Later that day, when Marc returned to the office after a meeting, Sally Johnson asked him what she should do about all the calls that Loren Wilmont was making.

"Nothing!" Marc said with a determined expression. "She'll get tired of me not taking her calls, and finally get the message."

"Some days I never hear from her, but on others she rings four times a day," Sally said with frustration.

"Look, Sally, it's something I want *you* to handle. I'm too busy to spend my day answering her calls."

"Should I start putting her through to your secretary?"

"No, it's something I want to quarantine at the front desk. It's bad enough that we're both involved in Loren's obsession; let's not involve anyone else in the place, for goodness' sake!"

"OK, boss, but that woman's pretty determined," Sally smiled ruefully.

"So I am, Sally," Marc said as he started to climb the foyer stairs to his office. "So am I."

* * *

Andrew Innes's bank readily agreed to provide the construction funding for the office park complex on the strength of the proposal. The Commercial Bank then gave Andrew's bank an undertaking that they would refinance the complex upon completion, which only added to his level of comfort.

Marc also involved Mary Arness and her people to oversee legal arrangements with respect to building contracts, lease agreements, and banking arrangements. She had no difficulty putting everything in place, and within a month, the builder was on site. Within two months, the complex started to rise out of the ground like a phoenix as the builder fast-tracked the construction by working on all three buildings simultaneously.

Marc's architect, Kenneth Carlisle, oversaw the work. This made it a very easy project for Marc to manage, as he had only to attend the weekly construction meetings to keep abreast of the project, which was scheduled to take nine months and cost $15 million. This meant that Marc would owe about $21 million on the complex after adding the construction costs to his existing land debt. Against this debt, the whole office park complex would be worth at least $30 million upon completion, and would appreciate every year thereafter.

The best aspect of the deal was that Marc would now have income from the rent of the office park's fifteen floors of commercial office space, rather than a sterile land asset that was costing him money in interest and property taxes every year. The rental income would cover all of the interest costs on the new, larger loan of $21 million, and still leave something to spare.

The ongoing construction of his complex was just one more reason why life at Vanity was so interesting in those halcyon days. Marc's can-do attitude permeated every corner of the operations. He changed the whole culture of the new enlarged Vanity Group, and everything improved as a result.

The working week started and ended with a strategy meeting with Marc and his trusted lieutenants. The meetings were a free and frank exchange of ideas and suggestions, as Marc insisted that anyone in the room be allowed to speak up without fear. Constructive criticism was encouraged, and in that spirit of openness, Marc was able to tap into the wealth of experience of his senior management team and thereby focus several good industry minds on the solution to particular problems.

Stephen James was also proving to be an excellent choice as general manager of the new group, and he too, brought about several revolutionary changes.

Within a few months, Marc was able to meet all of his loan repayments from savings made to the previously high overhead costs. The fact that his Hillsford office complex was right on schedule and its rental income would also reduce his ongoing costs was also reason to celebrate.

With his first objective of stabilizing the group now achieved, Marc was able to look for new and innovative ways of expanding turnover and increasing profitability. And without the constant pressure of trying to find loan repayment money, he was free to exercise his mind, allowing it to seek out lateral solutions.

* * *

It was now late in the autumn of 1992, and the happy couple's wedding day was fast approaching. Since Elisa insisted on involving Marc in the planning, she often met in his office and delegated tasks.

This day, Elisa happened to walk into the reception area while Sally Johnson had her phone on speakerphone and her back to her reception desk as she caught up on some filing. Elisa was intrigued when she overheard Sally telling a woman who identified herself as Loren Wilmont that Marc was not in the office. The woman was insistent and said that it was important, to which Sally responded offhandedly: "Well he's still not in."

"According to you, he's never in his office!" the caller responded angrily.

"All I can do is tell him that you called, Ms. Wilmont, " Sally said as the caller hung up.

Elisa wore a puzzled expression as she asked, "What was that all about, Sally?"

Sally spun around in her chair and was startled to see Elisa standing there. Not having time to devise a cover story to protect Marc, she simply told the truth. "She's apparently an old friend of Marc's who keeps calling him," she answered.

"Oh," Elisa mused as she started up the foyer stairs.

Marc smiled broadly as she entered his office. "Hi, honey," he said as he jumped out of his seat to hug her.

Marc noticed that Elisa seemed a little apprehensive. "What's wrong?" he asked.

Elisa looked preoccupied. "I don't like to pry, Marc, but who's this Loren Wilmont person who keeps calling you?"

Marc froze for a second. "Oh, she's just an old girlfriend," he explained quickly. "We're only friends now, of course, but she keeps ringing me. That's all. Certainly nothing for you to worry about, sweetheart," he said with what he hoped was a reassuring smile.

Elisa still looked unconvinced. "But why didn't you tell me about her?"

"Because she's not important," he insisted. "Anyway, who told you that she was ringing me?"

"Sally."

"Sally?"

"Yes. I just happened to walk into reception while she had the speakerphone on—I think she was trying to do two things at once."

"That sounds like Sally," Marc said, shaking his head disapprovingly.

"I'm intrigued. What does this Loren look like? Is she anything like me?"

"She has red hair, and a pale complexion. And she's nothing like you, honey, believe me."

"So I don't have to scratch this Loren's eyes out?" Elisa asked with a playful smile.

"Well not yet, anyway," he replied with a laugh.

* * *

Marc was bushed at the end of the day, and looking forward to some quiet time. He put his key in his front door and was surprised to find it unlocked. *How forgetful can you be?* he chastised himself. Entering the apartment, he noticed that a bedside light in his bedroom was on; a light he distinctly remembered turning off.

He froze in the doorway. *Great, I'm being burgled,* he thought as he picked up a heavy glass vase and moved gingerly through the living room. *Who would be stupid enough to break into a house at nine o'clock at night when everyone's still up? Maybe it's some kids looking for drug money,* he surmised as he moved toward the dim light streaming from the bedroom.

As he got closer, he began to pick up strains of soft music. *Elisa,* he thought as a big grin spread across his relieved face. He put the vase down and crept up to his bedroom door, eager to see what his beloved had in store.

Instead, he was shocked to see Loren naked on top of his bed, beckoning him to join her.

Marc turned white. "What the…"

Loren curled her naked body invitingly. "It's OK, Marc; I'm here to pleasure you."

He felt himself melt into rage. "Are you totally mad?" he shouted. "Have you lost all your marbles? Whatever gave you the idea that…"

Loren seemed to be in a dream world as she tuned out Marc's response. "I found the spare key," she purred. "It was where you always leave it. That's how I know you want me just as badly as I want you."

Marc's anger turned to bewilderment. "Is this some sort of bad stag-party joke or something? Can't you take no for answer?"

It looked like he was beginning to get through. Loren's jaw dropped. "You mean you really don't want me?"

Marc rolled his eyes. "That's what I've been trying to tell you, but you won't listen! You're married, I'm getting married, what part of that don't you understand?" he shouted. "Now for God's sake, get dressed and get out of here!"

Loren shocked expression underlined her disbelief. "You mean…"

"Yes, I mean every word of it."

As soon as she was dressed, Marc pushed her out the front door. He bolted it behind her, resolving to never again leave a spare key on the premises.

* * *

The next morning, Marc rang Elisa at home only to get her answering machine. *That's odd,* he thought. *She never puts her machine on this early in the morning.*

Later in the morning, he rang Elisa at work only to be told by the departmental secretary that she was tied up in lectures all day. Then he rang Elisa's office again in the afternoon only to be told that she was in a meeting.

That evening, Marc got Elisa's answering machine again. He had left several messages over the course of the evening, saying he understood that she was busy and telling how much he had missed talking with her. *What's happening here?* Marc asked himself. *Yesterday, we were a normal couple, and today I feel as though I'm being brushed off.*

Marc felt decidedly uneasy as he settled in to kill some time in front of the television. He eventually nodded off in front of the TV and was awoken at 1 A.M. by the end-of-transmission signal. He looked at his watch as he dragged himself into his bedroom, collapsing exhausted on top of his bed and into a tortured sleep.

Chapter Thirty-five

The next day, Marc decided to visit Elisa's apartment. He rang her intercom without answer and used his key to let himself in. There was no sign that Elisa had been in the apartment in the past few days.

Where the hell can she be? Marc asked himself. He was starting to become panic-stricken. *God, I hope nothing's happened to her,* he gulped as some dangerous scenarios played in his mind. *Maybe she's been called away for some urgent field assignment or something,* he tried to rationalize.

I'll ring her parents; they're bound to know where she is, Marc decided as he reached for Elisa's phone and hit the programmed key marked with parent's phone number.

"Hello Alexandra, it's Marc here. Do you know where Elisa is? I've been trying to call her for days," Marc said, his voice reflecting the strain he was under.

"She's safe and sound," Alexandria responded with an unusually frosty tone.

"Thank God," Marc said with relief. "I've been going out of my mind. I though something terrible had happened to her. Is everything OK?" he asked as he picked up on her strange tone.

"I don't know, Marc. That's something you'll have to ask Elisa," was Alexandra's cryptic response.

"What do you mean?"

"Look, Marc: Elisa saw another woman coming out of your apartment the other night and she's been upset ever since."

Oh, God, Marc anguished. It felt like all his nightmares were coming true at once. The ground dropped out from under him, and he began to feel sick.

"She's been staying with us and she won't eat, drink, or even go to work," Alexandra continued worriedly. "What's happened to you both?"

"She must have seen me with Loren—a *former* friend of mine," Marc stressed. "It was totally innocent—I swear, Alexandra!"

"I'll see if I can get Elisa to come to the phone," Alexandra said.

Marc held the receiver against his chest, chiding himself. *I knew that bloody Loren would stuff my life up, one way or another; why did I let her anywhere near me again?*

After several minutes of muffled discussion, Alexandra came back on the line. "I'm sorry Marc, but Elisa doesn't want to talk to you. There's nothing I can do at the moment—it's going to take a little time, I'm afraid."

Even when he was fighting for his life on the harbor, Marc had never felt so panic-stricken and helpless. "Alexandra, please tell Elisa I love her and *only* her. I would never do anything to upset her. She is the most important person in my life, and I would do anything for her," Marc declared as the horrible sinking feeling permeated his entire being. "It isn't as it looks. Loren Wilmont means nothing to me—I was just pushing her out of my life once and for all, and Elisa got the wrong impression."

Alexandra sighed. "Give it a couple of days, Marc. I'll see if I can talk her around. But I'm sure that nothing will get resolved unless you two start talking to each other again."

"Please believe me, Alexandra—I would never do anything to hurt your daughter."

"I know, Marc, I know," Elisa's mother said before saying goodbye. But there was still a note of uncertainty in her voice that cut him to the quick.

*   *   *

Marc was lucky that he had a general manager to take care of the day-to-day running of his operation, which allowed him to drop out for a short while without disrupting the business too much. While Elisa sought refuge with her parents, he went to stay with Maddie and Robert.

"I'm sure when Elisa saw Loren coming out of my apartment, she assumed that I invited her there," Marc told his sister over their third cup of morning coffee. "Compared to what she thinks, the truth looks pretty far-fetched. How do I get through to her with what really happened? And why does she think that I would want another woman when I have her?" Marc asked with childlike innocence.

"Women feel things more deeply than men," Maddie replied, her brown eyes filled with grave concern. "Elisa may feel a sort of 'emotional betrayal.' It's sometimes worse than actual betrayal, because you put so much of yourself into your partner that you leave yourself wide open to being emotionally crippled if they let you down, or somehow turn out to be less than you thought."

"I made a mistake, all right," Marc said with a shudder. "I just hope it doesn't end up costing me everything."

"I know," Maddie murmured with a reassuring look. "But you can't rush things. You're just going to have to wait your chance to explain to Elisa what really happened."

"Can you ring Elisa and put my side of the story, Sis?" Marc asked anxiously.

"I'll try, but I have to time it right. She needs to be in the mood to listen. If I call before she's ready, she'll just pay me lip service."

"God, this is worse than the agony of any business deal I've ever done," Marc said disconsolately. "What if she wants to cancel the wedding? It's only eight weeks away!"

"Don't you start getting paranoid on me!" Maddie said firmly, shaking him gently by the shoulders in an attempt to dislodge his negative state of mind. "It'll turn around, Marc—you'll see. Just give it time. The truth always comes out."

*   *   *

After a couple of days' leave, Elisa returned to work. She regularly had lunch at the academic-staff only restaurant on campus, and often sat at the same table as the dean of law, James Shearer. James seemed to have an ongoing crush on her, although she had made it clear long ago that they were to be just friends. They discussed a wide range of subjects over lunch, and often talked about aspects of their private lives. Since she was not in the mood to talk about her problems today, she kept the focus on James as much as possible.

"I've always wondered why you never married, James?"

James flashed a suggestive smile at Elisa. "Guess I never found the right lady."

Elisa shook her head in disbelief. "Come on; you must've had hundreds of women to choose from!"

He inclined his head modestly. "Oh, I don't know…" Then, his face darkened. "I think I found it hard to trust anyone after what happened to me several years ago."

Elisa was taken aback. "Oh, I didn't mean to pry…"

"No, no, that's OK. I really should talk about it more; it still burns me up." He lowered his voice. "You see, I fell for a student in a big way. She was the sort who burrows her way into you—I didn't really know how far until she pulled away. As difficult as it may be to believe, I'm still getting over her."

James allowed the familiar vision of Loren Wilmont to flash into his mind. "I still don't know how I came to be involved with her. Somehow, almost without me knowing, she found her way into my life. She probably just stroked the ego I always pretended not to have.

"She had an indestructible quality about her, and it seemed to rub off on me. Although she always talked about the importance of keeping secrets, she happily flaunted the fact that she was sleeping with me to anyone who might give a damn. I suppose she figured that you had to be good to make someone as straight-laced as me forsake all my values and standards.

"The worst part was dealing with our vice chancellor. Ben Allsop pounced on me like a lion protecting its pride when he heard rumors about my involvement with a student. You know Ben; he likes to have his university run like clockwork. Heaven help anyone who upsets his natural order of things.

"He called my into his office and sat me down on his famous olive green leather sofa, before starting his careful cross-examination. Within five minutes, we had reached a point where I held my whole future in my hands. He was smart enough to stop the meeting and give me a couple of days to consider my position before I could back myself into a corner.

"The showdown with Ben made me realize how strongly I felt about Loren, and how much I wanted to keep her in my life. I would have gladly thrown my career all away just to be with this lady, but when I tracked her down and told her what had happened, she acted as if I were from another planet. Over the next twenty-four hours, her undying devotion disintegrated into complete indifference, and I found myself stranded with a problem she'd helped fashion."

As James continued, a flood of bitterness drenched his senses. "I now realize that her life is a sad, pathetic excuse for an existence—one that will inevitably lead to self-degradation and a falling from grace. I have come to realize that it was her beauty and youth that disguised so many of her flaws. She's like a Dorian-Gray type who has several more brush strokes added every day to a secret portrait that is constantly disfiguring itself to reflect her true image." James paused for a moment to reflect on that sobering image before continuing.

"Although it ripped me to the core, I finally saw her for what she really was. The veil that had clouded my thinking had suddenly been lifted, and I couldn't help wondering how many other poor fools had trod the same path."

I wonder if I'm now seeing the same thing in Marc? Elisa thought as her friend's words hit home.

"The next day," James continued, "I called a meeting with the vice chancellor. I decided to tell him the truth and take my chances. After I confessed, Ben was very understanding about it, but he made me promise that nothing like that would ever happen again. I think he let me off because he knew I would continue to suffer. He was right— hardly a day goes by that I don't think of her."

Elisa readily empathized with James's feelings of betrayal. Her emotions showed in her face as she leaned closer to show her support. "I had no idea," Elisa said compassionately.

"Well, I'm still here, Elisa!" James said with a brave smile. "You know, I remember walking back to my office after meeting with Ben. It was a beautiful late spring day, and the birds were full of song. Their chirping was set against the clear, bright blue sky, and gave me a renewed optimism for life. This is where I belong, I remember thinking. I'm sure that any artist painting that scene would not have left me out of their canvas. In that moment, I realized that I was an integral part of it all, just as it was an integral part of me." He shook his head ruefully. "Yes, thankfully, you only meet one Loren Wilmont in a lifetime."

Elisa dropped her spoon and looked at James with disbelief. "What was her name again?"

"Loren Wilmont. She was a final-year law student. She now works in her father's practice. Why do you ask?"

Anything involving Marc was still difficult to talk about, but Elisa decided to push past her reluctance. "My fiancé knows a Loren Wilmont. Apparently she was his girlfriend before we met," she added with a sour look. "Surely it's not same woman…"

"Is she a lawyer?"

"I don't know."

James' brow furrowed as his curiosity began to compete with his concern. "So, your fiancé was her old boyfriend?" he asked. "How long ago were they together?"

Elisa shrugged. "We've been together for just over a year, so I guess it was sometime before that."

James shook his head slowly. "Well, I only hope it's not the same woman. *My* Loren Wilmont is bad news, and I wouldn't wish her on my worst enemy."

*　　*　　*

After Elisa returned to her apartment that evening and cleared her messages, Maddie's was the only call she chose to return.

"How are you?" Maddie asked with obvious concern.

"Terrible!" Elisa confessed. "I don't know what to think anymore. I may have overreacted when I saw that woman coming out of Marc's apartment. But the more I thought about it, the more hurt and betrayed I felt. Every day since has been a downward spiral."

"That woman was Loren Wilmont, Marc's previous girlfriend," Maddie informed her. "It was all over between them when he met you."

"But Marc didn't tell me until I *made* him tell me," Elisa said with a tone of hurt in her voice. "Why didn't *you* tell me about her, Maddie?"

"I don't know…we were all so glad to get her out of our lives, I guess. She was a dark force in Marc's life, and you were the light. The minute you came into my brother's life, everything changed for the better, whereas he seemed to continually struggle when he was with Loren."

"What does this Loren do for a living?" Elisa asked her friend.

"She's a lawyer in her father's city firm, I think…"

"So it *is* her!" Elisa exclaimed.

"What do you mean?" Maddie asked, puzzled.

"It turns out that I know someone else who's had a bad experience with her," Elisa told her. "From what I've heard, she sounds like a terrible woman."

"She is. It doesn't seem important to her that she's married," Maddie told her friend in disapproving tones. "She seems consumed by an obsession for Marc—she's reckless, and doesn't care whom she hurts as long as she can get what she wants. Marc's been trying to shake her off over the past few months, but she just won't let go. Marc didn't want to worry you about something he thought he could control. He loves you, Elisa, and would never be unfaithful to you…and certainly not with that Loren Wilmont woman!"

"Oh Maddie, I've been such an idiot. What should I do? I miss Marc so much, but I'm afraid I've driven a wedge between us."

"Do you trust my judgment, Elisa?

"You know I do."

"Good. Then get in your car and drive straight up here."

"Why?"

"Because Marc's staying with us and he is going round the bend without you, too. You two need to go for a walk along the beach and sort this out."

"I'll grab my bag and come straight up. Thanks so much, Maddie, I'll see you in about an hour."

"Drive safely, sweetie."

*　*　*

That evening, Marc and Elisa found the same weather-worn rock that they sat on their first night together on Whitefeather Cove.

Elisa remorsefully looked into Marc's face and whispered: "Marc, I'm so sorry that I didn't trust you. I should have known better."

Marc smiled ruefully. "I don't think I've ever felt so helpless as when I couldn't contact you," he said openly. "I've been going crazy without you in my life. Please don't ever do that to me again—I didn't tell you about Loren pestering me simply because I didn't want to worry you unnecessarily—and look what happened," Marc said with self-admonishment.

"It's my fault, too," Elisa said, looking sheepish. "I should have at least allowed you to explain. I feel so stupid about the way I jumped to conclusions—love seems to make fools out of even the most sensible of us."

"Let's not dwell on this too much, Elisa. It was our first real spat— but was a beauty, wasn't it?" Marc joked. "Let's just make sure that we can always talk things over if anything ever comes between us again."

"It's a deal!" Elisa said as she turned and kissed Marc's lips.

"Do you still want to marry me?" Marc asked tongue in cheek.

"Well I didn't cancel the church or the caterers, if that's what you mean," Elisa smiled back. "I just couldn't bear to do it. Deep down, I was hoping that this would work out."

"It's only seven weeks this Saturday, but I really wish it were tomorrow."

"Me, too," she said sincerely. "All this has only made me realize how much I want to be your wife."

"I've never been so motivated to do anything in my life, so I guess that makes me just as keen to make you my Mrs. Braddon," Marc responded joyfully.

"I think we have some lost time to make up—why don't we go back up to the house and climb into bed?" Elisa said with a cheeky smile.

"I thought you'd never ask," Marc laughed as he jumped down off the rock and held out his hand to assist Elisa to climb back down to the fluffy white sand.

Chapter Thirty-six

Elisa and Marc's wedding was to be a very swish church affair, with over three hundred and fifty guests invited to the wedding. As the couple drew up the invitation list, they were amazed at how many friends and relatives they both had.

Marc sent his old friend Billy Kennedy a first-class airline ticket with his invitation. When Billy accepted, he was immediately given the job of best man—Robert having graciously stepped aside at the last minute so that Billy could have that privilege.

Elisa chose Maddie to be her matron of honor. Robert accepted a role as one of the two groomsmen and was matched up with Amy Andrews, one of Elisa's oldest girlfriends. It was probably the first time he and Maddie had been parted, but they took it in stride as they muddled through the rehearsals. Marc's old pal, Jim Daniels, accepted the role as the other groomsman and was paired with Susan Reynolds, another of Elisa's old school friends.

Billy arrived from New York a week before the wedding and stayed at Marc's apartment. Marc spent most of that week entertaining him, as Elisa was fully occupied with last-minute wedding arrangements. It took a couple of days to reacquaint Billy with the city that used to be his home.

"I can't believe how some parts of this town have changed," Billy said, shaking his head in amazement as he struggled to recognize parts of the city he used to know.

"I think it's what they call progress," Marc quipped as he took delight in Billy's reaction.

It became a joy for Marc to see the expressions on Billy's face as he showed him all of the new and rejuvenated suburbs. He enjoyed it so much that he decided to take the whole week off to show Billy around. Marc pointed out the houses, townhouses, and other edifices he had built or was now building. At night they talked for hours on end, either at home or with Elisa over dinner at her place or at a restaurant.

Elisa liked Billy, and the feeling was mutual. But her understandable preoccupation with the wedding arrangements meant that she had little time to spend with either Marc or Billy during the week leading up to the big day, which gave both men a chance to revisit old times again.

On the third day of Billy's visit, when Marc took him on a grand tour of his finished projects, the Hillsford office park construction site, and some of the housing estates that Vanity was working on, it was clear that Billy was still trying to come to grips with what Marc had achieved.

"I tell you, Marcy, you've surprised the bejesus out of me," he told him. "I never doubted you'd find a way to make it, but my God, boy, have you found a way to make it!"

Marc's face was a mixture of wonder and pride. "You know, Billy, it wasn't until I started taking you around that I realized what I've done over the years. I just did one thing after the other, and never seemed to look back or think too much about my achievements."

Billy nodded sagely. "That's always been your problem, Marcy. At least *that* hasn't changed. You've never stopped long enough to take in your own achievements. You just keep plowing ahead on to the next big thing! Maybe my coming back will force you to stop and take stock of what you've accomplished."

"Yeah, you've always been able to do that for me, haven't you, you old coot!"

"Hey, hey, hey, a little less of the 'old' if you don't mind," Billy said with a belly laugh.

*   *   *

The wedding went off like clockwork. Marc stood at the altar with his best man and groomsmen, feeling more nervous than he ever had in his life. When the organist began to play the processional march, he turned to face the congregation. He smiled warmly at Alexandra, who was close by in the front row before turning his gaze to Elisa and her father, who had just entered the church and were starting to make their way down the aisle.

Peter was ramrod straight. He wore a proud smile and pushed his chest to its full extension. He was a proud father, an image he worked to maintain as he checked his stride to stay in time with his daughter, who was a vision in her full-length white wedding gown.

The world's most stunning bride! Marc marveled as he caught Elisa's eye. Her broad smile was apparent, even through her lace veil.

"You look stunning!" Marc whispered as Elisa moved next to him.

"So do you," Elisa smiled in return.

"Are you nervous?"

"Not anymore," Elisa whispered. "You?"

"Not anymore."

Once the minister finished reading about the sanctity of marriage, he asked, "Who gives this woman to be married?"

Eyes clouded with emotion, Peter stepped forward and choked out, "I do," as he guided Elisa's hand to join Marc's.

After reading the vows and asking in turn if they each agreed to take each other in holy matrimony, the minister asked for the wedding rings.

Billy was woken out of his daze and immediately started rummaging around in his pockets. Just as he was starting to fluster, Robert pointed to his own top coat pocket, allowing Billy to find the wedding rings in the nick of time. Maddie, who had proved invaluable as she guided the bridal party through all the rehearsed moves, kept very cool, but couldn't resist smiling at the shenanigans.

After the minor hiccup, the minister announced that Marc and Elisa were man and wife. "You may kiss the bride," he said in a rich and well-rehearsed voice.

With his heart in his throat, Marc tenderly lifted Elisa's veil and kissed her ruby lips to the robust applause of the congregation.

After they led the congregation out of the church, the newlyweds found a spot at the bottom of the church steps where they could greet their guests and accept their best wishes and congratulations. Next, there were the endless photographs with each guest and the wedding party before Marc and Elisa could relax and make their way to the reception in the vintage Rolls Royce that they had chosen as the wedding car. Marc smiled as he and Elisa accepted the congratulations of his favorite concreter, Milo Lombardo, and his wife as they posed with the bride and groom for a photograph.

At the wedding breakfast, Peter stood up and spoke about how much Elisa meant to him and Alexandra.

"Elisa is our most precious blessing, and we couldn't be happier that she and Marc are now married. And we welcome him as the son we never had." Peter paused and smiled benevolently at both the bride and groom.

As he thought about the past, his eyes clouded over again. "It now seems like a such a long time ago that my young family stood at the Shanghai docks trying to get passage on the first ship that would take us away from another dangerous communist uprising," he said with a quiver in his voice. "Alexandra and I thought only about Elisa's welfare, and we wanted to find a country where she could grow up to be happy and safe. Thank God, we eventually found our way to Australia."

"Thank God," Marc mouthed silently to his new bride, who smiled back.

"It was a struggle to establish ourselves in a new country, but we were always fired on by our desire for our beautiful Elisa to find true happiness." He turned to look at the happy couple. "Today, I believe that she has found a big chunk of that happiness with her new husband, Marc." He looked lovingly at Alexandra nearby. "I believe my wife now has something important to say to Elisa."

Alexandra stood up and moved over to her daughter. With tears in her eyes, she smiled as she opened her hand to reveal a magnificent diamond brooch that had been in her family for several generations. Elisa's eyes widened and then quickly filled with tears at the sight of the treasured object and the significance of this moment.

"Always keep this close to your heart, and always treasure your heritage," Alexandra said as she kissed Elisa's cheek before pinning the brooch on to her daughter's wedding gown.

Peter beamed as he turned back toward the guests and raised his glass. "I would like to propose a toast to both Elisa and Marc, and their life together."

There was hardly a dry eye in the house as the guests rose to join his toast.

Robert lightened proceedings with a clever, tongue-in-cheek speech about Marc and Elisa's quirks that had everybody in stitches. "And it's just as well that Marc is flying out for his honeymoon tomorrow, because his secretary has sent his desk away to be repaired—it'll take them at least a week to get rid of the deep fingernail scratches he left as he was dragged away from his desk," Robert said in a deadpan voice, to hearty laughs.

"Now, Elisa's not any better," he continued. "When they decided to go to New Zealand for their honeymoon, she immediately dispatched two teams of student archaeologists, one to each island, so that she could visit them on the way around and keep her hand in!"

As the levity subsided, Robert remembered he had also been given the task of toasting the women in the wedding party, as Billy said he was too nervous to speak in public. He became more serious as he noted how beautiful his wife looked as matron of honor, and also how lovely Amy and Susan looked as Elisa's bridesmaids. All the guests raised their glasses and readily endorsed Robert's comments.

The reception was a high-spirited affair, which turned into a big happy party once the formalities were out of the way. Champagne flowed and people danced the night away as they admired the newlyweds, who happily posed for more photos with each of their guests. It was hectic, wonderful, and unforgettable.

*   *   *

Marc and Elisa had little time to themselves before heading off to New Zealand on their honeymoon. They did manage to see Billy off at the airport the next morning. He promised to come back again to see their firstborn. "Oh, Billy; you're such a character!" Elisa laughed. Billy left that as his parting thought before waving them goodbye and disappearing through the immigration gate.

The Braddons had time for only a fortnight's honeymoon before they both had to get back to work. Those days were spent blissfully touring New Zealand's two islands, each newlywed claiming a different island as their favorite. Marc liked the rugged beauty of the north island, while Elisa loved the snow-capped mountains and every baby lamb she saw on the south island.

"Where are we going to live when we get back?" Elisa asked as she snuggled up to Marc in bed on a cold winter's night in their hotel room at the base of Mount Cook.

"I think I should let my apartment go and move into yours. You've got those harbor views, which is better than the quiet seclusion of mine," Marc said, rubbing his forehead thoughtfully.

"But I like seclusion, too," Elisa said as she snuggled a little closer and began to drift off to sleep.

By the time they had returned to the city, they'd agreed to give up Marc's apartment and move into Elisa's abode before deciding where they really wanted to live. No sense in keeping two places so close to each other, they both figured.

They could always build a house, but the prospect of living in the suburbs didn't appeal to either of them. One day, when the time was right, they might find a block of land and build a country estate, but they were not yet ready for that. They didn't want to sacrifice their convenient city lifestyle just because Marc had the capacity to build houses.

*   *   *

Marc's time away from the office had worked wonders for his creative juices. He had been hatching a plan for the development of a brand new business that could operate in conjunction with Vanity, and wanted to evolve something that would increase production of the various manufacturing arms of the group without creating a debtor's problem. *The last thing we want is to spend our time chasing a lot of bad debts and end up working for nothing*, he thought.

As a result, he was now more convinced than ever that his emerging idea of a "kit-home" business offered the best solution—it was something Vanity could control, thereby ensuring there would be minimal risk to the group's overall cash flow. In his proposed scenario, Vanity would control all the sales and the associated businesses, and deal directly with the owners. Since these owners erected their own kit-homes, Vanity would contract directly with them, thereby guaranteeing payment for the goods.

Marc worked up a proposed system under which his "kit-home" clients would make an up-front payment of ten percent when placing an order, with the balance payable upon delivery of the kit components. A new kit-homes division seemed to offer a way of increasing the manufacturing output of Vanity's factories while also closing the loop in terms of control and risk.

"I think it's a brilliant idea," Stephen James told the strategy meeting.

"Have I missed anything?" Marc asked.

"No, I don't think so. It'll give us a way to increase factory throughput, turnover, and profit while also allowing us to control who we give credit to. I think it's a marvelous bit of lateral thinking," Stephen declared.

The other managers agreed that, if properly implemented, Vanity would have a valuable new business—one that would further expand its current level of vertical integration. It would also allow the other divisions to grow proportionately without the need to take a great deal of risk.

It was almost a year since his takeover, and Marc now had some surplus cash in his working capital pool. He decided to use it to develop the new business rather than make extra payments against his takeover loan, figuring it would be better in the long run to use this money to expand and strengthen the overall cash flow rather than retire the debt.

* * *

As the pace picked up at Vanity, a number of casualties occurred in its workforce. Marc's secretary, Margaret, was among them when she announced her retirement.

"I know it's only been a little more than a year since the takeover, but I feel the time is right for me to retire. You're well and truly over the transitional problems, and I can now bow out with a clear conscience," Margaret told Marc as she broke her news to him one Friday afternoon.

"If that's what you want, Margaret, I certainly won't try to talk you out of it. I'll miss you, though. You've been invaluable to me this past year," Marc said sadly.

"The time is right, Marc. I need to spend some time with my grandchildren. And I think my husband wants me to slow down so that we can both travel a little and enjoy the rest of our lives. Not that I haven't enjoyed working for you."

"I understand, Margaret. Thank you for all you've done for me," Marc said as he rounded his desk to give Margaret an appreciative hug.

This left Marc with the unenviable task of finding a replacement. He decided to look outside the company, feeling that his role had changed significantly and that he now needed a high-powered personal assistant rather than a private secretary.

At the end of a long day, his mind turned to Jennifer Watkins, the young woman from Whitney Whyte's with whom he had worked to secure the finance for the Vanity takeover. It was nine-thirty in the evening, and he guessed she was still at her desk. *She'd make an ideal PA,* he thought. He found her direct phone number in his desk drawer and punched her number in.

"Hello, Whitney Whyte, Jennifer Watkins speaking."

"Why did I know you'd still be in your office?"

"Is that you, Mr. Braddon?"

"Well, at least you still remember my voice. How are you, Jennifer?"

"I'm fine, but very busy. How's everything at Vanity?"

"Everything's going well here. I was just thinking about you, and how you were probably still at work at this ungodly hour."

"So what's new? What about you? I'll bet you're calling me from your office instead of being at home with that beautiful wife of yours."

Marc smiled sheepishly. "OK, you've got me. I believe you owe me a lunch date. Do you remember that rain check? There's something I'd like to talk to you about, and lunch will get us both out of our offices."

"OK, then. How's this Thursday?"

"I can manage that."

"Good. How about I meet you in our foyer at, say, twelve-thirty?"
"I'll be there."

*   *   *

Marc stood in the foyer of Jennifer's building, scanning the sea of faces emerging in regular waves from the elevators. They spotted each other simultaneously and hugged warmly. After the usual inquiries about health and work, they headed off to a nearby restaurant.

It was a favorite haunt of the city's lawyers and was decorated in dark blues throughout. The dark wood chairs were upholstered in a navy blue cloth, and heavy wood tables covered with navy tablecloths and napkins. The walls were decorated with oversized photographs of political and business personalities, who appeared to be looking down on the chattering groups of business people gathered for lunch.

"Are you pressed for time?" he asked as their meals arrived.

"No, not really, but there's always something that needs to be done. You know what it's like, Marc. There are never enough hours in a day."

"That's what I wanted to talk to you about. I'm looking for a high-powered personal assistant, and I think you'd be ideal. It'd be a fulfilling role, and the hours and pressures would be a lot saner."

"It's very tempting, Marc, and I'd love to work with you, but I'm torn between working and going back to school. You see, I'd love to get my master's degree. My problem is that I can't seem to find a way to tell my boss I want to quit."

"If I know old Adam, he'll keep loading you up with work until your legs buckle. If you really want to go back to university, then you should make that decision and stick to it. It's your life, after all, and you only get one crack at it." He paused for a moment. "Don't worry too much about old Adam. He'll get over losing you, eventually. But you'll never forgive yourself if you don't follow your heart."

As Marc heard his words resonate inwardly, he realized that he could be giving himself the same advice.

*   *   *

Marc went to an employment agency and also put out the word around the industry to see if there was anyone out there who might suit his purposes. Within a few weeks, the agency called to say they had found the perfect person. Marc agreed to meet her at eleven o'clock the day after next.

Clare Eddings was a smartly dressed woman who appeared to be in her mid-twenties. She was trim, well groomed, and knew how to emphasize her best features. She was attractive without being beautiful, and seemed perfect for the role of a high-powered personal assistant.

"Do come in and take a seat," he said as he guided her into his office. "Can I get you a cup of something?"

"No, thank you, I'm fine."

"OK, then, let's get down to business. Do you have your résumé?"

"Yes, but the agency told me they had already sent it to you."

"Yes, they did, but it was only the short version. I was hoping to see your full résumé today. I always like to look at letters of reference and any certificates you might have."

"Fair enough," Clare said as she handed over the documents to him.

"Umm. I see that you've had experience as a personal assistant to a number of chief executives and managing directors in several industries."

"Yes, I've been lucky enough to work for some great people, men who were real achievers. I really like to work for dynamic people."

"Your qualifications and references are excellent, Clare."

"Thank you, Mr. Braddon."

"What do you know about the building industry and its related manufacturing areas?"

"I've worked in several industries and found that these roles, at least at my level, are not all that different. You have to come to grips with the terms that relate to the particular industry, but otherwise they seem very similar. I've had experience working with two building-related manufacturers whose business was to supply the commercial end of the building industry, which I believe gave me some exposure."

"Yes, I see here that you're currently with Austin Brick and Ceramics. They're a large listed company, aren't they?"

"Yes. They're an international firm with offices and plants in every capital city. They also have several offices in the Pacific Rim. I'm the personal assistant to the chief executive of the whole group."

"Very impressive, indeed. Tell me, why do you want to leave that job?"

"Too much travel. I seem to be on planes two to three times a week, and find that it plays havoc with my personal life."

"I can relate to that. The job here will require your total dedication, but it's still only a job. The working week may be long, but the weekends are your own, at least most of the time."

"That would be fine with me. I'm looking for a better balance of work and a social life. I take it there's no real travel in this position?"

"That's right. Our operations are currently all within the state. At worst, you might be expected to accompany me on a short trip around the state."

"It sounds ideal to me. May I ask you what sort of a salary you are offering?"

"Between $50,000 and $60,000 a year, depending on the applicant's quality and experience. Is that in the range you were expecting?"

"Yes. I am currently earning $57,000, and would like to increase that salary to make a move worthwhile."

"Tell me, when would you be able to start?"

"Within a month of giving my notice, I expect."

"Great. I'll be in touch with you or the agency in the next couple of days."

Marc rose and lightly shook Clare's hand before escorting her down the stairs. He noticed that she pressed the alarm button on her key ring as she went through the front doors. The indicator lights on a black, late-model series 5 BMW flashed to indicate its owner had just returned. *She must be doing well if she can afford a car like that,* Marc thought.

* * *

Marc made his own inquiries, based upon the references that Clare had supplied on her résumé. Everything about her checked out and confirmed she had an exemplary work record and was well thought of wherever she had worked. Marc decided to call her in for another interview. If all went well, he planned to offer her the job.

Clare arrived at his office at six o'clock the following evening. She looked very smart in a crimson designer suit with black trimmings. The purpose of this meeting was to gauge Clare's personality and determine how the two of them would interact if they were working together. Therefore, the conversation was light and varied. After about an hour, Marc said, "I want to offer you the job as my personal assistant and am prepared to pay you $60,000 a year to start. I'd like you to start as soon as possible."

"I accept, Mr. Braddon. I'll give notice tomorrow, and should be able to start a month from today."

"Any chance it might be sooner?"

"I'll call you in the morning and let you know. My boss can sometimes be difficult about people leaving. He often asks senior people who give notice to leave immediately. If this happens to me, I might be able to start sooner."

"I'll wait to hear from you, then. And if we're going to be working together, you should get used to calling me Marc."

Clare called at ten the next morning to say she had been asked to stay on by her current employer for the full month of her notice period in order to finish up a number of important matters.

"Oh, well, you can't blame me for trying, I suppose. I guess I'll see you on the tenth of next month. In the meantime, we'll send you a formal letter of employment, setting out all our conditions of employment for you to sign and return," Marc said as he reluctantly accepted her news.

"I'm sorry I can't start earlier. I'm very keen to work with you, Marc, and I'll be there on the tenth with bells on," Clare said as she bid him goodbye.

Chapter Thirty-seven

Clare's first day as Marc's personal assistant coincided with the completion of the three-building office park complex at Hillsford. Marc had little time to welcome Clare to the office before hurrying out for his final site meeting, at which the office park was to be officially handed over to him.

Marc met his architect, Kenneth Carlisle, and his project manager, Larry Symes, on site to sign off on the completion of the complex—which not only signified the end of the construction phase, but also the start of his term as a commercial landlord.

"I'll bet you're glad to be getting the keys today, Marc," Larry said with a grin.

"Absolutely! Thanks to you and Kenneth, I think I have something to crow about—you've both done a marvelous job!"

"I must say, Marc, you've been the model client," Kenneth said appreciatively. "I hope you start developing buildings like this regularly—I could use a good client to offset some of my bad ones."

All three men laughed heartily as they made their way over to the builder's construction sheds for their final site meeting.

The day was full of activity, with the builder organizing drinks on site as part of the traditional end-of-project barbecue. This allowed Marc to break away with Kenneth and Larry to take a closer look at the premises and, after they inspected each building, everybody agreed that the builder had done a first-rate job. Marc's new tenants were now free to move in over the next few days, and their rent would be a most welcome addition to Marc's cash flow.

I guess it was worth all the financial shenanigans and heartburn, Marc thought as he eyed his completed office park complex from the street before climbing into his car for his return to Vanity's office.

* * *

Time moved on, and Marc's businesses were growing in strength. It was now well over a year since his takeover of the Vanity Group, and he had consolidated his operations into a new, better-managed entity. The group's inherent strength was in its ability to manufacture and supply almost every building item used in the construction of its homes, such as the timber frames and trusses, kitchens, windows, and shower screens. All the critical items needed to build a house or supply one in kit-form could be manufactured within the group, thereby ensuring certainty of supply while capturing all available profits.

But Marc felt they had only just scratched the surface. Vanity's kit-homes and project homes were identical in that they used exactly the same designs and fittings. Therefore, it took almost no additional setup costs to produce either a hundred or a thousand kit-homes a year, since Vanity's factories were already tooled up and capable of manufacturing that additional number of homes. Marc recognized that the Sydney market could never grow quickly enough to fully utilize Vanity's manufacturing capacity, so why not bring the larger market to Vanity?

He brought it up at one of his regular strategy meetings, which included all of his sales, building, and manufacturing managers. "I'm pleased with the way the kit-home division is going, but we're still only selling kit-homes from our metropolitan display home network—and only to people who are building largely within Vanity's geographical boundaries," he observed. "I believe that this new division has massive potential outside our normal building area, and that we're now at a point where we can set about finding these new markets. Any ideas?"

Stephen James took up the challenge. "One way would be to target regional builders, who traditionally have difficulties in procuring building materials and hardware in the more remote locations of the state."

"You read my mind, Stephen," Marc said with a smile to his right-hand man. "These regional builders also have the added burden of having to pay high freight costs on any goods that arrive by rail in their remote country towns," he explained to the group. "Because of their relatively small populations, there is insufficient economy of scale to justify less expensive modes of freight, such as high-volume road transport."

Stephen stood next to a map of the state that hung from one of the boardroom walls. "We can pick out several target towns around the state," he suggested, "and set about contacting builders in these towns in order to recruit them as kit-home constructors or as franchise builders of Vanity homes."

"That's good," Marc told him. "But we need to do more than that. I believe the best way to penetrate these new regional markets is to build a series of Vanity display homes in prime, well-trafficked locations around key towns. This will give these franchise builders a measure of support, while also promoting the new kit-home division and expanding the Vanity brand name at the same time."

"That's a great idea!" Stephen acknowledged. "This ultimately allows Vanity to build its homes in areas where it has never been able to afford to build before. Whether it's a kit-home or a normal project home, the result will be essentially the same—a greater turnover and larger profit for the overall group."

So, Marc and his team set out to acquire the necessary display home sites. Mary Arness, now the group's solicitor, was asked to prepare a series of option-to-purchase agreements so that, should Marc find a parcel of land that suited his display home needs, he could secure it on the spot. He planned to take his new personal assistant, Clare Eddings, with him, and asked her to load all of these documents in her laptop computer. This on-the-road approach would allow Marc to close a deal before the seller thought too much about it, or before some local real estate agent forced him into a Dutch auction.

Within two weeks, Marc and Clare had visited six out of the initial ten target towns, securing six excellent display home sites along the way. He had also obtained signed commitments from five franchise or kit-home builders in each town. Many of the country towns he visited looked a little down in the mouth as they struggled through yet another drought, as well as the aftermath of the nation's recession. The builders Marc signed were all anxious to be connected with Vanity Homes, and immediately saw the benefits in being part of such a large and well-respected city organization.

Signing these builders was a lot easier that I had imagined, Marc thought as he drove out of the last town. *Now, I can think about getting on and building the display homes to fire up sales.*

This was the first stage of the grand plan—to penetrate these remote markets. But the capital required to fund the acquisition and construction of six display homes on these sites had used up most of the excess working capital in Vanity's coffers. And although Marc and his team had already earmarked the remaining four towns within their grand plan, the Vanity Group could not afford to buy any more land or fund any more display homes until it had built on these first six sites.

Before heading back to his Sydney office, Marc decided to survey the four remaining country towns to identify the best possible sites. By the middle of the following week, he had picked a site in each of the remaining four towns, and had Clare enter their details into her computer for future reference.

Marc and Clare had been constant companions for the past two weeks, and therefore had gotten to know each other a little better. Marc was impressed with Clare's professionalism and the way she polished up her appearance each day, even though she was essentially living out of a suitcase.

"Let's hit the road," Marc said to Clare as they cleared the city limits of the last of the four towns.

"I can't wait to get back home and into my own bed. There's nothing special about motel accommodation!" Clare said ruefully as she pushed her shoulders back to straighten up.

"Thankfully, we're only about eight hours' drive from Sydney. Settle back and I'll have you home before you know it," Marc told his personal assistant as she snuggled into her seat.

* * *

When Marc finally got back to Sydney, he set about establishing Vanity as quickly as possible in the new regional markets. To that end, he ensured that all property details were immediately handed over to Mary Arness, who was asked to speed up the legal side of purchase and transfer of these key land acquisitions.

Marc also had to ensure that his managers were prepared for the influx of work that these new markets would create. He directed that Vanity's best city-based building teams be dispatched to the country to build the display homes. He could have used the new franchise builders he'd just signed up to build these houses, but felt they lacked the necessary experience with the extensive range of Vanity's designs to deliver the quality he wanted and needed in the shortest possible time.

His decision acknowledged the need to get these homes built, landscaped, and in front of the public as soon as possible. "Nothing works with Joe Public like being able to walk through a fully furnished house," Marc told his team. "They need to see and touch the finished product. They're no good at visualizing things off plans."

Within three months, the first batch of display homes was up and running, and sales were streaming in. Their completion meant that Vanity had six new assets it could mortgage, and it could raise the additional capital it needed to fund the acquisition and construction of more display homes. Marc knew that this meant taking on more debt, but this was consistent with his overall plan for the group. Since he ultimately wanted to put Vanity on the stock exchange, it was imperative that Vanity be truly established in the public's mind as the premier building and manufacturing group in the country.

Time was of the essence, because he knew he had to keep expanding the group to coincide with the resurgence of the stock market—which he foresaw as happening within the next two years, once it finally absorbed the effects of the recent recession.

Accordingly, Marc and his managers revisited the original plan for the development of the kit-home division to make sure their original target locations were still valid. They now had some early sales data from their new regional sales centers, which assisted them in making more educated predictions.

After a great deal of discussion, they all agreed that their original target locations were still their best options. This left Marc with the task of revisiting all of these towns to try to secure the necessary display home sites.

"That means you'll have to get on your bike again, Marc, and sign up the next four towns," Stephen said with a grin—knowing how little Marc enjoyed being cooped up in a car traveling the state's roads.

"Thanks, Stephen," Marc replied with a rueful smile. "I'll have to find some equally arduous job for you to do while I'm away."

"I'll wash your car when you return," Stephen offered with a hint of mischief in his face.

"Thanks, but I can drive through the car wash myself," Marc shot back with a chuckle.

* * *

Prior to embarking on the next mission, the Vanity team had to be sure that all the financial arrangements were in place, so Marc and Stephen planned a visit to the bank to offer them the deeds to the six new display homes. They reasoned that these unencumbered titles would allow Vanity to raise another $1.5 million, which would then be put back into the construction of more display homes that would also be made available to the bank as additional security.

David Rhodes, the chief commercial manager of the Commercial Bank and the group's personal banker nowadays, was keen to see the group grow. He understood Marc's grand plan of turning Vanity into a larger, better integrated entity before making it a publicly listed company. And because Vanity had performed so well under Marc's stewardship, he had no difficulty in agreeing to their request for another secured loan.

In fact, David agreed to advance the necessary funds before they took him out to lunch—a very good sign indeed. Marc had found bankers traditionally difficult to pin down on most things, especially when it came to extending existing loans, but David's posture proved that he was more than happy with the way things were going at Vanity.

Well, at least I've got David and his bank on side! Marc surmised as the group made their way to lunch.

Chapter Thirty-eight

In no time at all, Marc's first wedding anniversary was upon him. He dared not start his business trip before celebrating the event, so he planned a quiet little dinner and asked Maddie and Robert to join him and Elisa at Di Petro's, their favorite Italian restaurant.

The restaurant held many good memories for them all. It was where he, Robert, and Maddie had sealed their deal to build what was now a very successful retirement village. It was also where he had consummated many of his best deals, and where he liked to take Elisa on those special occasions. Marc wasn't looking forward to being chastised by Sophia, the owner, for not coming around more often. But for those good memories and the great food, Marc figured he could tolerate Sophia's slings and arrows.

"What a lovely idea for the four of us to get together tonight!" Elisa told Robert and Maddie on the way to the restaurant.

"Are you two sure that you want us along?" Maddie asked. "After all, it's your first anniversary, and..."

"Absolutely!" Elisa interrupted resolutely. "You two are more than just family. After all, if it wasn't for you inviting me to Whitefeather Cove, Marc and I would probably have never met, so you have a legitimate stake in this celebration!"

"We both want you along to celebrate our first year as an old married couple, so let's not hear any more about it!" Marc added.

When Marc pushed open the solid timber door, he was immediately engulfed in the Di Petro's special ambience. He guided Elisa and

Maddie in ahead of him and stood back as the indomitable Sophia consumed the two women in a huge welcoming hug. Eventually, she got around to greeting Robert, and then Marc.

"Where have you been, you naughty man?" she interrogated.

"Too busy with my new building group to go out for long boozy lunches at Mama Sophia's," Marc replied with a hangdog expression.

"You've forgotten me!" she lamented, spreading open the palms of her hands in a gesture of mock broken-heartedness.

"No, I haven't!" Marc protested. "I picked your place for my most important dinner—my first wedding anniversary. And in my book, that puts you and your restaurant at the top of my list, doesn't it?"

"You always have a good answer for me, don't you, Mr. Marc?" Sophia said with a belly laugh, crushing him in a warm bear hug before directing everyone to the best table in the place.

After they were seated and the waiter had taken Marc's order for a bottle of champagne, Mama Sophia told them to enjoy their dinner and scurried off to greet another batch of newly arrived guests.

"She's quite a character, isn't she?" Maddie said with a wide grin. Everybody nodded while looking at his or her menus.

"Well, let's have a toast, shall we?" Marc suggested as the waiter poured the Bollinger into the last glass on the table. Smiling benevolently at Elisa, he raised his glass: "To my lovely wife. Long may she remain happy, healthy, wise, and of course, beautiful."

Robert proposed another toast. "May you both always be as happy together as you are today, and may good fortune follow you every day of your lives."

It was the start of another memorable night at Di Petro's. The conversation was stimulating, and the discussion topics wide and varied as the red wine flowed freely. *Quiet dinners with a select group of friends or loved ones often have a way of liberating one's deepest thoughts, even before they've fully hatched,* Marc marveled to himself. Dinners with Elisa, Maddie, and Robert in a wonderful atmosphere like Di Petro's only ensured that such a thing would happen.

"You know, I've been thinking about my life lately," Marc said quietly. "I've come to question all the effort I've been putting into work over the years. I mean, it's not that I want to stop right now in the middle of everything, but I'd like to have some sort of plan for the rest of my life."

Maddie put her glass down with a look of surprise. "This isn't the Marc we all know and love. Of all of us, you've always been the most single-minded one, hasn't he, gang?"

"Yeah," Robert concurred. "You've always been the one who drags the rest of us along in your wake. You've made me think about doing a number of things I otherwise wouldn't have done!"

Elisa laid a hand on her husband's forehead, pretending to look for signs of a fever. "What's this new side of you?" she asked incredulously. "I can't believe you've had enough of your beloved businesses. I'm not sure I'd recognize you without your chief executive's hat on!"

Marc shrugged apologetically. "It's just something I've been thinking about ever since Billy came over for the wedding last year. He made me take stock of everything I had achieved, and now I'm starting to see my life differently." He looked longingly into Elisa's blue eyes. "For one thing, I often find myself resenting having to spend so much time away from you. It always seems like the priorities in my life are dictated by a constant pressure to make my businesses successful…"

"Darling," she interrupted, "I sensed that capturing Vanity would change you…that it might turn you into even more of a workaholic, if that were possible. I knew that's the way you were when I married you, and it works for us since I have my own career to contend with."

"Yes, but I find myself wanting us to be together more. I'd love to have a business or some endeavor that we can do together."

Elisa shook her head in frustration. "I'd love to do that, too, but how? Our roles are so different…"

"Yeah, I suppose so," Marc conceded with a sigh. "It's not that I'm going to throw everything away tomorrow—just food for thought, that's all."

"I guess we must all do what makes us the happiest," Maddie offered. "Most people have to work for a living, doing what they can to survive, so I suppose in that sense, we're all lucky. We've been able to choose what we want to do with our lives," she said with a smile.

"You're right, Maddie," Marc said as he topped up everybody's glass with the last of the red wine.

*   *   *

They had just finished dessert, and coffee was being served when Robert said to Marc and Maddie, "It's not often that we get you two together in this sort of environment. I've always been intrigued by that amazing childhood of yours, even from the little I know about it, and I hoped that you might tell us more about it."

"What can we tell you?" Marc said. "You already know that we both grew up in a little sleepy place called Evans Vale."

"Come on, Marc; even I know there was a lot more to it than that!" Elisa prompted.

"Well, for starters, there was that huge mansion where we lived in Algiers," Maddie offered. "*You* remember, Marc—it had those three-story-high courtyard walls you used to walk along in your death-defying high-wire act!" she finished with a mischievous grin at Elisa.

Elisa's blue eyes widened. "What!" she exploded in surprise. "Are you kidding?" She turned to grill her husband. "How old were you then, Marc?"

"About five or six," he answered sheepishly.

"I have my doubts about you, Mr. Braddon!" his wife told him, shaking her head in mock disapproval.

Marc looked to Robert for support, but his brother-in-law silently made it clear that Marc was on his own in this one.

"It was just one of those stupid things that kids do," Marc said with a shrug. "I guess it sounds totally insane when you look back on it."

"It should have looked *totally* insane to you then," his sister said as Marc winced, looking decidedly guilty.

"OK, what else can you remember?" Robert asked with a wink.

Marc nodded his thanks for finally changing the subject. "Our family lived there as expatriates. We were there while our father served out his military posting. Our mother, Millie, was the perfect English army wife, with her impeccable twin sweater sets, her sensible tweed skirts, and her two peaches-and-cream kids," he delivered with a cheesy grin.

"We lived a good life, with servants to fetch for us as one can on ex-pat wages in a Third World country. Our parents rented that amazing mansion from a banished millionaire for pennies in exchange for looking after the place. Apparently, the owner lived in constant fear that the local Arabs would squat in his house and destroy it if left vacant.

"Although our parents told us about the many other exotic places we had lived in during our father's army career, this was the first home I can really remember. I don't know about you, Maddie?"

"Me, too," Maddie replied. "Keep going; you're doing a good job so far!"

"Well," Marc continued, "our favorite servant was a man called Brahiem, who would ride off to the local shops on his bike and bring us back all sorts of goodies. It didn't dawn on us that our mother was really paying for all the things he was buying us, so Brahiem got most of the credit. We thought he was the kindest man in the world."

"Yeah, I remember Brahiem," Maddie exclaimed with a smile that lit up her face.

"Although Brahiem did most of the family's shopping, we still went to the local markets ourselves on occasion," Marc told the group. "I always looked forward to going there, even if we had to drag our reluctant mother around the stalls. I can still smell the freshly brewed coffee and roasted peanuts there. The markets had an energy and life all their own, or maybe it just seemed that way to a tiny boy.

"We always created some excitement as we wandered through the stalls. The Arabs would stand and stare at us, and the local women would stop our mother and admire us. No matter how often they saw us, they'd always put their hands to their cheeks to express their amazement at our fair skin and blond, curly hair."

"Yeah," Maddie chimed in, "I remember seeing photographs in one of the family albums and being struck by the way we looked then. We were perfect-looking Aryan children, and made a striking pair. No wonder we were such a novelty on market days!" she quipped. "Do you remember how we used to get a special treat of roasted peanuts in a cone made of rolled-up newspaper? That cone always seemed to make them taste extra good."

Marc's eyes flashed. "That's right! We used to check each other's cone to make sure we both got the same amount. Everything had to be equal, and we weren't going to let some street vendor upset the natural order of things. If he tried to cheat us out of a single nut, we'd make him top up the offending cone."

Elisa, who had been listening to Marc and Maddie's account in spellbound silence, reached for her husband's hand and squeezed it. "When did you two leave Algiers?" she asked.

"Our dad had a way of dropping things on us out of the blue," Maddie replied with a wry smirk. "One day in 1963, he said we were going to return to England because he had been posted to a new position. He also felt it was a good time to leave Algiers because there was more trouble brewing over the Suez Canal. I remember him saying that being British in a Middle East hot spot was not a good idea."

"Remember the day we left Algiers?" Marc asked Maddie. "The mayor was standing on the front steps of our mansion, waiting for us to give him the keys. He was going to turn the house into his official residence, and was very anxious to take possession."

As the scene came back to life for him, Marc took a deep breath. "I still recall the scene as we drove away for the last time. My lasting memory will always be the image of a sea of navy blue uniformed policemen and police cars as they flooded our courtyard, hemming in the mayor and his entourage. The place was so full that most of the policemen could only stand next to their cars. Even then they filled most of the available space, making it look more as if they were laying siege to the place rather than waiting for a set of house keys."

Marc shook his head a little, as if to dislodge that memory before continuing. "I don't know about you, Maddie, but England was a far more interesting place for me. The schools were much bigger; the teachers seemed to know a lot more than the ones in Algiers, and the kids seemed much brighter, too! I seemed to fit right in."

"Yes, I remember England," Maddie said. "Dad was posted just outside Liverpool, so we rented a house in a middle-class part of the city. It was a three-bedroom tenement house, one of about forty attached to each other and stretching from one end of the street to the other. They all had an identical design and were distinguished only by their differing color schemes. All of the houses were old, and although most had been done up by their various owners, they still looked sort of dark and sad to me. It was a huge step down from the big, bright, airy mansion we had become used to in Algiers."

"I don't think we lived in Liverpool all that long," Marc said, "but I can still remember the freezing winters. The Beatles had just taken off and Liverpool seemed like the center of the world, even to an eight-year-old kid. Do you remember what it was like at that time in Liverpool?" he asked his sister.

"Yeah, everybody was into the Beatles," she responded with a smile. "The city was so proud of them that they were everywhere—I even remember my teacher in infants class playing their records for the kids at every opportunity."

Marc shared her smile for a moment. "Just when we were getting used to England," he told them, "our father accepted a post at a military college run by the Australian Army and was promoted to colonel. He said that Australia was a land of opportunity—a place where a family could grow up in an egalitarian society. Although he was an officer, he really didn't like the class structure so prevalent in England, and wanted us to be free of it. So with that, we packed everything up in 1965 and got on a boat to Sydney.

"I remember leaving Liverpool on a cold, rainy day. It seemed a fitting farewell as we all jumped out of our taxi and dashed for the shelter of the Lime Street Railway Station. Our train was waiting at the platform, and we barely had enough time to organize our hand luggage and tickets as we scurried on board. As our compartment door slammed shut behind us, the stationmaster whistled and flagged the train away.

"The train ride took us to the Southampton docks. Neither of us had thought much about Australia, and expected it to be just another Liverpool that happened to be on the other side of the world with lots of sunshine and strange animals," Marc said with a chuckle. "At worst, we expected it to be a cross between Liverpool and Algiers."

Marc closed his eyes in consternation. "You know, I've tried to remember coming into Sydney Harbour that first time on our liner, but no matter how hard I try, I can't seem to picture it. Anyway, everyone disembarked at the international passenger terminal at Circular Quay and, after clearing immigration, we were all bused to a migrant hostel in an outer suburb called East Hills.

"The first sight of our new home left us all gob-smacked. We were amazed to see dozens of neat rows of identical, semicircular corrugated iron huts that looked like an organized cluster of half-tin cans. These huts were called 'Nissin huts.' We arrived at the height of summer, and the idea of living in an oppressively hot home, no matter what it was called, didn't hold immediate appeal," Marc concluded with a grimace.

"Remember the looks on our faces when we first saw the hostel?" Maddie asked her brother. "We were bewildered, and looked at our parents as if to say, 'What the heck did we do wrong!' It was one thing to leave that mansion in Algiers for a three-bedroom tenement house in England, but moving into a tin can on the other side of the world…now, that was a real step backwards in *anyone's* book!" she said as they all laughed.

"Thankfully, our time in the migrant hostel was very short. We were only there for a few weeks while our parents found their feet," Marc continued. "Our father had bought a property near Canberra on the eastern side of the Great Dividing Range near the military college, where he was to become a senior instructor. We think he bought it because he always wanted to be a farmer, and own his own parcel of land. Maybe it grew out of a deep-seated need connected to his army days, when he was always on the move and had no permanent home.

"We loved the country, with its acres of open space and clean, sweet air. The farm was about two and a half thousand feet above sea level, in a sleepy little village about a three hours southwest of Sydney and an hour from Canberra. The town consisted of a general store and post office that doubled as somebody's house, and wasn't a bit like the big English towns we knew like Liverpool, Manchester, or Birmingham. Still, we survived. By then I was nine, and Maddie six.

"Our farm wasn't really a farm, but a property with a hundred acres of native eucalyptus trees," Maddie remembered. "The homestead was a comfortable old timber house, which was a lot better than the hot hostel huts. The local school was a two-room building, two miles from home. The primary school classes were held in one room, while kids under seven were taught in the other."

"I remember how strange this was at first," Marc said as Maddie's words took him back. "It really took some getting used to, and I found it hard to concentrate when kids in the next row of desks were doing more interesting work.

"This was probably the one time in my life when felt like an outsider, different from the others. At a young age, it really gave me a small insight into what it must like to be black in a white man's world. None of the other kids would play with me because I was different. My crime was that I spoke with a thick Liverpudlian accent.

"I really can't remember why, but I decided it might improve matters if I fought these thick-headed farm boys. I guess I got sick of being an outcast. It didn't help when they taunted Maddie and me about everything we did—especially about the way we spoke. We were even picked on for the way our mother packed our lunches! A more patient person might have weathered the storm, but suffering fools gladly was never my strong suit."

"You can say *that* again," Elisa joked.

Marc smiled. "Well, enough was enough, I thought, so I punched their lights out! You'd think I'd have realized that their big brothers also went to the same school and sat only a couple of rows away from me, wouldn't you?

"Anyway, I survived an uneasy truce with the older boys until my tenth birthday. That morning, before school started, my enemies gathered under the goalposts on the playing fields next to the school. They wanted to give me a special birthday present: All six stepped forward, saying that they each wanted a piece of me. I agreed to fight them all, but only if they'd fight me one on one. That's probably where it all started for me." He took another sip of coffee in perfect silence.

"Come on, Marc, don't stop there; tell us what happened," Robert said eagerly. "You have to tell us how you're still in one piece!"

"All right, all right," Marc agreed with a chuckle. "Well, after negotiating the terms of engagement, I began to fight each of them in turn, with the toughest waiting in line until last. My dad had taught me some boxing, and I dispatched the first kid, who was about my age and build, with a right-left-right combination. The next two boys went the same way, but my opponents kept getting older, bigger, and smarter, causing me to use up more punches and energy to defeat them. The fights were progressively turning into a cross between a wrestling match and a boxing match, and I had to keep coming up with new wrestling holds and boxing combinations, or at least try to better disguise my old moves with every new and tougher opponent."

"And I thought I had it tough with the bullies at my private school," Robert said with an incredulous look on his face. He looked across at Elisa who wore a stunned expression.

"Finally," Marc continued, "after vanquishing the last boy, I realized I had beaten every one of them, except the biggest one, who was also the ringleader. He eyed me up and down. I must have looked a sight, having just about fought myself to a standstill. And to my eternal surprise, he said, 'I'm not going to fight you, you tough little Pommy bugger. You've probably got enough fight in you to kill me, too!' With that, his face turned into a big friendly smile, and he reached out his huge farm-boy hand and pulled me closer. He shook my hand hard for a few seconds before yelling out 'Geronimo!' Then, he and the other five kids jumped on top of me in a strange initiation tribal rite that left me with a broken right arm."

"It's all true. Your husband was a bare-knuckle brawler," Maddie told Elisa, who was still frozen to her chair in disbelief. "After that, his reputation as a pugilist grew, and anyone who knew of the legend of the Evans Vale primary school fight stayed well away from him. You were such a terror," Maddie said with a grin.

"You could have told me about your brother the boxer," Elisa said as she struggled to assimilate what she had just been told.

"That's an amazing story. I'm glad I finally got you both to tell it. It makes it all the more real," Robert said as he slid back into his chair, having found himself perched on its edge.

"On a totally different note, Robert and I have some great news to share with you," Maddie said with a gleam in her eye.

"I hope you don't want us to guess what it is; I'm hopeless at that sort of thing, and Marc is even worse," Elisa said with a big smile.

"Well, OK, I'll spare you both the suspense," Maddie replied brightly. "Robert and I are going to have a baby!"

"That's terrific!" Elisa and Marc exclaimed simultaneously, jumping up out their chairs and running around the table to hug Maddie and Robert.

"So you've finally decided to make me an uncle!" Marc said, shaking Robert's hand enthusiastically.

"Yes, old boy. We thought it was about time to extend the genealogical line," Robert said mockingly.

"I'm nearly two months pregnant," Maddie told them. "We wanted to tell you both tonight, and I've been busting to get it out all evening!"

"Well, congratulations," Marc said warmly. "I know everything will work out beautifully for you both. You deserve it!"

"This calls for another bottle of that wonderful Bollinger champagne, and I'm buying this round," Robert said magnanimously.

"Steady, now. Maddie shouldn't drink in her condition," Elisa pointed out. "Ah, so *that* explains why you've been on mineral water all night!"

"I did have a tiny sip of champers for the toasts," Maddie confessed. "I think the baby will forgive me!"

"She can have a another sip to wet the baby's head," Marc joked. "Anyway, one of you charming ladies will to drive us old drunkards home tonight, won't you?"

"I'll drive," Maddie said. "After all, I have to set a good example, now that I'm going to be a mother!"

They hardly needed another reason to extend their celebration, but Maddie and Robert had certainly provided them with a good one. Sophia and her family, most of whom worked at the restaurant, joined in the impromptu party and donated another bottle of champagne to the festivities. Everybody had a rollicking good night as they swapped more stories and good wishes while the restaurant slowly emptied.

Thankfully, Marc and Elisa had the rest of the weekend to recover. Sunday morning was a sedate affair, with both of them nursing hangovers.

Chapter Thirty-nine

It was Monday morning again, which meant business as usual at Vanity. Marc was about to embark on another trip to secure the remaining four sites he had identified on his last excursion. These acquisitions would complete the kit-home division's initial marketing strategy, and give it ten regionally located display homes in ten significantly important and different marketing areas.

Marc and his managers had also looked beyond these locations, identifying another five townships for possible expansion when, and if, the kit-home division needed to further expand its markets. These locations were only secondary in that they offered access to relatively small markets and, as such, were not in his immediate plans.

As Marc drove out of the city with Clare in tow, he had a clear mandate to secure the remaining four sites and complete the agreed marketing plan.

"Here we go again," Marc told Clare as they reached the start of the western freeway. "I've decided to start at the furthest town and work backward across the state until all four locations are in the bag."

"At least that way, we'll end up closer to home when we finish up," Clare said as she looked at a map of the state.

"Settle in, Clare—you're in for a long drive," Marc said as he set his car on cruise control.

*　　*　　*

Marc's timing for the trip couldn't have been worse. The winter days were cold and short. The temperature was made even less tolerable by the unforgiving gusts of wind that blew up from the southern ocean, cutting one to the very marrow.

Hearing a beeping sound, Marc looked down at his dashboard to see that his Jaguar needed gas. He managed to find the right button to shut off the beep, scolding himself for not stopping to refuel at the last town. He scanned the horizon until he spotted a gas station in a little town just a few miles down the road.

He parked the Jaguar next to its only pump, leaving Clare to enjoy the comfort of the warm car while he huddled against the chilly breeze. Just as he started to fill the tank, a sharp gust of icy wind cut through him; he instinctively ducked closer to the car in an attempt to shield himself from the cold.

He shuddered as he got back in. "Cold out there?" Clare asked impishly.

"C-c-cold out there!" he agreed, shivering.

By the middle of their second day on the road, they reached Wentworth, the first town Marc had planned to visit. Wentworth was tucked away in the southwestern corner of the state, and offered access to two other nearby states. Part of this new regional market was expected to come from those states whose terrain, building rules, and basic consumer needs were essentially the same as Vanity's home state of New South Wales.

As soon as Marc and Clare arrived in Wentworth, they checked into their motel rooms and headed out to see the owners of the selected block of land. Like almost all the other parcels Marc had bought, this one was in a prime location, and big enough to accommodate several homes.

"Land in these far-flung towns is not normally expensive unless someone's got wind that a big-city firm has a particular interest in it," Marc told Clare as they prepared for their first meeting at Wentworth. "That's why I never approach anyone unless I'm ready to close the deal on the spot."

When Marc spoke with the owner of the Wentworth land, who had been identified by searching the land titles office's data bank in Sydney, he was taken aback: The man told Marc that he had already entered into an option agreement with someone from another company for a two-year period. The owner wouldn't tell Marc what price had been agreed upon, but did give him the name of the company.

Marc returned to his motel room and told Clare to track down the directors of this rival company. "We can look the company up in the public records of the Australian Securities Commission's database," he said.

"I'm afraid we don't have access to those sort of databases out here in the boondocks," Clare told her boss.

"Most city solicitors maintain a direct computer link with the ASC or a search company. Ring Mary Arness's people and get them to fax me the information as soon as possible."

*   *   *

Marc and Clare dined at the motel's tiny restaurant, the walls of which were decorated with striped red, black, and silver wallpaper that was beginning to peel at the seams. The "antique" wood fittings, stained a dark mahogany, were clearly imitation and a poor match to the dark laminated tables that furnished the restaurant. The eclectic mix of furnishing and fittings offered no help to the place's tired décor: a perfect reflection of Marc's state of mind.

"I can't believe this!" Marc said dejectedly to his personal assistant as the prospect of being beaten to the chosen Wentworth land began to sink in.

"You can't let something like this defeat you, Marc," Clare told him encouragingly. "Once we get Mary's report and you find out who's behind this company, you'll surely be able to cut a deal with them."

Clare had dressed for dinner and had obviously spent a great deal of time on her hair and makeup. She looked quite fetching, and although Marc noticed her appearance, he was in no mood to compliment her.

"Yeah, I suppose so. I just find it hard to believe that anyone else would have an interest in land out here in the boondocks!"

"Stranger things have happened," Clare replied after a slight pause. "You picked out this land, so why wouldn't someone else? Anyway, you don't know what their purpose was for optioning the land, and that in itself might explain things."

Marc nodded, his spirit returning. "OK, so we're not beaten yet! I'll just have to find an alternative site in case I can't work out a deal with this other buyer. We'd better try to tie up the local builders while we're here, so the journey's not wasted."

Clare smiled at her boss's determination. "That's what I like to hear! I like the way you recover after suffering a setback. You don't wallow in self-pity like so many other people; you just get on with it."

Marc shot her a rueful expression. "Believe me, Clare, that comes from overcoming many setbacks over the years."

Clare looked into Marc's eyes with a new intensity. "You're such a strong-minded man, Marc. I love that about you. I hate working for weak, self-serving people. They turn me right off." She lifted her wine glass to her grinning lips. "You, on the other hand, turn me on!"

"What would you like for dinner?" Marc asked, attempting to change Clare's dangerous line of conversation. *It's probably her drinks talking, or the fact that we're together in this motel so far away from home,* Marc reasoned with himself. "We should probably avoid the seafood this far inland. I think it'd be safer to stick to beef. At least they're grown in these parts!" he added with a smile.

Clare seemed absorbed in her plastic-covered menu. *She's probably trying to disguise her embarrassment at her little outburst,* Marc thought.

"I think I'll have steak and salad," she stated, wriggling a little in her seat and sitting up a little straighter. "Have to keep the girlish figure, you know."

"I think I'll have the filet steak with mushroom sauce," he said. "Can't go wrong with the specialty of the house, I suppose."

Still feeling a bit awkward, Marc buried himself in the wine list. "Funny thing about a lot of these out-of-the-way restaurants; they often have a fabulous wine list. It's almost as if they don't know about the real price of wine or the scarcity of particular vintages. Look, here's a bottle of 1965 Barossa Valley Cabinet-Sauvignon for twenty-five dollars. This same bottle in Sydney, if you could get it, would cost about three times as much!"

"Sounds almost too good to refuse," Clare commented with a polite smile.

Marc couldn't resist a bargain. "Yeah, let's order it, shall we?"

Clare made no other personal comments over dinner, but her remark about him turning her on gave him cause to think back in his motel room. He hoped he hadn't said or done anything to cause her to believe that his interest in her was anything more than professional. *Maybe it was just a slip*, he thought as he tried to snuggle into his unforgivably hard motel pillow.

*   *   *

After a couple of days, Marc and Clare had signed up six local builders who were happy to either become kit-home erectors or franchise Vanity Home builders. Marc had picked out an alternate display home site on the other side of town and had put an option on it, recognizing that it wasn't as good as his first choice, which he still hoped to find a way to secure once he got back to the city.

They went on to the next town and set up again in the local motel. They had contacted a number of local builders before leaving the previous town, which meant they could minimize the amount of time spent in this next town. Their motel served as a handy temporary office, and its facilities allowed them to have meetings and process agreements on foot.

Most of their time in the second town was spent signing up local builders. Toward the end of the second day, Marc went to meet the owner of the land he had earmarked for acquisition and left shaking his head. Someone had again beaten him to the punch. They, too, had signed a two-year option with the owner two months earlier.

"This is becoming very frustrating," Marc told Clare after their meeting with the landowner.

All Marc was able to find out was the name of the party who had entered into the option with the landowner. It was a company again, but different than the one that had beaten him to the Wentworth land. Again, all he could do was to ask Clare to get their solicitor to search out the directors of this company so he could contact them on his return to Sydney.

In the meantime, he again set about identifying an alternate site in this town. He was in a foul mood, and wasn't much company in the evenings. He bumbled through his dinners with Clare, preoccupied and mostly disinterested in whatever he ordered.

They moved on to the next target town, and immediately went to see the owner of the land he wished to buy. As he entered the house, his heart was in his mouth. He was almost afraid to ask about the possibility of purchasing this property for fear that someone else had already beaten him to it.

To his relief, no one had; the owner was very receptive, and readily signed the option agreement. Marc's mood perked up considerably, as his luck had seemed to change. He was a much better dining companion that night, and more relaxed as they went about signing up all the town's suitable builders.

"I was starting to despair there for a while," he told Clare over dinner that night. "It seemed that someone was second-guessing my plans, which gave me a very sick feeling."

Clare shook her head. "Marc, you're becoming paranoid."

Marc rubbed his chin with his thumb and forefinger. "Easy for you to say, Clare. You're not the one whose future depends so heavily on certain things falling into place."

"You need to lighten up," Clare said in an empathetic tone. An impish grin then ran across her lips. "Maybe you need a little female companionship to give you something else to think about!"

A look of dismay overtook Marc's previously worried expression. "Come on, Clare!" he protested. "I'm a happily married man. I have no desire to cheat on my wife. Anyway, you're a very attractive lady and don't need to sleep with your boss just because we're spending a lot of time together out here."

Clare reeled back in her chair. "Gee, lighten up, Marc. I was just joking, you know!"

Marc's serious expression underscored his resolve. "That's OK; as long as you know how I feel about the subject."

Her reply was muffled. To him, it sounded like: "Shame, though."

*   *   *

From that point on, Marc began to look at Clare differently. He had never seen it before, but when she came on to him with such single-minded determination, he couldn't help but be reminded of the same qualities that Loren Wilmont had in abundance. *Danger! Danger!* was his immediate thought.

No way did he need someone else in his life. He shuddered as he imagined the consequences if he did have an affair with Clare and she decided do something silly, like tell Elisa all about it to have him all to herself. *Oh my God*, he thought as the prospect kept him awake for hours, while tossing and turning in another lumpy motel bed.

The next day, he and Clare packed up and headed for their last town in the northwest part of the state. The two weeks in the wilderness were starting to take their toll on him, and Marc wanted to get this lot over and done with so that he could get back home to Elisa. This time away from her was clouding his thinking, making the reality of his life with her seem almost like a surreal memory. Although he called her every night, he still missed her terribly.

Again, Marc and Clare went through the ritual of checking into their motel, unpacking their bags, showering, and going to their first meeting. This was getting tedious, and they both wanted an end to it.

"Let's hope this town is as easy as the last one," Marc said as they prepared to go through their routine of interviewing and signing up local builders.

He couldn't get an appointment to see the owners of the property that he had earmarked until late the next day, and his spirits fell when this owner told him that another company had approached him some months earlier and signed a two-year option. The company was Jumonka Pty. Ltd., another strange-sounding name and as equally foreign to him as Abalpo Pty. Ltd. and Bebbok Pty. Ltd.—the other companies with options on the properties he had sought. *This is very strange*, he thought. *Three out of four of the properties I'm interested in, all in completely separate locations, being optioned by three different companies. Very odd indeed!*

He scouted for an alternative site without much conviction, found one, and signed them to an option before packing his bags.

"I'm really worried about this trend," he told Clare on the way back to Sydney.

"I know it looks a bit odd, Marc, but obviously someone else has identified these blocks for their own particular requirements."

"Yeah, maybe, but something just doesn't smell right!"

Clare cast Marc a reassuring smile. "Let's wait until we get the results of the company searches. It should tell us who's behind them, and give us a clue about what's going on."

*　　*　　*

Back in his office, and after a good night's sleep in his own bed with Elisa, Marc was ready to take on the world again. He called a staff meeting and told them about the strange happenings. During the meeting, Clare produced the anticipated company searches. The reports were distributed around the table, but no one could find any parallels in the ownership or the directors of these companies—they all appeared unrelated and separately managed.

The reports revealed the names and addresses of the directors, which allowed Clare to contact them in an attempt to arrange meetings for Marc without revealing his connection with Vanity. She tried to arrange these meetings in hotel foyers or restaurants, so that their expectations wouldn't be raised by the prospect of a large building company trying to buy their land options.

Oddly enough, all three company representatives were happy to sell. Each set a price of around $100,000 more than what they had agreed to pay the current landowners. This made each property about fifty percent more expensive than Vanity had expected. After weighing the various options and considering the long-term pros and cons, Marc agreed to pay the extra money.

What also struck him as strange was that these transactions were completed using only Vanity's solicitors. These companies wanted no legal representation of their own at the options transfer. "Oh well, that's their business, I suppose," Marc said to his solicitor when told of the situation. "As long as we get the properties, they can do as they like!"

He wasn't happy about having to pay a premium for these three key sites, and had to find the extra money to fund them from his normal cash flow. He agreed to go ahead with these purchases only after Stephen James and his financial whiz kids assured him they could find the funds. "It might be tight for a while, but these sites will pay it back and a lot more once they begin to operate," Stephen assured him.

There's nothing like being rich and having no money! Marc thought, realizing he would have to wait even longer to enjoy the fruits of his labor. All he had in the world was tied up in his business, and it seemed that every time he got close to being able to take something out, another black hole appeared to gobble up the surplus. It was going to be a matter of reining in a number of nonessential expenditures while also trying to hold off the creditors for another fourteen days or so to cover the extra $300,000 that must be found.

Vanity had a strong reputation for paying its bills in full and on time. Stringing out their major creditors for another fourteen days over a relatively short period wouldn't be a major problem, as long as everything went according to plan. Marc offered to tackle the creditors to gain their consent for his group's proposed approach.

Even the best plans need some luck to succeed, and this somewhat risky approach was no different. Marc knew it was possible for a big company to go broke as a result of a small cash flow hiccup. Once confidence was lost, based on a company's inability to deliver on a certain promise or time frame, it could snowball, with creditors and lenders withdrawing their support and leaving that company completely exposed. He knew that this scenario could happen to anyone at any time, and needed to be prevented at all costs. This was why he had decided to tell his key creditors himself.

*   *   *

Luck was on Marc's side. Within three months, the new batch of finished display homes were up and running, producing good sales and easing the financial difficulties their acquisition had caused. Three months after that, everything was blossoming.

Vanity now had enough cash to allow it to look at modernizing some of its factory equipment, or consider the acquisition of additional sites to replace some of its older metropolitan display villages.

It was a fact of life that Marc's business was capital-intensive, and it meant that, as the owner, he had to keep feeding the profits back into the business to give the group what it needed to keep it growing.

Sure, the business could support Marc's lifestyle and he never wanted for much, but he could never go out and buy something really extravagant, like a big boat or a house on the harbor. That would have to wait until he had a personal bank account with money of his own in it.

Elisa's professorial salary was significant, and between them, they had more than enough to live on. Still, Marc wanted to have a separate chunk of money in his account that was the result of his business endeavors—money that he could then spend as he pleased on whomever or whatever he wanted.

One day it'll happen, he kept telling himself. *One day!*

Chapter Forty

It seemed like only a couple of months since Maddie had announced her pregnancy. Yet here they all were standing at the nursery window in the maternity ward, waiting anxiously to see the newest addition to their family.

Robert was very animated as he recounted his midnight dash to get Maddie to the hospital. "She made me rehearse the whole thing over and over until I got it down pat," he told Marc and Elisa, "but as soon as she screamed in pain, I forgot the lot and just bundled her into the car. Maddie remembered her bag and made me go back into the house to fetch it. I dashed inside, knocking over potted plants and furniture as I went—I was more panicked than she was," Robert said with a big grin.

"And after all that drama, you both have a beautiful baby boy to show for it," Elisa said joyfully as Marc looked on in wonder.

Robert was bursting at the seams with new fatherhood's pride and joy. He pressed his name card to the nursery's viewing window, and the duty nurse obliged by wheeling over a clear plastic crib.

"The baby's name is going to be Jerome Francis," Robert told his in-laws. "Jerome was the only name Maddie and I could agree on, and his middle name was inspired by his great-great grandfather, François, who first brought the family to Australia."

"Not a bad moniker: Jerome Francis LaPont," Marc recited aloud as he nodded approvingly.

"It's a lot better than Pepi LaPont, which was Marc's contribution on the way up here," Elisa said, playfully punching Marc's arm.

"Well, I can tell you that Pepi was definitely not on our list," Robert said with a knowing smirk.

The nurse maneuvered Jerome's crib to position directly in the center of the viewing window. Elisa seemed to melt when she saw the baby for the first time before saying, "Look, Marc—he's the image of Robert, although he's got Maddie's cute little nose!"

"Yeah, I see that," Marc replied dutifully. He shrugged and looked incredulously at Robert, who was smiling back.

"Don't worry, Marc, I can't see any resemblance either!" the proud papa admitted with a laugh. "The poor little guy looks more like a sunburned prune to me, all wrinkled and red. It's going to take a while before I can see anybody in him."

"You men are hopeless!" Elisa said impatiently. "You can never see resemblances in anybody, can you?"

After watching little Jerome for several minutes, the family headed off to see Maddie, who was now back in her private room down the hall from the nursery. Marc and Elisa had brought armfuls of baby presents in honor of the momentous occasion.

Marc immediately approached Maddie's bed and gave his sister a huge hug and kiss. "You look positively radiant, Sis," he told her. "This motherhood thing seems to bring out something special in you."

"I'm just pleased to get the little mite out into the world," Maddie said with a tired smile. "This poor body of mine was getting too small for both of us!"

"You do look terrific, Maddie. Maybe you should do this more often," Elisa said in jest.

"Whose friend are you again?" Maddie shot back as everybody broke up.

After spending two hours with Maddie and Robert, filled to the brim with good humor and genuine affection, Marc and Elisa declared their intention to head back home so that mother, father, and baby could enjoy some quality time together.

"Feeding time is the really fun part of the day," Maddie told them with a laugh as they prepared to leave. "I'm only just getting the hang of it; he's such a hungry little mite, you know. Anyone would think he was starved!"

Elisa turned to Marc with a pleading expression. "I don't feel like driving home just yet. Maybe we could have dinner up here?"

"Why don't you stay at our place overnight?" Robert suggested.

"What a good idea!" Maddie exclaimed. "Robert would appreciate the company, and you can save yourselves a long drive home. Anyway, Robert's exhausted. He's been up for over twenty-four hours, and I would consider it a favor if you two would take him home and stay the night. There's a stir-fry chicken dish in the fridge that's all prepared and ready to cook; it was meant to be yesterday's dinner before I was carted off unceremoniously to this house of torture!"

Elisa's smile lit up the room. "How can we say no?" she replied.

"We'd love to stay over," Marc chimed in. "I don't have anything special in the morning, and Elisa doesn't have to be at the university until late afternoon, so that'll work out well."

After dinner, Robert retired almost immediately, apologizing for not being able to entertain his houseguests as he wearily climbed the stairs to his bedroom. Marc and Elisa reassured him by telling him they intended to visit Whitefeather Cove's sandy beach anyway, letting their host off the hook.

*   *   *

As Marc and Elisa wandered hand in hand along the path stretching down from the house to the beach, a soft, balmy breeze accompanied them, bringing with it a familiar blend of summer scents enveloped by the salty air. Scents and sounds combined to make their visit to this particular beach feel more like a magical homecoming than a casual evening stroll.

As they approached from a vantage point well above the beach, Elisa pointed to the rock they had come to claim as their own. They made their way across the fluffy sand to "their" weathered rock.

"Where has the time gone?" Elisa wondered aloud. "It seems like only yesterday that we sat on this rock on our first night together, but it was nearly three years ago!"

"Meeting you was probably the most significant thing that's ever happened to me," Marc said softly. "Yet, it still seems like only yesterday to me, too."

Elisa turned her head and smiled warmly at her husband. "Well, I'm happy, my love. How about you?"

Marc shot Elisa a look of mock amazement. "Are you kidding? My life with you is very special—so much so that I often wish we could spend *more* time together. It seems like we've become the typical business couple: you with your demanding life in academia, and me with my business. We seem to spend more time going to each other's functions than we do just being alone and enjoying one another."

Elisa nodded. "I know what you mean. Sometimes, I long to just be with you without any distractions. I keep telling myself that it'll happen one day, but until then, I'm just making do...and it often hurts to feel I have to compete for your attention."

Marc's expression became more resolute. "We should take an afternoon off during the week, just to be together. We could go to a movie or walk around the city or a park somewhere. I'll even go shopping with you!" he offered with an air of mock self-sacrifice as Elisa giggled. "Whatever we decide to do," he added with conviction, "we'll make sure that absolutely nothing gets in the way!"

Elisa's eyes lit up. "That sounds great! Wednesdays are good for me. I have only a morning class, and I always end up hanging around the university, just killing time. I'd love to spend the afternoon with you, just doing our own thing."

He nodded. "Consider it done."

Marc was silent for a moment while he mulled over a new line of thought. A few minutes later, he began to smile like a Cheshire cat. "Tell me, honey: if you were financially free and could do anything that you wanted with your life, what would it be?"

"I can answer that in a flash!" Elisa replied, sitting up straight. "I'd love to fund my own dig somewhere around the Mediterranean Basin, and maybe find some previously undiscovered artifact that might prove some of the myths about the Greeks or the Phoenicians."

Marc's smile grew even broader. "If you can organize a long-term dig on one of those Greek islands and promise me that I can come along, then I'll see if I can find a way to make it happen."

Elisa smirked. "Yes, it's nice to dream, isn't it? Tomorrow I'll go back to my associate professor's job, and you'll go back to your Vanity Group."

This triggered something that had been brewing in the back of Marc's mind for some time.

"You know, Elisa, a long time ago, I realized the truth in the saying, 'No man is an island.' No matter who you are, someone along the way will always help you up—often by making you see beyond the boundaries of your own thoughts and self-doubt. They dare you to be great...to see over the ridge into the next valley. It's as though they are your own private giants who hoist you up high on their shoulders to allow you to see beyond the limits of your own vision."

He looked earnestly into her eyes. "I remember once telling old Billy that he did that for me, but I think that you, more than anyone, are my real giant."

Elisa's cheeks suddenly became flushed with emotion. "Marc, honey, that's the nicest thing you've ever said to me," she said, swallowing hard.

Marc cuddled Elisa closer to him. "Yeah, well, I've been thinking more and more about the future lately, particularly after seeing little Jerome and listening to you tonight. I know now that I need to take some positive steps to get a hold of my life. Aside from you, the other parts of my life have really run me. I've been forced to do as I have as a result of problems within my businesses. Even before that, I was driven by the desire to prove myself worthy to those I thought mattered."

I know, honey," Elisa murmured softly as she ran her fingers soothingly through his hair. "I know how rough it's been on you...and us."

He squeezed her shoulder and kissed her tenderly on the top of her head. "Tonight," he announced, "I've decided to do something about getting more control of my life."

Elisa looked up quizzically at her husband's face. "Sounds like you have a particular plan in mind."

"Nothing set in concrete yet, but I'm working on it," he said as they continued to gaze at the silvery moonlit sea. Their rock was far enough up the beach to escape the rising tide, so they just watched without any real concern as the frothy edges of dying waves slowly inched up closer and closer to their rocky island.

They hugged and kissed in the moonlight. Each kiss was greeted by a knowing smile as they absorbed the warmth they offered each other in that kind moment. The long silence was broken only when Elisa mused aloud, "It must be nice to be a beach bum, not having to worry about any of the things you and I do and just sitting on the beach, taking in all of this wonderful, intoxicating sea air."

"I think that the sea air is making you drunk, honey. You could no more become a beach bum than fly," Marc playfully chided her. "I can't imagine you sitting on a beach somewhere, wasting your life away!"

"You can't even let me pretend, can you, you rotten old realist?" Elisa said with a smile. "But you're right. I couldn't stand the idea of doing nothing. I suppose it's just the way I'm made. I think you and I have that in common."

"Come on, Mrs. Braddon: I'll take you home before you have us catching the next piece of driftwood out to sea in search of that desert isle of yours!" he teased as he climbed down on to the sandy beach. "Nice thought, though—you and me alone on a deserted island," he added, stretching out his hands to her.

"I'm not ready for bed yet, sweetie," Elisa said, her face glowing in the soft moonlight. "Let's walk along the top of the escarpment for a while. This is a perfect night for walking, talking and just being together."

That night on their beach, sitting on top of their own rocky island, was significant in their short time together, and set the agenda for their future. Elisa was not the sort of person who spoke lightly. Marc knew he could rely on the way she felt today, and that she would more than likely feel the same way tomorrow.

* * *

After Elisa had cooked breakfast for Robert and her husband, she and Marc set off on their return trip to the city and their respective jobs. They listened to the car radio and made small talk over the strains of pop music as they headed down the Sydney-Newcastle freeway

After about a half-hour, Marc turned the radio down and smiled at his wife. "I was thinking a little more about our conversation last night, honey, and I think I've figured some of it out."

"Are you going to share it?" Elisa asked.

"Sure. As a first step, I'm going to actively instigate a program of debt reduction. I've decided to prepare the Vanity Group for a public float. By selling off about half the shares to the public, we should be able to become totally debt free. This will be my first step to reclaiming my life back from the corporate monster I created."

Elisa digested the information for a moment. "How long do you think it'll take you to organize a public listing?"

"Twelve to eighteen months. It'll probably take that long to get the group's current financial performance accepted in the market. I'll also have to complete a managerial restructure to show that the group is not a one-man band. People don't seem to like companies that are too heavily dependent on only one person. They want to know that their investment will produce dividends, no matter who's running the company."

"OK," Elisa said, her interest aroused. "Keep going."

"Well, my original plan was to float the Vanity Group within two to three years of acquiring it, and this fits into that plan. I'm going to have to reorganize the debt structure to take back the Hillsford office park, which I want to keep for us as a little nest egg."

"Don't you owe a lot of money on it?" Elisa asked, her brow furrowing. "Why would you hold on to it and not include it as part of the public float?"

"Even though I still owe something like $20 million, it's worth well over $30 million, and the tenants are paying it off. We'll own it outright within the next ten years anyway, but this float should give me enough money to pay off most of that debt as well. Once the mortgage is paid off, we'll have the full complex's rental income to live on!"

Elisa shrugged. "I guess you know best about these things, Marc. But have you thought about how you're going to handle answering to a group of interfering shareholders and directors after being your own man for so long?"

"Yeah," Marc replied with a slight grimace. "It's not much of a thought, I'll grant you, but at least I'll be out of the Vanity debt, which is something like $35 million. Unlike Hillsford, I don't have a guaranteed way of paying it back. For that, I'd have to ensure that the company performs above expectations, and that's where all my efforts are going these days. I'll pay it all off, I have no doubt about that—but it'll take another ten to fifteen years, and I really want my life back long before then."

"It's not a bad plan, I suppose. You'll still own the majority shareholdings, wouldn't you? And that'll give you effective control of Vanity?"

"*We'll* own it!" Marc corrected sweetly. "I don't recall signing a pre-nuptial agreement with you, my love. Everything I have is yours." A wry smile crossed over Elisa's pretty face. "Same with me, although you're well ahead of me in that department. I'm only a poor academic. We're used to being broke!"

"So what if I have to put up with a few difficult directors on the board?" he asked aloud. "As long as we control most of the shares, I'll still get to run the group! This way, we'll be debt free while still retaining ownership of at least half of the shares in a publicly listed group of companies. More importantly," Marc added with an air of longing, "I'll finally have control of my life."

"It sounds good to me, as long as it's what you really want," Elisa said with a look of concern. "Please don't do it because you feel you have to on my account, although you just made me realize how much money we owe. Fifty-five million dollars!" she said soberly. "That's more money than some African countries generate in a year!"

"It's not really as bad as it sounds," Marc told her reassuringly. "We have massive assets to cover our debts, and the cash flow they generate covers the interest payments on all our loans. As long as they're managed properly, we won't have a problem."

"As long as you're managing our situation, I guess I can stand the pressure. After all, I suppose we were in as much debt yesterday, and I lived with it then. But gee, Marc, did you have to tell how much we owe all at once!" Elisa half-joked.

Marc gave his wife a sly wink for a reply. "You know, Elisa, I've always believed I could work well in a more regulated corporate structure," he continued. "Taking Vanity public will allow me to prove that once and for all."

"I suppose the other good part is that once Vanity Group is publicly listed, its shares become immediately tradable," Elisa remarked. "You've always said that private building companies are notoriously hard to sell, and this should make it easier if ever you wanted to sell your interest in the company. So I guess it means that you could get out at almost any time if you didn't like the goings-on of a public company."

Marc did a double-take. "I didn't know you knew so much about this sort of stuff, Elisa. Have you been studying the stock market or something?"

"I do like to keep abreast of things," Elisa said with a satisfied smile. "Anyway, my father always told me about his investment portfolio and how the market works. He used to get all excited when he got a good deal, and would delight in explaining it in detail to Mum and me. And don't forget that I get regular reports from my pension-plan people discussing their share portfolio and investment strategies—you're not the only whiz-kid in this family, boyo!" she said, grinning.

"Well, pardon me, mam!" Marc said as they both broke into laughter.

Chapter Forty-one

Marc spent the next few months looking at all the areas where Vanity's management needed to be streamlined. After making himself the executive chairman and promoting Stephen James to the position of chief executive officer, Marc decided to go further and create two new group general manager positions: one in construction and the other in manufacturing. He hoped the restructure would illustrate to the share market that Vanity was run by a group of professional managers, and did not rely solely on Marc Braddon for its management energy and ideas.

With Stephen's help, Marc set about selecting his two best managers to fill the new positions. The final choices surprised no one. Andy Hollings was a tough, experienced construction manager in his early forties who had demonstrated real expertise in his role as a divisional manager. He had become one of Marc's best operators and was a key man. Paul Charmers was a few years younger than Hollings, but equally valuable to the group's manufacturing area. He had been responsible for many of Vanity's latest manufacturing innovations, and he was one of the people upon whom Marc had come to rely in recent times.

These two managers, together with Stephen James, formed Marc's new inner cabinet. Clare Eddings, Marc's personal assistant and the only other person allowed to attend their meetings, acted as the minute-taker for the group.

Marc decided to present his plan to eventually float the Vanity Group on the stock exchange at the first inner cabinet meeting.

"If this float is going to succeed, it's important for all the companies within the group to operate autonomously through an arms-length system of professional management," Marc told the group. "While this is the main reason for my management restructure, it's not the only one. All three of you have earned your new jobs, and I want you to dazzle me with your brilliance now that you each have new and wider horizons."

All three managers happily agreed to play their part in Marc's plans.

"We're behind you one hundred percent, Marc," Stephen said on behalf of his new management team.

Now free to focus on the public listing of the group, Marc decided to enlist the help of Whitney Whyte and Partners, the same firm that had helped him secure the finance for the Vanity acquisition just over two years ago. He called Adam Boyd, who listened intently as Marc outlined his plans. The two men made an appointment for the following day to discuss Marc's listing options.

"It's really good to see you again!" Adam said as he greeted Marc at the foyer.

"Likewise, Adam," Marc responded with a smile as he was escorted into Adam's office and shown to a chair across his desk.

Adam's eyes shone as he relished the opportunity to become involved with Marc again. "I hear only good things about your management at Vanity. You've increased production by well over fifty percent and doubled the profitability. Pretty good for someone who has been in the chair for only two years!"

"Thanks." Marc bowed his head modestly for a moment. "It's nice to know that my efforts are appreciated by the big end of town. I hope this will make my next assignment a little easier."

"Ah yes—the floating of the group on the stock exchange," Adam said. "I'd like to involve Jack Bennents in this meeting. He's our resident expert on public listings…that's if you don't mind."

"No problem," Marc said.

Adam left the room and returned with a heavy-set, middle-aged man in tow.

"Jack Bennents, I'd like you to meet Marc Braddon," Adam said as both men shook hands and exchanged pleasantries.

"Marc owns the Vanity Homes Group, among other things, and he has approached us to help him float the group on the stock exchange," Adam explained to Jack. "We organized the acquisition finance for his purchase of Vanity, and he's really made the group hum since." He turned to Marc. "Did you bring those figures we discussed yesterday?"

"Yes, I have them right here." Marc pulled a plain manila folder from his black leather briefcase.

"Good," Adam said as he thumbed through the financial reports. "The figures look good to me, Marc. You really have done a good job. You've increased group turnover from $150 million to a healthy $250 million, and the net profit from just under $7 million to nearly $15 million. That's a phenomenal performance that's really going to be noticed by the market."

"How many years has Vanity been under your financial management?" Jack asked Marc, his interest piqued.

"I've had the company for just on two and a half years," Marc replied, "but I'd like to go to the market with three full years of solid financial results behind us."

"Yes, that would be ideal," Jack agreed. "You should be able to produce your third year's results well before we have to present the final prospectus. You see it takes at least six, maybe nine months to prepare all the paperwork required to support your float. Presuming that everything is satisfactory with the underwriting stockbroker and the regulators, it should then take an additional three months to get the offer to market—a total of about nine to twelve months."

Marc nodded his understanding. "That's about what I figured— that's why I've spent the past few months reorganizing the management structures within the group before coming to see you. I really want to do this in the shortest possible time. How do you see the stock market in a year's time, Jack?"

"I think it'll be even stronger than it is now," Jack said.

"That's good to hear," Marc said with a relieved smile. "What's the traditional ratio of market capitalization to net profit for a group like mine?"

"Building groups often vary, depending upon the perceived strength of their turnover, profitability, operational strength, market share, and brand name," Jack explained, "but a high-quality operation like yours should sell for about ten times its net profit expectations."

"So based on last year's sales of $250 million and a net profit of around $15 million, the whole group should be worth something like $150 million on the market?"

"That seems about right," Jack confirmed. "It could be a little higher if your third-year profit figures turn out to be the $18 million you have here in these financial predictions."

"I'm confident about our forecasted figures," Marc said resolutely, "and it's my job to make them a reality. When can you start working on the float?"

Adam grinned as he became reacquainted with his old client's impatient streak. "Marc," he asked, "I have to ask you why you don't just keep the group for yourself? After all, it's making around $15 million a year!"

Marc shrugged. "Almost every dollar I've ever made from Vanity has gone back into it one way or another. It takes a tremendous amount of investment to keep an operation like this running properly, and it means that I've hardly made a dent in the personal debt I took on when I bought the group. I'd like to take advantage of the rising stock market so that I can clear my own debt. Maybe I'm just getting edgy, but I want certainty in my life."

Adam and Jack nodded. "Fair enough," Adam said. "I don't have to tell you about some of the things that you'll give up when you become a public company. For instance, you won't be able to write yourself a check for anything personal. All the money in the company becomes public money, and there are whole ranges of corporate watchdogs out there keeping their eye on you...not to mention all of the difficult shareholders and investment funds that you'll inherit," he warned.

Marc winced. "You make it sound all very unappetizing, Adam."

Adam shrugged, his palms outward. "Well, everybody wants to become a public company, but most never realize the ramifications until afterwards."

"I guess I'm not looking forward to the downsides, but I figure there will be upsides, too," Marc argued. "The listed group will have a market capitalization with tangible value. It'll give my ownership a liquidity I don't have now as the owner of a private group of companies. And I'll get enough money, I hope, to clear all of my debts. Now that can't be all bad!"

Adam pursed his lips. "True, and who am I to talk you out of it, anyway? You must have considered this decision carefully. It's just that we don't want you backing out at the last moment as a result of something you haven't taken into account," he said candidly. "That would ruin everything."

Marc shook his head. "No, Adam, we're going forward," he said firmly. "What I need from you guys is some sort of a blueprint setting out time frames and costs, so that I can do my bit to help get this float to the market as soon as possible."

"We can do that," Adam replied. Turning to Jack, he asked, "Do you think that Daintree's will be interested in underwriting this particular float?"

"Yes," Jack replied instantly. "I think that a group of this quality will fall nicely within their parameters. They'd probably be my first choice, particularly since we do so much business with them."

Adam turned back to Marc and flashed a confident smile. "Marc, Daintree and Partners are probably the largest brokers on the Sydney Stock Exchange. Their pedigree and proven track record would help promote this float to the institutions, not to mention the mum-and-dad investors."

"I'm totally in your hands, gentlemen," Marc said, realizing that their meeting had probably achieved all that it could. "Just get back to me as soon as you can with an outline of your requirements so that I can get on with my end of things."

Marc began packing his papers into his briefcase. When he was finished, he looked across the desk to Adam and said with a smile, "I was hoping to drop into Jennifer Watkins' office and say hello while I'm here. She'd never forgive me if she knew I visited your offices and didn't stick my head in, particularly after all the hard work she did on the Vanity acquisition."

"Jennifer's away on an assignment in Melbourne at the moment," Adam said somewhat apologetically. "We've got a big job down there that will keep her out of town for the next few weeks. I'll tell her you were here and wanted to see her. I'm sure she'll be sorry she missed you."

Poor old Jennifer; still working like a dog! Marc thought as he checked his watch before picking up his briefcase.

As Marc was preparing to leave, Adam invited both him and Jack into Whitney Whyte's large boardroom for a drink. Remembering the ornate bar and the plush furnishings, Marc gleefully accepted. He settled into a green leather lounge chair to celebrate the birth of their new assignment while Adam ordered their drinks from the white-coated barman.

This is my favorite bar—the scene of my greatest achievement, Marc thought, savoring the room's ambience as he sipped his vodka and tonic.

Adam and Jack spoke with great enthusiasm about Marc's upcoming public float and the part each of them would play in it, making for a congenial end to their meeting. Marc felt assured that he had again chosen to link up with the right people for the job. As the three men relaxed in each other's company, they all agreed that today was a day for reflection. Tomorrow, the real work would begin.

* * *

The Pressani family lived together in a three-acre compound at Bradley's Head in Mosman, on the northern shores of Sydney Harbour. Their hundred and thirty-year-old mansion had been extensively renovated over the years, and was now a blend of modern convenience and Victorian elegance. It was a huge twenty-five thousand square feet, and had north, east, and west wings.

Martello, the family's patriarch was a slight man, five-foot-eight, and always dapper. His closely cropped silver hair framed a small gaunt face from which two penetrating, poker-black eyes peered out at the world. To his family, Martello was a warm man who believed in the old principles of family, duty, and honor; but in business, he was as hard as nails.

Martello insisted that the family live together under one roof, and that included his son, Antonio, and his daughter-in-law, Loren. His daughter and six-year-old granddaughter had also moved back into the family home a year earlier after a messy divorce. Martello also insisted on family harmony at all costs—a veneer that often camouflaged deeper feelings of resentment between people like Loren and her sister-in-law, who let it be known that she thought Loren wasn't good enough for her brother or her family.

Breakfast was often the only time all the family got together for a meal, and it was always served in the solarium overlooking the harbor. The family had an uninterrupted view across the rolling lawns and sparkling waterway to the city skyline in the distance. As each family member carefully trod on eggshells, trying not to incur the wrath of anyone at the breakfast table, their efforts lent the room an air of disquiet.

"What do you have planned for today?" Martello asked Loren toward the end of breakfast.

"I'm in a Supreme Court case at Parramatta, Martello. I hope I just have to make an appearance; it's mostly procedural."

"It'd be nice if you could get home early. We could all have dinner on board the cruiser."

A slightly pained expression ran across Loren's face. Her husband, Antonio, cast her a scolding glance. He always accepted his father's directive without question, along with all the other immediate members of Martello's family. Loren was the only rebel in the ranks.

Loren relented this time. "I'll see what I can do, but I can't promise anything. It depends on the judge."

Martello smiled his approval. "See what you can do."

Chapter Forty-two

On her way back from her Supreme Court appearance at Parramatta, Loren decided to call in unannounced to Vanity's offices. She burst through the office doors and into Vanity's reception area in a whirlwind of red hair and perfume. "I'd like to see Marc Braddon please," she told Sally Johnson, the receptionist.

"May I tell him who's calling?"

"Yes: Tell him that Loren Wilmont wishes to see him."

Sally cocked her left eyebrow. *So you're the woman who keeps ringing Marc*, she thought. This was the woman who had bombarded Sally with several calls a day for the past year until Marc finally took her call or she gave up in frustration.

"Is he expecting you?" she inquired in her frostiest tone.

Loren shot her a depreciative look and said forcefully, "No."

Sally dutifully called Clare Eddings, who then relayed the message to Marc. A few seconds later, Marc emerged in the reception area. Clare couldn't help peering over the edge of the landing above to steal a glimpse of the woman who couldn't leave Marc alone.

"How nice to see you, Loren," Marc said with a politeness that was more for the sake of bystanders than Loren's feelings. "What brings you to Vanity?"

Loren offered Marc her most inviting smile. "I was just in the neighborhood and thought I'd drop by."

"We can go outside and talk," Marc said, guiding her through the doors.

"I thought we could talk in your office," she protested as she followed him into the parking lot.

He whirled around. "Not a chance, Loren. Look, you've got to stop stalking me! We're both married, and I don't know how else to get the message across. I have no interest in you beyond friendship, and you've strained it to breaking point!"

"But Marc…"

"'But Marc' nothing. You seem fixated on me—probably because I was the only man who ever left you."

"No! It's nothing like that!" she said indignantly.

Marc shook his head impatiently. "I don't really care what your problem is; I just want you out of my life. Now are we going to do this like sensible adults, or am I going to have to get tough?"

Loren looked down at the asphalt in resignation. "OK. I guess I know when I'm beaten."

"I doubt that very much," he said as they reached her car.

"I really thought there was a way back for us," Loren said with tears in her eyes.

"Loren, you're going to have to wise up," Marc said with genuine concern. "You're married to a man who will stop at nothing to keep you. You can't flit around town chasing some crazy notion that you and I are ever going to get back together. Imagine what would happen if your husband found out that you've still got the hots for me! My God, Loren, I shudder to think what Antonio would make of it if he saw us standing here talking, let alone doing anything else!"

Reality began to impede on Loren's dreamy expression. "I suppose you're right," she said softly.

I think I'm getting through, Marc noted with relief as he prepared to give her some more good advice. "The best way for you to get me out of your system is to totally ignore me—pretend I no longer exist, and dedicate yourself to your husband until it becomes a habit. Now promise me you'll do as I ask."

Loren looked into Marc's eyes, her mascara beginning to run. "I am going to forget you, Marc," she vowed quietly as she climbed into her car. "It's going to take me a long time to get over you—but I will get over you."

"You have to do it, Loren, for both our sakes, otherwise you'll end up destroying both of us," Marc said as he closed her car door.

As he watched her drive out of Vanity's car park, he felt as if he'd finally seen the last of her.

*　　*　　*

Whitney Whyte's documents arrived by fax late that day, setting out the various action plans and time frames that had to be followed in order to bring the Vanity Group to the stock market in the minimum amount of time.

Marc had just enough time to glance through them, since he was about to leave for the day. He tossed the documents into his briefcase, resolving to study them at home at his leisure.

He always passed Clare's desk on his way out. Today, for some reason, he was struck by her dedication to the job and to him personally. He also realized that he had consciously kept her at arms length lately, and had become detached from everything she was doing.

"Aren't you going home tonight, my dear?" he asked her as she worked studiously on a pile of papers on her desk.

Clare looked up. "Yes, I'll be off soon. I just have to tidy up these last few things so I can go home with a clear conscience."

He sat down on one corner of her desk with a friendly smile. "I just wanted to tell you how much I appreciate everything you do around here. You're here well before anyone else, and you're the last to go home. I'm really pleased with you, Clare; you're invaluable to me."

Clare's whole demeanor brightened, like flowers after a much-needed rain. "That's so good to know. I thought I was out of favor, because you haven't said boo to me lately."

"No, no. It's just that I've been preoccupied," Marc said with a nervous laugh. "Well, I'll see you in the morning bright and early," he added as he left for the parking lot.

"Yes…good night, Marc," she replied, her smile growing wider.

*　　*　　*

The smell of home cooking greeted Marc as he opened the door. *Elisa's home; she must have got out of her lecture tonight!* he inwardly rejoiced.

"Honey, I'm home!" he called out in imitation of a fifties family sit-com.

"Just wait there, sweetie pie," Elisa yelled back. She hurried to the door, wearing a frilly pink apron she had quickly donned for the occasion. They embraced and kissed at the front door, Elisa bending one leg at the knee in keeping with the sit-com scene.

"I don't know which of those old shows suits us best tonight," Marc remarked. "Take your pick: *Father Knows Best* or *I Love Lucy*?"

"Rick-y!" Elisa let loose with a high-pitched whine as Marc collapsed in laughter.

"It's marvelous, the way you anticipate me," he told her when he could speak again. "It makes it nice to come home to someone who knows you so well."

"Ooh, I do love to make a home-cooked meal for my man at the end of long, hard day," she jested, still in her black-and-white role. "I'm just glad that you came home on time!" she said menacingly as she returned to her Technicolor self.

"Why would I stay in the office when I have a chance to be with you, my little darling?"

"That's good, then! Maybe after dinner, you can do that thing you're so good at!" she said cheekily.

"Oh, and I thought you told me I was good at everything!" he replied with mock indignation.

"You are! It's just that I happen to like the way it makes me feel, and you're the only one who can do it."

"OK, OK, I'll wash *and* dry the dishes again tonight!" He ducked as Elisa punched him playfully on the arm.

They weren't always this playful, but like most couples, they had their crazy moments. Dinner was great, and Marc whisked Elisa from the dinner table to the bedroom. The lovemaking that followed was momentous, and the bliss went on for what seemed like hours.

They sat up in bed to watch the late news, and then realized they still had to clear away the dinner dishes. They looked at each other and agreed that the first one out of bed in the morning would do it as they curled up under the covers and drifted peacefully off to sleep.

*   *   *

"I have circulated the notice I received yesterday from Whitney Whyte," Marc said to his inner cabinet as he opened a hastily assembled meeting. "It sets out what we have to do to prepare the group for public listing."

"I can see why it takes so long to get companies ready for a float," Stephen remarked as he scanned the pages. "Just look at the sort of information one has to get together!"

"I see a number of items I can handle," Andy said, "but I guess it would be better if we discussed each of them in depth before any of us goes away to do anything on our own. No sense in everybody working on the same things."

"Precisely, Andy," Marc said. "This is why I called this meeting— to sort out the tasks and delegate them among us all."

After two hours of friendly debate, a detailed list of tasks was agreed upon, along with a list of responsibilities for the completion of each specific task. Some had to be shared among the group, since they entailed too much work for any one person, and Marc took sole responsibility for some of the others.

Setting up an eight-week timetable, Marc suggested the group hold similar meetings at least twice a week to review progress and collectively solve any of the thorny issues that would inevitably arise as the members worked through this process.

Marc found himself working late most nights with Elisa's blessing, as she accepted the fact that this was a very important stage in their lives. After most people had left for the day, he and Clare were still working to compile the reams of financial and corporate information that the whole process demanded.

In addition to the initial list of requirements, Marc had since received two more requests for information: one was from stockbrokers Daintree and Partners, who would actually underwrite the float, and the other from Whitney Whyte. This only added to the difficulty of trying to meet his self-imposed deadline as he addressed an ever-increasing list of tasks.

*   *   *

During the next few weeks, every time Marc approached Clare's desk to get a document or hand her something to do, she would spin around in her swivel chair, legs slightly apart, her short skirt riding up around her thighs and exposing her panties. While Marc made it a point to look directly at her face, he couldn't help but catch the whole show. Clare smirked as if to say that it was no coincidence her skirts rode up when he was around.

Sometimes she would brush up against him whenever they were near the filing cabinet in his office. At first, these little brushes were fleeting, but became more overt and were accompanied by small groans of pleasure. Marc knew that Clare had done a lot for him and the firm, and he felt he needed to treat her with kid gloves, so he tried to ignore her advances.

All that changed one evening when they were the only ones in the building and Clare strode into his office with purpose. He was standing in front of his desk reading some papers she had just given him. She rushed up to him, knocking him backward onto his desk. Before he could react, she kissed him wantonly on the mouth as all of her bottled-up passion exploded. She whispered frenziedly that she had to have him.

"Whoa, whoa!" he shouted as he struggled to pry her off him. "I can't do this. I'm a married man, and I love my wife. This just isn't right, and it's not going to happen!"

Clare's face was flushed, and she looked if she were about to erupt. "I want you so badly, Marc! You're driving me insane!" She stood up and worked her tight dress back down over her hips. "No one will ever know. I'll be your own little sex slave. I'll do anything, anything you want!"

I'm surrounded by mad women. No sooner do I get rid of Loren than Clare goes crazy on me. Help! Marc anguished as he tried to assimilate the situation.

He took a deep breath, straightened his shirt and smoothed his hair away from his face. "For God's sake, Clare, how can I get it across to you that I don't want or need you that way! Everything I need, I get from my wife. I don't know where you got the impression that I wanted an affair!"

Clare ran an eager tongue across her lips. "If you're happy with your wife, then what was that redhead all about?"

"That was not what it appeared to be. Anyway, it's none of your bloody business. Now please go back to your desk and behave!" Marc told her sternly.

"But. . . but. . ."

"Look, there are no 'buts' about it, Clare. This must stop, or I'll have to let you go. I don't want to do it, but that's how it is! I can't have you coming on to me like this. It won't happen again, right?"

Clare's shoulders slumped, and she took an awkward step back. "Right," she said. She bowed her head and walked out of his office.

Marc breathed a sigh of relief as he heard her leave for the day. He decided to say nothing about it to Elisa: After all, he had gone to great lengths to convince Elisa that his and Clare's relationship was purely professional before she would let them go on their trips around the state. He resolved to have the matter out with Clare once and for all the next morning in the privacy of his office.

*   *   *

When Marc arrived at the office, Clare was at her desk, as usual.

"Good morning, Clare; let's talk about things, shall we?" he said, directing her into his office before shutting the door.

"Look, Marc," she said immediately, "I want to say how sorry I am about last night…"

"Me, too, Clare," he said kindly. "I don't want to lose you. You're a very valuable employee to me, but I'm not the one for you. You're a beautiful woman, and you should have no trouble finding a partner. Now please, do us both a favor and let's get our relationship back to where it should be."

A contrite expression ran over Clare's face. She looked down at the carpet in Marc's office before finding her voice. "Marc, I can't apologize enough; I promise you it won't happen again. I love working with you, and want to stay. Can we start again with a clean slate?"

"Absolutely," Marc said with a sense of relief.

After a few more minutes, Clare left his office to finalize some critical reports needed that day by Vanity's underwriting stockbrokers to move the public listing documentation on to the next stage.

With that disaster averted, Marc and Clare settled down to an even more productive working relationship, which helped them overcome the massive workload temporarily placed on both of them.

* * *

Within three months, Marc and his cabinet had met all the initial requirements of their merchant bankers and underwriting stockbroker. With all the paperwork now in those people's hands, Marc was assured that they would move as quickly as possible to produce a draft prospectus for comment and, hopefully, approval by the Securities Commission.

Three months later—and six months after his initial meeting with Adam Boyd—Marc, Clare, and Stephen went to Whitney Whyte's offices to collect the draft prospectus. Adam Boyd and Jack Bennents were there, as was Christopher Ambos, a senior partner from the underwriting stockbroker, Daintree and Partners. Marc had met him several times during the past few months while attending the numerous planning meetings, held in Whitney Whyte's offices.

Because of their previous business association, Whitney Whyte's had taken the lead role in this float, which meant that everything went through their office rather than through Daintree's, as would normally have been the case. This protocol had been followed throughout the whole process, and seemed to work.

"This looks good!" Marc said as he thumbed through the hundred or so pages of the draft.

"Yes, it does," Stephen agreed. "I can see where all the effort has gone. I recognize a lot of the base information, but you fellows have certainly polished everything up!"

"Well, that's what we do best, but we have to have something to work with in the first place," Christopher said with a smile.

"Yes, that's right," Adam added. "All the polishing in the world won't disguise a poor deal. You guys have got a group that we can show in its best light, so that makes our job a little easier."

"When do you expect to hear back from the Securities Commission?" Marc asked.

"Within two to three months," Christopher answered. "It'll take them that long to get around to reviewing the prospectus. They'll appoint one of their officers to look after this float, and we'll liaise with that person throughout the whole process, right up until they sign off on the whole deal."

"Sounds like a long process. Is it always this difficult?" Stephen asked.

"If the prospectus is straightforward, then it should take no more than three months to clear all of the commission's requirements," Jack responded. "If things get complicated, then it can take up to a year."

"Hmm. Let's hope it looks straightforward to them," Marc said.

"By the way, my estimate of $250,000 to get the group to market still looks good," Adam said. "It'll only change if there's some unforeseen delay along the way."

With that, the Vanity people picked up their copies of the prospectus and caught a taxi from the city back to their Silverwater office, breathing a collective sigh of relief as they realized that the first part of their task was over. Marc and Stephen talked enthusiastically about what would happen after the group became public, and each speculated on what the eventual share price would be after the initial float.

"I think we've finally nailed this deal," Stephen said gleefully as he thumbed through his copy of the draft prospectus.

"It took an amazing amount of work, but hopefully it will all be worth it in the end," Marc said, letting out a sigh. "What do *you* think, Clare?" he asked his personal assistant. "You seem to be off in another world."

"Hmm? Sorry, Marc. What did you say?"

"Nothing Clare; go back to wherever you were," Marc said as he and Stephen began to laugh.

*   *   *

Adam Boyd phoned Marc on Christmas Eve, 1994, almost exactly three months after filing the memorandum with the Securities Commission.

"Marc, I have some good news for you. The Commission has just signed off on the prospectus after requesting only a few minor changes. The matter is now in Daintree's hands, and they only need to negotiate a date for the float with the Sydney Stock Exchange."

"That's fantastic news, Adam. You've just given me what I wished for this Christmas," Marc said gleefully.

"Either Christopher Ambos or I will call you as soon as a float date is determined. Until then have a merry Christmas and a prosperous New Year."

Adam's news filled Marc to the brim with Christmas spirit, so he took the rest of the day off to shop for presents for Elisa and their family.

*   *   *

In the third week of January, Christopher Ambos called Marc to say that the Vanity Group was scheduled to become a publicly listed company in about four months.

"We've planned a listing for the last week of May, which will give us just enough time to properly promote the float while also coinciding with a rising market." Christopher said enthusiastically.

"Sounds good to me, Christopher!" Marc said with a big grin.

"Happy to oblige," Christopher said with a chuckle. "The stock exchange accepted my firm's listing recommendations: fifty percent of the group's shares, or twenty-five million shares, are to be offered at a price of between $3.00 and $3.60 a share. This offer would value the whole group at between $100 million and $180 million, depending on market sentiment."

A perplexed expression smothered Marc's earlier grin. "When will I know which end of the share price range I should expect?"

Christopher cleared his throat. "I know it's difficult for you to accept, Marc, but as I explained at the outset, the final listing price will be determined closer to the listing day. This was because Daintree's, as the underwriting stockbroker, has to be sure it can sell all the shares for the final underwritten price, or else foot the bill for those shares remaining unsold if the offer is undersubscribed."

Marc's mood suddenly shifted downward. "It's really difficult for someone like me, who's been used to controlling his own destiny, to accept this sort of uncertainty," he said as he fidgeted in his office chair. "It's even harder for me to place my future into the hands of the strangers who might want to buy our stock."

Christopher shrugged. "It's difficult to do it any other way, Marc, because Daintree's can't afford to be put in a position where it has to buy back unsold shares at the offer price before eventually reselling them at whatever share price the stock market dictates. If it did, these losses would be reflected in your return from the sale of your half-stake in the group."

"That doesn't fill me with much joy! I have to sell my half-stake for at least $75 million to have enough left over, after paying capital gains taxes on the money, to clear my personal debts."

"I shouldn't worry too much, Marc," Christopher assured him. "You have a terrific company, and I'm sure you'll get more than the $75 million you need out of this float."

The prospect of a no-win outcome made Marc nervous, but he had to take the gamble if he wanted to clear his debts and release the value he had locked up in the Vanity Group. *What can I do, I'm well beyond the point of return now,* he thought.

*   *   *

"You're a brave man," Elisa told him as they discussed his dilemma at the dinner table. "It'll work out. There is no point worrying until you have something to worry about."

"You're right, honey. I guess I've faced worse situations before, but God, I wonder how many more knotted stomachs I have to suffer before I can finally get clear of everything. It'd be so nice just to come home to you at night without the weight of the world and the national debt on my shoulders."

"You're nearly there, my love; just a little longer."

"Yeah, just a little longer!" he said as he stared into his wine glass.

Chapter Forty-three

Another day in limbo! Marc thought as he counted the days until the scheduled public listing. It was now only a fortnight away, and he was expecting to hear from Adam Boyd or Christopher Ambos any day now.

It was Christopher who called Vanity's offices two minutes later. "Marc, the partners met and agreed to back your float at a price-to-earning ratio of nine times your last net profit of $18 million. This means that they value the whole group at around $162 million."

Marc breathed a sigh of relief. "That's about what you said it'd be worth, Christopher, although it's still a bit less than the valuation that Whitney Whyte's people came up with. But I guess it'll have to do," he added philosophically.

"Once the company's listed, it'll find its own level in the marketplace. If people perceive it to be a well run, profitable company, then its shares will escalate accordingly," Christopher reassured him. "Anyway, a total value of over a $160 million for a group of companies that you paid less than $40 million for just three years ago is pretty impressive, if you don't mind my saying so."

Marc grinned. "I don't mind at all, Christopher. I knew a bargain when I saw it, although it's a shame the market's so wary of building companies. Perhaps they've yet to understand the real strength we have as a result of our vertical integration."

"You're probably right," Christopher replied, "but as the underwriting broker, we have to pitch the company to the market as it exists today."

"I understand," Marc conceded. "I still reckon that our new listed entity should really value at ten times its net earnings, putting its total value at around $180 million. And I hope to achieve that level of capitalization within a year or so of listing."

"A worthwhile ambition," Christopher said with a knowing smile. "If anybody can do it, you can. We'll have to put the Vanity Group on the top of our 'buy' recommendations if you're going to increase the share value by that much!" he noted with a chuckle.

"I guess time will tell, Christopher. In the meantime, I've got to go with what your firm is prepared to underwrite. If my half-share sells for $80 million and I clear $60 million, after the tax man and everyone else gets paid, it'll give me enough to pay off all my debts and have a little left over. So, I guess I'm giving you the go-ahead."

"I'll fax over a letter of authorization for you to sign and return, Marc. Then we can go ahead and advise the stock exchange. Oh, and good luck with the float, old boy!"

With that call, a large part of the uncertainty that had been dogging Marc for the past few weeks evaporated. At least he now had a firm sales figure to work on, and he could calculate how much he would net from his sale of half his shares after all the fees and commissions were deducted.

The underwriting broker had agreed to take a flat fee for his risk, which came to about $5.6 million, and another $400,000 was earmarked for fees to everyone else, including the stock exchange.

On the basis of the figures that Christopher had given him, Marc thought he might just clear his magic figure of $60 million. This meant that he could pay off all of his loans, which now totaled about $55 million, and have money in his own name for the first time in his life.

The prospect of everything finally coming together made Marc a very happy man indeed, so he took the rest of the day off and called on Elisa at work. He couldn't wait to tell her about the surprise he had planned for her. She squeezed in some free time, and they went off for a drink at one of the campus bars.

"I can't believe you'd do that for me, my darling," Elisa said, her beautiful blue eyes welling with tears.

Marc's face was filled with a schoolboy's delight; he could hardly contain himself. "That's the first thing I want to do, once I get the money. You've done so much for me—now, I want to do this for you."

"Wow, a million dollars of my own! I can't believe it!" she said excitedly, trying to come to grips with her sudden wealth.

"So, what are you going to do with it?"

Elisa knitted her eyebrows as she considered her options. "I really don't know; I suppose I could buy myself a new wardrobe," she said with a mischievous smile.

"How about the dream you told me about that night at Whitefeather Cove?" Marc suggested tenderly.

"Yes...I could do it now, couldn't I?" she mused, a look of revelation sweeping across her face. "I really miss being on a dig, but don't get me wrong; I can tolerate being at the university because it allows us to have a life together, and that makes up for everything else."

"Well, now that you're going to be independently wealthy, you don't have to do anything you don't want to do!" he said with a grin. "I'll get more than a million dollars' worth of pleasure just watching you figure out how to spend the dough."

Elisa's eyes took on a faraway gleam as she pictured putting her dream into action. "Yeah, I could fund a dig using seven or eight of my post-graduate students. I'd have to visit them only every couple of months, and I'd be away for just a few weeks at a time." She looked entreatingly into her husband's face. "Could you tolerate that, my love?"

"Sure I could, as long as it makes you happy," Marc said with an affectionate smile. "You know I'd do anything for you! Why, I'd even kill a grizzly bear if you asked me to."

"You crazy man. A grizzly! Your mind's a funny thing, isn't it," she giggled, as she tilted her head and looked at her husband in a funny way.

"Seriously...if that's what you want, then that's what you should do. I'll back you all of the way, just the way you've done for me over the years."

"And you wonder why I love you so much." Elisa leaned over the table and kissed his lips.

If I wanted a way to spend a million dollars in one afternoon, I certainly found an easy way to do it! Marc thought to himself with a chuckle. Now all he had to do was get the money so that he could make good on his promise. For that, he would have to wait another two weeks until his company was floated on the stock exchange.

*   *   *

Now that Elisa had more than a vested interest in the outcome of the Vanity listing, she arranged to take the day off to attend Vanity's debut on the stock exchange's boards. At nine-thirty that morning, She and Marc were looking down on the stock exchange's trading floor from behind the plate-glass window of Daintree and Partners' trading office.

"It's hard to believe that we're only moments away from listing Vanity!" Elisa exclaimed to her husband as she took in the high-tech surroundings. "Who would have thought you could have come so far so quickly?"

"I almost feel I have to pinch myself—it feels kind of surreal," Marc said, feeling a little like a duck out of water.

Christopher Ambos and a couple of his colleagues were there, as were Adam and Jack from Whitney Whyte's. All stood around drinking coffee and chatting as they awaited the start of the day's trading.

"We're quietly confident," Adam told Marc while Jack, standing next to Adam with his coffee cup in hand, nodded in agreement.

"We haven't lost a patient yet, Marc, and I'm pretty sure that this one will go just as well," Jack said, tapping the side of his nose with his forefinger to indicate inside knowledge.

Marc, too, was quietly confident, as Christopher had confided that Daintree's had been inundated with advance orders for the new Vanity Group stock.

Marc sidled up to Christopher, who had just moved away from the group of colleagues he had been chatting with to pour himself another cup of coffee. "Have you heard any more about the level of subscriptions by the institutions?" Marc asked quietly.

"My advice is that interest is very high. I expect your stock to be a star listing," Christopher replied with a smile. "It should be fully subscribed by midmorning."

As the exchange opened, everybody focused on the electronic boards. Within a few minutes, "The Vanity Group" appeared, and they all cheered. Then, they all did a double-take as the stock exchange board indicated that it was already fully subscribed. To their complete amazement, all the shares had sold out in less than a minute of being offered.

"There was no point in telling you guys that the stock was priced too low," Marc said to Christopher with a wry smile.

Christopher gave a shrug as he prepared to reply. *He does a lot of shrugging, doesn't he?* Marc noted cynically. *Then again, I guess that goes with the job.*

"My managing partner would simply say that we were the experts," Christopher told him with an amiable smile, "and that the stock must have been properly priced, or it wouldn't have sold out so quickly."

Marc recognized a no-win situation when he saw one, so he just smiled back.

"Oh Marc," Elisa shouted gleefully, "you've made it happen, just as you said it would!" She hugged him and performed a small jig to everyone's delight.

Adam and Jack left quietly after offering their congratulations. Christopher then settled the excited couple down with another cup of coffee before showing them into his office, where he passed a series of documents across his desk for Marc to sign. "After you execute these documents, we'll be able to transfer the funds to your nominated bank account within seventy-two hours," Christopher told him.

Signing those documents was probably the most enjoyable task Marc had ever performed in his business life; with just a few strokes of his pen, he had overcome all the previous hardships and taken a massive weight off his shoulders.

"So in three days, you'll be flush with funds," Elisa said with a coy smile.

"Yes," he replied, his eyes shining with triumph. "And I'll then be able to pay off on my promise!"

"I'll have to keep my eye on you, Mr. Braddon, to make sure you don't leave town," she replied, giving her husband a playful nudge as they made their way out of Christopher's office.

"Geez, if I'd known you were so concerned about your lousy million bucks, I wouldn't have told you about it in the first place!" Marc shot back with a wide grin.

"You know how money-mad I am," she replied with an equally wide smile.

"Let's go home and make love; that way, you can keep your eye on *all* of me," Marc whispered as they walked hand in hand out of the stock exchange.

"Only if it's as wild as it was the day we bought Vanity," she said half-jokingly.

"That's what I planned, my darling; that's what I planned," Marc replied as he hailed a cab.

* * *

When Marc sailed triumphantly into Vanity's office bright and early the next morning, nothing had changed outwardly—the same people were there at their desks, and everything was still where he left it the night before. Still, he couldn't shake the feeling that on some level, a change had occurred. *The place has a different feel about it somehow; maybe I can sense the expectation of the new shareholders,* Marc mused as he made his way to his desk.

"Congratulations!" Clare offered with a broad smile as Marc approached her desk.

"Thanks, Clare," he answered as he spun his personal assistant's office diary around to his side of desk and studied it. "What appointments do I have today?"

"You have an interview scheduled for 2 P.M. with the *Financial Review,* but apart from that, you're pretty well clear all day. I thought you might need some time to yourself to work on the restructuring before you met with the press."

"Good thinking, Clare," Marc replied gratefully as he picked up his briefcase and moved toward his office.

Stephen James stuck his head in a bit later to offer his good wishes, as did the rest of the managers and staff throughout the morning.

Marc's first day as the owner of a publicly listed company was off on the right foot. He called a cabinet meeting for eleven o'clock to bring his team up to date about the new *modus operandi*.

The transition from a private to a public company went smoothly, once everyone realized by the end of the first day that nothing had really changed about the way the company operated. It was just that the group now had a multitude of owners, of which Marc was still the majority stockholder.

Marc had to reformat the board of directors to accommodate the various interests on the company's share register, which brought in several new faces. He settled on a mixture of four executive and six non-executive directors.

The four executive directors—consisting of himself as executive chairman, Stephen James, Andy Hollings, and Paul Charmers—added stability to the board in that they could advise the six new independent external directors of the ramifications of certain decisions. This also gave the Vanity board a unique balance. Marc figured that this blend would afford the new board a genuine insight into the way the company ran, thereby ensuring informed decisions.

That approach seemed to work fairly well, and at the six-month review of its life as a public company, the Vanity Group was doing very well indeed. In fact, its share price, which had opened at $3.24, had now increased to $3.55, valuing the group at almost ten times its last published earnings figure.

*   *   *

And that's when it all started. Almost six months to the day after Vanity had been listed, Clare brought that morning's *Financial Review* into Marc soon after it had been delivered to Vanity's offices.

"Have you read this? There's a story in the 'market rumor' column that Vanity will soon face stiff competition with an unnamed national builder who is intent on forcing his way into the Sydney market by heavily discounting his houses," Clare reported with a worried expression. "The newspaper is predicting a bidding war as Vanity and this competitor fight each other for market share."

Marc calmly fixed his attention on the newspaper article, which concluded that "such an outcome would have a severe effect on Vanity's profitability if it had to cut its profit margins, as might be expected, to repel the invader."

Marc arched a perplexed eyebrow as he finished reading. "This seems odd to me," he told Clare.

"What do you mean?"

"We discussed something like this at a recent board meeting, but no particular builder was mentioned—only the fact that Vanity had to allow for such a contingency."

"That's right," Clare agreed. "Hmm, that *is* odd."

Marc knew there was no substance to this rumor, but he could do little other than watch the rumor's effect on the share price.

The report indeed had an effect: The share price fell from $3.55 to just above $3.00, wiping out nearly $27 million, or about fifteen percent off the group's overall value. Marc was horrified.

"Welcome to the wonderful world of publicly listed companies," Adam Boyd told Marc when he rang his adviser. "It's probably just a minor fluctuation; these things happen all the time. Anyway, you're a new kid on the block, and the market is looking for you to hiccup! Things will settle down just as quickly because the underlying fundamentals of your company are sound, and that's what counts in the long term."

Adam was right—things did settle down. There was no sign of the mythical builder who might threaten Vanity's existence, and the share price recovered as several new buyers appeared on the company's share register. In no time, the Vanity Group was again the darling of the stock exchange.

A couple of months later, there was another rumor that Marc planned to borrow heavily to extend Vanity's operations into every state in the country. This rumor was also communicated to the market via the same financial newspaper, which concluded, "Vanity's profit expectations could suffer as a result of high interest and borrowing costs if this were true, not to mention its exposure to the untested markets the company would face in such an expansionary move." The financial scribes warned shareholders that "Vanity had only recently been listed and that, in our opinion, it lacked the underlying financial strength to fund such a major expansion."

"These wild rumors are starting to worry me, Stephen," Marc confided as the two men held an emergency meeting in Marc's office. "Where do you think they're coming from?"

Stephen shook his head. "I honestly don't know. As you know, we discussed this option at an earlier board meeting, but nothing had been resolved."

"That's right; we only considered the implications, should we ever expand our operations interstate." He looked to Stephen with a grimace. "There's only one logical conclusion: It's starting to look like we have mole on the board."

Stephen nodded his agreement.

Marc and his board issued strong denials to the press. But in some people's minds, denial only confirmed substance, which in turn caused the share price to dip even further.

Three days later, another article appeared in the same paper from yet another unnamed source, reporting that: "Marc Braddon is about to dump his entire fifty-percent stake in the company on the market." The article went on to suggest that Marc could not tolerate the vagaries of the market, and wanted to return to the anonymity of the private business sector.

This had a devastating effect on the share price, coming on the heels of the earlier rumor about the group's unfounded expansion plans. Vanity's shares plummeted to a new low of $2.20. Marc was horrified anew as he saw how easily his newfound wealth could evaporate before his eyes.

He quickly got a press release out to the media, inviting them to a hurried press conference in Vanity's offices where he could again state that there was no truth in this or any of the other rumors about him or the company. In just a few hours, Vanity's boardroom was reorganized into a theater layout with a desk at the front of the room for the Vanity executives and forty-two chairs lined up in six rows for the media.

While the room was filling up, Marc held a private meeting with Stephen James, Andy Hollings, and Paul Charmers. Before he went on the record with reporters, he wanted to make sure if they knew anything about this amazing spate of rumors.

"Come in and close the door," Marc said to Clare after his three managers were seated around his desk. He fixed them with a steely look. "I need to know if any of you knows anything about the source of all these rumors. As I'm sure I don't have to tell you, each of these three rumors has had some basis, as they relate to matters we have discussed at recent board meetings."

Marc searched each of their faces for signs of nervousness or guilt. While Stephen, Andy, and Clare all wore worried expressions, Paul Charmers looked decidedly fidgety, and Marc's steely gaze was only making him more so.

Andy Hollings was the first to break the uncomfortable silence. "I know it looks pretty fishy, Marc, but I give you my word that I haven't breathed a word to anyone about what we've discussed at our board meetings."

"I—I can assure you I've said nothing to anybody either, Marc," Paul Charmers chimed in quickly. "All of my board files are kept under lock and key in my office."

"You know my position, Marc," Stephen said.

After pondering Paul Charmers' response a little longer, Marc gave up the interrogation. "I'll take your word for it, gentlemen," he concluded with a sigh. "If it's none of us, then it has to be coming from someone else on the board. Clare, I need you to get me some background material on each of the other six board members—check their other directorships and affiliations...maybe we can find something out there."

"I'll get on to it straight away," Clare said, jotting down Marc's instruction in her notebook.

Marc shot his staff a determined look. "In the meantime, we all have to demonstrate a united front at this press conference. I want you all to follow my lead and deny that there are any changes mooted at Vanity," he commanded as he and his managers made their way across the hall to face the room full of reporters.

Chapter Forty-four

Within a month, the share price had recovered and topped its previous highs. Ironically, the Vanity Group was worth more now than at any other time. The whole episode puzzled Marc because even though Vanity was a solid asset-backed stock, its share price had bounced around in recent times as if it were a lesser speculative stock, which should have never been the case.

Soon after things returned to normal, he told Elisa, "I know something's going on, but I can't put my finger on it."

"Are you sure you're just not jumpy? I mean, maybe there's no real explanation, and this is just the way things work in the public arena— you know, where the market thrives on rumors as it tries to second-guess share price trends."

Elisa's suggestion did little to ease Marc's worried mind. "Maybe," he replied uneasily, "but I have a sinking feeling deep down in the pit of my stomach that something's afoot."

"Oh, that poor old stomach of yours, Marc; it's still taking a beating, isn't it?" she teased with a broad smile. "I thought you planned to give it rest when you got out of the financial woods, and now you're at it again!"

"It's no laughing matter, Elisa!" he snapped in frustration. "These sort of rumors shouldn't just *happen*. And every time they surface, the share price dives, only to return even stronger than before. I smell a rat, I tell you!"

Elisa's smile was replaced with a concerned gaze. "Well, if you think that's the case, maybe you should investigate. You'll have to be very discreet, though, won't you?"

"You bet I will. I wouldn't want to start another rumor…or worse, undermine the confidence my staff has in me."

"Maybe you should talk to Robert and Maddie. Maybe they know someone who could check this out."

"That's a good idea. I'll call them now," Marc said.

*   *   *

"Did you bring the latest share register listing and those other reports?" Robert asked as he and Marc sat down in the living room at Whitefeather Cove late the next day.

Marc nodded as he pulled out several manila folders from his briefcase and handed them to Robert, adding, "On the face of it, there doesn't seem to be anything sinister, but I've got a bad feeling that I just can't shake."

Maddie came in with coffee, then stayed on to listen to the conversation.

"Experience has taught me not to take this sort of thing at face value. You'd be surprised who might be hiding behind some of these innocent-looking companies," Robert said as he thumbed through the reports. "The good thing is that these people have to identify themselves sooner or later, or they wouldn't be able to claim ownership of their shares. In the final analysis, no one likes to lose control of his or her money. Even if they hide behind a complicated web of family trusts, you can still identify the ultimate owner."

Marc smiled at Robert and Maddie. "Sounds like a good starting point."

"I'll get someone I know to make the initial inquiries, if you like," Robert suggested. "That way, no one from your immediate business circle will be involved."

"That'll also allow you to quarantine any information he uncovers and stop it from being leaked to the outside," Maddie added. "Do you have any theories about who might be behind this?"

"No, not really," Marc replied. "I've met and dealt with some real low-lifes in my time, but I don't think I've upset anyone in particular; well, not lately, anyway!" he said with a sheepish grin.

"This may turn out to be nothing, Marc, but you can never be too sure about these things," Robert cautioned. "Sometimes people have a completely different perspective, and hold grudges about all sorts of things!"

"Yeah, I hear you, Robert," Marc said as he scoured his brain for a lead. "I've had deals with some odd people...you know, those who operate legally, but in the gray areas of the law. But I don't think I've ever upset anyone to that extent. I've always paid my way..."

"Don't worry about it now, Marc. I reckon if there were such a person, he or she'd stand out once you saw their name on a list of suspects," Robert told him assuredly.

"How long will you need?" Marc asked.

"I should have all of these companies checked out within a week. And you should expect to be surprised, if I'm any judge."

*   *   *

The week passed fairly slowly, and Marc and Elisa struggled to find other things to talk about as they awaited Robert's call. Toward the middle of the week, Elisa managed to extract a promise from Marc that he would not mention the subject again until after he had heard from his trusted "investigators."

Once the prescribed week had elapsed, Marc couldn't get up to Whitefeather Cove fast enough; Elisa had to keep reminding him to take his foot off the gas or he'd end up getting stopped for speeding.

When they arrived, they all congregated in the LaPonts' living room, eager to find out what Robert had uncovered. Maddie, nursing Jerome on her knee, joined them in the living room to be part of Robert's briefing.

"Tell me what you found, Robert," Marc asked, his nerves on edge.

"Well, I eliminated all the big companies and institutional investors, since they're obviously not out to get you," Robert surmised. "That left me with something like two hundred and eighty other entities. Of those, just over two hundred own the shares in their own name, leaving us the other seventy-five or so companies and trusts to check out."

Marc shook his head at the weeding-out process. "I feel I should apologize for giving you such a tough week, but I assure you that mine's been worse."

"It's like I said: One name'll stick out from the list—so much so that even Maddie and I recognized it."

"Well, who is it?"

"Dan White."

Elisa immediately looked up. "Wasn't he the guy who also messed you around on several deals before getting involved with you at Hillsford?"

"The very same!" Marc replied as his jaw dropped. "Dan White! What's he doing in Vanity? I haven't had any dealings with him since I bought him out of the Hillsford deal."

"Well, he seems to be interested in you and what you're doing," Robert noted. "Ironically, his name was almost the last one we tracked down. He owns his shares through a complicated network of beneficiary trusts. But as I said before, no matter how people duck and weave, they never really let go of their ownership, so the trail has to end with a name."

"May I see that report?" Marc asked as he extended his hand.

"You'd better look through the rest of these names to see if there's anyone else you recognize," Robert said, handing him the individual pages of the report.

"I still don't see why Dan White would want to harm you," Elisa wondered out loud. "If he's bought into your company, he must want to be involved with you, right?"

"Yeah, maybe that's all there is to it," Marc replied, his frown still firmly in place.

"Maybe you should look at this other report," Robert suggested. "It's a printout of when your various shareholders bought their shares, and how much they paid for them."

"Wow! Would you look at that?" Marc exclaimed. "Dan White's trust owns nearly six percent of the company! He brought them in two blocks, both times right after the price slumped when those rumors hit the stock exchange."

"Wow is right!" Robert said. "If you accept that he's a shrewd investor, then maybe it rings true. But you'll notice that he's been able to acquire his stake at an average price of $2.35, giving him a current paper profit of about $4.5 million."

"Not a bad investment!" Maddie said skeptically while bouncing Jerome on her knee to keep him quiet.

"Not a bad investment at all," Marc concurred in the same vein.

"You'll also notice that he stayed miles below the fifteen-percent ownership threshold so that he doesn't have to declare his interest to the stock exchange," Robert noted.

"Yeah, this is all too coincidental. You know that bad feeling I had, Elisa? Well, it now seems to have a name attached to it," Marc announced.

Elisa looked intently at her husband's face. "Where do we go from here?" she asked.

"Well, now that we have a name to work with, we can set a professional investigator on to this," Robert suggested. "He could come inside Vanity and see if anyone is linked to this fellow White, or anyone else for that matter. If you can prove a connection, then it's dynamite."

"That would unearth a massive series of crimes, not the least of which is insider trading," Marc replied, stunned. "If someone inside Vanity has been feeding Dan information or leaking false rumors to manipulate the share price, then it's fraud on a grand scale!"

"There is another angle here, Marc," Maddie said, her brow furrowing. "Since you know Dan White personally, we have to make sure we do this properly, so that you can't be accused of any wrongdoing."

"My God, you're right, Maddie," Elisa gasped. "We hadn't thought of that. At least you two will vouch for Marc and so will I, so nothing will happen to him, right?"

"Relax, honey. I'm hardly likely to instigate an investigation if I committed the crime, am I? Don't worry, I'll be careful, and make sure everything is done by the book."

"Make sure that you do! I don't want to have to bring you a hacksaw blade in a loaf of bread," Elisa warned him as they all laughed nervously at the prospect.

Robert told them he had an old school chum who was a private investigator, and that he had used this fellow himself to investigate some business matters. He assured them of his discretion. "His name is Austin Brookwood, and he knows his way around every modern gadget known to man, and a good many that aren't," Robert told them. "Computers, computer networks, and the secrets they hold are his specialties, and the sources of a lot of his key information."

"Robert, I didn't realize you were such a man of mystery. I'm amazed at your mastery of this secret art," Elisa said, smiling.

"We all have our little secrets, my dear," he replied with a smirk. "Seriously though, Marc, I've taken the liberty of contacting Austin, and he'll see you on Monday if you wish. I've got his home number, so you can talk to him over the weekend."

Marc offered Robert and Maddie a grateful smile. "You've been marvelous, Robert. You too, Maddie! You two have always been there for me, for both of us for that matter, whenever we've needed you, and we won't ever forget it."

"We love you both!" Maddie exclaimed. "You're more than just family, and we're not going to stand by and let anyone hurt you; not if we can help it!"

Marc and Elisa had arrived after lunch, and the conversation went on for hours through several cups of coffee and tea. Late afternoon, the women said they were starved, and the conversation turned to where they would all go for dinner.

"How about the little restaurant where you guys took us the night Marc and I met?" Elisa suggested. "We don't get a chance to go out to dinner up here very often, and I'd love to go back there again."

"Sure, let's do that!" Maddie agreed. "I'll call them and make sure they cater to babies."

"Well, if they don't, I'll dress little Jerome up in one of my suits, and we can paint a moustache on him. He's sure to pass for twenty then!" Robert joked.

Chapter Forty-five

Austin Brookwood: funny name for a private investigator, Marc thought as he waited in the bar. Austin had been most obliging when they had spoken on the phone over the weekend, agreeing to meet at a little pub at Berowra Waters, halfway between his office at Gosford and Marc's Silverwater office at eight o'clock Monday evening.

At five minutes to eight, a stout little man walked in, his horseshoe-pattern baldness enhanced by the reflection from the low ceiling lights, giving him a kind of aura as his scalp shone through the last few strands of fine hair he had combed across as camouflage. He looked to be in his mid-to late forties, although Robert had told Marc that he and Austin had been at school together, which would make him thirty-something. *He certainly looks a lot older*, Marc noted doubtfully as all the heroic images of private investigators from his childhood were shattered.

"Marc Braddon? Austin Brookwood."

Austin is nothing like I imagined, Marc thought disappointedly, before he remembered Robert's warning that Austin's blank expression and rudimentary manners concealed a first-class mind. *He's here on Robert's recommendation, so he must be good*, he assured himself.

"Pleased to meet you," Marc said as he shook Austin's hand. "Can I get you a drink?"

"Thanks. I'll have a Chivas Regal with just a touch of water, please."

"Right, I'll be back in a minute." Marc slid out of the booth and went to the bar to fetch Austin his drink.

"Ta," Austin said as Marc placed his drink in front of him. "Do you mind if I smoke?"

"Of course not."

"Thanks." After a few flicks of his lighter, he continued through a light gray cloud. "Well, as I said on the phone, a problem like yours requires delicate handling. If someone inside your operation is undermining you, then you can't let on that you're on to them. It's been my experience that these sorts of people always get sloppy, particularly if they get away with things the first time. And this has happened what...three times now?"

"Yes."

"We have to hope that whoever this person is, he or she has fallen for the 'three-card trick,' and has inadvertently left a solid paper trail," Austin said in a Machiavellian tone. He then smiled and asked, "Did you bring those reports on your six external board members?"

"They're right here," Marc said, lifting the files from the seat next to him to the table. "I've had a good look at each of these files," he added, "and can't see any connection or pattern to suggest that it's one of these men."

"That may well be the case," Austin replied in a way that indicated that he wasn't yet convinced.

"When do you want to start?" Marc asked.

"How about right away? Is there anybody in your office?"

"Probably not, but there's one way to find out for sure." Marc pulled his cell phone out of his pocket and pressed the speed dial key corresponding to his office number.

The rings went unanswered. Marc then followed the same procedure twice to give anyone who might be there the opportunity to answer the persistently ringing phone.

"All's clear?" Austin asked after Marc's third attempt.

"Looks that way. Do you want to follow me there in your car?"

"Yep," Austin said as he downed the rest of his whisky and cleared the table of his smokes and lighter. "Let's go."

By the time they reached Marc's dark and deserted offices, it was just after nine o'clock. Marc unlocked the front door and moved quickly to the alarm keypad behind the reception desk to punch in the security code, disarming Vanity's sophisticated alarm system. A few minutes later they sat down in Marc's office, where Marc explained the hierarchical structure of his organization and the role of Vanity's key people.

"I don't know about you," Austin said, "but it seems to me that if we exclude your external board members for a moment, there are probably only four people within your organization who could've had access to the sort of information that was leaked to the press. These are all people who are close to you; the very people who have been beside you all the way over the past few years."

Marc shook his head incredulously. "It seems impossible. Why would any of these people want to hurt me?"

"I don't know. Maybe it's not anyone here, or maybe the whole thing's a happy coincidence, but I don't think so. It's all too coincidental for my liking!"

"So you'll start by investigating my CEO, my general managers, and my personal assistant?"

Austin nodded. "Do you have a computer network here with e-mail access?"

"Sure."

"Do you know the passwords for these four people?"

"I think I have Stephen's here in my desk, because we sometimes share files," Marc answered as he fished around in the top drawer of his desk. "And Stephen's probably got the two GM's passwords for the same reason."

"What about your PA's password? What's her name again?"

"Clare Eddings. I don't know her password."

"That's going to be tricky, but I can probably access her files from the computer that you guys use as the file server with a little program I've developed to unlock such secrets," he asserted with a smug grin.

Marc was starting to get a bad feeling about his investigator's methods. "This all sounds very sinister, Austin," he protested mildly. "I can't help feeling like I'm invading these people's privacy."

"Well, you *are*," Austin answered matter-of-factly. Seeing Marc's expression change for the worse, he continued hurriedly, "but only to the extent that they have placed things on your company's computer system. You must remember that you're their employer. As such, you're entitled to access whatever work-related information is on your company's computer system."

"I understand that, but I still feel bad about doing it!"

"You won't feel so bad if one of these people turns out to be the crook, will you?"

"No, I guess not."

"Well, lighten up, Marc. We can only expose someone who has something to expose."

Austin grabbed a couple boxes of new computer discs and set about accessing and downloading the information on the four suspect's computers. He also took the backup tapes from the file server, replacing them with blank tapes so that it would appear as if nothing had been touched.

The whole process took several hours, which had given Marc plenty of time to think. When Austin came back into Marc's office to tell him he had all of the information he needed, it was nearly two-thirty in the morning.

"Austin, there's another matter that's been troubling me."

"What is it?"

"About two years ago, when I was setting up the company's kit-home division, I got gazumped on three parcels of land I had previously identified as sites I wanted to buy in the future when the company could better afford the purchases."

Austin's blank expression was punctuated briefly by a blink. "Yeah, I'm with you."

"Well, by the time I got around to making offers on these particular sites, all three had been optioned by someone else. I made some initial inquiries, and it seemed that a separate company was involved with each transaction. In the end I was able to buy all three sites back, but the ease with which I bought them back has always made me suspicious."

"And you'd like me to look further into these companies?"

"Yes. I can't help thinking this all ties in somehow."

"OK, OK. Have you got the information on these transactions, or at least the names of the companies that you dealt with?"

"Yes. While you were downloading the documents you needed, I've been putting together a complete file on these transactions for you."

"I'm glad to see that you haven't been sitting on your hands waiting for me," Austin said with a smile as Marc handed him another large file.

"How long do you think it'll take for you to get to the bottom of this?"

"I really don't know. I think I'll investigate your direct staff first and then move on to the outside directors if that doesn't give me any joy. That should take at least a couple of weeks I think, but the whole investigation could easily take a month or so. I'll give you a progress report in a week or so. There's a mountain of work in just deciphering these files, let alone chasing down the phantom directors in the deal you've just given me."

"Like every job you get, this one's urgent, Austin. I have to know who, if anyone, is behind things."

"Sure, I understand. I'll shift a lot of my other investigations over to some of my colleagues. Robbie stressed how urgent this was, and I promise you I'll deal with it urgently and exclusively."

"I can't ask for more than that. Do you need a retainer or anything to start working?"

"No—you've agreed to my fees, and Robbie's vouched for you. That's all I need for now. I'll wait till the job's done. Besides," he added with a hint of a smirk, "I don't think you should draw a company check with my firm's name on it, do you? If someone is working against you here, then they'll be watching for anything out of the ordinary."

"Good point," Marc replied, kicking himself for being so naive.

They left the office and headed off to their respective homes. Marc felt more at ease, now that he had handed everything over to someone who could finally get to the bottom of matters. *Now all I have to do is wait. It seems that I spend half my life waiting for one thing or another,* Marc thought as he got into his car for the drive home.

He woke Elisa up as he climbed into bed next to her. "Did you get it all done?" she asked, half-awake.

"Yes, we did, honey. Now go back to sleep. I'll tell you all about it in the morning," he whispered as he cuddled up to her and quickly drifted off to sleep.

* * *

The next few weeks were difficult for Marc. He had to continue working with his close-knit group, all the while wondering if one of them was working against him. He adopted an arms-length approach—the fact that he was the boss made it somewhat easier for him, as his people wouldn't readily question him about any change in his behavior, even if they noticed. Stephen James did on occasion ask Marc if he was all right, and Marc simply answered that he had a few things on his mind, which certainly was true.

Austin called Marc several times over the next few weeks, stating that he was following up on a promising lead but refusing to elaborate, for fear that Marc would jump the gun and collar an innocent party. "You'll just have to give me more time," he would say when pressed.

Just over a month after starting his investigation, Austin called Marc at work.

"You're not going to believe what I've found, Marc. I now have clear and irrefutable proof—not just evidence, but proof—that one of your most trusted employees is actively working against you. This person is definitely in league with someone who's out to get you."

"What is your distinction between evidence and *proof*?" Marc quizzed.

"Proof is when I can tie a person in to a particular event, and when that tie is supported by irrefutable facts and a series of cross references that all come back with the same answer."

Marc took a deep breath and willed his pulse to return to normal. "OK, who is it?"

"Not over the phone. I've worked very hard on this case, and I want to present every piece of evidence to you in person. When can I see you?"

"As soon as you can get your scrawny little tail down here, man!" Marc said excitedly.

"What's the time now? Half past ten? How about I meet you for lunch somewhere? I don't want any of this getting out until you're in a position to move against these people."

"OK, let's meet at that little pub where we first met. It's on your way, and it's far enough away from here to ensure that we won't bump into anyone from Vanity. Can you be there at twelve?"

"Yeah, I can make it. See you later."

Marc had to calm himself. He suddenly felt vulnerable and betrayed—from his previous business encounters, he knew he must contain these feelings and move with stealth and care to win the battle.

* * *

Good, Marc thought as he arrived in the pub's parking lot just as Austin did, and parked alongside him in the only two shady spots left. It was a hot, sticky summer day, and Marc had worked up a good thirst.

"I'm having a cold beer. Can I get you one?" he asked Austin, who was carrying several files under his arm.

"I could murder a cold beer right now; thanks, old mate!" Austin replied in his usual, laconic Ocker style.

They collected their beers and drank deeply before ordering lunch from the menu behind the bar. They then scouted the place for a suitable table before settling on one in the back of the pub. By the time they sat down, Marc figured he had waited long enough.

"Well, what have you got for me, Austin?"

"I've prepared a summary that sets it all out," Austin replied as he handed Marc one of the dossiers.

After scanning Austin's report for a few minutes, Marc's expression froze into a mask of hard resentment. "Oh my God! I can't believe it."

"You'd better believe it!" Austin retorted. "And your suspicions about those land deals are borne out, too."

He handed Marc a second dossier. As Marc read through it, he went white. "Why would anybody do this to me?"

Austin's eyes widened knowingly, a portent of what Marc would find in the balance of the report. "Keep reading, and you'll find your answer."

"Unbelievable," Marc said, shaking his head when he reached the end.

Austin's inscrutable expression relaxed into compassion for a moment. "Yeah, I thought so too. Tough break, mate."

"What should I do next? I would never have picked that person in a million years!"

"Well, if it were me, I'd go straight to the cops. There's plenty here—fraud, insider trading, conspiracy to defraud, deception on a grand scale, etc., etc."

Marc sat back in his chair and pondered the situation for a moment. "I don't think I'll do that just yet, Austin. I want to sleep on it to see if I can work out a better solution."

The investigator looked up from his beer, the foam still on his lips. "Well, I can't do much more," Austin replied with a touch of incredulity, "and I certainly can't go to the cops if you won't."

"I didn't say I *wouldn't*, Austin. I just need some time to figure out my best option in all of this. There are other things to consider, such as the effect something like this would have on our share price if news got out. I also need to know if old Dan White wants to be involved with me running Vanity, or if he wants to try to take over himself. I need to find out things like that before I can work out my next move."

Austin shook his head in bemusement. "I can see why I'm not in business. Too much intrigue for me, old mate!"

"Yeah, it is a bit like that. In any negotiation, you always have to understand your opponent's motivation in order to force the best deal."

"It's the way you guys play with huge sums of money that scares me the most!" Austin confessed, his face twisting in mock horror. "*My* only desire is in doing a good job and getting paid at the end of the day!"

Marc smiled. "I'm extremely pleased with your work, Austin, and based on your earlier advice, I'm going to give you a personal check. I don't want anyone putting all of this together—not yet, anyway."

Their lunch arrived, and Marc kept reading Austin's report while they both ate their steaks. Marc would read something and ask a question, whether or not Austin still had a mouth full of food, the gravity of the whole situation overtaking Marc's concern for etiquette.

"Everything is in those dossiers, Marc. My reports are self-explanatory and should contain all the facts. I have attached copies of all the relevant e-mails, computer records, etcetera. I'd like to see their faces when you confront them with this little lot."

"How much do I owe you, Austin?"

"Well, with disbursements, associated costs, and my daily retainer, it comes to a little under twenty grand," Austin said, steeling himself for Marc's anticipated reaction as he handed him his invoice.

Marc nodded amiably. "Very reasonable, I reckon. You've done me a service beyond anything I could have ever imagined. In fact, I'm going to give you a check for $30,000," he declared as he took out his checkbook and starting writing in the amount. "Consider the extra a bonus for a job well done."

With that, Austin's blank mask crumbled into pleasant surprise. "Thank you, Marc," he managed in his most upper-class Australian accent as he pocketed the check. "You're a gentleman and a scholar."

"It is I who thank you, Austin. I'm already hatching a plan to extract my pound of flesh from those who had planned to destroy me!"

"I wish you well, Marc, but somehow I don't think you'll need much luck with this one. Goodbye; it's been great working for you. If I can be of additional help, just let me know."

Marc remained in the pub, quietly rereading all the reports from cover to cover and absorbing every detail of his investigator's fine piece of detective work.

He finished his second glass of beer and then called his office to say he would be out for the rest of the day. He headed home to await the chance to share Austin's incredible findings with Elisa when she returned from work.

Marc spent the whole afternoon sitting out on their balcony engrossed in every detail of Austin's report. After reading each section, he would drop it into his lap and gaze across the harbor for long periods, as if in a trance. He would then return to the report and repeat the same process, the various threads of thought beginning to weave the pattern of a plan in his mind. *I still can't believe that I've worked shoulder to shoulder with such a bloody-minded traitor,* Marc lamented as he finished reading Austin's reports. *How could I have engendered these feelings in someone who was so close to me?*

As the evening started to approach, Marc came inside and opened a cold bottle of his favorite Semillon. He poured himself a glass, and placed the bottle in an ice bucket on the coffee table next to Elisa's waiting glass. He then settled down on the sofa in the living room to read Austin's reports all over again.

Chapter Forty-six

Marc decided to let the matter rest for the next few days: an approach that had served him well in the past. Over those days, he sought Elisa's, Robert's, and Maddie's counsel on many issues, including those involving his life after dealing with the traitor within. He and Elisa had long talks on their balcony overlooking the harbor about the sort of lives they would want in an ideal world.

"I understand that you want to confront your enemies and force them to relinquish their shares in Vanity in exchange for your silence," Elisa told him with a concerned expression, "but this will mean an even greater commitment to the business. Have you stopped to think about what that will mean for us?"

"Yes, of course I have, Elisa," Marc said with a forced smile. "I want to find a way to have a normal life, just as you do. But I have to be strong and deal with these obstacles in order for us to get to that point. If I fail, we could easily end up with nothing!"

As Elisa looked into her husband's troubled eyes, her expression became graver. "I know it's a dangerous time, but promise me that you'll factor *us* into your thinking."

"I promise you that *we* will be uppermost in every decision I make, honey," Marc said softly as he gave his wife a warm hug.

"That's all I ask," Elisa whispered into his ear.

With that, Elisa steeled herself against this unappealing prospect of her husband's deeper involvement in Vanity. When things got tough, she consoled herself with the realization that since Marc was letting her do what she wanted with her imminent archaeological expedition, it was only fair to let him do what he felt he needed to do with the business part of his life.

Over the past few months, Elisa had become engrossed in organizing the dig she was personally funding in Crete, and was now almost fully occupied with planning every aspect of the trip and her post-graduate students' participation. She had managed to get the university to agree to sponsor this excavation under their aegis, allowing her student team of archaeologists to get full academic credit for their work in Crete.

"Universities may be bastions of great ethics and higher learning, but they have also learned over many generations not to look a gift horse in the mouth," Elisa had told Marc many times when discussing the issue. She knew the university would be crazy to pass up the reflected glory that would ensue if she found anything of significance—especially when their involvement came at no cost to them.

Steeped in his own preoccupation, Marc had not realized how advanced Elisa was in her planning. She was now due to leave for Crete in a week with the advance team to set up the dig, and would be gone for about three months. Elisa's imminent departure didn't help his stress levels as he thought about how much he would miss her when coming home to an empty house.

Sure, he could always revert to his old system of immersing himself in work as a means of blocking out the pain of their separation, but that prospect did not inspire him. After all, finding Elisa was one of the best pieces of luck he had ever had, and it had saved him from a lonely, single-interest life.

Marc wanted to take everything into account when making his decision about his and Elisa's future. He was not yet sure which way to go, and that forced him to delay confronting anyone. *This whole thing's going to take a lot more thought*, he realized as Elisa's departure inched closer.

*   *   *

The next day, Marc found himself sitting in his office, peering out the window into the clear blue yonder and thinking of nothing in particular. Prior to that, he had been turning over all his available options in his mind, and had reached the stage where he was in a sort of mental stalemate.

The receptionist interrupted him to say that Jennifer Watkins was on the line, and asked if he wanted to take the call.

Marc's face lit up with a grin. "Yes, of course!"

"She's on line six."

He pressed the flashing button on his phone, grateful for the chance to talk with someone far removed from his current troubles. "Hello, Jennifer, how are you?"

Unlike many of their previous conversations, her voice sounded upbeat and energetic. "I'm fine, Marc. I hope you've recovered from all of those recent market rumors?"

"Yes, I'm getting there," he said with a rueful chuckle. "What are you doing these days?"

"Well, I wanted to call to thank you!"

Mystified, Marc let out a snigger. "You're welcome, but what for?"

"For looking out for me, and making me see that I should do more of what I really want to do with my life!"

"It's my pleasure," he replied, still stymied. "So tell me again, just what have I persuaded you to do? Start a cult? Take up skydiving?"

Jennifer laughed heartily at Marc's disorientation. "No, nothing as exciting as that, I'm afraid. I'm going back to school to earn my master's degree in banking. Then, I'd like to find a position, either here at Whitney Whyte's or somewhere else, that'll give me more time to enjoy life. Who knows, I might even find time to accept some of those offers for quiet dinners with the opposite sex!"

A broad smile lit up Marc's face. "That's great, Jennifer! It's important to do what you really want, particularly if you're lucky enough to be able to make that choice."

"Well, thank you again for taking the time help me see what I wouldn't have otherwise seen. Your concern made all the difference to me, and I just wanted to tell you that!"

Marc shook his head, slowly absorbing the significance of Jennifer's news. "Jennifer, your timing is superb. I have almost the same decision to make regarding my future, and I think you've just helped me make up my mind!"

"I hope everything works out for you, Marc. I know it will."

"Hey, I hope that Adam isn't mad at me for taking you away from Whitney Whyte?"

"No, no. I didn't tell him where my inspiration came from," Jennifer said with a little chuckle.

That afternoon, Marc saw Mary Arness to discuss the several options swimming around in his mind. She was very helpful, and agreed to attend the confrontation meeting when Marc finally set the date. Mary outlined the possible outcomes he might expect if he went forward with his current thinking. After discussing several scenarios with Marc, Mary nodded thoughtfully as she considered Marc's most favored option and said, "I can see real merit in what you're proposing, but you need to give me as much time as possible to prepare the necessary documents well in advance of the meeting."

He now had to set up a meeting with Dan White. *This should set the cat amongst the pigeons*, Marc thought apprehensively as he waited for Dan to answer the phone. "Hello, Dan, it's Marc Braddon from Vanity Homes Group."

Marc sensed hesitation on the other end of the phone. "Well, hello, Marc Braddon," Dan responded in a tone that was a little less confident than usual. "What can I do for you?"

"Well, Dan, I'll get right to the point. I believe you own about six percent of the stock in Vanity. We were delighted to hear about it, and wanted to talk to you about the possibility of a seat on our board."

There was another short pause. "I suppose there's no point denying it," Dan said huffily. "You obviously have an excellent system of monitoring your shareholder register."

Not so marvelous that it picked up your ownership without Robert's help, Marc noted cynically as he primed himself for the next part of his delivery. "We feel that with your experience and substantial interest in the company, you would make an ideal director. I wonder if you could come to our offices at two o'clock next Wednesday to discuss matters?"

Once again, silence reigned on the line. Marc was about to ask if Dan was still there when he answered. "It's short notice, but yes, I'll be there."

"I'll look forward to it, Dan," Marc said as a wicked smile crossed his face.

*   *   *

It was Friday night, and the end of another stressful and hectic week. Marc and Elisa now had the whole weekend to themselves before she flew out on the following Tuesday. They felt that they needed to be together in a spot that would allow them real peace of mind, so they decided to go up to Whitefeather Cove for part of the weekend. This would give them a chance to see Maddie, Robert, and Jerome, and to commune with nature in one of the most beautiful spots on earth.

Marc didn't talk much about his proposed meetings, content to spend his last moments in Elisa's company without interference from the outside world. Elisa herself wasn't too concerned about how her husband was going to fix his enemy's wagons. She just knew he would.

Marc managed to get some time alone with Maddie while Elisa sat on the porch with Robert, reading the Sunday papers.

"I think it's terrific that you're supporting Elisa in what she wants to do," Maddie told her brother as he helped her make the morning tea.

"It's nothing compared to what she's done for me, Maddie. You know how my life changed for the better the moment we met."

Her large brown eyes shone with warmth as she realized the truth of what her brother was saying. "Yeah, I know. But it's still a lot for you to give up—not seeing Elisa every day. You're being very unselfish, and I'm proud of you."

"Stop it, Maddie, or I'll have to make Elisa stay home," Marc shot back with a laugh as he picked up the tray laden with the teapot and cake before making his way to the front porch.

Before they knew it, it was Tuesday morning, and Marc was driving onto the departure concourse outside Sydney's International Airport. He stopped in the three-minute parking zone, carried Elisa's bags into the terminal, and led her protectively to the correct check-in line. He left her there while he hurried to move the car to the short-term parking area, promising to be back in a few minutes.

"Three months is only a short while. I'll call every chance I get!" Elisa said as boarding time approached.

A sad expression filled Marc's face. "I'm really going to miss you, my sweet. Don't be surprised if I find it unbearable and end up on your doorstep," he said as they walked to the immigration gate.

Elisa smiled back stoically. "You've got plenty of other things to think about at the moment, sweetie. Just make sure you get those low-lifes tomorrow. I can't wait to hear what happens."

"I'll try to call you at your hotel, but with the time difference and the fact that you'll be traveling for the next twenty-four hours, it might be hard for us to connect. I'll leave a message at the hotel if I miss you."

"OK. I love you heaps, and miss you already." Elisa said as they embraced at the entry to the immigration gate.

Marc gave his wife a final kiss on the lips. Bye, my darling," he said as Elisa slipped from his embrace and disappeared through the immigration gate, waving as she vanished from sight.

* * *

The long drive back from the airport gave Marc time to think about what he still had to do in preparation for tomorrow's meetings, although most of his thoughts reverted to Elisa and where she was at this point in time. Checking his watch, he figured she was just about to board the plane. As he arrived back at his office, he looked at his watch again and guessed that her plane would have just taken off if it were on time. He parked his car in the lot and looked up to see what he believed to be her jet passing overhead.

Marc suddenly felt the pangs of separation, and instantly longed to be on that plane sitting next to his wife, jetting away from all of his troubles. *Can't do that*, he told himself sternly. *I have to earn my place in the sun.*

Entering his office, he congratulated himself for a job well done in hiding his disgust from the employee who had betrayed him. *Practice makes perfect*, he thought cynically when considering how much easier it had become to conceal his real feelings for the person with the passage of time. *Maybe one day I could become a half-decent actor*, he thought as he reached his desk. He found himself smiling broadly at the prospect.

He then opened his briefcase and pulled out a checklist of things to do before tomorrow's meeting. Everything on the list was just about done, but he still needed to deal with the sacking of his traitorous employee.

He wandered down to the personnel department and extracted the files of five of his senior staff members. Among them was the one he was specifically interested in. The other four were just a smokescreen, in case his foe had a friend in the personnel department.

Marc maintained an "open door" policy that allowed anyone to visit him at almost any time of the day to discuss an issue or seek his advice. His management style was a natural extension of his personality, and had worked well for him over the years. It also had its drawbacks, since it meant that anyone coming into his office could see what was on his desk, allowing them to draw conclusions about what he was planning. Most of the time, it didn't matter. He had very few secrets to protect from his key staff members, who were the only people who came in uninvited anyway.

Closing his office door, when it was usually open, denoted that he was working on confidential matters. To avoid that, he decided to review his traitor's personnel file by putting it inside one of the other dummy files he had selected. He placed the others randomly on his desk and picked up the jacketed file as if he were reading a book.

An uncomfortable-looking Stephen James knocked on the door as he entered Marc's office. "Marc, can I see you for a minute?" he asked, closing the door behind him.

"Sure, Stephen. Pull up a seat," Marc said, putting down the personnel file he had been reading. "What's on your mind?"

"I don't know if I'm doing the right thing, but I wanted to draw something to your attention," he said, clearly grappling with some inner conflict. "On one hand, I have my loyalty to you to consider, while on the other I have to be certain—which I'm not—of the impropriety of one of my staff before bringing it to you."

"You're almost talking in riddles," Marc remarked pleasantly, but his eyes were taking notes.

"It's just…it's just that I've come across a copy of an e-mail sent by Paul Charmers to the somebody outside this organization that deals with something we talked about at a recent board meeting," Stephen said as he handed Marc a hard copy of the e-mail.

Marc scanned the e-mail and sighed. "Look, Stephen, I haven't told you this before, but I had a private investigator go through our computer system in an effort to identify the source of the leak. I need to swear you to absolute secrecy if I'm to share those findings with you— you can't mention it to a soul until after I deal with this issue tomorrow, and even then, I'd rather you keep this knowledge to yourself."

"You have my sacred word, Marc," Stephen said soberly.

Marc opened his briefcase and pulled out Austin Brookwood's report. He talked Stephen through its findings regarding the offenses of the turncoat employee, and the various implications of what Stephen had discovered about Paul Charmers.

Marc looked anxiously at Stephen, whose lip was now curling in distaste. "Now remember, Stephen, you must act as if you know nothing about this. It's imperative that our 'traitor' not have any inkling that the axe is about to fall."

"You can rely on me, boss. I'm only glad I'm not that poor bastard," Stephen said as he left Marc's office.

Marc was interrupted soon after Stephen's visit by Clare, who came into to ask him if he wanted a cup of coffee. When she noticed the personnel files on his desk, she couldn't resist inquiring what he was doing with them. "I'm just looking them over to see who might be entitled to a salary review," he replied lightly.

She laughed, saying, "I hope you've got my file there; I could use a raise."

Chapter Forty-seven

Wednesday had arrived, and Marc felt good about things as he showered, shaved and donned his favorite dark suit and a crisply ironed cream shirt. He looked for a tie, flicking through the dozens on his tie rack until he came across an old favorite he hadn't worn for a while—the one he had worn when he had confronted Dan White at his property in the country.

How fitting, Marc thought as he held it up to the mirror and admired its distinct coloring and pattern—small dark red and gray diamonds housed in a matching field of larger, lighter diamonds, aligned to create a subtle criss-cross pattern.

Checking his watch, he noted that Elisa was probably still in transit. After debating whether or not to call her, he decided to phone her hotel on the off chance she had gotten in early. The hotel operator spoke with a heavy accent, but was able to tell him that Professor Braddon had not yet arrived. Marc left a message that he had called to wish her a good night's sleep, and that he'd call again tomorrow.

Marc arrived at his office at about eight-thirty, passing Clare on the way in.

"Good morning, Marc!"

"Good morning," he replied with his usual good cheer.

"I see you have two meetings scheduled for this afternoon. Is there anything I can do to help you prepare for them?"

"Thanks, Clare, but I've got everything ready. I'd like you be on hand, though, just in case I do need you."

This is going to be an interesting day, he thought, placing his briefcase on his desk.

He had arranged to meet Mary Arness at a local restaurant at noon, where they planned to grab a quick bite while going through the latest version of the agreements they proposed to use later that afternoon. Until then, Marc kept busy with a series of meetings with Stephen James and a number of other people. He checked production levels and outputs with them, checked sales and promotional campaigns, checked construction programs, and even examined the monthly profit-and-loss results. That was enough to fill any morning, and he soon found himself pressed for time as he hurried out to keep his appointment with Mary.

By the end of lunch, they had transacted all of their pre-arranged business. It was now one-thirty, half an hour before their first meeting, so Marc paid the bill, and they drove back separately to Vanity's offices. They met up again in the parking lot, and Mary followed him into his office.

They decided that it might be best if Mary set herself up in the boardroom just across the corridor from Marc's office before the meeting with Dan White. That way, when Marc showed Dan into the boardroom, she would appear to be nicely ensconced.

When Dan arrived, the two men shook hands and exchanged basic pleasantries in Marc's office. Dan looked older and more stressed than when Marc had last seen him. *I'm not sure that all this share market manipulation agrees with old Dan,* Marc thought, scanning Dan's craggy face. Before escorting Dan into the boardroom to start the meeting, Marc quickly unlocked his briefcase and retrieved Austin's report. He then introduced Dan to Mary.

Dan expressed his surprise. "I thought I was coming here to meet the other members of your board to discuss the possibility of me taking a seat on it!"

"Yes, the discussion of your future role in the company is still very much on the agenda," Marc responded soothingly," but I don't think you'll really want the other board members to hear what I have to say."

Dan's eyes widened innocently. "Why not?"

"For a while now, Dan, I've suspected you of sabotaging our share price in order to manipulate a cheaper price for yourself. I'd heard that you harbored some grudge about the way the Hillsford deal had worked out for you."

"That's nonsense!" Dan shot back indignantly. "I don't have enough money to manipulate the market, even if I wanted to." His expression grew decidedly sheepish as he continued. "OK, I admit I was a little miffed when you didn't involve me in the development of the office park. After all, you've now got an income-producing asset worth well over $30 million. Although I provided the initial capital to get you into the site in the first place, I ended up with nothing to show for it. I've always felt that you wanted it for yourself, and just elbowed me out of the way."

A look of disbelief crossed Marc's face. "You need to watch that you don't become a bitter and twisted old man, Dan. You've managed to reinvent history to suit yourself. You must remember turning down several opportunities to go into developments with me. When I finally got you into the Hillsford deal, you couldn't get out fast enough. Now, years later, you tell me you're aggrieved because you weren't invited to participate. Surely you agree that what I paid you at the time was what you said you wanted out of the whole deal. I don't know what else I could have done for you!"

"I always thought you had the Midas touch," Dan replied bitterly. "OK, I could have had more faith in you and your ability, but I still felt I had a stake in what you were doing. I just thought you could have done a bit more than you did, that's all."

"That's what I'm going to do right now," Marc said with a magnanimous smile. "I'm going to do a little more for you than you deserve! I now know that it wasn't you who rigged the share price. Sure, you got your shareholding when the price was down, but your purchase wasn't large enough to make it worthwhile for you to manipulate the market. Someone much bigger than you has been playing that game!"

Dan's eyebrows rose up a notch. "What are you telling me, Marc?"

"I'm saying there's been a secret battle going on for control of the group. I'm telling you this to give you a chance to decide what you want to do with your investment. If you want to hold on to your shares, then I believe that after today, they'll be worth a lot more once I isolate the cause of this problem and deal with it. I'm telling you this as someone who apparently feels I owe them something. I want the ultimate decision to be in your hands!"

"I'm not sure I understand," Dan said. Things were moving a little quickly for him.

"You don't need to understand, Dan. You just need to believe what I'm telling you."

He shrugged. "OK."

"In my opinion, you should hold on to your shares because, no matter what happens in the short term, you will still make a lot of money out of them. I believe Vanity's share price will drop significantly once the news of my next move hits the streets. But it'll jump back up again, probably increasing its value by twenty to thirty percent, once the market fully understands the ramifications."

Dan's eyes narrowed in suspicion. "What next move?"

"I won't tell you that. You'll just have to have that thing you've always had trouble with—faith. If you don't like the idea of volatility, you should divest yourself of the stock immediately after this meeting, or you could make a quick killing by selling your stock now and repurchasing it when it bottoms out."

"Ah, yes." Dan's false teeth emerged in a wily grin. "Thank you, Marc. That's worth knowing."

Marc shrugged the words off nonchalantly. "Well, the choice is yours...as is the risk of being caught for insider trading, if you chose the latter option."

The false teeth disappeared as his shady hopes were dashed. "Hmm."

"There is another option, Dan. If you decide to keep your shares, I can offer you a seat on the company's board of directors immediately. The only catch is that you have to decide what you are going to do before you leave this meeting."

Dan thought long and hard. "Every time I've ignored your advice, it's cost me dearly. Maybe it's time to change the habits of a lifetime and trust someone else's judgment. I really appreciate your taking the time to warn me, Marc."

Marc then handed him a "Consent to Act as Director" form, which Dan filled out, signed, and handed to Mary Arness. They all rose, shook hands, and filed out of the boardroom. Dan promised not to make mention of any of the things he'd just been told while still on the premises, understanding Marc's concern that his staff might hear things not meant for them.

Descending the charcoal marble stairs with Dan in tow, Marc nodded to the man sitting patiently in the reception area.

"Goodbye, Dan; all the best," Marc said, shaking hands with his old business partner.

"Yeah, thanks for everything, Marc."

As Dan went out the front door, Marc turned toward his next guest, who had been observing the two men's farewell.

"Thank you for coming today."

"You didn't give me much choice, Mr. Braddon," the stone-faced newcomer replied matter-of-factly.

Marc showed him into the boardroom and introduced him to Mary before ducking out and around the corner to ask Clare to join them. She picked up her pad and pencil and followed him back into the room, steadying herself as her eyes met the dark, cold gaze of Martello Pressani.

"So now that you've got me here, what is it that you want from me?" Martello asked impatiently. "You said on the phone that you'd go ahead with your plan whether or not I came. Well, here I am."

Marc raised his gaze to meet Martello's. "I've found out about your desire to control the destiny of Vanity," he delivered with smooth confidence.

Martello sat up straight in his seat and produced a saccharine-sweet smile. "Are you delusional, Mr. Braddon?"

"Just so that it's clear, I'm talking about how you came to acquire just under fifteen percent of Vanity stock in a very short time."

Martello threw Marc a contemptuous glance. "I buy all my stocks through the stock market, just like everybody else. I'd like to see you make something sinister out of that! If you can, then the whole share-buying community would have reason to feel guilty!" he added with a dismissive laugh.

"The whole 'share-buying community,' as you put it, doesn't go around manipulating the stock market so they can buy a stock cheaply and make a massive profit! Nor do they set out to create instability, as you have," Marc said forcefully.

Martello exploded. "I hope you can back up this slander. I should have my lawyer here, since I see you have yours," Martello said, pushing his chair back to indicate his intention to leave.

"I suggest you sit back down and listen, Mr. Pressani," Marc advised his opponent with a steely glare. "I intend to prove what I'm saying. I think you'd be very unwise to walk out right now. That would leave me in the awkward position of having to choose which of the authorities to call first."

Both Mary Arness and Clare shifted uncomfortably in their seats as they realized that the stakes had just been raised.

"OK, you've got my attention," Martello said, looking subdued.

"I ordered an investigation into the shenanigans that have been going on here," Marc began. "Oddly enough, these occurrences began about eighteen months or so after I bought Vanity..."

"What's that got to do with me?" Martello interrupted. "You weren't even a public company then!"

"I'm getting to that, Mr. Pressani," Marc chided. "This investigation proved conclusively that someone inside this company has been feeding you information. This same person fed false rumors to the financial press, ultimately causing the company's share price to plunge. Coincidentally, this was when you bought your first block of shares. You and your spy have twice caused the stock to plunge. Here's the proof of your purchases," Marc said as he handed Martello copies of pages from Austin's report. "The dates of your acquisitions correspond to the bottom of those two slumps."

Martello glanced at the executive summary and threw the pages back on the table. "So what does that prove—that I bought wisely at the bottom of a slump before the market recognized the underlying strength of the stock?"

"As I said, I have proof that connects you to an inside person through a series of e-mails and phone records," Marc said, placing those records on the table.

"Oh, and who is this person?" Martello said, ignoring Marc's evidence.

Marc looked up, wanting to see Martello's face when he delivered the fatal blow. "I'm surprised that you don't recognize your own daughter," he remarked sarcastically. "Shall I make the introduction? Clare Eddings, meet Martello Pressani."

As Clare began to splutter protests, Martello emitted a low, dangerous chuckle.

"You're delusional," he told his interrogator. "No child of mine would work for Marc Braddon."

"A child of yours would work *against* me, though—that was the idea, wasn't it?" Marc asked angrily.

"This is insane, Marc!" Clare shouted. "You know I'm single and that my name is *Eddings*, not…"

"Just because you're single doesn't mean you haven't been married before," Marc answered coldly. "As it turns out, you apparently continued to use your married name after your divorce. I pity Mr. Eddings, whoever he is."

Clare's face went white as she felt the full force of Marc's accusation. "How could you say something like that, Marc, after all I've done for you?"

Marc rolled his eyes in disgust. "Oh, please cut the act, Clare! All you've done for me? All you ever did was to position yourself here so that you could give your father information about the company and me. You even tried to seduce me so you could use it to either blackmail me or destroy my marriage. God knows how your script was to read!"

Martello tried to find a way to negotiate. "Marc, surely…"

"Surely what? Look at all of this proof. Not just evidence, but proof absolute. I have all the e-mails Clare sent to your home. I have her e-mails to the papers, showing what she sent them to initiate those market rumors. I even know that she worked with you to fleece me of about $300,000 by giving you the locations of the country properties I had earmarked to buy early last year. In the end, you two forced me to buy them back from you via your stooges. I'll wager that further investigation would show how my $300,000 found its way back into both of your bank accounts."

"Marc, what can I say?" a tearful Clare said.

"There's nothing for you to say, Clare. You took sides a long time ago, so don't try to soft-soap me. You're too transparent!"

"Looks like you've done your homework, Mr. Braddon. Where do we go from here?" Martello said resignedly.

"Between the two of you, I think you've managed to trample over just about every law known to man. The very least you can expect, Martello, is to be charged with insider trading, conspiracy to defraud, and grand larceny. Your daughter here is looking at the same charges, but her punishment will be even more severe. And when it all comes out, her reputation will be in tatters and you, who obviously put her up to it, won't be able to show your face in public. The Pressani name will be dragged through the mud, and you'll probably have the dubious distinction of being a father who not only put his own daughter behind bars, but is also able to join her in the exercise yard."

In the pause that followed, Marc became more circumspect. "You know, I've thought long and hard about why you're so desperate to get at me. I'd really like to know what I did to you."

Martello's expression grew more resolute, dropping all pretense of politeness. "I wanted revenge for what you did to my son, Antonio," he uttered with the quiet rage of a man who never forgets a slight. "You ruined his life by letting him marry that horrible woman. You gave me a tramp for a daughter-in-law, and poisoned my line. You cursed my family forever. I know you were still seeing her after they married. She even came to your apartment."

"She also used to ring me all the time and even came here to the office one day, but you'd know all about that, wouldn't you?" he said, looking directly at Clare. She immediately looked away.

"After she got married, she and I were nothing more than friends, Martello," Marc continued. "Surely, you don't expect to choose Loren's friends for her?"

"Maybe not, but you don't mess with another man's wife— especially a Pressani."

"You're mad. Do you know your son tried to kill me!"

"Pity he missed!" he snarled.

Marc's jaw dropped open. "You *are* mad!"

"Mad...maybe I am." Martello's face suddenly brightened. "Maybe I can use that as a defense."

"I don't think so, Martello. Besides, I've got something much more ironic planned for you. You see, I figured that if you wanted to be involved in this company so much, then you should own it!"

Martello squinted, as if he hadn't heard Marc correctly. "What?"

"I want you to buy me out. I want you to purchase my entire holding in Vanity at twice the current market price."

Martello fell back in disbelief. "Are you kidding?" he asked incredulously. "What makes you think I have that kind of money?"

"I think you do, or you can find it," Marc told his stunned adversary. "The current share price will cover the first half of the cost, and you'll have to rely on Vanity's management to improve the value of the stock over the next several years. Anyway, that's your problem, not mine. I want you to sign the deed of agreement that Mary has prepared to that effect."

By now, Martello looked as if he were caught up in a bad dream. "You want me to sign this now?"

Marc nodded. "It essentially says that you'll pay me seven dollars a share for my fifty percent of the company. It also says that you'll pay the first half, $90 million, within seven days from today. The next half is to be paid over the next three years at a rate of $30 million per year at ten percent interest."

Martello looked at the agreement and then, with a puzzled expression, looked back up. "But this means we'll be tied together for at least the next three years!" he exclaimed.

"No, it doesn't. You'll have no direct dealings with me after the first part of this deal is done. Thereafter, everything is to go through Mary. If you default on any of these payments, all the shares will revert back to me."

While Martello paused to think it over, Marc could feel his plans hanging in the balance. *What if he refuses and storms out?* he wondered. Marc pictured the renewed media blitz that would ensue when the report became public information; the additional damage done to Vanity's reputation; and the vengeful plots the Pressanis would hatch after Martello was taken into custody. Unless Martello signed now, Marc's and Vanity's troubles would be far from over.

"What guarantee do I have about your silence regarding this whole thing?" Martello finally asked.

Still in the game! Marc rejoiced. "I propose to sign a confidentiality agreement to give you my assurance that I won't divulge any of these matters as long as you hold up your part of the bargain," he told Martello. "Only the four of us here know all the sorry details, and Mary is constrained by her attorney-client confidentiality code. So unless you and Clare want to tell people about your parts in this fiasco, I think you're pretty safe! My copy of the agreement," he continued with a knowing smirk, "will be my insurance against any urge you may feel to revert back to your old Sicilian ways."

Martello's stony expression did not change. "What about Clare?" he asked.

"She's to resign immediately by signing this letter," Marc said, pulling out a sheet of paper and handing it to her. "And she's to leave this office immediately and not work for Vanity again, even if you own it. On that basis, I won't do or say anything about her activities to anyone outside Vanity, as long as I'm bound by the agreement. In other words, as long as you keep your end of the bargain and meet your payments, I'll be restrained from going to the authorities, so it's really up to you, Martello."

For the first time in her life, Clare watched her father bow his head in defeat. "Just give me a few minutes to read this," he said.

Marc worked hard to maintain his poker face as a feeling of relief washed over him. "There's one more thing I should explain, Martello. I'll still own this company until I receive your check. Between now and then, I'll sign employment contracts with all key staff members. These will be binding upon you as the new owner, so you can't fire any of them for the next five years. They can leave if they like, but you can't discharge them. This way, I can protect the company's best employees from your interference and save you from yourself at the same time. You may own the company, but this will allow me to safeguard my investment while you pay me off."

Martello shook his head. "You've really planned this very well, haven't you, Mr. Braddon?"

"I guess I've picked up a few pointers from watching people like you at work," Marc said with an easy grin.

Martello let out an involuntary huff. "Obviously!"

"Clare, you should look at your own agreement," Marc continued. "I've drawn a check to cover your salary and benefits. It's yours once you've signed the agreement."

Clare forced out a tight smile for a reply, but her eyes were full of poison.

After Mary Arness checked to ensure that they had both signed their agreements in the right places and witnessed the signatures, she gave each of them an executed set. Martello then asked Marc if he could wait for Clare while she collected her belongings.

"Of course," Marc replied, now that he could afford to be generous. But inside, he was doing a victory dance. *That'll teach you Pressanis to mess with me. Pack up your traitorous daughter and crawl back to the deep hole you crawled out of!*

Chapter Forty-eight

Marc and Mary walked back to his office. He went over to his small bar and poured two glasses of iced mineral water. They were almost there, and the cool drinks marked the halfway point in a busy afternoon.

"You were *brilliant*, Marc," Mary said with a look of genuine admiration. "You were so composed, so measured—you simply blew poor Martello away. I've never seen anybody handle anybody as clinically as that, and I've been in plenty of similar situations."

Marc smiled. "Thanks, Mary, but I knew I had you as my back-up."

"I don't think you needed me today," Mary replied, shaking her head modestly. "You were masterful."

"So, do you think Martello will deliver the check on time?"

"I don't think he would dare do anything else!" Mary exclaimed with a laugh. She then went to her briefcase and pulled out one of the several employment agreements she had previously prepared while Marc called Stephen James in.

"Stephen, I've just sold all of my interests in Vanity to a fellow called Martello Pressani."

Stephen sat wide-eyed for a moment as he tried to assimilate what his boss had just told him. "Martello Pressani. Isn't he the fellow who owns the Multi-Grid Group?"

Marc smiled. "Yes, the very same. In seven days' time, he'll be the new owner. That's why I want to sign a five-year employment contract with you and the other managers now to guarantee your tenure. The new contracts will be binding on Pressani or anyone else who might own Vanity."

Stephen was still struggling to accept Marc's news, and he appeared to be only half-listening to what Mary was saying as she explained the very favorable terms of his proposed employment contract. He didn't hesitate.

"I know you're only looking after my best interests," he said as he signed the document. "My more pressing concern is how I'll get on without you to guide me."

"Things are certainly going to be different around here, but nothing that you can't handle, Stephen," Marc assured him. "Clare has gone, as I told you would happen yesterday, so you won't have to worry about having a viper in your midst, setting up your staff as she tried to do to Paul Charmers. That should make your life a lot easier than mine was," he said with a shudder. "Apart from that, your new employment contract will ensure security of tenure, so you should have a free hand to run the place as you wish."

Later in the day, when Marc told Paul Charmers about Clare's attempt to set him up with the fake e-mail, Paul was shocked and wounded. "This would certainly explain why Stephen was looking at me oddly a few days ago," he noted with a sigh. "It was absolutely awful, coming to work day after day, knowing that one of our team was working against us. When you confronted us all before the press conference, I could barely sit still; I was so distraught that someone could be doing this to you after you've given us all so much. What really puzzled me was that I simply couldn't imagine Stephen or Andy having anything to do with it—they're such nice blokes. Never thought about Clare for a moment. Isn't that strange?"

"None of us did," Marc replied. "I'm glad those dark days are behind us at last."

Paul's face flooded with earnestness. "Marc, I would never betray the faith you put in me. You promoted me and gave a huge break. I feel I owe you so much."

"Even if I hadn't had the proof about Clare, I wouldn't have been able to bring myself to believe that you were a turncoat. Some people are just beyond reproach, and that's always how I've seen you, Paul."

"Thanks, Marc. Coming from you, that means a lot to me," Paul said with a huge grin.

By six o'clock, every employment contract had been signed. Marc opened the bar in his office, this time pouring himself and Mary a double scotch. They discussed this remarkable day and how well everything had gone before Marc invited Stephen back in for a farewell drink.

Marc said, "I've decided to move up my departure. I'm leaving town for a while; this will be my last day at Vanity."

"Oh," Stephen said with dismay, as he reluctantly absorbed Marc's latest shock.

Marc smiled generously. "Yes, and I want to say that you've worked out to be an even better chief executive officer than I ever imagined."

"Thank you, Marc. Coming from you that's high praise, although I don't know how well I'm going to do on my own."

"Come on, old friend, you'll be fine. You've really been running the place, I've just been a spectator this past year," Marc said reassuringly. "Anyway, I'll still have a financial interest in the group for the next three years, and I'm relying on you to ensure that the profits keep growing."

"OK," Stephen smiled, accepting Marc's vote of confidence.

Marc packed some of his belongings into cardboard boxes and asked Stephen to arrange for someone to gather the rest and store them for him.

He then hugged Mary, who assured him that she would put everything they had discussed in place during his absence. All three grabbed their briefcases and some of Marc's boxes, and left the office together.

As they stood next to Marc's car, Stephen said, "It's not going to be the same around here without you, boss."

"You'll soon get used to it. You'll have a free hand without me looking over your shoulder. Now you'll be able to really enjoy yourself!" Marc smiled as they walked over to Mary's car to see her off.

After Mary drove off, the two men embraced and patted each other on the back. They wished each other well, while promising to stay in touch. Marc then drove away, looking back at Vanity's smart façade one last time. He couldn't help remembering the circumstances that had brought him here in the first place, and how it had become such a fixture in his life.

When he got home, there was a message on the answering machine from Elisa. "I couldn't get hold of you at the office because you were still in your meetings, and I didn't want to disturb you. Just wanted to say hello and remind you that I'm off to the dig location and won't be back at the hotel for about a week. Love you, sweetie, and already miss you badly," Elisa cooed into the phone.

Marc replayed the message several times just to hear his wife's familiar voice, saving it before walking into their bedroom. He opened his bedside drawer and pulled out a first-class airline ticket to Crete, confirming his six o'clock departure time the next morning. He then threw his suitcase onto the bed and started packing.

*　　*　　*

He looked out of the cabin window as the plane left the ground, started on its steep ascent, and reduced everything he had left behind to miniature size. *It's hard to believe all that's behind me now,* he marveled, sipping at the first of several celebratory drinks. *When I started out, I had nothing but a burning desire to succeed. My ambition carried me over all the hurdles that would have paralyzed me had I stopped to think about them. In a way, my ambition saved my life; in another way it nearly killed me. Thank God I came out of it with something. I think I'm a better person for the experience.*

Marc's thoughts then turned to the people who mattered most to him—the people who had been loyal to him through all of his many trials and tribulations. His mind filled with images of Maddie, Robert, Billy, and the Vanity managers who had always stood by him. After silently giving thanks for these supporters, he fell into a much needed doze—his first effort at catching up on the sleepless nights that had led up to the finalization of his affairs.

After twenty-one hours of relentless travel, punctuated by two stopovers and a change of planes, he finally landed at the Crete airport. He immediately hired a car and a driver to find Elisa's dig by trial and error, explaining its approximate location to the driver, who spoke only broken English. After ten minutes of pointing to a map on the hood of the rented car, the driver felt sufficiently briefed to allow Marc into the back seat.

*   *   *

After two hours in the scorching sun, exploring three dead-end trails, they finally came across a group of young people dressed in Hawaiian shirts and khaki shorts, scurrying around as they marked the ground with string lines and chalk.

"This has to be it," Marc told the driver as sweat drenched his clothes all over again.

As the car rattled to a stop, Marc recognized the unmistakable curves of Elisa's body. She was bent over, surveying something on the ground. He paid the driver with a wad of local currency and grabbed his bag out of the trunk. Finally, he was in the only place in the world he wanted to be.

He walked toward Elisa's camp, his figure silhouetted in the blaze of the setting sun. Focused on the task at hand, Elisa didn't sense him at first, but as he got closer she raised her head.

She peered over her shoulder toward the blinding sun, almost as if knowing someone she knew was approaching. She tilted her head in an attempt to filter out the sun's harsh light and thought she saw her husband's figure through the blinding rays. *Am I dreaming?* she asked herself skeptically. *It must be a mirage, or maybe the sun's playing tricks. How could it be…?*

"Marc, is that you?" she heard herself ask, half-expecting a negative response.

"Yes!"

A rush of euphoria engulfed them both as they instinctively ran towards each other, knowing the power and warmth that they would find in each other's embrace.

"What on earth are you doing here?" Elisa asked from the middle of their embrace as she came to grips with her shock of seeing him.

Marc offered Elisa a huge smile. "I sold my entire interest in Vanity to Martello Pressani and made the jerk pay me twice the market price.

We'll have a check for $90 million by the end of the week, with another $90 million to follow over the next three years. After tax, we should still clear well over $125 million, not including our Hillsford assets." He stood back, opened up the palms of his hands, looked into his wife's eyes and rocked his shoulders in a show of delight. "We're rich, baby! We're now free to do whatever we want with the rest of our lives!" he told her as she struggled to take it all in.

Marc's expression became serious and he said soberly, "You've dedicated so much of your life to me and my business interests. You've given me so much of yourself so willingly that when I saw the chance to get out of Vanity, I took it. There's no reason why we should deprive ourselves of each other for the sake of a business that was sucking the life out of us. From now on, I want us to live for each other and take all the time in the world to figure out what we want to do next. I don't know what it will be, but for now, I'm going to help you dig as many odd-shaped holes as you want, my love. The rest will take care of itself." Marc smiled warmly at his wife. "I just want to give you the kind of support you've given me since the first day we met. Please believe me when I say you're the best person I've ever known, and that I don't want us to be apart ever again."

With tears welling in his eyes, he added, "Like I said that night on the beach, you've been the real giant in my life; you let me stand on your shoulders so that I could see forever. And what I've seen from way up there has freed my spirits. I could never have walked away from the business or seen the real possibilities in life without you. It's because of you that for the first time, I feel completely liberated, completely open to new challenges. I believe in you and our love, and it's allowed me to break the shackles of a lifetime. And I don't fear any of our tomorrows, just as long as we're together."

Elisa struggled to get out the words but managed to say, "Marc, if you could have looked into my heart and found my deepest, most treasured hope for us, you couldn't have answered it in a more perfect way.

"You know," she continued, "I got a fax from the vice chancellor yesterday offering me a full professorship when I return…"

"That's great!" Marc shouted. "It's about time those small-minded twits saw you in the proper light."

Elisa's smile could have lit up the whole desert. "Better late than never, I guess. But I think you've just helped me decide whether to take it or not. We're good enough to find a way to work together in some worthwhile enterprise—you as an ex-business genius and me as a soon-to-be professor emeritus."

A look of genuine delight covered Marc's face as he realized the implications of his wife's career decision. "I'll do anything as long as we do it together, my darling, but you must first finish your work here in Crete, and I'm going to stay here with you until you do."

Elisa's deep blue eyes glistened with tears as she looked into the eyes of the man she loved so completely. She knew he could look into the very reaches of her soul, and she could do the same with extraordinary ease. She felt more closely bonded to her husband than ever before.

"In all my quiet moments, long before we met, in all my times alone with my innermost thoughts, I never thought anyone could be as close to me as you are at this moment," she said as they fell again into each other's arms.

This is where I want to be. Marc thought as he drank in the warmth of Elisa's embrace. *This makes all those years of struggle worthwhile.*

Nearly overcome with emotion, he pulled Elisa in a little closer. "Everything before this moment is already history—something that another generation of archeologists can dig up if they want," he whispered tenderly in her ear. "For us, every moment from now on is what our lives should be about."

As Elisa drew back her head and nodded, the tears in her eyes belied the joy and hope that would define all the years to come.

Acknowledgments

I would like to extend my thanks to all those people who provided great support during the development of this novel.

I had great help in the initial editorial stages from Nicole Bentley of A-1 Editing Service, who took a personal interest in the book and worked tirelessly to help me polish up my rough diamond. Later, American Book Publishing assigned me two excellent editors. The first of these, Dawna Simpson, helped me take the book to its next level. However, my second editor, Adrienne deNoyelles, deserves most of the credit for helping me fashion the book into the finished article. We worked for almost a year cutting, rewriting, re-plotting, and then editing all over again—Adrienne proved to be a true and consummate professional.

I would also like to thank those friends who gave so freely of their time in reading the various versions of the manuscript. I took particular notice of my good friend, Lorraine Ettridge, who generously read the manuscript three times yet always managed to give me some new and interesting insights after each reading.

Finally, I would like to thank my wonderful family: My wife, Leah, my children, Luke and Erin for always being prepared to lend an ear while I ran off with another plot development, or to read my next batch of prose as I glued together another set of ideas.

To all of you, I give my heartfelt gratitude for helping me deliver what I hope will be an enduring story.

About The Author

Peter Verinder is a consulting structural engineer who lives in Sydney with his wife and their two adult children. He spent his formative years attaining his various formal qualifications through an exhaustive combination of part-time study and working for a living, before setting up in business.

Peter has since seen business from many aspects, having developed, managed, and nurtured businesses for himself and others. This unique background has equipped him with a broad band of experience from which he is able to create realistic stories. *Ambition* is his first novel.